SHILOH VALLEY

Doris Dumrauf

This book is a work of fiction. All characters, dialogue, locations, and events portrayed in this novel are either products of the author's imagination or are used fictitiously.

Copyright © 2020 Doris Dumrauf

dorisdumraufauthor.com

ISBN: 978-0-9976767-3-0

Cover design: Historical Fiction Book Covers

Editing: Historical Editorial

Those who deny freedom to others deserve it not for themselves.
- Abraham Lincoln

Chapter 1

June 1849

Martin rode into Homburg's market square, his horse's hooves clattering over the cobblestones. Halting in front of the imposing town hall, he tethered his roan to a ring in the wall. After mopping his forehead with the sleeve of his blue tunic, he took the two steps at once and opened the wooden entryway. Inside, he knocked at the first door and stepped into a musty office where a bearded turner was seated behind a mound of files.

"Yes?" the man asked, barely looking up from the paper in front of him.

"I have a dispatch for Colonel Schimmelpfennig," Martin said, gasping for breath.

The turner pointed to a chair in the corner and left with the orders, returning a minute later. "You're to wait for the colonel's reply."

He sat down behind his desk and scrutinized Martin.

"What was your name again?" he asked.

"Private Dupree," Martin replied.

"Dupree? Are you related to Hermann Dupree?"

"He's my father," Martin said reluctantly.

"Well, I hope you're more useful than he is," the turner said.

"Why? Did something happen?"

"You could say that. Today we received news that the weapons your father purchased in Belgium were confiscated in Köln."

Martin was startled. He had not even been aware that his father, a member of the provisional government of the Palatinate, had been sent to Belgium to purchase much needed weapons for the revolution. Shame over his father's role in the confiscation and anger over the loss of the rifles fought within him. With those weapons, the irregulars might have

1

been able to delay the Prussian soldiers until another party offered help with an influx of troops. Now, an army of men brandishing scythes had to face the new breech-loaders of the Prussian troops and everyone knew how accurate those rifles were.

"Do you know where my father is now?" Martin asked.

"As far as I heard, he's in Sarreguemines. He should have sent the rifles through France, too."

The turner entered the colonel's office and returned with a letter to General Sznayde. Martin grabbed the message and fled the building. After exchanging horses at a nearby stable, he shoved the dispatch into his saddlebag. A throng of housewives had gathered around the fountain filling their jugs. Ignoring the chattering women, he pushed around them to fill his canteen before splashing his face and hair with the cool water. If only he could wash off his embarrassment that easily.

Why would his father even consider sending weapons through enemy country? Was he so eager to shed his responsibilities that he did not consider the lives of the rebel fighters, including his youngest son? And now he would sit out events in safety while innocent men paid the price for his ill-conceived decision. Could Martin even hold his head high again once people learned about his shameful connection? Martin was certain that his father would fall on his feet again, but he was not so sure about himself. He had given up too much to join the revolution. It had all begun with such promise . . .

Chapter 2

April 1849

"I bring exciting news," Martin burst out as he arrived at the Weber farm on horseback. Young Nikolaus and his father looked up from the barn door they were repairing.

"*Guten Tag,*" he added after dismounting his horse.

Father and son gave him expectant looks as they approached him.

"Kaiserslautern is abuzz," Martin said. "There will be a public assembly next Wednesday and all Palatine towns are to send delegations. They will force the government in München to accept the constitution." He smacked his right fist into his left palm. "They must."

He opened his jacket to cool off after his ride. "You've heard that the Bavarian government rejected the constitution this week?"

The previous month, the Frankfurt parliament had drafted a constitution and even elected an emperor. So far, twenty-eight tiny German states had acknowledged the document, but Bavaria had refused.

"Yes, we heard about it." Herr Weber pushed his cap back. "I hope our village will send a delegation. Most of us have republican views."

Martin tapped his hand on his leg. "I can't wait to get back to the city. I don't want to miss a minute of the excitement." Catching a longing look from his friend, he asked Nikolaus, "Why don't you come to the meeting?"

Nikolaus took a deep breath. "Papa, can I go?"

"We'll see," his father replied before he returned to the barn.

3

Nikolaus strolled to the trough with Martin, who had tethered his horse on the pump handle. "We haven't seen you for a while."

"Work doesn't allow me much time to visit anymore," Martin said. "We celebrated my mother's birthday during my last visit, and I had to get fitted for a jacket for my sister's wedding tomorrow. By tonight, the house will be full of guests. I decided to tell you the news first before facing everyone."

Martin's stomach rumbled. It was time to approach the other purpose of his visit, spending a few precious moments near the daughter of the house. He asked, "Have you had dinner yet?"

"Yes," Nikolaus said.

"Is there anything left over?"

"I don't know. Ask Katrin. She's in the kitchen. Don't they feed you at home anymore?"

"Yes, but I rode away before dinner. I wasn't in the mood to meet the whole family yet. I'll see them all tonight; that's soon enough."

The stale smell of sour milk mingled with the stench of cow dung in the hallway that separated the barn from the living quarters. Martin wiped his boots on the doormat and knocked on the kitchen door. His hand shook as he touched the door handle. He heard a voice inside and slowly opened the door. Taking off his cap, he stepped into the spacious kitchen where eighteen-year-old Katrin was drying dishes at the corner sink by the window to his left. She touched the stoneware plates as gracefully as if they were Meissen porcelain. Her honey-colored braids formed a crown at the back of her head, but a few strands of hair had escaped her plaits and framed her milky face.

Katrin's hazel eyes sparkled when she repeated Martin's greeting. His shy smile froze when he became aware of another visitor. Old Babette, the town gossip, sat on one of the six well-worn chairs at the table.

Her tongue sliced through the marital life of a village couple like a butcher's knife. "He's always the last one to go home from the *Gasthaus*," she rattled on, "and she's the worst-dressed woman in the village. . ."

Martin wished her to the moon and debated what to do next.

"Did you want something?" Katrin asked him when Babette's torrent of words ebbed for an instant.

Martin's hands twisted his cap. "I was wondering if I could get something to eat."

"There's some bread soup left, but the potatoes are gone," Katrin said, wiping her hands on her blue apron. "You wouldn't believe how much two men can eat."

"Oh yes, I would."

"Have a seat," Katrin said, pointing at a chair. "Should I make you a liverwurst sandwich?"

"Yes, please."

Katrin fetched bread from the cupboard. She swatted at a fly before putting a bowl of soup and a small wooden board for the sandwich in front of Martin. He could hardly keep his eyes from the dimple at the right corner of her mouth while she spread wurst on a slice of bread. As she headed back to the sink, he stared at the nape that was visible above her collar. Babette's gaze darted between Katrin and Martin, and he quickly gave the soup his full attention.

The kitchen door swung open and Katrin's mother entered. Frau Weber was in her early forties and of stocky build. Her brown hair was covered by a white day cap. A tart "Guten Tag" escaped her thin lips when she became aware of Martin. He felt a sudden chill under her scrutiny.

Babette watched Katrin's movements with a keen eye. "Your betrothed is a lucky man. When are you getting married?"

"Next fall," the girl replied listlessly, "after the potato harvest."

Martin choked on his soup and coughed.

"Is the soup too hot?" Katrin asked.

"No," he said when he could speak again. "It just went down wrong."

Martin hastened to empty his bowl and rose. He had been looking forward to this encounter for weeks. Now he could not wait to leave the presence of the girl he adored before he betrayed his feelings. He trudged to the courtyard and sank down on one of the stone steps, staring at the ground. A black barn cat soon rubbed her fur on his legs and he absentmindedly petted her. All the joy of the sunny spring day had left him.

* * *

Nikolaus stepped out of the barn and joined his friend on the cool stone. "Something's on your mind, isn't it?"

Martin continued to brood in silence.

"Is it a girl?"

Martin's answer was almost inaudible, "Yes."

"Do I know her?"

"Your sister."

Nikolaus gaped at Martin and raked his fingers through his sandy hair. "Katrin is promised to marry Alfons Weigel from Weidenbach in the fall."

"I just heard. I almost choked on the news."

Nikolaus scratched his head. "I thought I told you about the engagement weeks ago."

"I must have been daydreaming." Martin rested his head in his hands. "Ever since I first came here last year, I can't get her out of my mind."

"If you ask me, the engagement happened rather suddenly. Our parents arranged everything with the Weigels." Nikolaus lowered his voice. "I think my father owes Herr Weigel money and believes he won't have to pay up if Katrin marries his son."

"That sounds like horse-trading to me," Martin said as he lifted his head. "How does she feel about it?"

Before Nikolaus could reply, the rumble of wheels rolling over the cobblestone street interrupted their conversation. A large four-wheeled wagon with a white canvas roof appeared on *Hauptstraße*, the main street. A middle-aged man, dressed in a linen travel shirt, and a youth of Martin and Nikolaus's age strode alongside the wagon. Women and children peeked out of the holes of the shack, singing an emigration song.

They waved at Nikolaus and cried, *"Adieu!"*

He waved back until the wagon disappeared behind a house. "What do they expect to find in America? How can they leave all this behind?" His outstretched arm took in the nearby houses.

Martin doubted that Nikolaus had ever been farther from home than the neighboring villages and perhaps Kaiserslautern. "I think I can understand them. A farmer's son does not have a secure future under our inheritance laws. The fields are getting smaller and smaller with each generation. People are desperate. And when the Mackenbachers return home from their travels and talk about all the countries they've seen and the money they have made, many people get restless." He hesitated for a moment. "I didn't want to tell you this yet, but lately I have thought about immigrating to America."

Nikolaus's jaw dropped. "You want to go to America? But your father is one of the richest landowners in the Palatinate. All doors are open to you here."

Martin shook his head. "As the eldest, Joseph will succeed my father one day. That has been decided already, and you know how I loathe my job as an office trainee. I'm not suited to be a businessman, and I have never forgiven my father for forcing me into this profession. I've tried to obey him until my apprenticeship is over, but I can't endure it any longer. I would much prefer to oversee our forest and farm properties, but my father refused to consider me."

"And what do you expect from America?" his friend retorted. "Do you think it's the land where milk and honey flow?"

Martin took a deep breath. "I want to decide for myself where I live and how I earn my living. Of course, it would be easier to stay at home. But, as much as I need freedom in my career, I am also unhappy with our political situation. The public meeting is my last hope."

"So, you'll stay here if we become a democracy?"

"Probably."

The friends fell silent until Nikolaus asked, "Why did you never tell Katrin that you like her?"

Martin shrugged his shoulders. "She doesn't seem to care about me," he said in a flat voice. "I think she is only polite because I'm your friend. Besides, I'm much too young to court a girl. My family would never agree to such a match."

Nikolaus cast a long look at Martin. "Do your parents know we're friends?"

Martin slowly shook his head. Nikolaus's face drooped and Martin hastened to say, "I don't tell them where I'm going for my rides, but I'd much rather spend time with you than with my father's rich friends."

Nikolaus's smile rivaled the sun's warming rays.

"Carolina is the only sibling I can confide in, and she'll be leaving tomorrow. Forever," Martin said. "Perhaps that's why I'm in a bad mood today."

"I wish I could help you, but I don't know how."

"You've helped just by listening to me." Martin rested his head on his hands. "I am so tired of being trapped in a musty office and I don't want to work there for the rest of my life. On my days off, I want to go home, but the moment I get there I can't wait to leave. I don't know what's wrong with me for feeling like this."

"There are times when I would like to get away from my father for a while. But this is the only life I know. At least you have your own room in Kaiserslautern and can do what you want after work."

Martin sneered. "It's not as good as it sounds. Now I have to obey a landlady instead of my parents."

Friedrich Weber called his son back to work, and Martin took the opportunity to take his leave.

Nikolaus asked, "Are you riding home now?"

"No, I have to pay another visit first." Martin mounted Nelly and patted her neck. "Will I see you at the meeting on Wednesday?"

"I hope so. How will I find you?"

"The assembly is on the *Stiftsplatz* at one o'clock. I'm sure we'll see each other somehow. Auf Wiedersehen!"

* * *

Mist rose from the moors as Martin approached the first houses of Landstuhl. The peat cutters plodded homeward after a hard day's labor, carrying spades over their shoulders. Martin returned their polite greetings with a tilt of his head.

He rode onto the courtyard of the *Sickinger Hof* inn that had belonged to his family for twenty-five years. The lounge faced the bustling main street on the long side of the two-story Dupree mansion while two wings stretched into the garden. The east annex above the kitchen served as sleeping quarters for paying guests and the domestic staff while the west wing housed the family's bedrooms.

Two elegant one-horse carriages stood in the courtyard. The inn would be full tonight with family and friends.

"Wait, I'll help you," Martin shouted, dismounting to aid the stable lad who was unhitching one of the horses.

Martin led Nelly and the second horse into the stable where he curried and fed them. Bracing himself, he stroked Nelly's neck, took a deep breath, and strode toward the great house.

Luise, the young downstairs maid, was polishing doorframes in the hallway.

"Has my family eaten supper yet?" he asked her.

"No, Herr Martin."

"Thank goodness. Where is Carolina?"

"She's upstairs in her room."

Martin mounted the stairs and knocked on Carolina's door. He opened the door slowly, gaining courage from his sister's warm smile. She looked lovely as ever in an azure housedress with a white lace collar. Her raven hair was shaped as a coronet twist at the back of her head. She stood in front of her open wardrobe while Minna, the elderly maid, was busy packing a huge trunk.

"Hello, Martin," Carolina said. "We could have met at lunchtime. Why did you go for a ride straightaway?"

"I needed some fresh air. Can I speak to you alone for a moment?"

"Yes. Go ahead, Minna, I can finish this up myself."

Martin closed the door behind the maid. At Carolina's encouragement, he sat on the edge of the bed and took a deep breath. "I just wanted to say good-bye to you. We may not see each other anymore after your wedding."

Carolina laughed. "Well, if that's your only worry. . .! Of course I will come home from time to time. I love you all too much to stay away for long."

"Maybe I won't be here anymore."

A line formed across her forehead. "What do you mean?"

Martin forced himself to meet her gaze. "Will you promise not to tell anyone what I'm telling you now?"

"Yes, but please let me know what's on your mind."

"The last time I came home for a visit, I found an old straw suitcase up in the attic. There were old letters inside, letters from relatives and friends to our parents. One of them came from America. Did you know that Father has a cousin in America?"

She shook her head.

"The letter was written in 1836 by a man who emigrated some years before and settled near the Mississippi River, along with many other Germans. I took his letter into my room and read it over and over until I knew it by heart. It has encouraged me to ponder my future. I am thinking about going to America."

A cloud seemed to travel across her face as Carolina sank on a chair. With trembling hands, she straightened out the folds of her dress.

"When did you first think about leaving?" she asked.

"About three or four months ago. You know how I always hated this office position Father forced me to accept. I am not suited for it at all."

Carolina bowed her head. "That's not a good enough reason to leave your Fatherland. You could always get into another trade, couldn't you?"

Martin groaned. "That's not the only reason I'm unhappy with my situation. I feel as if I'm suffocating in this country."

Carolina gave him a sympathetic smile. "You're certainly not the only one. I have often eavesdropped on our patrons and their complaints. I can see why a young man like you would be unhappy under the current government."

"I knew you would understand me," Martin said, breathing a sigh of relief.

Carolina looked intently at her brother. "You know it would be a blow to Mother if you left. Is your mind set already?"

9

Martin shook his head. "I want to wait and see how things will progress after the assembly."

Carolina lowered her eyelids and Martin knew that she would accept his decision, whatever it might be. Moreover, she would defend him against his parents' inevitable objections. This was probably the reason why Martin idolized his sister: never did a reproachful word cross her lips. She was equally friendly to everybody: family, staff, and patrons.

"Whatever happens, you should always know how dear you are to me," Martin said. "I wish you all the best. May you be very happy with Ludwig."

He rose and kissed his sister on the cheek. Then he went to his chamber, changed clothes, and hurried downstairs to the dining room to meet his family.

* * *

The two-story manor house in the center of Landstuhl was gleaming for the upcoming wedding. A fresh coat of white paint on the shutters brightened up the warm red of the stones. Its tavern sign, bearing a knight with his shield, had been polished to a shine, greeting travelers from afar.

Hermann Dupree had built the manor from the red square stone blocks of the demolished city palace of the von Sickingen family. He had constructed the mansion not only to demonstrate his status to the world, but also to accommodate his large family.

At last, the wedding party gathered in the courtyard and climbed into the carriages. The horses wore shining harnesses and the coaches were decorated with colorful spring flowers and sprigs of green. Many onlookers lined the streets of the small town that hugged the Sickingen hills to watch the cheerful ride to church. They were not disappointed. The young bride who sat next to her father was as radiant as the April sun.

After the wedding ceremony, the whole party returned to the Sickinger Hof. Before everybody sat down, they presented their gifts to the new couple. Only Martin congratulated them with empty hands.

"Aren't you going to give your sister a gift for her wedding?" asked Aunt Amalie with arched eyebrows.

Martin blushed at the reproach. "Of course, but my gift is so large that it doesn't fit into any box. Besides, it hasn't arrived yet."

"Well, I'm dying to know what it is," Carolina exclaimed.

While the guests mingled and admired the presents, maids placed an array of yeast cakes and cream tortes on the tables.

Feeling stifled in the stuffy, crowded lounge, Martin stepped to the window facing the courtyard and peeked outside. For his sister's sake, he was dressed in a black frock coat, gray pants, and a crisp white shirt. He had even tamed his black curls with a wet comb.

The maids served wine and Martin's father signaled his brother-in-law to give a speech. Martin groaned. His uncle was famous for long-winded talks, and he hoped that his surprise would get noticed to interrupt what was sure to be a lengthy speech. He perked up when he heard a commotion in the courtyard below.

Hermann Dupree opened a window. "Well, if those aren't Mackenbachers." Three itinerant musicians had appeared in the courtyard, tuning their instruments. Martin hurried outside to meet them and beamed at the delighted faces in the windows. Carolina rushed outside and hugged her brother.

"Thank you so much, Martin, for remembering my love of music."

As the musicians became aware of the beautiful bride, they put more swing and momentum into their act to show their admiration for her. Suddenly, Carolina let go of him and whispered something to the trumpeter. The band began to play a lively polka and she said to Martin, "Come on, dance with me."

"But you can't dance on the cobblestones in your wedding gown," Martin protested.

"Why not?" Carolina pulled him along.

Martin smiled and placed his right hand on her hip. She sang off-key into his ear while he twirled her around the band. The courtyard quickly filled with dancers. Maids hopped with servants and stable boys, Martin's sister Emma twirled around with her husband and the laundry maid's little girl spun around a broom stick.

When the polka ended, the groom reclaimed his bride and Martin ambled towards a cluster of people at the edge of the courtyard. The father of the groom, a wine merchant, had brought several casks and began to tap wine for the musicians and guests. Martin waited patiently for his glass and turned to watch the party. His parents stood a few feet away observing the dancers.

"What a splendid idea to hire Mackenbachers," he overheard his father say to his mother. "Come on, Margarethe, let's give it a try."

Although not directed at him, Martin felt heartened by the rare praise and finished his glass to join the revelers. He danced with Emma, his mother, and his cousin Franziska, but most of all he whirled Luise around the yard. She was always there when he happened to be available.

It was late at night when Martin wearily climbed up to his room on the second floor, wondering whether he would ever see his entire family again. Was he selfish for thinking about leaving? He slowly shook his head to dispel the doubts.

Chapter 3

Martin's hand caressed the stones of the dilapidated Castle Nanstein high above Landstuhl. He had been here so many times by himself or with his friends that he thought of it as *his* castle. After all, his grandfather had purchased it during the auction of national properties. The nobility had ceased to exist in the Palatinate since then, but that had not deterred young Martin and his friends from storming the fortress in battle or engaging in peaceful jousting.

Martin stepped through an arched doorway and sat down on the remnants of a wall. He rolled a small rock between his hands and let his gaze wander from the bare castle mount to the moor at the foot of the Sickingen Hills. He closed his eyes and tried to imagine the castle as it had looked during its heyday. Before, he had no trouble conjuring up images of knights and damsels, beggars and jugglers, farriers and cupbearers.

Yet, this time he did not succeed. It made no sense to imagine life during the Age of Chivalry when the present demanded his attention. What was his life's destiny? Would the upcoming meeting give him the answers he was seeking? He sighed and patted the dust from his pants before he rode downhill into town.

* * *

The entire family had gathered in the courtyard to see Carolina off as Martin rode into the courtyard. Mindful of his dusty old breeches and sack coat, he dismounted and hastened to the carriage. Carolina stood next to the coach, a brave smile on her face, and bid farewell to her family. Her face conveyed melancholy when she shook Martin's hand. He had to turn quickly away before betraying his feelings.

The young couple's carriage drove off and the family went their separate ways again. Martin packed his traveling bag and took the stagecoach to Kaiserslautern to report for work the next morning while his brothers returned to their university studies.

* * *

On May 1, Hermann Dupree stood on the flight of steps in his dark blue militia uniform waiting for his carriage. His thoughts turned to the Hambach Festival of 1832. He had been one of thirty thousand men and women who ascended the castle that overlooked the Rhine Valley. Political demonstrations had been prohibited by the authorities, and the press club had called for a festival instead. Artisans and burghers, farmers and winegrowers, Frenchmen and Poles had gathered to celebrate the birth of democracy in Germany. Flags featuring a black, red, and gold tricolor had fluttered on a wind of freedom that excited the crowd.

Back then it had been fashionable to be a Democrat, so Dupree became a Democrat. When the first excitement was over and a second storm did not follow on the heels of the first one, people quietly returned to their businesses and old lives as if nothing had happened. Yet, under the surface, unrest was brewing. Could the volcano of public dissent finally be erupting?

Seventeen years after Hambach, dissension once again began to stir in the Palatinate. Not surprising, since they had enjoyed greater liberties under French rule before falling to Bavaria after Napoleon's defeat. Yet in his opinion, the Frankfurt parliament had made a mistake in offering the imperial crown to the Prussian king in the first place. While he lacked Martin's youthful passion for change, and felt a twinge of apprehension about the upcoming meeting, he had been relieved when the Prussian king rejected the offer.

Margarethe stepped behind him and asked, "How long will you be gone?"

"I don't know. It's possible that I'll be home in two days, but I may have to stay longer. I will write to you if that is the case. Ah, there's the carriage at last."

* * *

Martin looked down on the great room of the *Fruchthalle* from the balustrade of the gallery when someone tapped on his shoulder. He turned around and beamed at Georg, his fellow trainee at a lumber and coal merchant.

"I'm sorry for being late," his friend said. "Did I miss anything?"

"The gentlemen wish to be addressed as *citizens* from now on," Martin replied, stifling a yawn. "And they elected Member of Parliament Nikolaus Schmitt as their president."

He paused for a moment. "Now they are debating how they can force München to recognize the constitution."

"What do they suggest?"

"Some propose a state defense committee, others want to go one step further and elect a provisional government," Martin replied.

"Is your old man down there?"

"Yes."

"Has he given a speech yet?"

"No," Martin said, "my father is not a gifted speaker, even though he could hardly fare worse than the other gentlemen I've heard so far. I am struggling to keep awake."

Georg, an energetic young man with a cheerful demeanor and a perpetually tangled mop of blond hair, glared downward onto the assembly. The colors were dominated by black frock coats and blue militia uniforms.

"Speeches, speeches, nothing but speeches," he uttered. "The Frankfurt Parliament did nothing but talk instead of acting. For sixteen years, Germany was as quiet as a grave and when they finally stirred, what did the Germans do? Instead of joining arms and chasing all rulers out of the country, they elected a few poets and dreamers as their representatives. Those daydreamers had nothing better to do than develop a constitution. I want action, not speeches!"

Martin nodded, thinking of his conversations with Nikolaus and Carolina. "I agree with you, but isn't the fact that we are all here today a sure sign that something big is going to happen? Just look around us. There is unrest everywhere: in Hungary, Saxony, Rhenish Prussia, and here. I'm sure that many Germans only wait for a sign to rise up. Why shouldn't that sign come from us? We Palatines know about liberal laws. Why shouldn't we fight for their introduction all over Germany? Whether it is a state defense committee or a provisional government, we cannot leave it to a few men to push through our demands. Each one of us has to stand up for our convictions. You say that you want to see action. Well, go ahead and do something."

"If it were up to us, this movement should win all over Germany," Georg declared. "And if fighting breaks out, I'll be the first volunteer."

"I'll be the second," Martin said. "But what will our poor master do without us?"

"We can't worry about him. If tomorrow's People's Assembly is serious, they will elect a provisional government and not a state defense committee."

The president's bell interrupted the friends' agitated conversation. Despite Georg's wishes, the leading politicians of the Palatinate decided to propose the appointment of a state defense committee to the People's Assembly.

* * *

The next day, Martin and Georg sat at a small table near the entrance of a beer garden. A militia band drowned out the animated conversations of the mostly male guests with lively tunes. Men of all ages, from the downy bearded youth to the shaky veteran of the Spanish War, had gathered here to quench their thirst and gain courage for the upcoming meeting. Infected by the boisterous mood, Martin and Georg talked animatedly about the upcoming assembly.

Martin was reaching for his beer mug when his hand froze in midair. Nikolaus and Katrin appeared on the other side of the picket fence that separated the beer garden from the sidewalk.

"You made it. How splendid," Martin greeted the friends and beckoned them to come in. Georg, every inch the polite son of a wine merchant from Neustadt, jumped up and introduced himself to the siblings. He hurried away to find chairs for the newcomers while Martin sent bashful glances at the girl he adored. Questions swirled through his head at seeing her so unexpectedly, and without her parents or prying neighbors. Could it be that she came to see him? No, that was out of the question. She was engaged, after all.

"I am happy that you could come," he said.

"It took me three days to talk Father into it," Nikolaus confessed. "When our neighbor offered me a ride, he could not refuse."

He had barely finished when Georg returned with two garden chairs. Martin asked him how he had managed this trick, but he said mischievously, "I pulled them from the bottoms of two militia men."

Laughing loudly, the siblings sat down.

"Don't believe a word he says," Martin told them. "He probably promised one of the waitresses a kiss if she gave him her last chairs. When he looks at a girl she melts like butter in the sun."

Georg smiled. "Of course, no girl is a match for my charms. I had to promise, though, to wait for her at the end of her workday."

Martin chuckled. As always, Georg's zest for life and his cheerful nature were contagious. He had a way of seeing only the sunny side of life that entirely escaped Martin. When the two were together, the young man from Neustadt talked most of the time and probably did not even notice how shy his friend was.

For as long as Martin had known Georg, he wished to be like him. Yet, he had no taste for his friend's attitude toward girls. Georg treated every girl as if she were his intended, but he never became emotionally involved. Martin, on the other hand, had not set eyes on any other girl after meeting Katrin.

Georg turned to Katrin, "I am delighted, *mein Fräulein*, that the concern for our Fatherland is so great that even young ladies spared no trouble to come here today."

Georg may have really meant what he said, but Martin suspected that he had just complimented Katrin to make conversation.

"Well, to be honest with you, I'm just as much concerned about my own welfare as I am about the Palatine people," Katrin replied.

Georg and Martin gave her puzzled looks.

"My sister came to Kaiserslautern to find work," Nikolaus chimed in. "I already explained to her that this is not the appropriate day to look for a position, but I couldn't get the idea out of her head."

Martin gaped at Katrin. It had taken him a few seconds to comprehend the full meaning of this announcement. He finally grasped that the wedding was off, as far as Katrin was concerned. His esteem for her grew immensely, even if he would not have an opportunity to talk to her alone. Only then did he notice the bundle in Nikolaus's hand. Those must be Katrin's belongings.

"What kind of position were you thinking about?" Georg asked.

"I'm not afraid of any work."

"Well, let's have a look around. Last week I wouldn't have had to beg for two chairs in any Gasthaus in town, but today it's the Peoples' Assembly, tomorrow it's the Militia Congress, and who knows what will be in store next week? It's quite possible that a beer garden or Gasthaus is understaffed and needs another kitchen help or waitress."

Katrin's face lit up. "What a wonderful idea! I'll ask right here."

Georg pulled his gold watch out of his vest pocket and glanced at it. "I'm afraid you won't have time until later. We have to hurry if we want to get to the assembly in time."

A throng of people had gathered at the Stiftsplatz when the foursome arrived. Georg, Martin, and Nikolaus were able to find a space near the podium, but they lost Katrin in the crush and had to turn back. They found her engaged in a conversation with a stranger from the eastern Palatinate, judging from his dialect and his supply of wine.

"Would you care for a sip of wine, young lady?" he gallantly offered his pitcher.

Katrin declined the offer but the young men gladly accepted.

* * *

Hermann Dupree exited the hotel *Zum Donnersberg* together with his fellow delegates to walk the few steps to the Stiftsplatz. Despite the sun's warming rays he suddenly shivered when he thought of the upcoming meeting. He chided himself for feeling uneasy. Apart from his attendance of the Hambach Festival, he had always made cautious decisions without stepping on anyone's toes.

Yet, this very morning he had written a letter of resignation as post expeditioner to the postal administration in Speyer. He could no longer remain in the service of the hated Bavarian government while participating in the revolution. The winds of change were blowing through the German provinces and it was best for a man of his social standing to take the winner's side.

Meanwhile, the dignitaries had reached the square and Dr. Hepp, who was walking at his side, said, "Do you see all these excited people, my dear Dupree? This time we won't be content with a refusal from München. We're quite serious about our demands."

"And what do you intend to accomplish with a state defense committee?" mocked another delegate from Neustadt. "No, I can't stand these half-measures. If we want to dissociate ourselves from Bavaria, we have to elect a provisional government today. Should our movement come to a different end than we are hoping for, we will be held accountable one way or the other."

His laugh sounded bitter.

Dupree tried hard not to show his surprise. To give account for the uprising? Didn't this whole delegation consist of respectable Democrats who had no other wish but to build a new life for themselves and their children, free from oppression?

* * *

Katrin sighed as she shifted her weight from her left to her right leg. She could not see anything but the backs of the people in front of her.

"Aren't you bored with these endless speeches, Fräulein Weber?" asked Georg.

"To be honest with you," she said, "yes. The last five or six speakers haven't said anything new."

"You're right. One should put an end to this prattle before we all fall asleep."

Martin grinned at his colleague's outburst. "Georg thinks that speeches are a waste of time," he told Katrin. "I believe he would much rather start marching toward Bavaria tonight."

"I don't know whether the Bavarians are our greatest enemies," Georg said.

"Who else could it be?" Katrin asked.

"It is us and our indecision."

"I will recommend you to the president as a member of the State Defense Council," Martin replied, teasing him.

"Quiet, here comes the voting," Nikolaus said.

The first poll raised the question whether the people wanted to appoint a state defense council or a provisional government. The lady in front of Katrin raised her arm with the men. Feeling encouraged, Katrin followed her example and lifted her right arm when they called for a state defense council. After all, she had defied her parents and her engagement today, so why not defy the authorities as well?

The first round showed no majority. After a lengthy discussion, the election committee decided on a second voting. This time, the people were to raise both hands. The crowd accepted the proposal of a state defense council and voices of protests sounded over the square.

The president informed the crowd of upcoming elections for members of the State Defense Council before closing the meeting. "Brothers! Our province must be transformed into a camp. Everyone must be armed. Each house must become a fortress. Each tree must turn into a line of defense. Brothers, let us arm ourselves for the holy battle of self-defense. Join us in the battle cry: Long live Germany and its eternal rights!"

"Hooray!" shouted Georg, his eyes glowing with enthusiasm.

"Hooray!" yelled Martin and Nikolaus and thousands of others.

The dignitaries hurried into the Fruchthalle to elect the State Defense Council while the crowd streamed into Kaiserslautern's beer gardens and taverns.

"Hooray!" echoed Katrin, invigorated by her choices and encouraged by the infectious optimism of the crowd.

* * *

The four friends left the Stiftsplatz, dispersing in different directions. Georg made his way to the Fruchthalle to learn the result of the voting while Nikolaus and Martin looked after Katrin. They agreed to meet again at the *Sonne* in an hour. When Katrin and the two young men arrived at the beer garden, they could not find a single empty chair.

"What shall we do now? Do you really want to ask for a position today?" Nikolaus asked.

"Yes," she replied, "wait for me here."

She made her way between the chairs and tables and disappeared in the inn. After a while she returned, beaming all the way.

"I'm in luck. I start working as a waitress tomorrow morning at eleven."

"Will you come home with me tonight?" asked Nikolaus.

"No," she said. "If I go back home our parents won't let me leave again. I'm sorry, but you'll have to explain everything to them. Tell them that I believe I can be most useful to the family by working here in the city and making my own living."

Martin turned away from his friends and pretended not to listen to their family discussion. Yet, he could not leave Katrin's side, not when there was a flicker of hope burning in his heart that he might win the girl's affection someday. At last, Nikolaus assented.

"And where will you sleep tonight?" he inquired.

"I don't know yet." Katrin looked forlorn. "They don't have any empty beds because of the assembly."

Martin cleared his throat and faced Nikolaus. "Maybe I could help Katrin, if you agree."

"Do you know somebody who has a room available tonight?" Nikolaus asked.

"No, but I could ask my landlady whether Katrin can sleep in my room tonight. I'll find a place to sleep somewhere. Georg has an old chaise longue in his room, I believe."

Nikolaus shot a look at his sister.

"Very well," he finally said, scratching his chin, "take Katrin to your landlady and ask her permission. I'll wait here for your return."

Martin and Katrin walked through several narrow side streets until he became worried that Katrin would get lost.

"Do you think you can find your way back tomorrow morning?" he finally broke the silence.

"I don't know. If necessary, I will ask somebody for directions," Katrin replied. "Thank you for helping me out."

"It's no more than anybody else would have done," Martin interrupted her. "I'm only doing for you what I would do for any other friend. We are friends, aren't we?"

"Yes," Katrin said in a trembling voice.

They arrived at the house in Salzstraße where Martin had lodged for the past year. His landlady, the widow of a court clerk, was a sourpuss like her late husband and strictly refused Martin's plea. Exasperated, he gathered his work clothes in his bag to prove that he did not intend to spend the night. At last, the widow gravely nodded her approval and the friends set off back to the *Sonne*.

"I don't mean to appear nosy, but what gave you the idea to look for work in the city?" Martin asked.

"I want to help out my family, and I refuse to get married just because my parents are poor."

"I can understand that very well," Martin replied.

"You don't understand anything," Katrin suddenly snapped at him, her eyes glittering with anger. "How can you possibly understand? You never had to live from hand to mouth. We can't ride through the countryside on a mount. Oh no, we have to worry what to put on our table tomorrow. Times are damned hard. Three families from Moorbach left for America this year already, and it's only the beginning of May."

Katrin stumbled over a cobblestone and Martin offered her his arm for support.

"Thank you." She lifted her skirt with one hand. "I almost fell, and what would I wear tomorrow if my dress was ripped and dirty?"

Martin's cheeks began to burn when she placed her hand on his forearm. He turned away from Katrin and pretended to look at a hardware store's window display.

"I know that times are hard, and I understand your anger," he said after composing himself, "but you have overlooked a very important point: It isn't my fault that my father is rich. Ever since I realized the difference between rich and poor, I've tried to spend as little as possible of my father's money. I dress as simply as my position allows, and I like a blood wurst sandwich much better than a saddle of venison. The only thing you cannot accuse me of is that I behave like a rich man."

Katrin shook her head so vigorously that her bonnet tilted to one side.

"I didn't want to hurt you," she said while adjusting her hat. "I spoke about your class. Of course it's not your fault that your father is rich. But it's also not my fault that my father is poor. Do you think that I enjoy it? I want to wear nice dresses, stroll in the park and have many admirers just like your sisters."

"Nevertheless, you should be aware of men like Georg," Martin retorted.

"Why? He seems very nice."

"He's nice to every girl," he grumbled. "He makes eyes at one today, but he'll forget her by tomorrow."

"I promise I'll be careful."

They continued their walk until Katrin said, "When I think about tomorrow, my stomach feels queasy."

"Come on, you're not afraid of work."

"That's not what I'm dreading. I have always worked hard, but I'm not used to being alone after work. Here in the city, everything is foreign, and I don't know a soul, except for you."

They waited for a swineherd and his charges to pass before crossing the street.

Martin steered Katrin around a group of three tipsy young men. It was best not to tell her yet that he might be leaving the city soon. "But you shouldn't lose heart. Everything will look different in a few days. Perhaps you'll find some colleagues you can talk to after work."

"You're probably right."

Katrin released his arm as they arrived at the beer garden where Nikolaus and Georg waited near the gate for their return. Georg chatted with a turner about the election results while Nikolaus listened.

Katrin relayed that she had lodging for the night, and Nikolaus wished her luck before hurrying away to meet his neighbor.

"I have news for you," Georg said, turning to Martin. "Your father is a member of the State Defense Council. What do you say now? I didn't think he was capable of holding a public office after everything you told me about him."

Martin shrugged. He doubted that his father would hold his new position for long. Hermann Dupree had inherited his wealth and had not made much effort to increase it. Perhaps the dignitaries assumed that Dupree would bring in collections from his rich friends.

"Let's wait and see," he said. "This won't last very long, or I don't know my father very well." As ever, his father hung his coat in the wind. After the Hambach Festival, he had soon stepped back into line and no doubt he would do the same now. "Who else is in the council?"

Georg rattled off the names.

"You aren't among them?" Martin teased his friend.

"No. I wouldn't be able to criticize the council if I were a member."

"That's a pity. A few outstanding gentlemen are among them, but in my opinion, a defense council can't be radical enough, especially when things begin to heat up around here."

"No," Georg said, "that would not be a job for me. I told you yesterday that I'd rather dance than set the tone. And now, I suggest we don't talk about politics anymore since it must surely bore Fräulein Weber."

"Don't mind me," Katrin said. "I'm interested in other people and like to listen to them."

"Starting tomorrow you'll have many opportunities to do just that," Georg replied.

"Perhaps that's why I'm attracted to this job," she said.

"Just a moment, I see an acquaintance who I must speak to," Georg said. "In case we won't see each other again, I wish you the best of luck tomorrow."

He shook her hand and turned to leave.

"Wait," Martin called after him. "Can I sleep in your room tonight?"

"Of course. There's a key under the empty flowerpot in the window left of the front door. You don't have to wait for me tonight, I'll be late."

He disappeared into the crowd and Martin was once again alone with Katrin. He shoved the tip of his boot into the ground to hide his embarrassment.

"What do we do now?" he asked her at last. "Do you want to stay here?"

"No, I want to go to bed early so that I'll be well rested tomorrow," she replied.

Martin took Katrin to his landlady's house where they shook hands and bid good night to each other. He wished he could hold her hand forever, yet she seemed determined to go inside. He asked himself whether she was worn out from the day's events or wanted to avoid him.

After she closed the door behind her, he spun around and set out looking for his father. He expected to find him at the *Donnersberg* and turned his steps to the hotel. Arriving, he asked a young waitress where to find the State Defense Council members.

She pointed toward an oak door. "The gentlemen are dining in the adjoining room."

When Martin opened the door, he found the table cleared and the dignitaries in animated conversation over the rims of their wine glasses. Dupree was relating the wedding of his youngest daughter as Martin appeared by his side.

"I wanted to congratulate you on your appointment," Martin said reluctantly when Dupree greeted him.

Dr. Hepp gave the newcomer a closer look. "Is this your son Martin? I haven't seen you for several years. My, you've turned into a handsome young man. Did you go to the meeting?"

"Of course."

"Are you willing to fight for the freedom of the Palatinate?"

"Yes." Martin's voice sounded more self-assured than he felt. He searched his father's face for a reaction to that last remark, but his father showed no signs of alarm. Martin began to wonder why he had come here at all if not to get his father's permission to join the rebel forces if an armed rebellion was imminent. He doubted that his father would be equally indifferent if one of his older brothers decided to join the fight, if it came to it.

He grew tired of the gentlemen's attention and took his leave as soon as he could without appearing impolite. As usual, his father had barely talked to him.

He wandered around the city, drinking a glass of beer in one place, exchanging a few words with an acquaintance in another before heading on his way again.

He felt a profound confusion he could not blame on political events, and midnight had long passed when he finally arrived at Georg's lodgings. No, it was Katrin who had stirred too many emotions in him. For the first time since he knew her, he had been alone with her and she had talked about nothing but her poverty and her new position. He doubted that he could ever win the girl over after today and concluded that fighting in the inevitable uprising was probably a special form of forgetting.

Chapter 4

May 3, 1849

After attending the first official gathering of the State Defense Council, Hermann Dupree was exhausted when he left the Fruchthalle in the late afternoon. He had planned to eat supper with the other council members. Yet, he found himself ambling past his hotel. For an outdoorsman like him, it was unbearable to pass a whole day in a closed session under a thick cloud of cigar smoke.

Dupree consulted his pocket watch. Martin should be home from work by now, and he resolved to have a serious conversation with his son. Ever since Martin had moved into the city, he had become very reserved toward his family. Carolina was his only confidante nowadays. Martin's behavior had been especially peculiar last night. When he congratulated him on his appointment it sounded more like condolences.

Although this was only the second time that Hermann Dupree visited Salzstraße, he immediately recognized the house with its double gable windows. Widow Hoffmann slowly opened the door when he knocked.

"Good afternoon," Dupree said. "I would like to see Martin. I'm his father."

"Come on in," the widow replied, her chin jutting out of her stern face.

He stepped into the hallway and she firmly closed the door.

"I guess you've heard already what happened here last night?" she grumbled. "It's about time someone finally came to see after things."

"What's the matter? What on earth are you talking about?"

"I'm talking about the fact that your son brought a girl home yesterday," the widow said, disgust dripping from her voice. "She slept in his room last night."

A girl? That did not sound like Martin at all, but it could explain his odd behavior.

"And he, did he sleep here, too?"

"He packed a few things and left again."

"Well, then everything is alright," Dupree said matter-of-factly. "Now, may I see him?"

The widow gasped at his indifferent response and bumbled ahead to Martin's room. Martin sat on the only chair and looked out of the window, obviously lost in thought. He turned and jumped up when his father stepped inside.

"Guten Tag," Dupree said, and Martin reluctantly returned the greeting.

"I need to talk to you," his father said while surveying the room.

The entire furnishing consisted of a short bed, a nightstand, a double-door wardrobe, a washstand, and a small square table. Martin's clothes were scattered over the bed and on the floor. The only object in the room which gave a glimpse of the inhabitant's character was the painting of a horse's head leaning on the nightstand.

"It doesn't look very cozy in here," Dupree remarked, thinking about his son's room in Landstuhl. There, his youngest son had gathered everything that delighted a boy's heart: a hunting rifle, a willow pipe, marbles, and rocks.

"I know," Martin said, "the old woman doesn't allow a nail in the wall. She believes the house would collapse."

Dupree shifted his weight. "She told me that you brought a girl here. Is that true?"

Martin briefly explained the circumstances. "Did the widow call you here because of Katrin? That's just like her."

"No, no. I came here for another reason," Dupree assured him. He could not find the right words and paced around the small room with his hands clasped behind his back.

Martin remained by the window, his arms folded over his chest.

"I've been wondering about your strange behavior for quite a while now and I asked myself why you came to see me last night. What do you hold against me? Why do you avoid me like a leper? Your mother has also complained that you don't come home very often anymore."

Martin scowled. "You know exactly what I have against you. You forced me into this apprenticeship against my wishes because you want to groom me to become a merchant. I begged you to let me work at one of your estates, but you refused. I'm sorry that Mama has to suffer, but I can't help it. I'm not happy at all with the life you forced me to lead and have therefore decided to change it completely. Just so you know, today I resigned my position at the Schwarz Company."

Dupree felt like Martin had slapped him in the face. None of his older sons would have ever dared to go against his wishes. Hadn't he always wanted what was best for them and the family? "And what will you do for a living? You have no skills other than riding a horse."

"I'm young enough to learn something new. For the moment, however, I will not seek work. Coincidentally, you have just signed an appeal to call the youth of the Palatinate to arms. I have decided to join the irregulars. One thing I would like to make perfectly clear," he said, looking Dupree in the eyes, "your involvement in the State Defense Council has nothing to do with my decision."

Shattered by his son's outburst, Dupree left without uttering another word.

* * *

Martin sat down, motionless while listening to his father's fading footsteps. How could he tell his father what had changed in their relationship when he ignored his dearest longings? As a boy, he had adored the stocky man who would take him on hunting trips or for visits to one of his estates. His love of the open air had developed during these outings and he had hoped to manage one of his father's properties someday.

Everything changed for Martin when he attended the *Gymnasium* in Kaiserslautern. Here, he was exposed to the company of boys from the whole province. They were often outspoken and did not mind criticizing their elders. Martin gradually realized that his father was not the omniscient presence he had always thought he was.

Then, unbeknownst to Dupree, Martin's grandfather confided in him that his father did not have any reason to boast about his participation at the Hambach Festival as he frequently did when the children were young. From those stories, Martin had believed that his father was a crucial figure during the demonstration. Now it turned out that he was just one of thousands of bystanders who had sung freedom songs and listened to speeches. As the last song faded away, Hermann Dupree quietly slipped back into the role of a landowner who had inherited his wealth. When he applied for the position of postal expeditioner a couple years later,

Dupree denied any participation in the festival. And this was the man who now held a crucial role in the revolution!

Stifled by the small, spartan room, Martin donned his jacket and roamed the streets. He walked past his workplace without greeting the laborer who was just closing the main gate.

The important decisions he had made earlier today would probably determine the course of his entire life. Martin was relieved that he had gotten off lightly during the conversation with his master. Herr Schwarz had obviously been relieved to let the reluctant trainee go. He simply nodded as if he had realized early on that Martin was not cut out to be a businessman. His eyes had grown sad, however, when Georg resigned right after Martin.

* * *

The next morning, Martin climbed into the stagecoach to pick up several items from home. He was surprised to see that the chaise stopped in front of the *Seibert* inn instead of Sickinger Hof. Then it occurred to him that his father must have submitted his resignation as a post expeditioner to the Bavarian government, so his parents' home was no longer a stagecoach stop.

Martin crossed the street and prowled around the rear of the house, eager to avoid being seen. He peaked through the open kitchen windows and was relieved to see Luise at the sink, scouring a pan. His plan would have been more difficult if one of the older maids saw him.

"Psst," he whispered and then a little louder, "psst!"

The maid looked up. "Oh, Herr Martin, you gave me a scare. What's the matter?"

"Is my mother at home?" he whispered.

Luise shook her head. "No, she went to her seamstress for a fitting."

"Good," Martin said and entered the house.

Upstairs in his room he rummaged through his wardrobe until he found what he was looking for: a large, old brown leather bag his grandfather had once given him for hunting trips with his father. He crammed two shirts, a pair of shoes, a light jacket and two pairs of socks into the bag. Then he picked up his rifle from the wall and scanned the room. His willow pipe had been lying on the bookshelf for years, all but forgotten. On a sudden impulse, he grabbed it and placed it in the bag. Finally, he slung the bag and rifle over his shoulder and hurried out of the room without looking back. He walked past the kitchen, then changed his mind and entered.

"Listen, Luise, if my mother happens to go into my room and sees that the rifle is missing, don't tell her that I took it. Just make up an excuse. Tell her you moved it while cleaning or something. Would you do that for me?"

"*Ja,* Herr Martin. I won't tell her that you were here today."

"Splendid," Martin said and left the house for the last time.

* * *

Georg and Martin were among the first volunteers of the revolutionary army. The registration and medical examination took place on the first floor of the Fruchthalle while the State Defense Council met upstairs.

Georg was fortunate that his father supplied him, an only son, with a generous allowance. He shared the money generously with Martin, who could not expect anything from his own father anymore.

Since they both owned a rifle and were respectable marksmen, Martin and Georg were immediately accepted into the riflemen company and spent the greatest part of each day with shooting and drill practice. In the evenings they strolled through the busy streets of the city, always on the lookout for news. One night, they passed a crowded beer garden and Georg nudged Martin. "Isn't this the Gasthaus where your friend works?"

"Yes," Martin said reluctantly. He had not been here since the day of the Public Assembly to avoid an encounter with the girl he adored. His life was complicated enough without thinking about Katrin, especially when they might be leaving any day now.

Georg said, "Come on, let's go in there," and Martin had no choice but to follow his friend.

They found an empty table in the rear of the garden. A short time later, Katrin approached them to take their orders. Martin sat with his back to the girl. Her face turned an attractive shade of pink when she recognized her patrons.

"Good evening, Fräulein Weber," Georg charmed her. "That is your name, isn't it?"

"Yes," Katrin said. Martin noticed with delight that she looked at him while answering his friend's question.

Martin plucked up his courage and asked her, "When do you get off work?"

"In about fifteen minutes," Katrin replied, "why?"

"Would you like to sit down with us for a while when you're finished?"

A smile stole over Katrin's face. "Yes, I'll be glad to come. See you soon."

She hurried away and returned with their beer mugs. Martin turned his chair around so he could follow her with his eyes as she moved between the tables. At last, she came back and dropped on a chair the friends had reserved for her.

"How are you doing, Fräulein Weber?" Georg asked.

"I'm doing fine, only my feet hurt dreadfully," Katrin replied, grimacing.

"Have you seen Nikolaus lately?" Martin asked.

"Yes, he came on Saturday and brought me my clothes," Katrin said with glowing cheeks. "My parents thank you for putting me up for a night."

Georg pointed at the hustle and bustle of the inn. "There are many strangers in town nowadays. I'm sure you have had quite some excitement here?"

"Yes, we have. I would have never believed that there are so many crazy people in the world! It is quite normal to hear loud singing at all hours, but I have never seen so many old hats and worn-out shirts in my life. On the other hand, I learn all the news here and almost at the same moment as they occur."

"Well, I hope you don't think we're crazy," Georg joked.

Katrin shook her head and pointed at Martin's hat on the table. "Is that a Hecker hat?" The young men chuckled.

"It is when you don't have any other," Martin said and pointed at the chicken feather in the hatband. "I don't think there are many chickens in town that still have all their feathers."

Katrin laughed and the two friends joined in.

Then she asked Martin, "I heard that your father was sent to Belgium as a weapons buyer. Aren't you proud of him?"

"Proud?" Martin asked. "Just so you know, I have moved out from home and will not return there, no matter how this revolution turns out."

"I'm sorry," Katrin said.

A comrade from Martin's and Georg's company appeared, unable to find a seat. Katrin used the opportunity to get up and say good-bye.

"I've had an exhausting day today and would like to go to bed soon. Goodnight," she said. Martin's face drooped as she disappeared in the crowd. Yet, was that a look of admiration he had detected when he told her he had left home for good?

The exhausted newcomer sank on the chair and wiped the sweat off his forehead with a blue dotted handkerchief.

"My, is it hot again today," he groaned. "The only good thing about the heat is that one can drink more than usual."

The two friends roared with laughter and Georg voiced the suspicion that Anselm had only joined the irregulars to find drinking buddies. Anselm protested vehemently before admitting that he would much rather bivouac in the eastern Palatinate than sleep in a feather bed in Kaiserslautern.

"You may get there sooner than you think," Georg replied, sobering.

"Yes, I have learned that irregulars from Kaiserslautern are to move to the siege of Landau. I hope I'll be one of them," Anselm said.

"I don't care where I'm going as long as I have something to do and won't have to linger in town anymore," Martin said.

"That's true," Georg agreed. "As long as I'm in Kaiserslautern I feel like a civilian."

At that moment Karl Morgenstern, another irregular, approached Anselm. He wore a blue cotton blouse, black trousers made of cloth, and old leather boots. The dark colors reflected the stern expression on his face. His hat looked like an uglier cousin of Martin's hat.

He had heard Georg's last words and said bitterly, "Many of the irregulars feel like civilians because they don't have any weapons. I myself don't even own a scythe. Is it a great surprise when we refuse to drill?"

"The weapon buyers of the council are already in England and Belgium to purchase rifles," Anselm tried to appease him.

"How will those weapons be shipped to the Palatinate, though?" Morgenstein asked. "And will we still need rifles when they get here?"

Martin interrupted them. "Don't talk like that. Don't we have the best chance to succeed? Our allies Württemberg and Baden are between Bavaria and us. By the time the Bavarian troops reach the Rhine River, we'll be well armed and beat them back with ease."

"I believe in the revolution, but my companions are getting discouraged," Morgenstern said. "Just this morning I overheard one irregular saying to another, 'I don't know why they talk of volunteers when we are forced to do things all the time.'"

Martin remained silent. It had never occurred to him that some young men did not volunteer to join the irregulars. Morgenstern kept talking incessantly but Martin stopped listening, lost in his own thoughts. He said good-bye to the others and proceeded to his quarters alone.

He crossed the street and walked a few steps when he suddenly heard someone calling his name. He turned around but did not see any acquaintances.

"Psst, Martin!"

There it was again and this time, Martin looked up. Katrin was leaning out of a window under the attic of the inn waving him over.

"Are you still mad at me for what I said on the day of the assembly?" she asked softly.

"Oh, no," Martin said, "I could never be cross with you."

"Well, then everything is alright," the girl said, "goodnight."

"Goodnight."

Bewildered, Martin continued on his way. When he had left the city behind, he sat down on the side of the road and thought about the encounter with Katrin. Earning her own money seemed to have improved her disposition and confidence. He had even detected a glint of joy in her eyes when she saw him earlier. Finally, he came to the conclusion that he may not have won Katrin's love yet, but at least he had gained her friendship. When the revolution was over, he would have time to think about his future. For the time being he would have to be content with seeing the face of his beloved girl in his dreams.

The revolution crept back into his mind when he mulled over Morgenstern's remarks. It was true that the passage from Bavaria to the Palatinate led through revolutionary provinces, but what about the long border facing north? This very day, he had read in the newspaper that Prussia had promised the King of Bavaria assistance in the "Restoration of Law and Order in the rebellious Palatinate" by dispatching troops. And even if they defeated the Prussians, how long would they be able to maintain their position against the rest of reactionary Germany? Or would the people of other German states, or even all over Europe, go to the barricades once a great victory was achieved?

Darkness came late at this time of year. When the last light faded, Martin rose and ambled back to the city. If he did not leave for camp soon, these somber thoughts would quench his enthusiasm for the cause.

Chapter 5

June 1849

After leaving Homburg behind, Martin guided his horse over Kaiserstraße. How he longed to talk to Georg right now. His friend would surely dispel the cloud that had formed over his head ever since he heard of his father's blunder. But Georg and Anselm had left for Landau ten days ago. Martin was alone again, delivering messages between Kaiserslautern, Kirchheimbolanden, and Homburg.

Outside Homburg, he passed a platoon of nearly thirty recruits. Two armed irregulars accompanied them on their way to camp. Their indifferent, sometimes even stubborn facial expressions showed Martin that none of them had volunteered to come along. He shielded his eyes from the glaring sun as he searched their faces for Nikolaus. It was only a matter of time until his friend would be drafted.

Before reaching Landstuhl, Martin steered the roan on a trail through the moor. He fingered the letter in his pocket.

"Since you joined the rebels, Mama walks through the house like a sleepwalker," his sister had written. "The management of our huge household rests on my shoulders now. Martin, I beg you. Please come home so that Mama will be happy again. I promise to support your wish for a different profession with all my heart. Your loving sister, Emma."

Martin shook his head. His mother would never understand that he could not turn back now. Better not to see her at all. With her husband in exile, she would plead even more strongly for Martin to return home.

In Kaiserslautern, an orderly handed Martin a dispatch for Colonel Willich in Landau. Martin's face brightened at the thought of meeting Georg again. With any luck, this would be his last mission as a courier.

* * *

Nikolaus was weeding the potato field when Fritz, the neighbor's ten-year-old son, ran along the field path.

"Nikolaus," he cried, "you have to come to town hall right away."

Nikolaus straightened his aching back. "Why?"

"You and all other young men are being drafted. Come, hurry."

Nikolaus broke into a run. At home, his mother had already packed a change of clothes into an old bag.

"Be careful," she said and her usually stern expression softened. "Come back safely, you hear me?"

A tear rolled down her cheek while Nikolaus kissed it.

"Don't worry about me," he said, trying to hide the rush of excitement that began to well up in him. "I'll be alright."

Friedrich Weber called his son to the barn. "Son, I want to show you something."

He pulled a scythe from behind a stack of hay. "I had it straightened for you by the blacksmith the other day. I didn't want you to be unarmed. It isn't much, but it's better than nothing."

Nikolaus suddenly felt a lump in his throat as he grabbed the scythe. It was a gesture of love for his father to give up a scythe right before the harvest began.

They shook hands and Nikolaus ran to the meeting place. His heart leaped when he saw the colorful group of young men gathered in front of the mayor's office. One lad held a pitchfork in his callused hand and boasted that he would stick it to any Prussian he saw. Nikolaus and his friends marched off laughing and singing. By the end of the day, they were in Kaiserslautern and waited in front of city hall until the lodging forms were written.

Nikolaus was billeted at the house of a pharmacist. His stomach grumbled as he trudged through the unfamiliar streets. At last, he found the address and a maid invited him into the kitchen. A fellow already sat at the kitchen table and consumed a portion of fried eggs, ham, and salad with great appetite. He introduced himself as Jakob Christmann and the red band wrapped around his hat showed Nikolaus that he had deserted his army post to join the rebels.

Nikolaus tucked into his supper, put his bag in a corner, and went to town. He wanted to use the opportunity to visit his sister despite his fatigue.

The waitress at the *Sonne* told Nikolaus that it was Katrin's day off. He climbed the narrow, dark staircase to the upper floor but found Katrin's room empty. Disappointed, he turned to leave when she appeared at the bottom of the stairs.

"Nikolaus?" she asked. "What are you doing here? Is there something wrong with our parents?"

Nikolaus explained why he had come, and she climbed the stairs, concern etched on her face.

"I didn't expect them to draft farm boys," she said. "How will Mother and Father get along without you?"

"They'll just have to make do," Nikolaus said tersely.

In her room, he sank down on the only chair. "I'm alright with the conscription," he admitted. "Now that I'm away from our village, I find it exciting. This will be quite an adventure."

"Is that all the revolution means to you? An adventure? At least Martin is fighting for a cause he believes in," she said scathingly.

"No, I didn't mean it like that," Nikolaus appeased her, "it's just that I hardly ever get out of Moorbach and now I have a chance to see more of the world." He surprised himself with these words. Had it only been weeks ago when he had told Martin that his village was the only life he knew? Back then he could not have imagined leaving it, if only for a brief time.

Katrin placed her bonnet on the bed and ran her fingers through her hair. "Has it ever occurred to you that you could get killed?"

Nikolaus winced as he tried to shrug off her concerns. "Don't worry, we won't get that close to the fighting, if there is a battle at all. I'll be alright, you'll see."

"Have you heard anything from Martin lately?"

"No, I haven't seen him since the Public Assembly, and I don't have the faintest idea where he is right now."

He searched her eyes for clues of her sudden interest in Martin, but she averted her gaze.

"I saw him once since the meeting," she admitted with rosy cheeks. "He came to the inn with Georg. They seemed eager to begin the campaign."

"They're probably not in Kaiserslautern anymore. How are you doing? Have you settled in yet?"

"I'm doing fine, thank you. I get along well with the other waitress but since only one of us can take a day off, I'm alone all day long. It can get very lonely in town when you don't know anybody."

Nikolaus looked at her with sympathy as she spoke. He could not image what it meant to be lonely. As far back as he could remember, he had never been alone, neither at school nor at work or in the evenings, which he often spent at the house of friends.

"I think the problem will solve itself over time." he tried to console his sister. "At the moment I urge you not to go out by yourself. There are a lot of strangers in the city."

"How long will you stay in Kaiserslautern?" Katrin asked.

"Nobody knows. Maybe we'll leave tomorrow or the next day. It's about time for me to go back to my quarters, though. I'm very tired after today's march."

Katrin accompanied him to the end of the street and grasped his hand. "Take care of yourself."

Chapter 6

The small town of Offenbach near Landau teemed with irregulars when Martin arrived with his dispatch. At the village square he found a Landau turner who led him to Colonel Willich. On the way, Martin asked him about Georg and Anselm, but the turner did not recognize their names. At the schoolhouse Martin handed the message to Colonel Willich and waited respectfully until he had read it.

"Very well," Willich said finally, "I don't have any messages for you at the moment. You may go."

Martin remained rooted on the spot.

"Is there something else?" the colonel asked.

"Yes, I wanted to ask you if you needed a competent rifleman?"

"And that competent rifleman would be you?" Willich said, considering as he stroked his beard.

"Yes."

"Report to my adjutant," Willich replied and turned his attention to the paperwork on his desk.

Martin was walking along Hauptstraße with a billeting form in his pocket when a squad of boisterous men approached. Martin thought they had had too much wine to drink when he discovered the object of the racket: one of the irregulars had speared a large hunk of fatty pork on the bayonet of the rifle he proudly carried. Martin broke into a wide grin when he recognized the joker as his comrade from Kaiserslautern, Anselm Scheuermann.

Anselm, however, was too preoccupied to notice his friend. Martin followed the group until they found an appropriate resting place in the village. Several young men fanned out to forage food. Meanwhile, a rebel hauled a bundle of brushwood for the fire, another one held a huge frying pan in his hand, and a third rebel carried two loaves of bread under his arms.

While Anselm cut the meat into the pan, Martin stepped behind him and said, "I'm hungry, too."

Anselm turned around and almost dropped the meat. "Martin, when did you get here?"

"Just a few minutes ago," Martin said. "I brought a message for Colonel Willich. Now I'm part of his corps. Do you mind if I eat with you?"

"By all means, share our meal. There should be enough for all of us. Sit down and tell me where you've been lately."

"Thank you, I'm famished," Martin said and sat on his bag. "Have you seen Georg by any chance?"

Anselm pursed his lips while stirring the meat. "I haven't seen him in days. We got separated before we even arrived in Landau. I'll tell everybody that you're looking for him."

Martin sipped from a wine pitcher one of Anselm's friends handed to him. He was glad just to see a friendly face in the confusion of retreating troops. Life as a courier no longer held any appeal for him. He had missed the company of his fellow irregulars to divert himself from the growing sense of unease over the course of the revolution. Less than two months ago he had all but decided to emigrate to America, and now he was hoping fervently to remain here and dream of a future with Katrin, but only if that meant shaking off the Bavarian yoke once and for all. It was up to him and his fellow rebels to make it happen.

* * *

The following day was payday. Martin picked up his one Gulden and nine Kreuzer at the mayor's office and proceeded to a Gasthaus. Several of his new acquaintances were already assembled around a rectangular table and eagerly beckoned him to join them.

"I guess you want to have another beer before we go into battle?" a French laborer said, sneering.

The insurgents all started talking at the same time, one shouting louder than the other. Everyone seemed to sense that their first clash with the Prussian army was imminent.

"Landau has been relieved this morning," cried one rebel. "And Colonel Schimmelpfennig is retreating from the Prussians."

"Yes, he's probably approaching the Queich Valley as we speak," said another.

"We're doomed," whined a third fellow. "The Prussians are moving in on all fronts and are surrounding our volunteer army."

"Is that true?" Martin asked the man next to him.

He nodded. "General Sznayde has ordered a withdrawal across the Rhine River to merge with the revolutionary army of Baden. I bet that Willich won't go for that. He's not finished with the Prussians just yet."

* * *

It was late afternoon when the drums sounded and the Willich volunteer corps marched off. Martin's feet grew heavier with every step of the way. He was not accustomed to hikes of such length and his heels soon burned with blisters. He disregarded his bodily aches, however, when he scrutinized the determined faces of his comrades.

Martin had chosen the Willich volunteer corps because it was the only corps that possessed something like a fighting spirit. Having traveled across the Palatinate long enough, he realized the neglected state of the Palatine irregulars. He appreciated the spirit of order and purpose this corps possessed and hoped it would make a difference when they faced the Prussians.

* * *

The huge clock of the Andreas church struck midnight when the volunteer corps finally marched into Annweiler. Unaccustomed as he was to the forced march, Martin could barely keep his eyes open by the time he received his billeting assignment. He was half asleep by the time he dropped down on a sack of straw, too exhausted to think of the day ahead.

The next morning, his hostess fried potatoes for Martin but he could hardly swallow a bite with his stomach tied in worried knots. He downed a cup of chicory coffee and thanked the woman for her hospitality. He chided himself for behaving so anxiously at the thought of the imminent confrontation. Wasn't this why he had joined the corps? He could have just left and gone back home, and nobody would have noticed. The thought of home strengthened his resolve. He was determined not to crawl home to his mother at the first sight of a Prussian helmet.

At the meeting place Martin barely had time to clean his rifle when Colonel Willich rode into town at breakneck speed.

"Quick," he called to his officers, "gather all troops, the riflemen first. The Prussians are near Rinnthal."

Hampered by his blisters, Martin could barely keep up with the fast march that ensued. His fellow insurgents fell silent, giving him time to reflect. He feared for the future of the revolution, more so than about his own fate. So much depended on the outcome of this battle. Too much. He took several deep breaths to calm his jittery nerves and kept marching.

Chapter 7

Rifle shots crackled in the distance as the troops hurried through Rinnthal. At the end of the village, Martin and his fellow sharpshooters came upon a troop of men armed with scythes who were blocking the highway. Screams and yells erupted when a bullet buzzed overhead. Martin frowned at the disarray of men when it occurred to him that Nikolaus may well be part of such an insurgent unit. After all, they were mostly farmers or woodsmen and could not be expected to perform like regular soldiers. What could they possibly accomplish without weapons?

Willich's vanguard had already opened fire against the 2nd Prussian Division. A bearded lieutenant ordered Martin's company to climb the ridge on their left. Martin clambered up a slope overgrown with shrubs and took cover behind a bush whenever he could.

The moment of truth had arrived, and Martin was ready. His hand remained steady when he grasped the rifle from his shoulder. He peeked at his fellow rebels. If they were nervous, they did not show it. One of them drank a sip from his flask while another checked for the last time whether his rifle was properly loaded.

Martin took aim at a Prussian on the opposite, wooded hillside. He pulled the trigger, but the weapon remained silent. The rifle that had served him for several years failed him now when he needed it most. He cursed and pointed it at a bush to set it off. At his third attempt, the rifle fired but the bullet landed in front of the bush. Martin concluded that he must have made a mistake while loading the rifle and forced himself to slow down. He pulled a cartridge out of his pouch and carefully loaded his weapon again.

For the next half hour, the Prussians and insurgents exchanged skirmish fire. Martin was unsure if he ever hit a target, but he was certain that the soldiers missed theirs. Did they miss on purpose?

At last, the main column of the Prussian army receded further into the valley. Martin set off to pursue them when a shrill scream stopped him in his tracks. He turned around and froze. The entire hillside teemed with Prussians who aimed their rifles at the sharpshooters from above. Several insurgents began to run away, tumbling head over heels down the slopes.

"Cowards," Martin gasped through clenched teeth.

The sharpshooter closest to Martin rose and dashed down the slope when his barrel was struck by a bullet. He dropped to the ground while another bullet whirred past his head. The rebel scrambled to his feet and scurried down the hill. Martin sensed that the riflemen could not hold onto their position and darted downhill after his shrieking companions.

The road was clogged with insurgents marching in wide columns. Martin lost contact with his sergeant as he trudged through a swampy meadow to get around the battalion. Never mind, he consoled himself. He would catch up with his company in Annweiler.

Wedged into a dense file of insurgents, Martin made slow progress. Every time a musket bullet struck the column, the men screamed in terror. Yet, the Prussians did not appear eager to pursue the insurgents.

Martin was struggling for breath when they arrived in Annweiler. The forced march after a heated firefight had taken its toll on him and he was glad for a respite.

A cluster of tired men gathered around the town well, gulping the cool water. Martin dipped his hand into the bucket and wet his cracked lips. Then he filled his canteen and stepped back to allow room for others. He longed to be alone with his thoughts. Were the other rebels as discouraged about the defeat as he was? And where was Georg?

* * *

Martin's eyes scanned the frightened faces of the irregulars until they rested on the three hilltops towering above the village. Ages ago, the three castles Trifels, Anebos, and Münz had grown out of them as if they were natural extensions of the hills. The wretched outcome of the Palatine revolution and the sudden retreat of the liberation troops to Baden did not seem to concern the old ruins in the least. Too many armies of various nations had marched over this soil since the first stone was put in its place high above on the hillcrests.

Martin tried to imagine what had gone through a knight's mind before he set off on a crusade to the Holy Land. Instead he saw a slope blanketed with a thick forest of spiked helmets.

"What are you staring at? Do you think the Prussians are here yet?" said a voice nearby.

Martin started as if caught in an illegal act, then he whirled around and looked into Georg's beaming face.

"I wonder why we haven't met any sooner. When did you join Willich's corps?" Georg asked.

"Since the day before yesterday. I was a courier until then."

"Well, I'm glad you came here. Let's stay together from now on."

Martin's grin was answer enough.

The irregulars had quenched their thirst and continued their march, bypassing the fortress of Landau in a respectful distance and heading southeast.

"You're very quiet today," Georg said, nudging his elbow in Martin's side.

Martin kept staring at the neck of the man in front of him without uttering a word. How could he explain his disappointment over the outcome of his first battle? His mind kept revisitng the events of the day, unable to think ahead.

"You're thinking about Rinnthal?"

"Yes," Martin murmured.

"You worry too much. Believe me, that gets you nowhere," Georg said precociously. "When we were still working at Schwarz's, I often thought that you'd try to convince a client who wanted to buy ten cubic yards of lumber that five would probably be enough. You will never make a good businessman."

Martin laughed in spite of himself.

"I can see that I have come at the right time to cheer you up," Georg said. "There is the Rhine Valley. Doesn't it look like one huge garden?"

Georg talked on and on and Martin listened to him with great pleasure, thankful for the diversion. His blond friend bubbled over with funny ideas. He stole a handful of strawberries in a garden, pulled the thick plait of a girl or simply begged for a bottle of wine. When the two friends were hungry, they bought bread and wurst in one of the villages they were passing through. Georg never seemed to take life seriously.

* * *

Darkness had closed in on them when the Willich volunteer corps marched into the small village of Impflingen. Georg and Martin were among seven rebels billeted at the mayor's barn for the night.

While Georg fell asleep as soon as he settled in the straw, Martin lay awake for hours despite his exhaustion. His thoughts revolved around Rinnthal and the fact that the revolutionary army, which he had respected so highly, had run away in disgrace as soon as the Prussians fired their first shot. Now they were spending their last night on Palatine soil and nobody knew when they would return.

Perhaps his expectations had been too high. After all, many rebels were equipped with nothing more than straight scythes, thanks in part to his father's bungled weapons purchase.

Martin was glad that no one seemed to hold the family relation against him, glad as they were for any man who knew how to operate a rifle. He also thought of his despondent mother. What must she endure once she learned that both her husband and her son had taken flight?

Long after midnight, Martin finally sank into a restless slumber. He was relieved when the trumpeter woke the men at four o'clock in the morning. He stumbled into the courtyard and held his head bravely under the ice-cold stream of the pump. Then he grasped his canteen and filled it with the invigorating drink: Palatine water for the difficult escape to Baden.

* * *

On this cool, misty day the sun was hiding behind leaden clouds as the men of Willich's volunteer corps marched toward the Rhine Bridge at Knielingen. The longer the rebels pressed on, the more they dragged their feet. No shout of encouragement could lift their spirits. Their faces, so determined and eager just yesterday, reflected the gravity of their mission. Even Georg had not uttered a word during the last hour.

With the Prussians at their heels, the insurgent army pushed on. When the company passed a tavern in Rheinzabern, Georg could no longer restrain himself.

"I can't go on any longer. I'm going in there right now to drink a cool beer and you are coming with me," he announced.

"But we can't do that," Martin protested weakly as his friend pushed him into the empty lounge with unexpected energy.

As soon as Martin had finished his beer, he fell asleep on the hard chair. Exhaustion from the forced marches and the skirmish had caught up with him at last. An hour later, Georg roused him gently.

"Martin, I think we have to move on."

Martin yawned. "What time is it?"

"It's almost three o'clock," Georg said, glancing at his pocket watch.

Martin gave a feeble cry. "What do we do now? We won't be able to catch up with the others."

"Not if we're walking," Georg pondered, "but if we had horses. . ."

"I handed in my courier horse days ago."

"The landlord has two beautiful horses in his stable," George mused, ignoring Martin's comment. "I just saw them a while ago. Hey, landlord, we need your horses."

The landlord shook his head as he approached, but eventually relented when Georg signed a credit note. Martin and Georg strode to the horse stable, saddled the two sorrels, and trotted southward. They passed several irregular companies without a sign of Willich's corps.

"Are you sure that this is the only road crossing the Rhine?" Martin asked.

"Of course it is," Georg replied, "we've been passing volunteers for the last half hour. Where else would they go?"

"Then we'll have to cross the Rhine alone. We'll leave the horses on this side."

Georg agreed. Martin had been annoyed when Georg had coaxed the horses from the tavern owner. Now, he couldn't help but laugh at his friend's ingenuity. It was a much easier way to travel. They left the mounts at the mayor's house in Maximiliansau and urged him to notify the tavern owner about his horses.

The two friends pushed their way to the bridge through a dense crowd of wagons, horses, and insurgents when someone tugged on Georg's sleeve. He spun around to face an old man.

"Good day, Herr Schneider," Georg said with a wry smile.

"Aren't you Friedrich Lingenfelder's son?" Schneider asked.

"Yes."

"Do you know where my sons Fritz and Ferdinand are?" the old man asked. "I've come to take them home with me."

"I'm sorry, I haven't seen them."

"Your father has also asked me to bring you home before it's too late."

"Please tell him I don't give up that easily," Georg snapped at the old man. "Send my regards to my father and tell him that I'm not capable of treason. All is not lost yet, and the tables of the revolution may still turn tomorrow. Now, if you'll excuse me, we have a long way ahead of us."

He turned and marched off so swiftly that Martin could barely keep up.

"Wait for me," he pleaded. "I don't want to lose you in this crowd."

"I'm sorry," Georg said, slowing his pace, "I just can't believe my father is giving up while there is still hope. All is not lost yet; I guarantee you that."

"Weren't you a little harsh on him? After all, he's an old man. What if he's right?"

Georg's face contorted. "Oh no, don't you start and get discouraged now."

"I hope you're right." Martin wiped the sweat off his forehead with the sleeve of his tunic. "I'm just a bit discouraged that we're withdrawing already."

"I heard rumors that the general wants to join our army with the Baden insurgents and throw us all against the Prussians."

"When did you hear that?"

"While you were sleeping," Georg said, nudging Martin in his side.

* * *

Martin gaped at the sight of the river. Like a gigantic dragon, the stream of irregulars stretched over the narrow Rhine Bridge all the way into the city of Karlsruhe. The temporary bridge, supported by innumerable boats, swayed dangerously from time to time under the weight of men and horses. Would it last or would it give way? Would the insurgents safely arrive on the eastern side of the river or would they plunge into the murky depths of the water to certain death?

In the middle of the river, he paused to look back. He paid no attention to the rebels who had to make way for him, their scythes, rifles, and elbows boring into his side. He fixed his eyes on the houses nestled near the shore. A heron stalked its prey in a shallow branch of the river while the poplars on the embankment stood motionless in the hazy air. He took in every detail as if he intended to paint the scene from memory. After several minutes, Georg gently put a hand on his shoulder.

"Come," he murmured.

Martin consented and followed his friend. He did not notice that the countryside in Baden was a mirror image of the Palatine Rhine valley. In his mind's eye, he saw the deserted moor near Landstuhl with its mist rising from the damp earth, lending an eerie contour to each crippled tree.

Chapter 8

Karlsruhe, the capitol of the Baden revolution, was teeming with men from all over Europe. In the crowded streets, Martin discerned Polish and French tongues as well as different German dialects.

Martin and Georg kept close together so they would not lose sight of each other. At headquarters, they learned that there was not one bed available for them in the entire city.

They shuffled toward the outlying districts of the city to find a place for the night. After being rejected at three houses, Georg came to a halt in front of a church.

"Should we ask at the parsonage?"

"Why not?"

The heavy oak door opened slightly after Georg rapped the doorknocker three times. The elderly housekeeper took one look at the two dirty figures and puckered her brows. Georg stepped forward before she could close the door on them.

"We're two Palatines helping the revolution in Baden and need a place to spend the night," Georg said with a smooth voice that seemed to soften the housekeeper's resistance.

"I don't know if it's alright with the parson, "she said. "He has been called to a death-bed."

Martin gave her a shy smile.

"Very well, you may sleep in the attic room," she said with a shrug. "Have you had supper yet?"

The young men shook their heads.

"Go into the kitchen and sit down. I'll make you some sandwiches."

Martin and Georg ate every crumb of bread and liverwurst before the housekeeper led them to the attic where they soon fell into a deep slumber.

* * *

It was past nine o'clock when they woke up. They staggered into the kitchen and dabbed their faces with cold water from a can sitting in the sink. Without eating breakfast, they set out to headquarters, losing their way several times in the unfamiliar streets. The former banker's office was sparsely furnished with three desks and two cabinets. It reminded Martin in a frightening way of the gloomy office he had escaped from just a few weeks ago.

A freckle-faced clerk sat behind a desk and leafed through a thick bound book. He raised his brows indignantly when he recognized the two irregulars from the evening before.

"We have lost contact with our company," Georg explained.

"Which company do you belong to?"

"Corps August Willich."

The clerk opened another book and said after a brief search, "Corps Willich withdrew to Blankenloch at half past seven o'clock this morning."

The friends exchanged puzzled looks.

"Is it really necessary to return to Willich?" asked Martin at last. "There are enough companies here in Karlsruhe who could use two good riflemen."

As they spoke, a young turner entered the room with quick steps and delivered a document to the clerk.

"Don't you belong to the battalion Kirchheimbolanden?" the clerk asked him.

"Yes."

"Very well, take these two riflemen with you and introduce them to your lieutenant. They would like to join your battalion. By the way," he turned toward Martin and Georg, "did you get paid this week?"

They shook their heads. Nobody had given any thought to paying the insurgents during the skirmish at Rinnthal and their withdrawal. The clerk jotted down their names and handed them their pay. Martin and Georg grinned while stuffing the money into their pockets. Perhaps their luck was changing now. They hastened to follow the turner to their new battalion.

The turner found his lieutenant bent over a map in a summer house. He was the spitting image of his adjutant. His white trousers were tucked into black, polished boots and his blue blouse was tied at the waist with a black belt. A black Hecker hat with a red feather, a black-red-and-gold sash, pistol, powder bag, and rapier completed the aggressive get-up.

He eyed Georg and Martin and said to his adjutant, "Very well, we'll accept them into the First Company."

"And where will they sleep?"

"Take them to the inn *Zum Hirsch*. The others will have to move closer together."

At the inn, the three rebels climbed over a worn-out wooden staircase to the dance floor, which was completely covered with straw. The turner remarked that today was a rest day, turned away, and left the two friends alone.

Martin stared at the white walls. "What shall we do now?"

"Sleep, what else would we do?" Georg yawned.

"But we just got up," Martin protested as Georg stretched out on the straw.

Martin shrugged, climbed down the stairs, and traipsed past the open lounge door into the street. He had not wandered far when he noticed quick steps behind him.

"Martin, is it really you?" asked a familiar voice, while a strong hand landed on Martin's shoulder.

"Nikolaus," Martin cried, and the two friends clapped each other's back.

"I couldn't believe my eyes when I saw you walking through the hallway at the *Hirsch*," Nikolaus said. "How did you end up here?"

Martin told him how he had fared since they had last met in Kaiserslautern. He did not dare asking about Katrin until he could look at his friend's face and see his reaction. Seeing Nikolaus again brought back all the memories of his last meeting with her.

They wandered the streets until they came to a park. Under a chestnut tree, they sat down with their backs against the trunk.

"They drafted you, didn't they?" Martin asked.

"Yes."

"Would you have joined the irregulars on your own?"

Nikolaus rested his head on his right arm and looked straight into Martin's eye.

"I doubt it," he said. "I support the cause, but my parents need my help."

"How is Katrin doing?"

Martin did not recognize his own voice when he asked the question that had been on the tip of his tongue for the last half hour.

"Katrin is fine. The last time I saw her she asked about you," he said with a grin.

"Are you serious or are you just telling me fibs?"

"Have I ever lied to you before?"

"I'm sorry," Martin said. "Now tell me about your adventures."

"I got to ride on the new railroad," Nikolaus said. "When the line ended, we had to build a barricade and march the rest of the way to Neustadt after the Prussians crossed the border. I've never been so far away from home."

The talked all the way back to the inn. Before Martin fell asleep that night he wondered if Kartin had only asked Nikolaus about him to make conversation with her brother or whether she was really interested in him? The answer would have to wait.

* * *

Martin was a changed man the next morning when the Donnersberg company marched northwards out of Karlsruhe. Ever since the skirmish at Rinnthal, he had been morose and quiet. Now, he was his old self again as he was flanked by his two best friends. For Nikolaus, the campaign appeared to be a welcome change from the monotony of everyday life. His carefree character and Georg's unshakable optimism gave Martin the support and security he had missed during the early days of the campaign and the first decisive battle.

Many years later, he would vividly remember the motley crowd of an irregular army gathered there from all over the continent. A sturdy young fellow carried a listless black, red, and gold flag in the still summer air, followed by a marching band that played lively tunes from morning until evening. By late that afternoon, the battalion had settled down in a rye field.

"What a waste of good crops," Nikolaus complained when he observed the flattened field the next morning.

Once again, the Kirchheimbolanden battalion marched all day long, but Martin and Georg resisted the urge to rest on their own authority. They did not want to lose contact with their troops again.

In a small village, a well-meaning vintner took pity on the thirsty rebels and handed out free wine at the village square. Georg ran to the nearest farm and returned with a dented milk can. Soon it was filled to the top with wine and he carefully brought it to his lips.

"Hmm, almost as good as my father's wines," he said before Martin snatched the can out of his hands.

After a monotonous day of marching, the irregulars bivouacked in a potato field near a copse behind Blankenloch. Two fellows foraged a wagon full of straw and Georg grabbed a load for his two friends and himself. The three lads sank on the straw and were soon fast asleep.

Martin woke up on bare ground, numb with cold. Freezing rebels had pulled the straw from under their bodies without waking them.

Unable to fall asleep again, Martin rose to stretch his legs. He carefully climbed over the sleeping insurgents until he reached the edge of the camp. A faint ray of light emerged on the horizon, enabling him to recognize silhouettes. Martin approached a nearby sentry to indicate that he was a friend.

"It sure is cold tonight," he said to the guard, rubbing his hands together.

"Yes, it is."

"Are there any Prussians in the area?" Martin whispered.

"I don't think so. They're further to the north."

"Well, what are we doing here then?"

"I've heard rumors that we'll be marching to Bruchsal tomorrow. Perhaps we'll gather there to fight the enemy," the sentry replied.

Martin could not help frowning when hearing the word "enemy." Enemy! What a simple, yet complicated word it was. Weren't they all Germans, and wasn't it quite possible that tomorrow the sentry might shoot a man from his own hometown?

The struggle of the insurgent army was indeed not directed toward the Prussian soldiers; it was rather a fight between the new, freethinking minds against the old German subservient spirit. It was just unfortunate that the new army was mostly armed with scythes while the old one had the most advanced breech-loaders at their disposal.

As the guard had predicted, the Donnersberg company marched into Bruchsal the following evening. In the morning, Georg, Martin, and Nikolaus had not even downed their coffee yet when the bugler sounded their departure. Georg stuffed a slice of bread in his trouser pocket and the three friends dashed on the double to the assembly point.

Soon they were lined up and the Kirchheimbolanden battalion marched to the north on the rutted country road. The tired men remained silent, except for an occasional complaint about the oppressive heat.

Suddenly, Martin became aware of a strange noise. He followed the example of his comrades and clambered into the ditch as the sound of hoofbeats grew louder. Envy stole into Martin's eyes as he watched a procession of horses covered in sweat, driven to an even faster gallop by their blue-frocked dragoons. The horsemen disappeared on the horizon, leaving behind a cloud of dust that enveloped the foot soldiers.

"What's the meaning of this?" asked Martin's front man.

"Maybe the Prussians are up ahead," speculated the man next to him.

Seeing the horses reminded Martin of the carefree life he had lived as a courier. Now he felt the hardship of the campaign very distinctly. The heavy leather bag on one shoulder and the rifle slung over the other one seemed to pull him to the ground and his shoes appeared to be made of pure lead. Working in an office had not prepared him for the hardships of the campaign. His only consolation was the thought that he would not have met his friends again if he had remained a courier.

Disappointed, he thought of the wonderful days of his childhood when he had devoured books about the heroes of the Peasant War, Florian Geyer and Thomas Münzer. Gone were the romantic days of the *Bundschuh*, but gone were also the times of murderous, plundering raids and burning villages. The new revolution tried to balance their lack of weapons with words and stole no more than the occasional pig or a keg full of cool wine.

Chapter 9

After two hours of strenuous marching, the Donnersberg company arrived near Ubstadt. A hush went through the troops when they learned that General Sznayde, the Commander-in-Chief of the Palatine irregulars, was personally leading them into battle.

As the whole battalion remained at a standstill waiting for the general to give the signal to attack, Martin took in the scenery before him. He had never been here and yet he was sure he would remember the battlefield forever. A millstream gurgled about two hundred yards to the left, edged by some poplars lined along the bank. Cut grass spread out on the meadows between the road and the millstream and a dog barked in the distance. Yet, the scene seemed surreal. After a while, he realized what was missing: he did not see a single person on this whole expanse. Would the Prussians appear out of nowhere as they had done in Rinnthal?

"Where are the Prussians?" Martin asked Nikolaus.

"I don't know. Maybe they're behind that hill?"

A baby-faced lieutenant ordered the riflemen company to split into two ranks. Martin's heart skipped a beat when he realized that he was the right flank man in the second row. He had never been so close to the front before and his hands felt ice cold despite the sun's warming rays. He hoped fervently that his rifle would not jam. After taking a deep breath, he clambered down the banks of the stream, slipped over small rocks and climbed up the other side.

The front-row flank man pointed at the spiked helmet of a guard in a rye field at the bottom of the hill and yelled at the top of his voice, "Brothers, they're retreating."

The whole troop of irregulars stormed uphill and Martin followed suit, even though an inner voice warned him that this might be a trap.

The rebels had not yet ascended to the top of the hill when Martin's fears came true.

A salvo of rifle discharge put an end to the rebels' advance, and they scattered in wild confusion. Many stormed down the slope while several musicians threw themselves on the ground, seeking cover behind their drums.

Martin fired his weapon whenever he spotted a glint of a Prussian helmet. He was so devoted to this task that he did not notice when Georg suddenly jerked.

"I think I've been hit," Georg said with a strangely calm voice as Martin reloaded his rifle.

"Where?" Martin asked. "Does it hurt a lot?"

"No more than an insect bite," Georg replied.

He opened his jacket and touched the bullet hole in his left side. When he pulled out his hand, it was covered in blood.

Martin turned to Nikolaus. "We have to retreat right away."

"You stay here. I can still walk by myself," Georg stammered.

"I'm afraid we can't stay here," Nikolaus said. "Look, our whole company is on the run. In a few minutes, we'll be the only ones left on this slope if we don't pull back in time."

The rebels were indeed scurrying downhill to escape the horrific case shot and rifle fire. It would be suicide for the scythe company to remain at their position because the enemy had shot all the scythes from their poles within minutes.

Martin and Nikolaus both slipped a shoulder beneath Georg's armpits, ignoring Georg's protests that he didn't need any help.

The friends retreated to Ubstadt, making slow progress with their patient. All doors and shutters were closed in the deserted village. Behind a barn, out of shot range of the Prussians, the two friends put Georg on the ground and checked the wound, uttering reassurances.

Martin surveyed Nikolaus's face. His eyes reflected the worries that filled Martin's heart. Blood had soaked Georg's tunic and Martin grabbed his friend's jacket to press it on the wound. Soon the jacket was stained, and blood began seeping through Martin's fingers. Nikolaus pulled a handkerchief out of his pocket and dabbed the sweat from Georg's forehead. Georg's eyes glistened feverishly, and his face glowed like embers.

He glanced at his friends and whispered, "You can't fool me. I'm dying, aren't I?"

"Be quiet," Martin said curtly, "don't say that. I'm going to find a wagon to get you away from here."

"Stay here," Georg murmured, touching Martin's arm. "I don't need a wagon anymore. I can feel how quickly my strength is leaving me. Oh, it isn't easy to die so young when one has not accomplished much in life yet. Martin, Nikolaus, don't be sad for me. You should laugh as I have always laughed. Hard times will come in Germany. But I beg you to wait until the moment of freedom has arrived. My poor fa. . ."

Georg writhed in obvious pain one last time and sank into Martin's arms.

"No," Martin screamed, "wake up, Georg. Come on, wake up."

Martin remained on the ground, staring at the lifeless features of his handsome friend. He was grateful that Nikolaus remained silent, allowing him time to say good-bye.

"Get up, Martin, we have to run," Nikolaus said at last. "The Prussians will be here soon."

Martin took a deep breath. "But we can't just leave him here."

"I'm sorry." Nikolaus gripped Martin's shoulder. "We don't have time to bury him."

Martin still did not stir. "Why him? Why not me? He was worth much more than I am."

Everybody loved you and you loved them. Why, oh why, didn't you listen to that old man and go back home?

* * *

"Martin, I hear shots coming from the direction of the church," Nikolaus said. "Come on, we have to leave. Did he have anything on him that we could send his parents?"

Martin obediently searched Georg's pockets, taking along his watch and wallet. He rose slowly, casting a last look at the still figure. Later, Martin could not remember how he had reached Bruchsal. His feet pushed forward as swiftly as those of his companions while his thoughts remained with his dead friend at Ubstadt. Emotionless, he looked upon the rifles, woolen blankets, and leather bags strewn on the ground during the flight, and the injured men crying for help in the ditches. He was tempted to throw himself down into a trench.

Martin reflected on his friendship with Georg. The previous spring Georg had invited him to his home in Neustadt. From there they had hiked to Hambach Castle. The air was filled with the fragrance of the blooming fruit trees and the buzz of countless bees flying from one blossom to the next in their search for nectar.

They had rested under a cherry tree and unpacked a bottle of wine and several sandwiches from their backpacks. Martin could still taste the spic-laden flavor of the liverwurst on his tongue and feel the beguiling fragrance of the cherry blossoms in his nose. Georg had stretched his arms and exclaimed, "This is paradise on earth."

Later, when they stood in the great hall of the old Maxburg castle, Georg gave such a rousing speech that it had rivaled editor Johann August Wirth when he spoke to a crowd of over 30,000 people sixteen years before. Back then, it had all been in good fun.

On another Sunday, Martin had invited Georg to Landstuhl. They had saddled two horses from the Dupree stable and gone for a ride. Martin had never told his friend about his castle. Yet, on this day the ruin high above the roofs of Landstuhl was the destination of their ride. At the crest of the hill, Georg had keenly explored the remnants of the old stone walls.

"So this is your hiding place, Sir Franz--or should I say, Saint Martin?" he had teased. "I didn't know you were lord of a castle."

"My grandfather purchased it from the French during the National Property Auction. Since then, it has belonged to my family, but nobody thinks about it anymore," Martin had explained. "The Sickingen family used to own a town palace in Landstuhl. Our house was built from the stones of that palace."

Martin told many anecdotes about the former lords of Landstuhl and Georg listened open-mouthed. From that day on, their friendship had rapidly grown until it ended abruptly in a tiny village in Baden.

* * *

The fleeing troops arrived outside the town of Bruchsal, disheveled and panting. They were not admitted into town and had to settle in a wheat field instead. Martin and Nikolaus sank down on a meadow away from the others. They sat motionless for a long time, alone with their thoughts.

"Martin?" Nikolaus finally said.

"Yes?"

"What are we doing here?"

"What do you mean?" Martin asked.

"I'm only a draftee, but I expected things to go a little different. Ever since the Prussians marched into the Palatinate, we have retreated from them. This is a very odd campaign. How can two hundred poorly- or unarmed men defend themselves against an army that is ten times as big? Why are we wiping ourselves out in skirmishes instead of throwing the whole revolutionary army against the Prussians all at once?"

Wasn't it strange that every ordinary country lad found a solution, but the general of their army could not think of one?

Nikolaus's voice grew agitated. "Day after day, hour after hour we pull back farther and farther from the Prussians and Bavarians. Pretty soon, there won't be a corner in Germany where we can hide."

"Well, what should we do in your opinion?" Martin asked hoarsely.

"Don't think that Georg's death has not upset me. I just said that we didn't have time to bury him because it was the right thing to do. This afternoon, I thought about our future. You and I, we only live once, and how can we be of use to the revolution when we're dead?" He took a deep breath. "I think it best if we go back home as soon as possible."

Martin glared at his friend.

"Go home?" he whispered, even though nobody could hear them, "How do you plan to do that? The Prussians have occupied the Palatinate and they'll arrest you when you take the first step across the border."

"You don't want to come with me?"

Martin rested his head on his hands. "Forgive me. I can't give you an answer tonight. I've been thinking about Georg's death so much that I haven't had a chance to think about my own future. Let me sleep on it tonight and we'll talk again tomorrow."

Martin tossed and turned on the hard ground for hours. Georg's death had shaken him to the core and Nikolaus had voiced the concerns he had not yet admitted to himself. At last he fell into a light, fitful slumber just before a gentle rain shower woke him up, soaking him and his comrades.

* * *

The battalion waited for hours outside the town gates until they finally marched off toward Weingarten. Surrounded by their companions, it was impossible for Nikolaus and Martin to exchange a private word. From time to time, Martin looked around. The eyes of the other rebels told him they were just as discouraged as Nikolaus was.

He searched his mind for a way out of a situation that appeared more and more hopeless every day. Then he remembered a conversation he had had recently. Nikolaus, who had remained silent all day, approached him in the evening.

"Well, have you made a decision yet?"

"Yes, I believe I have developed a useful plan. Where are we anyway?"

"We are in Durlach," Nikolaus replied with a rueful smile.

"Sorry. I didn't pay any attention to where we were going. Do we have a bed for tonight?"

"No." Nikolaus kicked the dirt with his foot. "They told us there isn't one bed available in Durlach and that we'll have to march to Krätzingen."

"Count me out," Martin declared. "I'm not walking one step further."

"What do you want to do instead?"

Martin mulled it over and signaled to Nikolaus. "Come with me."

In a dimly lit side street, he stopped in front of a little house and rapped at the door. After a while, an old, yet sprightly man opened.

"What do you want here?" he snapped at Martin. "Can't you at least leave me alone at night?"

Martin's heart sank. He almost turned away when he remembered how Georg would have reacted in his stead. He took a deep breath and said, "Excuse us, we just wanted to wake our comrades who are billeted here. The drummer has just sounded the departure."

"Well, in that case, come on in," the old man replied.

He led them through a tiny kitchen, where a young girl sat on a stool mending clothes, and into the bedroom. Two rebels were sleeping in the bed and Martin shook their shoulders. With feigned cheerfulness, he shouted at them, "Get up. They've sounded the departure long ago. We're all ready to go."

The two lads pulled themselves up drowsily, jumped into their clothes, and scurried away. Martin gave a bitter laugh.

"Well, now we have a bed," Martin said and took off his shoes.

The old man opened the door and sucked in his breath noisily. He took one look at the young men and his expression softened.

"Oh well," he mumbled as he left the room, "you may stay here if you like. You must be dead tired."

The two friends quickly undressed and lay down in the warm bed.

"I'm afraid we will lose contact with our battalion," Nikolaus admitted.

"No matter. It wouldn't be the first time. Besides, no one there will notice whether two fellows are missing or not. I can't walk any step further tonight."

"You wanted to tell me of your plans," Nikolaus said.

Martin rolled on his side and fixed his eyes on his friend.

"I've racked my brains how we can get out of this situation in one piece, but I could only come up with one possibility. Listen to me carefully: your idea of walking straight home from here is fine where it concerns you. If you get caught and tell the Bavarians that you didn't volunteer to join the irregular army, they'll probably let you go."

Nikolaus nodded.

"Very well, but that solution is out of the question for me because it would be far too dangerous. Don't forget that I am the son of a member of the State Defense Council and a dedicated rebel myself. If I fell into the hands of the Bavarians or Prussians, I would hardly escape with my life. That leaves exile in a foreign country. A life in exile costs money, though, and I don't have any." He paused to take a break before continuing. "What if we both flee across the Rhine into France as political refugees and keep walking along the Palatine border until we reach a place from where you can hike home. If you want to do me another favor, go see my mother and tell her that I need money for my flight. In the meantime, I will look up my father in Sarreguemines and wait there until my sister brings the money. Then I will travel to Havre and wait for the next ship that sails to America."

"You want to emigrate to America after all," Nikolaus said in a flat voice. "I've always been afraid of that."

"You must believe me, I have not thought about America for the past two months at all. It seems to be an irony of fate that I should enjoy the freedom I had imagined for Germany in America after all."

Martin closed his eyes to avoid Nikolaus's stare.

"What?" he asked at last. "Why are you staring at me? Do you think I'm giving up too easily?"

"No, I don't," Nikolaus replied, "it was my idea to quit. I'm just wondering what your mother will say when she hears your plans."

"We'll find out," Martin said curtly and turned his back to Nikolaus. He was embarrassed and relieved at once that he did not have to break the news to his mother himself.

Martin had brooded over the planned escape so intensely all day long that he completely forgot whose idea it was. After the pitifully lost skirmish of Rinnthal, he had been gripped by an unexplainable fear of the future. Only Georg's steadfast optimism had dissipated his misgivings. After Georg's death, he became even more aware of the hopelessness of their struggle. It did not matter anymore whether they fled a few days sooner or later and the opportunity presented itself here, less than a mile away from the Rhine.

Chapter 10

At daybreak, Martin and Nikolaus spooned the bread soup the young girl had prepared and asked for directions to Ettlingen. Out in the street, their faces turned toward the distant crackling of rifle fire from the north.

"Well," Nikolaus said, "are you sure about leaving?"

Martin sighed. "Yes, it makes no sense to keep on going."

He clenched his jaw while they turned southward.

"Wouldn't it be better to leave the rifles at the house?" Nikolaus asked.

"I don't think so. There are so many irregulars on the roads nowadays that we are probably more inconspicuous with a weapon than without one. Besides, as long as we're still in danger I feel much safer with a rifle in my hand."

Traffic on the road increased. Now and then, a hay wagon full of wounded men overtook them on their flight from Karlsruhe to Rastatt. Their eyes spoke of thirst and hunger, encouraging Martin to increase his pace.

When they felt they had hiked far enough to the south, the friends turned west toward the Rhine. They came upon a creek, dropped their bags and rifles, lay down on their stomachs, and gulped down the cool water. After they had quenched their thirst, they took off their boots and socks and dunked their hurting feet into the stream. Martin noticed the many bushes on the bank and said, "This would be a good place."

Nikolaus yawned. "For what? To sleep?"

"We probably won't have time to sleep tonight. No, we could transform ourselves from irregular soldiers to plain farm boys in those bushes."

"I've never been anything else."

"Now I'm glad we never had any uniforms. We'll tuck in our shirts and leave the rifles in the bushes."

Martin took off his dust-covered hat and plucked a red feather from the band. Had it only been a few weeks since he had proudly tucked the plume on his hat? He tossed the feather on the ground and marched on.

* * *

Nikolaus and Martin entered the first house in the next village and found several men dressed in plain clothing seated around the kitchen table.

"Which way to the Rhine?" Martin asked.

There was no need to tell the villagers that he and Nikolaus were fleeing rebels. The men just gawked at them. At last, a man rose slowly and led Martin and Nikolaus behind the house. He showed them a field trail that would lead close to the river. Martin and Nikolaus thanked him and strode away.

"How are we going to cross the Rhine?" Nikolaus brooded. "Even if there were a ferry, we probably couldn't use it, could we?"

"No," Martin replied, "to be honest with you, I don't know yet how we will get across. We'll have to rely on chance and mustn't lose heart. Do you have any money left?"

Nikolaus turned his pockets inside out and said gloomily, "two Gulden and six Kreuzer, that's all."

"I don't have much more myself. We'll just have to live on bread for the next few days."

Just before suppertime, they spotted a village in the distance. The river glistened like a silver ribbon in the afternoon light. They turned off the road and bypassed the parish on a track across the fields. At the banks of the Rhine, they found a bush that was large enough to protect them from discovery. Here, they crouched down and waited for nightfall.

While Nikolaus took a piece of bread and a wedge of cheese out of his bag and ate with appetite, Martin stared at the water pensively.

"Don't you have anything to eat?" Nikolaus asked with bulging cheeks. "I'll be glad to give you something."

"No, thanks, I'm not hungry," Martin muttered.

Martin looked away while Nikolaus munched on his meager meal. He could not eat a bite on the last evening he spent on German soil.

"What's the matter? Aren't you feeling well?" Nikolaus asked.

Martin tried to control his shaking hands. "It's just that we are sneaking out of Germany like two criminals. Is it such a crime to fight for freedom?"

"It's not too late to change your mind."

"Yes, it is too late, and you know it. We all dreamed a beautiful dream, and it was shattered when the other states betrayed us. They promised to support us in our fight for freedom and they let us down when it counted. Even if I were able to get back home without getting caught—which I doubt—I cannot live in this society any longer. Should I wait another twenty years until a new generation has grown up? One that has not lived through this humiliation and is willing to go to battle again?"

He shaded his eyes with his hands and shook his head. "No, no, I have to get away from here."

They watched the day fade away without uttering another word.

"It's almost dark now," Nikolaus said at last, swatting at a gnat that targeted his neck.

"Then let's go before we get eaten alive."

The friends left their hiding-place and crept along the bank. They headed straight for a cottage that stood apart from the village near the river. The house was dark, and a fishing net was hung over a rope in the yard for drying.

"Well, where there's a net, there's a boat," Martin said. "It seems that we're in luck."

They stayed put on the ground for several minutes and when all remained quiet, Martin said, "I'll go ahead and check whether the fisherman has a dog that could betray us with its barking."

He crawled away and returned a few minutes later.

"There is no dog around the place," he whispered.

The bank was flat at this side and a weathered rowboat lay bottom up in the sand. They turned the boat over and pushed it into the water. Then they jumped in, each one taking an oar. Martin sighed with relief when a cloud sailed in front of the almost full moon. Anyone watching the river on the French side would be hardpressed to detect them.

Almost immediately, the current pushed them downstream and they had to exert themselves to keep the boat on a straight course. Finally, they reached the Alsatian embankment and pulled the boat on land.

"What we just did is wrong," Nikolaus said. "How will that man get his boat back?"

"I don't know," Martin said with a sigh. "I feel bad about it too. You'll have to admit, though, that we didn't have any other choice. I suggest that we walk all night and look for a hide-out toward morning."

* * *

Although exhausted, the young men agreed that it would be sensible to hike at night to avoid all people, especially those in uniform. Martin did not rule out the possibility that he and Nikolaus could have obtained a transit visa for France from the police if they claimed to immigrate to America. Still, he decided to avoid all government offices. No French policeman would have believed that a man was immigrating to America with two Gulden in his pocket.

There was another reason, though, for Martin's wish to sleep during the day. The Alsatian landscape was such a mirror image of the Palatinate that he would have been gripped with homesickness at the sight of it. Not long ago he had been convinced that his future lay in America. Now that he was forced to leave his homeland behind or risk being executed, he felt torn to pieces. Torn between his desire for freedom and a life in Germany with the girl he would probably never see again.

* * *

Martin and Nikolaus tramped all night over lonely tracks across the moon-lit fields. Toward morning, they reached a copse and went to sleep in the undergrowth.

On the second day, they choked down the last bites of dry bread and debated where they could find something to eat. Luckily, Martin had indeed learned a thing or two from Georg and soon had a brilliant plan. He recognized the steeple of a Catholic church in the next village and told Nikolaus to wait for him at the other end of town.

Nobody was around as Martin strode across the cemetery and approached the back door of the rectory. At his knock, the door gaped open. The inviting aroma of freshly baked bread led him straight to the kitchen, where a young girl with flushed cheeks stood at the stove. She did not even jump when she caught sight of Martin, obviously used to frequent visits from petitioners.

Martin took off his hat.

"Excuse me, miss, that I have walked in here like this," he said with a steady voice. "My friend and I are two unemployed traveling journeymen and we're hoping to find work in this area. We haven't had any luck yet, though, and we're both very hungry. We'd appreciate it if you would give us something to eat."

She nodded sympathetically and gave him a loaf of the warm bread. Martin thanked her effusively but waited just the same.

"Oh, I beg your pardon," she said with a smile, grabbed a meat fork and speared a piece of pork from the chimney. Martin bowed, crammed the food into his bag and made off to meet Nikolaus.

* * *

North of Bitche it was time to bid good-bye. Martin dreaded the moment of departure. He was losing a second close friend within a short time and, moreover, he was about to embark on a journey into the unknown all by himself. Nikolaus would most certainly reach German soil unnoticed across the densely wooded border and would arrive at home after a few more night marches.

Martin had written a letter to his mother in which he asked her to send enough money for a passage to the New World to his father's address in Sarreguemines. He handed it to Nikolaus and said, "If you arrive in Landstuhl during the day, hide at the castle until it grows dark. At the inn, there is a small gate in our garden wall that leads you through the garden into the courtyard. The kitchen window is to the left of the back door."

Nikolaus motioned that he understood. "Should I send your regards to Katrin?"

A shadow traveled across Martin's face.

"You may tell her good-bye from me," he said with a trembling voice, "but don't tell her how much I adore her. She would be better off marrying a man who has both feet firmly on the ground, not a dreamer like me."

When Nikolaus still hesitated to leave his friend, Martin said harshly, "now go on, because I can't bear it anymore. Or do you want to see me cry?"

Nikolaus's hands quivered as he clapped Martin's back and murmured, "Please write to me when you arrive over there. *Leb wohl!*"

Martin stood rooted on the spot and focused on his companion until he disappeared between the fir trees. Now that he was alone, he blew his nose noisily into his soiled handkerchief. It occurred to him that, together with Nikolaus, his carefree youth had vanished from his life.

Chapter 11

Nikolaus felt so safe from discovery in the secluded villages near the border that he decided to hike during the day. Now and then, a farmer gave him a ride on his wagon, allowing him to make good progress. His yearning for home was so strong that he hardly allowed himself to sleep anymore Several days after leaving Martin he arrived at the Dupree house in the first light of dawn.

Luise was busy lighting a fire in the kitchen stove when Nikolaus rapped at the window.

"Yes?" she said as she cracked open the casement.

"I would like to speak to Frau Dupree. I have a message from Martin," Nikolaus said.

Luise blushed. "Is he alive?"

"Yes."

Her eyes sparkled as she hurried to the back door. She invited Nikolaus to have a seat in the kitchen while she ran upstairs to wake up her mistress.

Martin's mother darted into the kitchen where she froze in mid-step, Luise close behind her.

"You aren't Martin. Who are you?" she asked, her shoulders sagging.

Astonished, Nikolaus studied the women's expectant faces. Everybody in this house seemed to wait constantly for a message from father and son. Without a word, he handed Margarethe Dupree the letter. She struggled to maintain her composure while reading it.

"Where is he now?" she finally asked in a choked voice.

Nikolaus told her briefly about meeting Martin, Georg's death, and their decision to flee.

Frau Dupree sank on a kitchen chair and looked gravely at her son's confidant.

"Why did you come back and he didn't?" she asked.

Nikolaus tried in vain to find the right words. How could he explain the political motives of her son to his desperate mother?

"My father needs me," he said at last, "and I'm sure that none of the villagers will betray me. After all, I was drafted."

"Why couldn't Martin come home with you?" Frau Dupree interrupted him in a hollow voice.

"Martin thinks that the government will put him in jail because he was a rebel and your husband a member of the State Defense Council. Please excuse me now, I would like to get home as quickly as possible."

"But you will have breakfast first. Luise, fry some eggs for this young man."

* * *

After Nikolaus left through the back door, Margarethe Dupree read the letter again and said to the stunned girl, "Luise, I'm going to Sarreguemines myself and will try to bring Martin to his senses. Go tell Matthias, then come to my room to pack my traveling bag."

An hour later, Matthias drove up the Tilbury and she climbed in. He handed her her travel bag before climbing on the coach box. Then he drove westward, en route to the French border.

* * *

Now that he was alone, Martin felt safe enough to hike during the day. The rolling landscape of Alsace and Lorraine touched the horizon in all directions, and he quickened his steps to reach his destination. This far from the Rhine and any revolutionary groups he no longer feared being detected by authorities and had even hitched a ride with a peddler.

The sky hung sad and low over Sarreguemines when Martin arrived. It was noontime and the streets were deserted. The clatter of pots and pans told him that the townspeople were sitting down to dinner. From the open door of a *boulangerie*, the aroma of freshly baked bread teased his nose. He counted the coins in his pocket and stepped inside to buy a baguette. Martin devoured the bread in large chunks while he wandered the streets in search of hotels.

Near the center of town, he came to the imposing, half-timbered *Le Moulin* inn. He opened the heavy wooden door and spotted the familiar figure of his father in the lounge. Hermann Dupree sat at a window with his back turned toward the door, a newspaper spread out in front of him. Martin approached him from the side and said with more assurance than he felt, "Guten Tag, Father."

"What are you doing here?" Hermann Dupree asked, and a flicker of annoyance crossed his face. It seemed as if his son's arrival reminded Dupree of past times, a silly prank from his youth perhaps.

Martin studied his father. In vain, he checked the familiar features for traces of resignation or guilt over the failed revolution. Instead, he eyed the well-fed, carefree countenance of a prosperous landowner. Anger welled up in him. Anger that he had to flee because his father had botched a weapons transport that was crucial to the revolution.

"I have dispatched a message to Mother to send me money to your address," Martin said. "I will come here every day until the money arrives."

"Money? What do you need money for? And where have you been lately?"

"I come from a revolution that failed because you made a mistake," Martin blurted out, unable to control his anger. He turned on his heel and dashed to the door without looking back. Outside, he regretted his stormy exit right away. Why did his father always rub him the wrong way? He was nineteen years old, but his father treated him as if he were a child that had to be reprimanded. Yet, he still needed Hermann Dupree's money to start a new life.

* * *

Dupree was not in the lounge when Martin returned the next day. He asked the landlord for his father's room number and climbed the worn staircase to the upper floor. No one answered his knock. Martin opened the door hesitantly and winced at the sight of his mother. Dressed in a plaid traveling dress, she perched on a chair by the table, facing the door.

He had not expected her to come to Sarreguemines herself and braced himself for a confrontation. Indeed, his mother's glare penetrated his soul, causing him to lower his eyes.

"Close the door, I need to talk to you. I asked your father to let me speak with you alone," she said with frightening composure.

Martin obeyed and stood rooted in the middle of the room while his heart beat like the drummer of his battalion.

She leaned forward. "It won't do for you to stare at the floor and stand there as silent as a post. Sit down and tell me exactly what your plans are."

"I would rather stand," Martin said in a defiant voice.

"You can't be serious about wanting to immigrate to America."

"I've never been so sincere in my life, Mother."

She twisted her silk watch band between her fingers. "But why? Tell me for God's sake, why!"

"I'm not in the least interested to see the Bavarian casemates from the inside," Martin countered.

"They can't be such brutes. You haven't done anything evil."

"Oh no, the Prussians and Bavarians are real angels. I'm sure they did not enjoy shooting their prisoners in Kirchheimbolanden like birds from the trees. They only wanted to spare them a life under oppression." He took a deep breath. "Mama, they killed my best friend."

"Stop it," his mother cried, covering her ears. "Couldn't you stay here in France until everything has settled down in the Palatinate?"

Martin shoved his fists into his jacket pockets. "I don't wish to stay in exile for years like so many others and wait idly for the moment of return. And I don't want to live in the repression that is sure to follow at home. But to practice a meaningful occupation here, I would have to speak and write French, and I don't."

"Don't they speak English in America?"

"I learned some English from books years ago," Martin replied.

"And you think that is sufficient? What do you intend to do for a living once you get to America?"

"I don't know yet. I don't have the gift of looking into the future. But America is a land of great opportunity and an open society. I am sure that I will find my place in it somewhere."

He stepped closer to his mother and took her hand in his. "Don't you understand, Mother? I am suffocating here. I need to live in a free society." Martin pulled another chair close and sat down. He told her about his high hopes for the revolution, his adventures, and his deep sorrow over Georg's death.

A tear trickled down his mother's face. "I only brought three hundred Gulden because I was hoping to change your mind. I now realize that one should not hold back a traveler, because he would never be happy. If you want to leave, then leave," she said in a dejected tone. "I just ask one thing of you: If things go badly for you over there and you can't find work, don't be afraid to come back. Our house will always be open to you."

She rose with difficulty, bent over her traveling bag and put a money pouch on the table.

"Thank you." Martin picked up the purse and stuffed it into his pocket.

"Where are you staying?" she asked.

Martin told her the address of his rooming house.

"If you wait another day, your father can probably find the names of some decent emigration agents for you. One hears a lot of stories about agents who have a questionable reputation."

Martin considered the offer. He had heard the same rumors. As much as he hated to be indebted to his father, he did not have much of a choice until he could make a living for himself. He promised to return the next afternoon and left.

* * *

His father greeted him in the lounge when he returned the following day.

"Sit down."

Martin obeyed.

"Here is the address of an honest agent in Metz. At least, I'm told he's honest," Dupree said. "You will take the train to Paris and from there the stagecoach to Havre. I heard the coach is expensive, so here's some more money."

Martin was dumbfounded when his father handed him the French coins.

"Thank you," he mumbled.

"Your mother brought the passport you were issued a couple of years ago when we visited our relations in France together. She was so distraught yesterday that she forgot to give it to you."

Martin carefully placed the precious document in his pocket. Now he would not have to avoid officials any longer.

There was no trace of hostility in his father's voice as he continued, "Your mother told me of your conversation yesterday. She is taking this very hard. Believe it or not, I'm very sorry that you're leaving. I know we had our differences, but we could have resolved them somehow."

He cleared his throat. "Unlike your mother, though, I understand that you can't possibly go back home for quite some time. They would put you in jail for years, if not worse. I therefore approve of your decision to emigrate to the United States and to find your own way. Please write to us when you arrive over there. Don't leave us in anger."

Martin flushed when his father shook his hand.

"Good-bye, Father," he uttered and rose.

"Now go and say good-bye to your mother. She's upstairs in my room."

Martin took the steps one at a time, wishing to be anywhere but here. He had slept poorly after the talk with his mother the day before. It had never been his intention to hurt her. Didn't she realize that he had to leave or face great danger?

Margarethe Dupree sat by the window with a piece of needlework in her hands. It was a handkerchief on which she embroidered her favorite flower, a pink rose. As Martin stepped closer, he noticed that her eyes were swollen and red. She barely looked up from her work. "You spoke to your father yet?"

"Yes."

"I guess everything is settled then. When are you leaving?"

"Tomorrow morning. The earlier I go, the better."

She rose and placed her needlework on the bed. Her hands were shaking slightly when she rummaged through her bag.

"I've brought you a pair of socks. I'm sure you will need them come winter."

"Thank you," Martin murmured.

Tears began to well in her eyes as she handed him the socks. Martin stuffed them in his pocket. He was barely able to control himself any longer. He would rather face the entire Prussian army than have this conversation with his mother.

"Mama," Martin pleaded, "please don't make this more difficult for me than it already is."

His mother moaned and slumped back on her chair. Martin stepped close to her and bent his head. "Farewell, Mother!"

He kissed her on the cheek, eased away, and fled the room without looking back. In the hallway, Martin staggered to the staircase and clutched the newel until his knuckles turned as white as the walls that were closing in on him. He took a deep breath and climbed down the stairs.

* * *

Martin could not remember how he got back to his rooming house. He dropped on his bed, staring blankly at the ceiling. The thought of grieving his mother drained his strength. Parting from her was much harder for him than the defeat near Rinnthal.

In the past, Martin had sought solitude, but now that he was lonely by circumstance it took away his courage. He was more than glad when he sat in the stagecoach at last, even though he was cramped in between a corpulent merchant and a skinny watchmaker. He had tied the pouch around his waist and secretly checked whether it was still there. The money was all that stood between him and despair.

Martin had difficulty finding the address of the emigration agent. He had to show the note to several people before he found a clerk who spoke some German and guided him to the office. When Martin stood in front of the agent, he asked boldly, "When does the next ship leave for America and how much is the passage?"

"To New York or Baltimore?" the bored clerk asked without looking up from his papers.

"It doesn't matter to me."

"July 20, New York, *Milan* under Captain Snow, one hundred and fifty Gulden," the clerk rattled off.

Martin blanched. "That's very expensive."

If he had to spend that much money on the passage, he would arrive in America empty-handed.

"It's a new packet ship," the agent replied indignantly. "The furnishings are very comfortable and elegant, and the crossing does not take longer than twenty-five to thirty days."

"Don't you have anything cheaper?"

"Let me check."

Martin settled on the brig *Amelia*, which was to sail for Baltimore in ten days. The crossing cost eighty Gulden and included a bed and water. Each passenger had to bring enough provisions for sixty days.

Martin was on his way. There was no turning back now.

Chapter 12

Havre was the port of departure for most emigrants from southern Germany. Martin fought his way to the harbor through a confusion of horse-drawn wagons, carts, immigrants, proprietors, and seamen. He stood gaping at the forest of masts in the harbor. Vessels from all points of the globe were anchored there, causing his heart to race. Lust for adventure and fear of the unknown fought within him.

"Attention!" shouted a powerful French voice behind his back. Martin jerked around and made way for a packer carrying a sack full of grain on his back.

He found lodging at the *Helvetia* inn in the harbor district for two francs a day. Now it was time to shop for provisions.

At a barbershop, he met a German clerk who was working for one of the large business firms of Havre. While they waited for their haircuts, he told Martin the sad news that the siege of Rastatt had ended, and the entire state of Baden was occupied by Prussian troops. Martin barely flinched. It would have required a miracle to turn around the course of the revolution.

Martin asked his compatriot which provisions he should take on a long sea voyage. The young German answered, not in the least surprised, "That's very easy: a straw mattress and a straw pillow, woolen blankets, a plate, cup, cutlery, bowl, and bucket—all made of metal."

"And what food do I bring?" Martin asked.

"Bread, ship biscuits, ham, smoked sausages, preserved fruit, raisins, rum, and vinegar," the clerk said, using his fingers to list each item. "And don't forget to take some sea water soap to wash your clothes and yourself. It is made of white clay. Ordinary soap is only useful in regular water. Are you going to America?"

"Yes, I'll be sailing to Baltimore and don't know yet where to go from there. Thank you very much for your advice. You've been very helpful," Martin said, hoping he would remember everything. "Should I exchange my money here or in Baltimore?"

"I recommend that you buy a bill of exchange from a reputable bank. They are safer than cash and you can send a copy of it to your relatives."

"But how do I know which bank is reputable?"

The clerk told him the name of the bank his company dealt with and gave him directions.

"Do you speak French, by the way?"

"Only a little," Martin said. "My forefathers were Huguenots, but they've lived in Germany for ages."

"Then I advise you to be careful when shopping for your supplies. The merchants in Havre are very cunning and take everybody who doesn't speak French for a ride. When someone quotes you a price, don't say yes right away. Bargain!"

Martin thanked his fellow countryman and followed his well-intentioned suggestions. Over the next few days, sacks and boxes began to pile up in his hotel room.

In the streets, Martin detected several German dialects. There were Swabian, Swiss, and Alsatian emigrants milling around. Martin sighed at the sound of their familiar jabber. He seemed to be the only person traveling alone. Now and then, a family was camped in an alley, their household goods stacked around them. Were these poor souls short of money already or were they just being prudent?

"Do you need passage to America?" a greasy lad of no more than sixteen years asked in broken German while grabbing Martin's shoulder.

"No, thank you," Martin said curtly and shrugged the runner off. The clerk at the barber shop had been right. He had to watch out for shady characters every minute of the day.

He smiled when he detected a tavern sign with the familiar name *Zum Hirsch* and headed straight to the door. Martin devoured a pork chop with fried potatoes. It would be quite a while before he could enjoy such good food again.

The next morning, he was drawn to the harbor. While searching for the *Amelia,* Martin inhaled the breeze of salty air, dank wood, spices that tickled his nose, and human bodies in need of a bath. The clamor of hammering artisans, rolling wagons, screaming vendors, and the chatter of immigrants in dozens of dialects assaulted his ears.

His wanderings led him to the shop window of a bookstore. One of the books on display piqued his interest, *"Der Englisch sprechende Auswanderer in Gesprächen und Redesätzen."* The English-speaking Immigrant in Conversations and Sentences.

Martin stepped into the store, a tinny bell gaily tingling above the door. He pointed at the book in the display area and the owner wrote the price on a piece of wrapping paper. Martin nodded happily. Whatever the cost, it would be worth it. He put his coins on the counter and waited patiently while the elderly owner wrapped the book.

Each of the five days he waited, Martin strolled to the harbor and watched the sailors of the *Amelia* while they cleaned the imposing two-master. The air smelled of salt and adventure and he breathed it until his lungs were close to bursting. Life in the port city was expensive and Martin hoped that he could soon board the ship. Even though he lived frugally, the contents of his leather pouch became lighter every day.

While his days were filled with new impressions, the past occupied his mind when darkness fell. He sat on the only chair in his sparse room, gazing out the window. He thought back to the Palatinate where he once again saddled Nelly and rode to Moorbach where Nikolaus was waiting for him. Katrin gave him a cup of the still warm milk and they sat on the bench in the courtyard and talked away the hours until their mother urged everybody to go to bed so that she herself could get some peace.

Martin also thought of his kind-hearted mother. She did not deserve the grief he had caused her. Yet he quickly rejected the idea of writing to her from Havre to explain his hasty departure. He would rather wait until he had settled down in America. As long as he was on European soil, he was too torn by self-doubt and memories to make any plans for his future.

* * *

Finally, the big day arrived. Martin paid his bill at the hotel and hired a horse-drawn wagon and a porter to take his provisions aboard the *Amelia*. The two-master vessel teemed with passengers, sailors, and dock workers.

"Billet!" bellowed a deep voice behind Martin as he prepared to start up the gangway with his porter in tow.

Martin dug in his pockets and produced his ticket. He had barely entered the ship that would be his home for the next few weeks when he tripped over a water bucket one of the sailors had used to swab the deck.

He caught himself and moved on, his eyes fixed at the ground. He missed the hatch that led to the lower deck and had to ask a seaman for the way.

He bent down as he descended into the bowels of the ship over a narrow staircase, followed by his porter. Countless bunk beds in close proximity took up most of the first lower deck, leaving only narrow passageways open. Just a few months ago, Martin would have been startled at such a sight, but during the campaign he had learned to sleep anywhere and under the most unfavorable circumstances.

Martin searched for an empty bed in the semi-darkness, making his way through the cluster of fellow travelers. At last, he found an upper bed and flung his leather bag on it to reserve it. His porter lifted the mattress and the pillow onto the bunk and put his other possessions on the floor. Martin paid the Frenchman, feeling forlorn among his chattering fellow passengers.

Chapter 13

July 24, 1849

Martin climbed on deck to watch the ship casting off. He observed several immigrants bidding farewell to their relatives who had accompanied them to the port. The women wailed while wiping tears off their cheeks. Children clutched their mothers' skirts while the men inspected the deck. Martin averted his eyes. Now that the departure was near, he was surprised to discover that the loneliness no longer weighed him down. No one had accompanied him to the ship, and he knew that nobody would await him in the New World. But this reflection did not alarm him anymore.

Compared to most emigrants, he had the immeasurable advantage that he was not the head of a large household. For the first time in his life, he was free. He did not have to obey any orders and could choose his residence and place of work at his own discretion. This challenge appealed to him so much that his heart began to beat faster. From now on, Martin resolved, he would dwell less on past mistakes and live in the present instead.

Martin could not keep his eyes from the sailors who performed their duties like clockwork. They pulled the fenders aboard and threw the heavy lines over from the landing. A steamer towed the *Amelia* out of the harbor area, turned around and abandoned the vessel to the winds and waves of the seemingly infinite Atlantic Ocean. Most passengers had gone below but Martin stayed on deck. He watched in awe as the sailors climbed all the way up the standing rigging to the yards on the foremast to unfurl most of the sails.

After the mass of houses had disappeared behind the horizon, Martin descended with stiff legs and lay down on his bed. He supported his head with his hand and watched with amusement as his fellow travelers made themselves at home in the cramped space. In less than half an hour, though, his stomach began to rumble. He staggered to a bucket and vomited.

* * *

Two days later, Martin was well enough to be seized by agonizing boredom. He considered studying the English book he had bought in Havre, but it was too dark under deck to read. He climbed on deck and looked around, spotting a towheaded young man who was reading a well-worn book. Martin, who was still trying to acquire sea legs, stumbled close enough to read the title: *Gottfried Duden: Bericht über eine Reise nach den westlichen Staaten Nordamerikas. Report about a Journey to the Western States of North America.*

The fellow looked up and said to Martin, "Would you like to read my book for a while?"

"Oh no, I don't want to take it away from you. But it would be nice if you could read something aloud," Martin said. "I know almost nothing about America."

"Very well, I will continue reading where I stopped. 'You will probably be surprised that I have not mentioned the summer in Missouri before, even though an anxious remark had been mentioned in one of my previous letters. I mention casually that, just as the first winter had been unusually mild, this summer had been unusually hot and dry. Indeed, the Fahrenheit thermometer indicated 104 degrees in the shade (compared to 32 degrees Reaumur). That the heat has surpassed the temperature of blood is evident enough in that glasses and metal objects in the house feel very warm on touch. The nights, however, were usually cool and I found myself in perfect health the whole time. . .' That sounds disturbing, doesn't it? Can a person really work in such hot weather?"

"Do you suppose it gets this hot everywhere?" Martin asked.

The young man shrugged.

"I guess we'll have to cope with heat if we don't want to starve to death," Martin continued. "For my part, I don't have any other choice."

"Me either and I don't shy away from work. I'm a carpenter by trade and have been without work for months. At home there were more people sitting at the table than we owned acres of land and everybody was relieved when I left. My oldest sister immigrated to Ohio with her husband two years ago and they own a small farm. As soon as I'm settled somewhere, I may bring over my parents and younger brothers."

He spoke with the optimism of a man who had nothing to lose and everything to gain.

"My name is Daniel. I'm going downstairs now. Would you like to read the book while I'm gone?"

"Yes, I'd be happy to."

After he left, Martin realized that Daniel had changed from the formal *Sie* to the familiar *du*. He sat on the cover of the staircase and eagerly began to read the travel story. Now and then, a frown stole over his face as he reread a passage. He was so immersed in it that he jerked when a broad-shouldered, sandy-haired young man approached him.

"Excuse me," he said, "I see you're reading this book and felt like giving you some advice. I've lived in America for two years and I want to warn you not to have unrealistic hopes about America. That book has done more damage than good. It would be wise to throw it overboard right away."

"It doesn't belong to me," Martin said.

"I'm sorry, but I just can't stand by watching so many people headed for disaster. Believe me, America is not a country where milk and honey flow. Only those who work hard will do well over time. May I have a look?"

Martin handed him the volume wordlessly.

The stranger leafed through it and read a few sentences at random, "'One will and cannot believe it in Europe how easy and comfortable life in these countries is. It sounds too strange, too splendid. The belief that such places exist on Earth has long been banished to the world of fairy tales. One gives the hogs corn, more so to keep them in place than to feed them. The soil is so fertile that the corn harvest requires nothing but breaking the sod.'"

He shut the book with a thud. "Each of these sentences is pure nonsense. Fairy tales. Even if it were a fairy tale world, the stomach wouldn't get filled from it. Would you like to hear how I fared when I arrived in New York two years ago?"

Martin nodded.

"Soon after my arrival, I fell ill with yellow fever and was bedridden for an entire month. If the landlady hadn't nursed me, I probably wouldn't have made it. When I had finally recuperated, my savings were exhausted. I went on the road and played music to buy myself a loaf of bread. Finally, I joined a peddler on his travels because I don't like to be alone. After several months, he fell ill and died a short time later. He didn't have any relatives, so I decided to sell his goods and found that I have a talent for sales. When my English was good enough, I found a position as a salesman in New York and made enough money for this trip."

"Where are you from?" Martin asked because the dialect of his new acquaintance sounded very familiar to him.

"I come from Reichenbach in Rhenish Bavaria," he said. "By the way, my name is Ludwig Behringer."

* * *

Martin was glad to have found two acquaintances to help him pass the time on board. He and Ludwig spent a lot of time together during the following days and soon Martin knew the life story of his fellow countryman.

Ludwig had only returned to Germany to fetch his bride, but the girl had grown tired of waiting and had married someone else.

"Oh, well," he said with a shrug. "There are pretty girls in America, too, I just haven't had much time for them yet."

Martin could easily imagine how many girls would gladly marry the handsome young man.

"You've said so many negative things about America that I can't imagine why you're going back," Martin said during a lull in Ludwig's torrent of words.

"I didn't speak unfavorably about America, I just said that the immigrants have too many expectations of it," Behringer replied gravely. "You will probably understand better why I'm returning once you have lived there for a while. Two years is a long time and when I returned home, I found that my former friends had nothing to say to me. For that reason, and because my family will probably follow later, it wasn't too hard for me to say good-bye to my home country. Do you know which state you are going to yet?"

"I don't have any plans at all," Martin said. "So far, I don't even know whether I should look for a job in Baltimore or travel west before winter sets in."

"If you want my advice, travel west before winter comes. Work is scarce in the East once the cold weather sets in and then it's too late to travel. The future is out in the West."

"That sounds like sensible advice. Where are you headed?"

"I want to travel to Missouri and see whether it is suitable for my family. Would you like to join me? Maybe we could go into business together."

"Thank you for the invitation to travel together. I may take you up on it, but I don't think I would be a good business partner for you. I want to see if I can make it on my own at last. I have obeyed other people all my life. Now, I want to live life as it pleases me."

Ludwig sneered at him and Martin hastened to talk about the failed revolution and his crushed hopes for freedom.

"Do you speak any English?" Ludwig asked when Martin had finished.

"I've learned some English from books."

"Books," Ludwig said and spat over the railing. "If it were up to me you wouldn't be allowed to touch a book in the next few years."

Martin gave him a puzzled look.

"Well, learning from books is better than nothing at all," Ludwig said. "Most German immigrants don't speak a word of English. If you want to, we could practice your English from now on."

"I'll be glad to."

Ludwig kept his word. At an appointed time in the afternoon, Martin assumed the role of an eager student and Ludwig was a strict teacher. Martin came well prepared to these teaching lessons that were the highlights of this endless, deadly boring sea voyage. After just a few days, Martin was not allowed to speak a word of German but had to answer all questions in English. If a German word slipped out on occasion, he had to pay a fine of one sixth of a Kreuzer. The two friends enjoyed these lessons very much even though they were spawned by the gravity of survival.

Martin had little contact with the other passengers of the *Amelia* since most of them were families who kept to themselves. Even Daniel spoke to him less and less ever since they had had a disagreement over his book. Martin was inclined to believe the friend who had lived in America for two years while Daniel argued that the author could not have invented everything.

* * *

When Martin was not learning English, he was busy preparing his meals. There was only one thirty-foot long common kitchen on deck, and it was constantly crowded with passengers. The German immigrants did not deviate from their habits even when they were far from home and wanted to eat dinner at twelve o'clock. He therefore stayed away from the kitchen at that hour. For breakfast or supper, he ate only ship biscuits or bread and drank tea. Somedays, when the sea was especially rough, he ate nothing at all. He lay on the bed and tried to think of something other than his rumbling stomach.

From time to time, Katrin's familiar face appeared in his daydreams. At their last meeting in the crowded beer garden she had seemed almost happy to see him. Did she ever think about him anymore? He banished the thought. He had more pressing problems at the moment. Girls would complicate his dire financial situation even more.

Although he had brought provisions for seventy days on board, Martin could not wait to put his feet on firm ground once again. He longed to find a job that required physical labor so that he could feel his muscles again and was not forced to sit still.

* * *

Six weeks after the *Amelia* had lifted its anchor in Havre, her voyage came to an end. Martin was on deck with Ludwig when he spotted a lighthouse at starboard. As soon as the other passengers became aware of the shoreline, they were dancing with delight. Several ran under deck to tell their fellow passengers the joyous news.

Amused, Martin and Ludwig watched a group of dancers who were forming a circle. Two young girls became aware of the silent onlookers and challenged them. A girl of no more than fifteen years dragged Martin along and he followed her reluctantly while Ludwig hummed the tune all the while. When the dance ended, his partner kissed him on the mouth before Martin shrank back dumbfounded.

"What's the matter?" Ludwig laughed. "Have you never kissed a girl before?"

Martin blushed. He had attended a boys' school before his apprenticeship and therefore had had little contact with girls during his adolescence. Nikolaus would have understood, but he could not explain this to a stranger. Behringer stepped aside with him.

"I think you have a lot to learn," he said. "First of all, you have to stop making such a dour face. America belongs to the optimists and you'll make much more progress in life by smiling. None of us can look into the future so therefore we shouldn't worry too much about it. If I only knew what depresses you so much. Are you homesick already?"

Martin flinched. Just a few weeks ago he had resolved to live in the present instead of the past and now he had failed already. "No. I had thought about immigrating to America for quite a while. But I had never imagined fleeing from Germany in the dead of night. I will never forget the eyes of my mother when she handed me the money for the passage. They haunt me even in my dreams."

"Have you written to her yet?"

"No."

"Then do it now, as soon as we arrive at the harbor. She's waiting for it."

"Yes, I think I will."

Martin shifted away from Ludwig and fixed his eyes upon the horizon. He drank in the sights of houses, lush green fields, and trees heavy with fruit. Seagulls cruised the ship noisily and waited for the scraps the travelers threw out. Martin's gaze roved over his fellow passengers. Most of them, especially the children and women, looked haggard and worn out from seasickness and the lack of nutritious food. Their clothes, probably new when embarking, were dirty, frayed or torn from living in cramped quarters.

Martin and Ludwig used the opportunity of an empty kitchen to cook their last dinner. They ate beef, potatoes, rice, beans, and an apple for dessert.

"How does it taste?" asked Martin while chewing with dogged determination.

"Like leather. The wine is the best thing about this meal. Do you have another bottle?"

"No, that was the last bottle, but if you would like to have ship biscuits I can help you out. I have enough of them."

"No," Ludwig said quickly, raising his hands. "I would rather eat meat for the rest of my life than have another biscuit."

Martin chuckled. "Tomorrow I'll throw everything into the sea. And do you know what I'll do first when I get to Baltimore? I'll go to a bakery, buy a loaf of fresh bread and eat it all at once."

In the evening, the *Amelia* dropped anchor before reaching Baltimore and Martin ascended his bunk one last time. The captain had ordered everybody to rise at four o'clock the next morning to get washed and dressed. Martin worried if the rumors of a quarantine were true. What would he do if he were denied entry? He could not return to Germany after his involvement in the revolution.

Finally, he shook his head to dispel the gloomy thoughts. He was in better health than most passengers and concentrated on the journey that lay ahead. Where would he go from here?

Ludwig had told him of St. Louis and the large community of Germans who had settled there. Since the discovery of gold in California, it was also the starting point of many treks out west. Martin had therefore decided to try his luck there.

"Would you like to search for gold in California?" Ludwig had asked him once. "It's a long and treacherous journey, though, if you sail around the cape."

Martin had laughed. "No, thank you very much. I've had enough of ocean travel and fruitless efforts. I'll travel no farther than St. Louis."

The two ship companions had decided to stay together until they reached the city on the Mississippi River.

A ragtag group of mankind gathered on board when the ship's officers and a doctor inspected them the next morning. Martin's heart skipped a beat when the doctor checked out his eyes, ears, and mouth before passing on.

"What would you like to do first when we get off board?" Ludwig asked him.

"I would like to get a haircut, a shave, and take a bath," Martin said without hesitating.

"You do need it."

Martin punched him in the side.

Since none of the travelers was rejected, the deck hands raised the anchor, unfurled most of the sails and the *Amelia* headed to the city of Baltimore. A new official came aboard and inspected the luggage for taxable items. It was afternoon when the brig finally berthed in Baltimore harbor.

Of all the disembarking travelers, Martin Dupree carried the least luggage. His whole outfit consisted of the single old leather bag which had survived quite a few hunting adventures in the Palatine woods before he used it during the campaign, the flight through Baden and France, and finally the crossing to America. The baggage he carried was mostly in his mind.

"If I ever become President of the United States, this bag will have a place of honor in my office," Martin joked. "It shall always remind me that I started at the very bottom."

"If you have a job to fill, think of me. I'm always up to try something new," Ludwig replied dryly.

Chapter 14

Captain Heller instructed his passengers about transportation from Baltimore. Most of the Germans on board, including Martin and Ludwig, decided to take the railroad to Columbia, Pennsylvania, and from there on canal boats to Pittsburgh and beyond. Martin's knees buckled when he stepped off the gangway with his luggage. His first steps in the New World!

He almost lost Ludwig in the throng of seamen, porters, hacks, wagons, and vendors selling everything from apples to newspapers. The two shipmates proceeded to a German hotel, the *Darmstadt Inn*, to take a brief rest before moving on. It was stiflingly hot under the slanting roof of their one-bed attic room, but it afforded a privacy they had missed on the crowded ship. They asked their landlord for the location of a bath house and he replied, "You could have a bath right here if you wait for hot water." The young men gladly accepted and drank a cool beer while they waited. Afterward, they visited a barber shop for a haircut and a shave. Back at the inn, they ate a hearty supper of pork roast, potatoes, gravy, and cabbage accompanied by fresh bread.

"Ah," said Ludwig while wiping a piece of bread over his plate, "I haven't eaten such good food in a long time. If I never see a ship's biscuit in my life again, I won't shed a tear."

Martin chuckled. He had no idea which provisions to bring on a canal boat, but he intended to buy apples and bread before embarking. The next morning, he took the landlord aside and asked him for the location of a reputable bank where he could obtain American money for one of his bills of exchange.

"Don't take any state bank notes," Herr Frank urged him. "They call it wildcat money because it's usually worthless. Accept only gold and silver dollars."

Martin set out alone since he did not even want Ludwig to know how much money he had. The teller at the bank spoke only English and it took Martin a while to explain that he wanted gold and silver coins. Martin carefully stuffed the money into his pouch, leaving out some small coins for food.

* * *

The locomotive which was to take the immigrants into Pennsylvania looked smaller than the coal train Martin had once seen in Landstuhl. Women and children shrieked when the whistle screeched above their heads. Families gathered all their youngsters around them and heaved their luggage into the tiny railroad cars. Martin and Ludwig squeezed themselves onto rough-sawn benches next to a mother and father with their three noisy children. A little boy wanted to climb over Martin's legs, but he fended him off. He was still tired from the long sea voyage and wanted to be left alone.

The locomotive steamed past rolling farmland, forests, small towns, and log cabins in the woods. Toward the end of the journey, the mountains grew higher and rockier. Martin gaped at the tallest trees he had ever seen; they seemed to touch the sky. After weeks on the ocean, he was delighted to see green again, even though the once-lush color seemed to have faded and shriveled in the relentless summer heat.

The canal boat appeared to be a house on top of a barge. It was so small that there was no room for sleeping arrangements of any kind. Two scrawny mules pulled the boat on a towpath along the canal. During the day, Martin often traipsed along the towpath, together with most other men and children. The children ran back and forth with relentless energy, covering the distance the boat traveled several times while peering into fruit and vegetable gardens for edible treasures. They were not shy about climbing on a tree to pick apples if the branches hung close to the path. Martin stayed away from the rough-looking crew with their long beards and wild manners. They did not hesitate to pick fights at the numerous locks the boat passed through.

"Where are we all supposed to sleep?" Martin asked Ludwig.

He found out when the passengers squeezed themselves on deck, men on one side and women on the other like herrings in a barrel at the market. This much humanity was uncomfortable to Martin, who had always shied away from strangers. Even during the campaign, he had had more sleeping space.

"We pay one and a half cents a mile for this," he complained to Ludwig.

"You could have traveled in a packet boat for four cents a mile," Ludwig retorted, "And you would have been fed, too."

"I can't afford that. God knows when I'll find work."

"Then you and I will have to make the best of it."

When he was tired of studying his English book, Martin drank in the passing countryside. Black-eyed Susans, meadow sunflowers, and asters grew by the wayside, turning their gay faces toward the weary travelers. He thought he had never seen anything so enchanting until he spotted a bright red bird on a tree branch.

"Look," he pointed to Ludwig, "that's the most beautiful bird I've ever seen."

"That's a cardinal, they're everywhere. You'll soon grow tired of them."

"Oh no, I'll never stop admiring them."

After that, he looked out for other species of birds and soon distinguished between robins and chickadees. He did not know their names but that did not diminish his enthusiasm. A drilling noise alerted him to look up at a dead tree where he spotted a red-bellied woodpecker.

"What's the matter? Have you never seen birds before?" laughed Ludwig.

"Not these kinds of birds. And I must do something to pass the time. How I wish I could draw them, but I have never been good at it and I don't have any paper anyway."

"Well, you could look at girls instead."

"What girls?"

The oldest girl on board was no more than fourteen years old.

Ludwig chuckled and pointed at the houses of the next town they approached. A comely, scarlet-haired girl of about eighteen years was hanging laundry in a garden. Ludwig whistled at her and she turned away giggling.

Martin was embarrassed about his new friend's behavior and plodded on. He could never behave like Ludwig when he was in a girl's company.

* * *

After three days of traveling, the canal boat arrived at Hollidaysburg. Here, the sections of the boat were taken apart and floated onto railroad cars, and then stationary engines pulled the cars out of the water.

Workers joined three cars together in a hitching shed and a locomotive pulled the train up an inclined plane with the help of a wire rope. At the same time, another train descended on the second track to counterbalance the weight.

Martin drew in his breath at the sight of a steep drop. As the train climbed higher and higher, he watched hawks gliding above the majestic trees and for a moment he envied them. It would be a thrill to view the world from above, looking down on the ancient mountain range, interrupted by valleys and streams and now and then, a cabin in a clearing. There, he spotted children running back and forth; cows grazing and pigs foraging; and men chopping firewood, completely unfazed by this engineering marvel. This spectacle repeated itself four more times. In between, the boat sections were pulled by horses or locomotives. At each stage Martin felt the excitement of the journey anew. Anything seemed possible in a country with such majestic landscapes.

The children on board screamed when the train chugged through a 900-foot long tunnel. Another time, it crossed a beautiful viaduct and Martin watched a boy fishing in the creek. On the other side of the mountains, the cars descended five more planes and eventually, the sectional boat was floated into a canal basin in Johnstown and connected with the help of irons. The journey to Pittsburgh continued without incident. Martin treaded along the towpath and squinted at the hills covered with maples, oaks, and elm trees. He doubted that he would ever see a range as high as the Allegheny Mountains again in his life.

As the boat neared the sooty city, the number of smokestacks and blast furnaces increased. Their haze blocked out the sun and some passengers coughed when the fumes reached their lungs.

"Would you like to look for a job here?" Ludwig said to Martin.

"No, I don't think so. This is too grimy for me."

The boat crossed the Allegheny River by an aqueduct before spewing out its passengers. The two friends decided to spend a night at a tavern since the steamboat *William Clark* did not leave until the next day. The young men scratched themselves bloody in their flea-ridden bed and could not wait until the night had passed.

After a hefty breakfast of eggs, sausages, potatoes, cheese, and bread and butter, the two companions set out to buy soap and other toiletries. At an agency on Market Street, they purchased tickets for the steamboat to Louisville, where they would have to change boats. A steward took them to a simply furnished cabin, where Martin dropped his bag on the bed before setting out to explore the ship.

Now that he knew he would be leaving Pittsburgh soon, he wanted to take in the sights for posterity. A steep mountain rose from the riverbed almost straight up to the south, blocking his view in that direction. It loomed larger than the Sickingen Hills that surrounded Landstuhl.

The Ohio River valley reminded him of the Rhine River, but this waterway was wider than its Old World counterpart and no castles graced its wooded hilltops. Its treasures were hidden beneath the surface. They were coal and ore, promising back-breaking jobs to countless immigrants.

Martin, however, had no desire to work underground. The Midwest beckoned him with its open spaces and fertile land. Maybe someday he would be able to buy a farm and be his own master.

Chapter 15

In the early evening hours, the St. Louis levee swarmed with people and Martin pushed on until he reached a quieter part of town. He roamed through the unfamiliar streets, unable to find the boardinghouse Ludwig had recommended to him.

On the steamer from Louisville to St. Louis, Ludwig had made the acquaintance of a wide-eyed brunette from Switzerland. She was traveling with her entire family and her father had invited him to accompany them to Little Switzerland, a thriving colony on the Missouri River. Ludwig was truly smitten with the girl and did not hesitate for a second. He half-heartedly asked Martin to come along but Martin declined. It was time for him to make it on his own.

At last, Martin asked a policeman on a street corner for the way, slowly pronouncing each word. The officer did not appear the least fazed by his accent and pointed Martin in the right direction. He was exhausted when he reached the two-story white frame house of Bertha Lingenfeld. The middle-aged landlady scrutinized Martin up and down and nodded. They agreed on a board of six dollars per month and Martin was allowed into the house.

"Are you hungry?" Frau Lingenfeld asked.

"Yes. I haven't had anything to eat since breakfast."

She put a bowl of cornmeal mush in front of him and laughed at Martin's face when he first tasted the strange fare. He gobbled down the mush and asked Frau Lingenfeld to wash his second shirt, since he needed it for his job search. By and by, the other boarders came home from work. Their loud voices and boisterous card games kept Martin awake for hours.

Every morning, after a breakfast of cornbread and milk, Martin put on his fresh shirt and went looking for work. Every evening, he sank onto his bed, defeated and bone tired. With winter approaching, many immigrants who arrived here by boat competed for jobs before setting out west in the spring.

On the sixth day of his search, Martin gathered all his courage to inquire about employment at city hall. He waited for an hour before someone noticed him. The personnel clerk who called him into his office looked him over and turned back to his paperwork.

"One of our street sweepers died of yellow fever a couple of weeks ago," he said. "He was paid seven dollars a month. Is that alright with you?"

Martin swallowed hard. Seven dollars pay would mean that he only had one dollar of pocket money left over after paying for his board. Even as a rebel he had received a higher pay, but he had no other choice.

"I'll take it," he said, vowing to resign as soon as he could find better paying work. He picked up his tools and set out to clean the St. Louis streets of debris. At least he had an opportunity to get acquainted with the street names of the city.

He considered what his mother would say if she saw him sweeping streets, but he quickly put the idea out of his mind. Wasn't every job honorable, as long as it was honest work? He had no illusions that this would be a position for life.

Two weeks later he was called into the office. "I was told this morning that the city can no longer employ all street sweepers," the clerk said without looking up from his ledger. "Since you're the last sweeper we hired, we have to let you go. Pick up your pay at the treasurer's office."

Martin shuffled back to his rooming house and dropped wearily on his bed. He wanted to think about what to do next but fell asleep instead.

When the other boarders returned from work in the evening, he told his roommate of his misfortune. Joe, a stocky Polish man, scratched the back of his head and said cheerfully, "No problem. Just come down to the dock with me tomorrow. There's enough work for anybody who wants to work."

Martin was not so sure about that, but he told himself that he should give it a try unless he wanted to starve.

The foreman skeptically inspected Martin's physique and consented at last that he could work on the dock. The pay of one and a half dollars per day was handsome; the work itself was not.

From early morning until evening Martin was now busy loading and unloading the many steamers that anchored at the levee. Bales of hay, kegs of whiskey, barrels of flour, and mailbags passed through Martin's hands now. Martin was especially careful when he handled the mail. In many cases they were letters from immigrants to their families who had remained in the old country. He imagined that they told of homesickness or unexpected success, depending on the circumstances of the writer.

Each time Martin lugged a mailbag on board he wondered whether it contained the letter he had written to his parents. He had not mentioned his occupation as a dockworker because he knew that his family would consider that an outrageous social descent. For him, however, it was nothing more than a brief employment until he could land a better position.

One morning, a colleague had not reported for work and Martin had to pick up his load.

"Come on," the foreman shouted. "You'll have to carry two bails instead of one. The ship doesn't wait for you."

Martin hesitated briefly. How would he manage to lift a double pack when he was already struggling with the bundles he had to carry? He stumbled up with the load on his back when a porter with a handcart rammed him in the side. Martin staggered and his load began to tumble to the ground, taking him with it.

What am I doing here? I am not a dockworker and won't live very long if I keep working here. He clambered back on his feet and slogged to the gangway where he had last seen the foreman.

Chapter 16

Martin could not have explained why he stopped in front of *Flaherty's Inn*. Was it the sign in the window that invited every patron to play fiddle if he mastered the instrument? Or perhaps the small metal harp which hung over the front door?

A man was sitting in a wicker chair under the green awning of the tavern, watching the morning traffic on Pine Street. Assuming he was the proprietor, Martin stepped up to him and asked, "Do you know where I could find a job around here?"

"Have you ever worked in a pub before?" the man replied.

Martin gaped at him, unable to understand a word of the Irish brogue. He almost turned around and left. The man repeated the question slowly until Martin's face brightened.

"Yes, I often helped at my father's inn," he said, carefully pronouncing every syllable.

"Can you handle horses, too?"

"I grew up with horses," Martin said with confidence.

Flaherty knocked out his pipe and rose slowly.

"Well, we could give it a try," he said. "The name's Ray, by the way. You'll get twelve dollars pay per month with free board. Come, I'll show you everything before the noon customers arrive."

Martin followed the Irishman inside. In the hallway, a narrow staircase led to the guest rooms on the upper floor. At the back of the house, Flaherty opened a door to a courtyard spacious enough for several Conestoga wagons.

Ray pointed to the stable. "Most guests take care of their horses themselves, but there is always work to be done in the stable."

He showed Martin the lounge. Wood panels on the rear wall of the large rectangular room created a contrast to the yellowing white walls.

Several spittoons were scattered about the room, but the floor was still littered with puddles of chewing tobacco.

"These have to be emptied several times a day," Ray said, pointing at a spittoon.

On the walls hung several paintings recording the rise of the city from the small French settlement of Laclede's Landing to the most important metropolis in the American West. Curious, Martin stepped closer to inspect each picture thoroughly and decided to get better acquainted with St. Louis. Afterward, Flaherty led Martin through one of the many doors into another hallway and from there to a small room.

"This is your room," he said. "I'll call you when I get busy."

The room was sparsely furnished with a bed, nightstand, and washstand. A wooden cross was the only decoration on the wall besides a brown tobacco stain. At least it was clean. After wandering the streets for two days, he had almost given up hope of finding a position in St. Louis. He had even considered looking up Ludwig in Little Switzerland. Still, by doing that he would have admitted that he could not make it in life without help. Martin's pride forbade him to give up on his dream just yet. Perhaps fate had led him into a part of the city he had never entered before. He returned to his boardinghouse to fetch his bag and settle his bill.

* * *

Martin had not lied when he claimed that he knew how to run a public inn. Before working in Kaiserslautern, he had often helped at his parents' inn. Therefore, Ray only had to explain the names of the offered food and drinks and their prices. Martin saw at once what work needed to be done and promptly began to wash the glasses that had accumulated behind the counter.

Thanks to Ludwig Behringer's help, Martin's English was now good enough that he was just barely able to understand the Irishman, although with some difficulty. When Martin returned to his room late that night, he was more than satisfied with his day. His mother would have been mortified to see him emptying spittoons, but then she would have never set foot in such an establishment at any rate. Maybe his luck was changing, he reflected, hoping that he could find a second home in St. Louis.

* * *

During the following days, Martin strolled about St. Louis in his free time. Within a short while, he knew his way around the business district. Every now and then, he walked to the Mississippi River where an endless row of boats spewed a colorful mixture of travelers onto the shore: businessmen and gold diggers, soldiers and actors, farmers and cattle traders.

It was impossible to command a view of the whole river, and so Martin hiked until he didn't see a boat berthed on the shore anymore. He surveyed the panorama before his eyes and his heart sank. The mighty Mississippi River, his final goal after months of travel, did not quite conform to the image he had formed in his mind. Yes, it was twice as wide as the Rhine River near Knielingen. But back then, the Rhine had seemed much wider to him than it was because by crossing it, Martin began a new phase of his life.

The Rhine had been lined by poplars while the tranquilly flowing waters of the Mississippi were rimmed by grass and a few shrubs. On the Illinois side of the river, the prairie stretched all the way to the horizon and was only interrupted by several hills shaped like a trapezoid. From what he could see, they did not appear to have been formed there naturally, but rather as if a giant hand had dropped them there for unknown reasons.

Martin rested on the banks and mulled over his life. There was no one around as far as he could see, and the loneliness enveloped him like a woolen blanket. For the first time, he began to have doubts whether he should stay in St. Louis. He did not want to go west, but he doubted that he would find a companion like Nikolaus or Ludwig in the city. Every human being needed a friend to share his pleasures and sorrows with, and Martin was no exception. *Perhaps I should have followed Ludwig to Little Switzerland after all*, he thought wistfully.

He decided to ask about German settlements in the area. On his way back to town, he walked into a general store and bought a notebook and a few sheets of paper. The same night, he wrote a detailed letter to Nikolaus and started a diary in the notebook.

* * *

On Saturday nights, many Irishmen frequented Flaherty's Inn because it was famous for its liveliness. From time to time, the clumsy fingers of a brewery worker coaxed a quavering melody from the fiddle, but no one could master the instrument as well as Flaherty himself. They never had to ask twice before he brought out his fiddle or his uilleann pipe, a bagpipe which was operated with the left elbow. It was the only luggage beside the violin that Raymond had brought from his homeland.

When the Irishmen begged Ray to play a tune for them, Martin realized that they suffered more from homesickness than he did. Famines and overpopulation had driven them to far-off shores while Martin had emigrated by choice. The Irishmen formed a loose community while he was all by himself. Trying to form friendships with them was impossible since he could not understand most of what they said and had to work when they were off. After being employed at Flaherty's Inn for two months, however, he had a chance encounter that would lead his life in a new direction.

Chapter 17

Early one afternoon, Martin was alone in the inn when two gentlemen entered the lounge. The younger one wore a black suit and a broad-rimmed hat. Sandy hair and a full beard framed his face while the other gentleman's hair and mustache were silver. Martin approached the pair to take their orders.

"Lager," said the younger one while his elder asked for a glass of wine.

"I'm sorry, we don't sell any wine," Martin replied.

The patron shrugged and also ordered a lager. While Martin filled their order, he overheard the gentlemen speaking German. Pleased to hear his mother tongue again, Martin debated whether he should dare to address such fine gentlemen.

"How much for the two glasses?" inquired the gray-haired customer. His companion protested, but he cut him short. "That's alright, Hecker, next time it will be your turn."

"Zehn Cents, mein Herr," Martin replied in German, pondering what he had just heard. Could it be that the man in front of him was Friedrich Hecker, the famous revolutionary, who had to flee to Switzerland last year after a failed uprising in the southern Black Forest? And if it was really him, what was he doing in St. Louis at Flaherty's Inn?

Hecker asked with genuine interest, "You're German? What state are you from?"

"I'm from the Palatinate in Rhenish-Bavaria."

"Have you lived in St. Louis very long?"

"Almost three months," Martin said.

"And your parents and siblings are here also?"

"No, I'm here all by myself."

"Why don't you come over to Illinois? Many Germans live over there," Hecker suggested. "Have you ever heard of Belleville?"

"No, I've never been on the other side of the Mississippi," Martin said. "How do I get to Belleville?"

"That's easy. You take the ferry to East St. Louis and then board a stagecoach to Belleville. It is just fifteen miles away from here."

Martin resolved to have a look at this town before deciding to move.

"Excuse me for asking, sir, but are you Friedrich Hecker?"

"Yes, that's me," the latter replied with a smile.

The rebels had often sung Hecker songs during their raids through the Palatinate. Martin had particularly liked this one: *Wenn die Leute fragen, lebt der Hecker noch? Werd' ich ihnen sagen: Ja, er lebet noch! Er hängt an keinem Baume, er hängt an keinem Strick, er hängt an seinem Traume der deutschen Republik.* When people ask, is Hecker still alive? I will tell them: Yes, he is alive! He does not hang on a tree, he does not hang on a rope, he hangs on his dream of the German Republic.

"We could have used a man like you in Baden," Martin mused. "Perhaps the revolution might have turned out differently."

"Are you talking about the uprising in the Palatinate and Baden?" Hecker asked, his voice rising in excitement. "Were you involved in it?"

"Yes, I was a rebel from the very beginning."

"My fellow countrymen and I would like to hear what really happened in Germany this year—not what was written in newspapers," Hecker said. "Why don't you come to my farm in Illinois and tell me about your adventures?"

Martin had met many important gentlemen during the revolution in Kaiserslautern, yet he had often had the feeling that they only talked to him for his father's sake. An invitation from a famous politician was a new experience for him.

"Thank you very much. Where do you live?" he uttered.

"My farm lies east of Lebanon in the Looking Glass Prairie. Can you remember that?"

"I think so," Martin replied, bidding good-bye to his compatriots as a customer called him away.

For the rest of the day Martin was preoccupied with the conversation with Hecker. After the last patron staggered home, Martin made the longest entry ever in his notebook. He decided to travel to Belleville as soon as the weather was agreeable. The chance meeting with two Germans had reminded him how much he had missed speaking in his mother tongue. Perhaps he could even look for a position during his visit.

During the first week of January, the temperature plunged to a deep freeze. Martin had to deplete his savings to buy a winter coat and gloves.

In early March, though, the thermometer climbed as drastically as it had dropped, and Martin once again planned his journey. He asked Raymond for several days off and strode to the mooring of the ferry. In East St. Louis he asked for the way to the stagecoach station from a man who happened to be a German on his way home from delivering building timber to St. Louis.

"Why don't you ride with me?" he asked. "The trip will be just as uncomfortable as in the stagecoach and you can save the fare."

Martin did not have to be asked twice and climbed on the wagon.

"My name is Karl Leibrock, by the way. What's yours?"

He gave Martin a blanket to put over his knees before urging the horses on. Leibrock had not exaggerated the poor condition of the road. After a short time, Martin's entire body hurt, but the view compensated him for all discomforts.

The seemingly endless prairie stretched all the way to the horizon, now and then interrupted by an impenetrable copse. Despite the few isolated farmhouses, which hinted at human life in this untouched wilderness, Martin felt he had never seen a more desolate land. The profound peace that enveloped the vast valley remained undisturbed even by the jangling of a cow chain or the barking of a dog.

"Do you know anyone in Belleville?" Leibrock asked when the wagon approached the first houses of West Belleville.

"No, I don't know anybody," Martin answered without looking at his compatriot.

He almost pinched his arm to make sure he was still in America. Each one of the plain one- or two-story brick houses could have stood in a German village. Even the names on the store signs sounded familiar: There was the small drill machine factory of Philip Gundlach, the butcher store of the Reis brothers, and Merck's bakery. Main Street was immersed in mud, except for the brick and wooden sidewalk in front of the stores.

As dusk deepened, Martin pondered where he could spend the night. As if Leibrock had read his thoughts, he said, "Do you know where you'll be staying tonight?"

"I don't know, but I see many inns and hotels here. It shouldn't be difficult to find a room."

Leibrock surveyed his passenger.

"You don't seem like somebody who can afford that," he said with a shake of his head. "You know what, I'll take you home for tonight. You're looking for work, right?"

Martin hesitated. "I might, but first I want to take a look at the town."

Leibrock reined in his horse in front of a whitewashed brick house, set the brake, and jumped off the wagon board. With stiff limbs, Martin clambered off the wagon and sank into the mud almost to his ankles. The thaw of the last few days had turned the streets into sludge. Leibrock's front door was painted the same green color as the shutters and a chimney jutted out of each end of the shingled roof. The home could have been located in any Palatine village, with the sliding windows as the only concession to the new American home.

Leibrock opened the front door, invited Martin to enter and called into the dark house, "Lena, I'm home again and I've brought a visitor."

A short, stout woman came to the door and greeted her husband with a smile. Then she turned to the stranger with a puzzled look on her face.

"He's looking for work here in Belleville and didn't know where to sleep tonight," Leibrock explained.

"It's alright," she replied with a soft voice and beckoned Martin into the kitchen where she had kept the cornmeal for her husband warm on the stove.

Before he drifted off to sleep that night Martin thought how much the bread his hostess had served with supper reminded him of home.

* * *

Slightly stiff from the night spent on blankets on the floor, Martin walked out into the sunlit day. He already felt at home in Belleville and was determined to find a position, even if it was not his first choice. The shopkeepers on the north side of Main Street seemed perfectly able to handle their workloads by themselves.

At last he crossed Main Street, carefully avoiding the largest puddles and horse-droppings. Safe on the planked sidewalk, Martin looked down at his muddy boots that were beginning to fall apart. He would need new ones soon, another unexpected expense. There were numerous saloons, inns, and hotels in this street, but Martin wanted to do something different this time. Around noon, he had success at last. The general store owner, Mr. Ellis, was willing to hire Martin as an assistant.

Oscar Ellis's general store took up the first floor and basement of a three-story building. Citizens of Belleville and the farmers of the vicinity could buy everything imaginable here: cigars from Virginia, pottery, china, glasses, flour, coffee, eggs, salt, sugar, flour, salted meat and fish, butter, and much more. Kentucky whiskey and vinegar were dispensed from barrels.

Once again Martin had to resort to the profession of a merchant because he had no other qualifications for making a living. Shy as he was, he was ill-suited to be a salesman. That had been Georg's specialty, he thought with a pang of sorrow.

Revolutionaries such as Friedrich Hecker were not able to work in their original profession either, but at least they owned enough money to make a new life for themselves. Martin did not own more than the clothes on his body and would have to remain an unskilled assistant until he had saved enough money to buy a farm or other property. Being his own master was his ultimate goal, no matter how long it would take.

Now that he had a job, it was considerably easier for Martin to find a boardinghouse. Just one block away from the store, he rented a bed in Glanig's boardinghouse and did not need to take advantage of Leibrock's hospitality any longer. The next morning, he returned to St. Louis on the stagecoach, eager to begin a new chapter in his life.

Chapter 18

One of Ellis's regular customers was newspaper editor Bartholomew Hauck.

"How's work?" Ellis asked him one morning while he handed him two cigars.

"Everything is topsy-turvy," Hauck replied. "My printing apprentice took a fall and broke his leg. Not only will my newspaper be printed later than usual, but I don't have anybody to deliver the papers on Saturday evening. I can't deliver them myself since I'm invited to a friend's birthday."

Recognizing an opportunity to make more money, Martin stepped up to the newspaper man.

"When I'm finished with my work here, I would like to deliver the newspapers for you," he said, his eyes fixed on Mr. Hauck.

"Fine. Come to my office on North Illinois Street on Saturday around five o'clock."

Hauck promised to write a list of subscribers so Martin would find their houses. Martin had two reasons for accepting a part-time job. He could well use the additional, if meager, pay, and he hoped to get better acquainted with the citizens of Belleville.

* * *

Martin knocked at the office door of the *Belleviller Zeitung* but received no answer. He drove his fingers through his hair and cleared his voice before tapping again. At last, he cautiously opened the door.

Hauck was seated at his desk. "Why are you knocking? Come on in."

"My parents taught me to knock before entering a room," Martin said in German.

Hauck handed Martin a stack of newspapers.

"You'll get paid next Saturday," he said curtly. Hauck's list proved to be useless and Martin decided to ask his way from one subscriber to the next. In this way, his work extended late into the evening hours, but allowed him to become familiar with the hospitality of his compatriots abroad.

Many housewives recognized him from the store and gave him a piece of sausage, a slice of honey bread, or an apple. A woman in Jackson Street even urged him to sit in her kitchen and drink a cup of coffee with her. While Martin warmed his cold hands on the cup, the curious widow asked him about his background.

Another time, a lovely about sixteen-year-old, fair-haired girl opened the door. When Martin asked her where Adam Friess lived, she remained mute and fixed her eyes on him. Martin knew by her facial expression that she had understood every word he said.

"What's the matter? Don't you know or don't you want to tell me?" he said, feeling uncomfortable under her scrutiny.

"It's the third house on the left," she whispered.

"Thank you," he stammered, hurrying away while the girl giggled behind his back. He had the feeling that he had behaved clumsily, but why in the world had she stared at him?

After he had delivered his last newspaper, Martin returned home, his pockets stuffed with the delicacies of Belleville's kitchens. For the second time during his brief stay in town he felt reminded of home. Depositing his fragrant treasures on a small table, he nodded, satisfied with the outcome of this day.

The following Saturday, Martin put the newspapers on porches or dropped them in front of doors. Eventually, he came to the two-story, square house of book dealer Wilhelm Ruppelius. Martin plunked the paper on the porch and turned away when the blond girl slipped out of the front door and ran toward the garden gate.

"Are you coming to Eimer's Hill tomorrow evening?" she asked in a low voice.

"Where in the world is that?"

"You really haven't been in Belleville very long, have you? Everybody in town knows Simon Eimer's amusement park where they hold dances every Sunday evening. I'll be there tomorrow with my girlfriends."

"Anna, where have you got to?" called a woman's voice from inside the house.

"I have to go now," Anna said quickly. "Well, are you coming tomorrow?"

"If I'm able to find this attraction, I'll come," Martin said with a laugh.

"Eimer's Hill lies on South Sixth Street on a hill. You'll see it from afar. Good-bye."

She turned around swiftly and ran along the garden path.

After Anna had disappeared into the house, Martin stood thoughtfully at the garden gate. A girl he had just met had asked him out and he had accepted it. Were all American girls so outspoken or was she an exception?

He had to admit that she was a lovely creature. Her blond hair framed an angelic face with a small, well-formed nose and rosy cheeks. He had not dared to look at any girl since he had last seen Katrin in Kaiserslautern. When he longed for a confidant who could help him through his loneliness and his lack of direction, he always imagined young men such as Nikolaus and Georg.

He consoled himself with the thought that Katrin was surely married by now and lost to him forever. Besides, he had not promised to go out with Anna. In fact, he did not have to go at all.

Martin spent Sunday writing overdue letters to his mother and to Nikolaus. He seldom wrote home, unless he had to report a change of address. When writing to his mother, he had to weigh every word carefully because her letters always implored him to come back home. This was impossible under the current political circumstances and he took his time answering these accusations. Even with a husband in exile, his mother just did not understand why Martin had emigrated. Returning home so soon would not only mean imprisonment, but also losing the last thread of self-esteem. No, he was not ready to give in just yet.

* * *

After supper, Martin washed up and put on a fresh shirt. Before he could change his mind about attending, he set out for Eimer's Hill, a small elevation in the midst of the prairie. Martin could not discern the lovely park in the darkness, but the brightly lit windows of the dance floor greeted him like an inn welcomed a weary traveler. Before entering the hall, he looked out toward the direction of the town.

"In the summer one has a beautiful view from this spot," said a female voice behind him.

It belonged to Anna, who had approached him unnoticed. She wore a vine-patterned wool dress that accentuated her small waist. Her flaxen hair was twisted into a coronet crown at the back of her head. Together, they entered the dance hall, which was splendidly adorned with colorful paper garlands. Anna asked Martin to join her and her girlfriends at the table, but Martin declined. As much as he admired her smile, he did not want to sit with a group of giggling young girls all evening.

He approached a fellow resident of Glanig's boardinghouse. The young man, a Hessian named Karl Seibold who worked at a distillery, sat amid his friends and offered a chair to Martin. When Martin ordered a glass of lager from the waiter, Seibold asked, "Don't you want to try our wine?"

"Wine?" Martin asked in a tone as if the Hessian had mentioned leeches. To him, Palatine wine was superior to all others.

"Oh yes. The hill we're sitting on is actually a vineyard. Of course, the wine doesn't taste as good as our Rhenish wine, but when you don't have anything else it isn't that bad."

Martin forced a smile.

"I brought a keg of wine from home," A watchmaker from the Odenwald said.

"Splendid! Be prepared for an invasion tonight," Seibold teased him.

"That would be pointless since I emptied the keg a long time ago."

"What a waste of good wine," said the Hessian dryly and rose because the three musicians were beginning to play a lively polka.

Martin did not take part in the stomping and asked himself over and over why he had come if it was not for Anna. All evening long he was content with watching the merry dancers until Anna appeared in front of him and curtsied.

"Ladies' choice," she said.

Martin took his place as Anna's partner while the musicians elicited the sweet melody of a waltz from their violins. He was surprised that the energetic little lady was light as a feather in his arms. After the music ended, he escorted her back to her chair and asked, "May I sit down with you?"

"I'm sorry, but I have to go home now," Anna said. "I'm only waiting for Charlotte. Who knows where she is." She frowned and looked around the room. "I think she left with that young man she danced with."

"I'll take you home," Martin said quickly, quietly thanking Charlotte.

He fetched his jacket, helped Anna into her coat, and the two young people walked toward the dark town under the faint glow of a half-moon.

"I think spring will be here soon," Anna said. "Do you like spring?"

"Oh yes. I'm tired of freezing and I don't have many winter clothes. When I left my parent's house in May, I didn't think about taking my wardrobe along."

Anna tumbled over a branch and Martin quickly placed his arm under hers.

"Why did you ask me for a dance tonight?" he asked. "A pretty girl like you could have ten admirers on each finger."

"Who says I don't?" Anna retorted. "You provoked me because you weren't interested in me. I'm tired of all these young men who only admire my looks and think I have a chicken's brain. I'll show them all that's not true because I have a brilliant idea."

"What idea?" Martin asked.

Anna smiled mischievously. "I'm not ready to discuss it yet."

"Well, you brought it up."

"I just want to say that I liked you from the beginning even though you're very shy. Maybe I can help you to take life less seriously."

Martin almost let go of her arm, amazed at how fast she had evaluated his character.

"But, if you're not interested in my company, I'll never bother you again," Anna continued.

"Oh no, it matters a lot to me," Martin hastened to say.

They had arrived in front of her parents' house and Anna gave Martin her hand in parting.

"When will we see each other again?" Anna whispered to avoid waking her parents.

"Next Saturday," Martin replied and kissed Anna's hand gallantly.

* * *

The following Tuesday, Martin went for a stroll as was his habit every other evening. He paused when he reached Maus Tavern on the southwestern corner of the square. The big frame house was a unique structure because it possessed a bell tower from which a bell rang every time dinner was over.

Martin entered the lounge and sat down at the counter. Two gentlemen in the rear of the lounge were engaged in a lively conversation. Martin was surprised to recognize Friedrich Hecker, the man who was responsible for Martin's move.

Hecker looked up and, seeming to recognize him, beckoned him over. "Hello, my young friend. I see you have followed my advice to come to Belleville. Please, sit down with us for a while and tell us how you are doing."

"This young man and I are fellow sufferers because we are both revolutionaries disappointed in life," he said to his companion. "You, my dear Krafft, were smart enough to leave Germany so early that your name could not appear in any black book. We, on the other hand, hesitated a while before turning our backs on our homeland because we didn't want to leave Germany without a fight. But we don't want to philosophize, let's hear what our young friend has to tell us. What's your name, young man?"

Martin introduced himself and told briefly about his new job.

Hecker listened with interest. "Pardon me, I forgot to introduce my friend, Theodor Krafft, to you. He is a Palatine like you and is about to become the mayor of Belleville."

Krafft made a dismissive wave of his hand to interrupt Hecker's flow of words, but Hecker had already found a different topic.

"By the way, have you forgotten my invitation back in St. Louis?" he asked Martin.

Martin confessed that he had been too busy for any visits. Furthermore, considering the weather and his inappropriate clothing, the journey would have been impossible just yet.

"How do I get to your farm anyway?" he inquired. "Is it too far to walk?"

"Can you ride?"

"Yes."

"Why don't you rent a horse," Hecker suggested.

Martin had never considered that possibility. "Very well. With your permission, I shall visit you this coming Sunday."

After he had finished his glass, he took leave from his new acquaintances claiming to be tired. Truthfully, his financial circumstances did not allow a second drink if he wanted to rent a horse on Sunday.

* * *

On Saturday, Martin delivered the last paper at the house of Wilhelm Ruppelius so he could talk with Anna.

"I told my parents about you," Anna said eagerly. "Mother has asked me to invite you for dinner tomorrow."

"I'm sorry, but I already have an invitation for tomorrow."

She pouted. "I thought you didn't know anybody in Belleville."

He explained the chance meeting to her, but she did not know Friedrich Hecker.

"How is your brilliant idea coming along?" Martin asked.

Anna's mouth widened into a mischievous smile.

"Yesterday, I finally talked my father into helping him in his bookstore for a few hours every day. I'm so excited! You'll see, I'm going to be a real merchant."

Anna urged Martin to take part in the simple family supper, giving him an opportunity to meet her family. Elisabeth Ruppelius had combed her blond hair back into a tight bun which gave her features an expression of severity. Nevertheless, Martin discerned that she must have been a beauty in her younger days. Anna's father was a well-read man who was knowledgeable in science, history, and politics.

After supper, Martin reluctantly bid farewell to his hosts and made his way to the bathhouse, feeling content with the day that had passed and excited about the trip that lay ahead.

Chapter 19

It was still dark when Martin trudged through the empty streets to the stable. The stableman had already fed the horses and was about to curry them. The dapple-gray mare Martin had reserved resembled a farm horse more than a mount. While Martin soothingly patted the horse's neck, he thought wistfully of the sorrel he had left behind in his parents' stable.

Martin led the horse out into the street, mounted and rode northeast until he reached the hamlet of Lebanon where he stopped to drink a mug of coffee at the local tavern.

After he had left Lebanon behind, he instinctively drew in the reins. The Looking Glass Prairie spread out in front of him as far as his eyes could see.

Like a calm lake, the undulating plain stretched from Silver Creek to Sugar Creek, only now and then interrupted by an isolated copse or the bushes that suggested a brook. In the faint radiance of the March sun, it greatly resembled the Landstuhl moor in its bleakness. Martin almost believed that he was on his way to see Nikolaus to pour out his heart. It did not matter much that the man who awaited him today was Friedrich Hecker and not Nikolaus Weber when one had not had a confidant in almost a year.

At last he reached Hecker's farm. He lived in a two-story brick house with a porch that stretched along the whole side of the building. The wooden barn and stables were larger than the farms in Martin's homeland. The former Member of Parliament seemed to do well for himself, Martin concluded as he spotted several horses in a spacious paddock.

Hecker met him on the porch, followed by a seven-year-old boy, unmistakably his son. A laborer led Martin's horse to the stable while

Hecker escorted Martin to his study. He offered Martin a chair, took a seat behind his oversized oak desk, and lit a cigar.

"Now tell me what happened in Germany last year," he said.

Unaccustomed to being the center of attention, Martin began with an unsteady voice and almost faltered until the words flowed freely.

Now and then, Hecker interrupted his guest with shouts that meant approval or anger, but when Martin paused for a moment he said, "Go on, go on."

Just as Martin was telling of the battle of Rinnthal, Frau Hecker stepped into the room and asked the gentlemen to dinner.

"I'm sorry," Hecker exclaimed. "I never even offered you refreshments."

"That's alright, I had a cup of coffee on the way here."

Obviously, prairie life had not altered Frau Hecker's sense of propriety. She wore a black silk dress with a white lace collar as she led the men to the dining room. Martin had not savored such a good meal in a long time and paid it its due respect. There was a whole chicken wrapped with pork slices, thick gravy, a mound of yellow potatoes, and sweet corn. As a dessert, Frau Hecker served canned cherry preserves and dished up coffee in the study.

Martin continued to tell anecdotes from his rebel days that seemed to entrance his listener. His voice trembled when he talked about holding Georg in his arms and how Nikolaus had to tear him away from the body. He hastened through the rest of the events: the retreat of the insurgent army, the flight over the Rhine River, and the long march through France.

"When did you arrive in America?" Hecker asked when Martin had finished.

"At the end of August."

"Well, I guess I missed you by several weeks then."

Martin gaped.

"Yes, I did go to Europe last year," Hecker replied, rubbing his beard between his thumb and forefinger. "When we learned about the uprising in Saxony, the Palatinate, and Baden, we immediately collected money for the equipment of the rebels. In Belleville our ladies organized a bazaar where we collected four hundred seventy dollars. The money was sent to Lorenz Brentano and, as I later learned, was used to support the rebels who had fled to Switzerland.

"One of the first acts of the provisional government of Baden was to call me back. I hurried to Europe as fast as I could, but when I arrived at

Southampton in July, I learned that the rebels had fled to Switzerland or France. I pressed on to Strasbourg, hoping for the impossible, yet at the end I could do nothing but turn around and go back.

"It was probably the last time that I have seen Europe, because I don't believe that there will be another revolution in Germany in the next few decades. The time for action is over forever. We Forty-Eighters must finally accept that the United States is not merely our exile, but our new home."

Martin sighed. "If only it were that easy." He did not possess Hecker's ability to let bygones be bygones so quickly to focus on the future and American politics. "Sometimes I reproach myself for leaving the rebels before our defeat was certain. My only excuse is that Georg's death shattered me so much that I lost heart. He was the born optimist and always made the best of every situation. I simply could not understand that he left me behind, helpless and without a purpose. At that time, I worked as a trainee in the timber trade and was more than happy to give up the job I hated to join the irregulars. The revolution became my purpose in life and when it failed, there was still the worry about reaching the shores of America safely. Since I have arrived in America, I have worked in a variety of jobs, but I haven't been able to gain a foothold because I don't know a trade."

Friedrich Hecker once again lit a cigar and said calmly, "You are certainly not the only one with this problem. Look at me: I used to be an attorney, but I am already resigned to the fact that I will never work in my profession without an American partner who will take care of hearings and trials. My English just isn't good enough for negotiations. So, I have gladly retreated to my farm because here I can take part in public affairs without having to make a living off the law."

"At least you had enough money to buy a farm," Martin replied, not concealing the bitterness in his voice.

Hecker rose from his chair and paced about the room. "Are your parents well-off?"

"Yes."

"Why don't you ask them for your inheritance?" Hecker suggested.

Martin brightened up, but his expression darkened again. "I think that life on an isolated farm would be too lonely for me in the long run. What I need is the company of people my age."

"I could imagine that there are quite a few young ladies who would love to keep a fine, well-bred young man company," Hecker said with a smile.

Martin blushed.

"Ah, I see you've already met someone," Hecker said and settled back in his chair. "You should ask the young lady to study English with you."

The wine that had been served with lunch had loosened Martin's tongue and he began to talk about Anna.

"Her father owns a bookstore, you say?" Hecker asked. "Why don't you ask him to give you some books about America to read? It is always a good idea to know as much as possible about the country you live in."

He leaned back and pressed the tips of his fingers against his temple.

"Didn't you mention that you deliver newspapers?" Hecker asked.

"Yes."

"What if you apprenticed as a typesetter? You would then have a profession that is more respected than a salesclerk."

"And what should I live off in the meantime?" Martin brought the conversation around to his most pressing problem.

Hecker shrugged. "Think about my suggestion and let me know what your decision is. As you can probably imagine, I have many influential acquaintances."

Martin tilted his head but resolved not to accept Hecker's generous offer of helping him to find a suitable position. He wanted to remain true to his principle not to ask anyone for help. At least in this aspect he would be a true American.

He bid good-bye to the Heckers, wanting to return to Belleville before nightfall. He mulled over Hecker's advice during the lonely ride home. Hecker may have gotten the impression that Martin's thoughts revolved around money. He was not entirely wrong. In the past, Martin had believed that money played no role whatsoever in his life, but since he had immigrated to America, it had become tremendously important to him. He had to learn what poor people had experienced since early childhood: the art of survival.

* * *

Several weeks later, Martin's temporary job as a newspaper delivery boy ended because Mr. Hauck's apprentice had recovered from his broken leg. Martin accepted the news without regret, although he was thankful for the opportunity to meet Anna and for getting acquainted with the citizens of Belleville. Many female customers at the store recognized Martin as their paper boy and asked for the polite young man's assistance.

Ellis had therefore good reason to offer Martin a raise of two dollars a month. Anna had settled into working at her father's bookstore and her family's resistance had gradually given way to pride in their competent daughter. Anna's father was not only a book dealer but also owned an extensive library. Seeing these books reminded Martin of Hecker's suggestion. He asked Ruppelius whether he could borrow books about American history and Anna's father enthusiastically complied. With few exceptions, they were German books printed in America. While Martin looked forward to reading them, he appreciated the book dealer's conversations even more.

During mild spring evenings, the family would sit on the white porch, the father in a rocking chair and the mother and Anna busy with some needlework or sewing by the weak, smoky light of a lard oil lamp. Martin listened attentively when Wilhelm Ruppelius told of the founding of the colonies of New England, of trappers, scouts, and the repelling of Indians to the West. He could imagine the days of the War of Independence much more vividly, though, and places like Valley Forge, Germantown, Brandywine, and Yorktown were soon as familiar to him as Rinnthal and Ubstadt. His interest in American history was aroused.

At other times Anna and Martin took a walk or rode out into the country. Anna's favorite spot was a hill near the Mascoutah road. From the highest elevation, the eye commanded a view of miles and miles of fertile plain unrestricted by forests or hills.

Martin and Anna sat in the grass while devouring the sandwiches they had brought, and he thanked his destiny that had brought him here. As much as he appreciated a conversation with men like Ruppelius or Hecker, there was no lovelier company for him than Anna. Occasionally, a girl with honey-colored hair and an inviting smile appeared before his inner eye, but he quickly pushed the thought out of his mind. Katrin was probably married by now and out of his reach forever.

Chapter 20

In 1850, Belleville received its town charter and Theodor Krafft was elected mayor, just as Hecker had prophesied. The young community celebrated this special occasion with a festival on Eimer's Hill. For three days, the proud inhabitants of Belleville and the surrounding towns strolled along the fairground stalls, basking in their new status with food and drink.

Martin accompanied Anna and her parents to the fair. The mouth-watering aroma of spit-roasted oxen competed with the tantalizing scent of freshly baked pancakes, waffles, and cakes for their attention. Martin bought a plate of beef chunk with corn on the cob while Anna decided on a waffle. Afterward, they visited a puppeteer show before heading to the dance floor, where a brass band blasted a lively polka over the heads of the twirling crowd.

After Martin won a bouquet of paper flowers for her at the shooting gallery, her father beckoned the couple to join him. He introduced his companions at the table, lawyer Gustav Körner and county treasurer John Scheel.

Ruppelius asked Körner, "I have often wondered why a man of your talents has settled in this tiny prairie town. In Germany, all doors must have been open to you."

Two tiny lines formed on Körner's high forehead. "If it doesn't bore you too much, I would be delighted to tell you the story of my emigration."

"Yes, do tell us," Martin and Anna exclaimed, settling on the bench.

"In 1833," Körner said, "A year after the Hambach Festival, several conspirators—I myself among them—decided to capture the city of Frankfurt. It was our hope that the uprising would spread to all German

115

states, but our daring adventure only went down in history as the Assault on the Frankfurt Guardhouse."

His audience listened spellbound as he talked about the ill-fated adventure, his bayonet wound, his escape dressed in women's clothing, and the journey to America. "When we saw Negro slaves for the first time in Louisville, we knew we could not settle in Missouri. I remember writing into my diary that day: 'As long as the southern states keep slaves, I believe that the beautiful structure of the United States will collapse, and until then, the freedom that the whites are enjoying right now will only be a half-earned blessing.'"

* * *

Darkness closed in while Martin walked Anna home. She said thoughtfully, "Mr. Körner has been through a lot, hasn't he?"

"What has he done that was so extraordinary?" Martin asked her. "I never heard of this uprising before, but I know enough about politics to recognize an ill-conceived deed. A few half-crazed people stormed a guardhouse and believed that all Germans would be so upset about it that they would rise up."

He shook his head fiercely. "Körner was injured in the process, but my best friend died in my arms and nobody cared about his death."

Anna hooked her arm in his. "You're crying."

Martin jerked his head away from her. "I'm not crying. I apologize for being so upset, but Körner has stirred up many painful memories in me. I have tried not to dwell on the past, but when I'm not with you I spend many hours brooding over the mistakes I have made."

Much later, it occurred to Martin that he was probably not a very amusing companion for a young girl. Even though Anna handled books every day, she was quite indifferent about their contents. Although she had mentioned early on that she did not care for boys who only admired her good looks, Martin talked more with her father than with her during his visits. There would never be another girl like Katrin for him, but Martin determined to change his behavior if he did not want to lose Anna.

* * *

A week later, Martin took Anna to a dance and talked at great length about funny occurrences at the store or at the boardinghouse. Anna appeared to be pleased that there was no end to Martin's volubility. They danced almost every dance and did not go home until the musicians packed away their instruments. Before they bid good night, Martin bent his head and gingerly planted a kiss on her rosy lips.

"I'm sorry, I shouldn't have done that," he stammered as he pulled away.

"There is no need to apologize," Anna replied before she returned his kiss.

* * *

"My girlfriend Charlotte became engaged to a baker from Mascoutah last Sunday," Anna said during their next walk.

"Is that so?" Martin asked coolly.

She shot him a vexed look and he hastened to say, "Excuse me, I wasn't listening. What did you just say?"

Anna repeated the news and Martin understood. She wanted to get married. Deep inside, he had feared that it would come to this. At age twenty-one he considered himself too young for the financial responsibilities of marriage, even if it were the love of his life. And while he enjoyed Anna's company, their temperaments seemed to be too different to make such a commitment.

"If Charlotte's betrothed is a baker, he can well feed a family," he said. "But I cannot. My earnings are just enough for my needs and I have to be very thrifty to buy myself some clothes now and then."

"You could be more successful if you asked your father or your friend Hecker for help," Anna reproached him.

"I don't want anybody's help."

"Papa said you're a very proud young man and he was right," she said, running away crying.

Martin chased after her and clutched her shoulders.

"Dearest Anna," he declared. "I don't want to hurt you, but there is no sense in fooling you. Last year, when I joined the rebel army, I had decided to never again enter the merchant's trade. Back then I had great plans, but none of them have materialized yet. My experiences during my early days in St. Louis have drained my courage to make any plans for the future. Since then, I've been drifting through life like a hickory branch in the Mississippi River. All I have left is my pride. Don't you understand that I only want the best for you when I ask you to wait before making a big decision like this? We are still very young. We have all the time in the world."

Anna appeared reconciled by his soothing words.

"You're right," she said, wiping away her tears. "I will never mention it again."

Chapter 21

In early 1851, Martin became worried. His mother's letters were overdue for almost two months. On a Saturday in February, his landlady met him in the hallway and handed him a letter.

The envelope was covered with several postmarks, yet Martin realized that the handwriting was not his mother's, but his sister's. Ignoring Widow Glanig's call for dinner, Martin went up to his room and settled on the chair by the window. He carefully opened the envelope with a pocketknife and pulled out two sheets of paper.

"Dearest Martin!" he read, "When you read these lines, our kindhearted mother will no longer be among us." Shaken, he read the rest of the letter quickly.

> None of us children have yet comprehended why she was taken from our midst at a premature age. In late November, she suddenly decided to inspect all our properties. A day later, she asked Matthias to get the carriage ready and drive her to our estate in Hornbach. It was cold and on the way back it began to rain hard. Within a short time, so much rain had fallen that the carriage became lodged in the mud. The coachman went for help while Mother waited in the cold carriage as darkness set in. When she arrived at home, she already had a fever. The doctor diagnosed pneumonia and I hurried home to nurse Mother, but all our prayers were in vain.
>
> On the evening of December 6, she closed her eyes forever. While looking through her chest of drawers, I found two letters. One of them was addressed to me and the second to you. In the former letter, Mother asked us siblings—in place of our father who is living abroad—to send you the sum

of 3,000 Gulden, which you should consider your inheritance. I hope with all my heart that this money will help you overcome the difficulties that fate has dealt you. Mother's thoughts were always with you and so are mine. Please let me know as soon as possible how I should transfer the money to you.

Your loving sister, Carolina

Martin stared out the window before he unfolded the other note.

My dearest boy,

My life is coming to an end and what I have only feared until now has become a certainty: we shall never see each other again. It almost seems as if the children who have left me are dearer to me than the ones that remained with me. When you asked me a year ago to get you the traveling money, I implored your father to give you your inheritance, but he refused his consent. I hope that the last wish of a dead woman will be respected. May this money help to make your future a blissful one and dispel the shadows of the past.

May the Lord protect you always, Mother

Martin folded the two letters, put them in his pocket and stepped out of the house. He plodded down the street, his eyes fixed steadfast on the ground, until he had left the houses of Belleville behind.

His legs carried him to Walnut Hill cemetery. He slipped through the creaky gate and read the inscription on the gravestone in front of him without emotion. He did not know how long he had been standing there when he sank on the tombstone and rested his head in his hands.

"Mother, forgive me for causing you grief," he murmured.

At this hour, nobody besides Martin disturbed the quiet of the dead. A row of young pine trees looked silently down on the graves and the distraught youth. At last, the peaceful stillness of the cemetery passed to Martin and he breathed the freezing air into his lungs. He roamed among the graves until a sudden breeze sent a whisper of cold across his neck. He pulled the collar of his overcoat tighter before trudging home.

Widow Glanig had kept his dinner warm but he ate without appetite. In his room, he sank on his bed and closed his eyes. He thought in anguish that he had seldom written to his family since his departure. Now it was too late to tell his mother how he felt about her. But there was one person he could tell. He swung his legs over the side of his bed and sat at the table to write a letter to Carolina.

Chapter 22

Nikolaus bid a bewildered Margarethe Dupree in Landstuhl good-bye and hurried home as fast as his legs carried him. He paused when he entered the family farmyard. His father approached the barn from the other side with slow and measured steps.

"Good afternoon, Father," Nikolaus said, stepping up to him.

Friedrich Weber grabbed his son's hand and pumped it as if sawing wood.

"My boy," he said, "It's good to have you back again. We didn't know whether you were still alive or not."

"I didn't have writing paper, so I hurried home as fast as I could," Nikolaus replied. "Come into the kitchen so I can tell you and Mother how I fared since I left."

"Your mother is not in the kitchen," his father said almost inaudibly.

"Well, where is she?"

"Over there," Weber answered, pointing in a vague direction.

"Is she out delivering laundry?" Nikolaus asked, slightly worried about his father's odd behavior.

"Your mother is dead," his father said in a flat voice. "We buried her two weeks ago."

Nikolaus blanched.

"How is that possible? She wasn't even sick," he mumbled.

"She must have had a heart attack in her sleep. When I woke up in the morning, she was dead."

Nikolaus swallowed hard. "Then you have worked here by yourself the whole time?"

"No. Katrin came home immediately after Mother's death."

"Katrin is here?"

"Yes, she's been home ever since I sent for her." His father eased his fingers out of Nikolaus's grip. "Go inside to see her. I'll join you in a few minutes."

Katrin's sad eyes lit up when Nikolaus stepped into the kitchen. They shook hands silently.

"Where have you been all this time?" she asked. "Are you hungry?"

Nikolaus nodded. While she placed a cup in front of him, he told her about the course of the campaign and Martin's decision to emigrate to America. Her hands trembled when she poured chicory coffee into his cup. She spread butter on a piece of bread and placed it on a wooden board in front of him. Dropping on a chair opposite her brother, she said solemnly, "I guess father told you already what happened?"

"Yes."

"What choice did I have but to return home since I couldn't leave him in a lurch. My employer had given me notice anyway because business was slow after the rebels retreated."

She heaved a deep sigh.

"I wanted so much to earn my own money," she said in a choked voice.

"How did father pay for the funeral?"

"I used all my earnings to help."

Nikolaus placed his hand over hers. "Don't worry, this situation can't last forever. Now that I'm home, perhaps you could earn some money with seasonal work. Maybe father will marry again and then you can look for a position elsewhere."

Katrin jumped up from her seat. "If Father gets married again, I will move out. I can't imagine another woman ever taking Mother's place."

Nikolaus shrugged. He was exhausted from weeks of marching and wanted nothing more than sleep. He yawned and excused himself to go to bed. Toward evening, he woke up to help his father with chores. After washing up, he told Katrin that he wanted to go to the cemetery.

"I'll go with you," she said, taking off her apron. He would have preferred to go alone, but she seemed to need his company. She leaned on him heavily as they stood in front of their mother's wooden cross.

"Mama could be a stern woman sometimes," Katrin whispered. "But I'd do anything to bring her back now. Our father doesn't show it, but he is clearly lost without her. I don't know how we can go on now."

Nikolaus patted her arm. "We must. We have no other choice."

He scrutinized the fields that abutted the graveyard. "Tomorrow, I'll talk to him about the harvest."

"Yes, do that. The other farmers have already begun harvesting wheat."

During the following weeks, Nikolaus's thoughts often turned to Martin, who had probably arrived in Havre by now. He did not believe for a second that Margarethe Dupree had changed Martin's mind, yet he listened to every hoofbeat that approached the farm. He missed his quiet friend very much.

He was glad that Katrin had returned home, and the siblings bonded more than ever before. Nikolaus took Katrin along when he met his friends at the linden tree or at one of their houses.

"I haven't seen Alfons since I came back," Nikolaus said one Saturday evening. Their friends had all gone to a dance and they were sitting on the front steps after supper.

"I wrote him a note from Kaiserslautern telling him about my move to the city and haven't heard from him since," said Katrin. "Can you drive me to Weidenbach tomorrow so I can talk to him?"

Nikolaus shifted on the hard stone. "What are you going to say?"

"I'll tell him the engagement is off," Katrin said, her voice not revealing any emotion. "I cannot possibly leave you and Father alone right now."

"Is that the only reason?"

"No. I never loved him and only agreed to the engagement because Mother pressured me into it. With her gone, there is no reason to keep him waiting."

Nikolaus slapped his leg. "Very well, I'll take you tomorrow."

He was secretly relieved that his sister was not getting married yet. Together, Katrin and Nikolaus could help each other through their loss. Their father was not a good companion at the moment. Overnight, he had grown old and tottered about the barn, mumbling to himself for hours on end.

* * *

Nikolaus drove Katrin to Weidenbach and waited by the wagon while she disappeared into the house. Ten minutes later she returned, her chin set in defiance.

"That went better than I hoped," Katrin said and clambered on the wagon. "He said he never loved me either and was thinking of a way to end the engagement. I believe he has his eyes on another girl."

"Are you alright?" Nikolaus asked, giving her a smile.

"Yes, I'm fine," Katrin said while grabbing the board as the wagon jolted over the rutted road. "But I never want to be forced into an engagement again. If I can't find anybody to fancy me as I am, I'll remain a spinster."

Nikolaus wondered whether he should tell Katrin how much Martin loved her, but he remained silent. If Martin did not have the courage to do so, it was not his place to tell her.

* * *

Nikolaus could not fathom that everyday life in the Palatinate moved along as if there had never been a revolution at all. The steps of the fleeing rebel army had barely faded away when the royal Bavarian authorities commenced their operations once again. The Royal General Prosecuting Attorney of the Palatinate immediately launched an investigation against the leaders of the revolt "because of armed rebellion against the armed power, high treason and state treason, etc." The indictment that was completed in 1850 eventually listed three hundred thirty-three defendants, among them Hermann Dupree. All members of the provisional government were sentenced to death in absence as they were all abroad.

After the suppression of the revolution, more than ten thousand Bavarian occupying forces were stationed in the Palatinate. It was therefore no wonder that it struck Nikolaus as a tranquil garden. Everyone avoided discussing politics, preferring instead a safe game of cards.

Chapter 23

The funeral costs had depleted the Weber family finances and Katrin had to find employment by doing the laundry for several families after the crops were harvested. Nikolaus also wished to improve the lot of the family, but he had learned no other trade besides farming. He helped by picking up the laundry in the surrounding villages and delivered it after it was washed. Nikolaus began to worry more and more about his future, wondering whether Martin had not made the wiser decision by immigrating to America.

* * *

On a chilly November day, Nikolaus was returning from a laundry delivery when Katrin ran out into the yard to greet him.

"I'm so glad you're back," she cried. "Father had an accident while he brought the cattle home from pasture. He's in a bad way."

Nikolaus's heart raced as he hurried to his father's bedstead. Katrin had not exaggerated. Their father was moaning, his body distorted from the agonizing pain.

"One of our oxen kicked him in the stomach when he tried to put them in the barn. Herr Scheuermann and his son helped me bring him into the house. Fritz went to fetch the doctor," Katrin said, pressing a cool compress on their father's forehead. Nikolaus paced through the bedroom and the kitchen, unable to work or even to scrape together enough energy to light a fire. They took turns at the bedside, exchanging looks of utter despair.

Darkness began to descend on the distraught household when Doctor Mehler finally arrived. After examining the patient, he shook his head silently. Friedrich Weber, who had never been sick in his adult life, had

125

succumbed to his severe internal injuries. Katrin and Nikolaus stood petrified at the bed of their father whose features looked strangely contorted.

Nikolaus asked the doctor at last, "What do we owe you for your services?"

"Nothing," Mehler said with a dismissive wave of his hand. "Unfortunately, I have not been able to help your father. I am very sorry for your loss."

He issued the death certificate, quietly pressed the siblings' hands, and trudged to his carriage.

After his departure, Nikolaus and Katrin emerged from their numbness long enough to finish their chores. Nikolaus lit a fire in the kitchen stove and took care of the livestock while Katrin went to tell the neighbors the inconceivable news. Frau Reis accompanied her to the parish church to discuss the details of the funeral with the priest. In no time, the whole village learned of Friedrich Weber's death. When the two women returned, the house was crowded with people.

Katrin accepted the expressions of sympathy as if in a daze.

"About the funeral," Frau Reis asked. "Are you able to pay for it?"

Katrin shrugged her shoulders helplessly. "I guess we'll have to sell something."

"Don't you worry. I will start a collection for you," Frau Reis said. By next evening, she had accumulated twenty Gulden thanks to the Webers' popularity in the village.

* * *

Nikolaus and Katrin did not come to their senses until the funeral meal had passed. Only then did Nikolaus realize what a great loss they had suffered within just a few months.

After the funeral, their uncle and guardian, Sebastian Weber, sat down with them to discuss their future. He had discovered that his brother had signed several promissory notes for small amounts through the years in order to keep the farm afloat. Now that the father was dead, the creditors demanded their money.

The law of real division demanded that the estate of the parents was to be divided in equal parts among the two siblings. If they split up a farm of fifteen *Tagwerk*, none of the parts would be large enough to support a family.

Silence reigned and the threesome pondered, their faces darkened by the strain.

"It will probably be best for you to sell the farm," Sebastian Weber said at last and countered his niece's and nephew's indignant looks with imperturbable calmness.

"You're underage, and which one of you would work the farm when Nikolaus gets drafted? No, you have to sell and make a living somewhere else."

These words hit Nikolaus hard since he had never worked anywhere but on his parents' farm. He would likely have to enter service as a laborer on an estate.

"Please, give us some more time to make a decision," he begged his uncle.

"Alright, I'll give you four weeks' time."

Chapter 24

Nikolaus had not made up his mind about the future of the farm when he received the much-longed-for message from Martin. He sighed with relief when he learned that Martin had safely arrived in the United States and had soon found work.

He read the letter several times and gradually, a new idea occurred to him. What if he immigrated to America with Katrin? Land was cheap over there, he had heard, and perhaps they could purchase a small farm with the proceeds of the sale of their parental farm and a loan.

He brooded over this idea for two days before he proposed it to Katrin.

"I have no ties here," she said without hesitating. "Perhaps it is best if we tried our luck in a new country."

For the first time since their parents' deaths, Nikolaus detected a sparkle of hope in his sister's eyes.

Now that he had Katrin's approval, Nikolaus began to think about the details of immigrating. He had not forgotten that he once vehemently opposed immigration, but how much had changed since then. If he remained here, he would have to accept a position as a poorly paid laborer. It made no sense to learn a trade when so many artisans were unemployed.

* * *

Like many immigrants before him, Nikolaus had only vague ideas about America. It never occurred to him that he would probably have to work as a farm hand in the New World. He expected to receive so much money from the sale of the farm that he and Katrin could purchase land in America. His visions about the future were no more detailed than that.

Nikolaus had ample time during the winter to plan the journey. He eagerly studied newspaper advertisements in which numerous shipping agents painted a crossing aboard their sailing vessel in glowing colors.

Nikolaus also talked to his friends Michael and Dietrich about his plans because both had relatives in America. Michael told him that his cousin lived in a small town named Manheim in Ohio and that many immigrants from Moorbach had settled there.

"If you need help of any sort, each of them will be more than willing to help you. You just have to tell them that you come from Moorbach."

"Do you know where they are working?" Nikolaus asked.

"Most of them either work as farm hands or own their own farm."

Nikolaus was satisfied with the answer. He knew what he wanted and did not shy away from any work to achieve his goal.

* * *

In mid-February, the Weber farm was auctioned off. The farmyard had filled with many curious onlookers from Moorbach and the surrounding villages who had learned of the imminent emigration of brother and sister.

While the few prospective buyers inspected the farm, Nikolaus and Katrin remained seated next to the auctioneer's table, unable to move or speak. At last, the auctioneer rose and began the proceedings. Katrin's eyes rested on her folded hands while the auctioneer accepted a bid.

After deducting the debts and fees, a sum of one thousand two hundred Gulden remained for the heirs. Nikolaus arranged with the new owner that they could remain on the farm for another month before leaving their childhood home forever.

The very next day, Katrin and Nikolaus paid a visit to town hall. Jakob Mantes, the secretary, kept them waiting before he condescended to look up from his files.

"What do you want?" he snapped.

"We would like to apply for an emigration permit and a passport," Nikolaus said firmly.

"Birth certificate," the clerk replied, and the young man fished the document out of his pocket.

"I need a certificate about your financial assets and a confirmation by the tax collector that all liabilities toward the township have been met," Mantes continued.

Nikolaus handed him the form that had been issued yesterday. To apply for a passport, Nikolaus had to fill out an application in duplicate and hand his passport credentials to the official. The same procedure was repeated for Katrin.

Mantes demanded the approval of the siblings' guardian since they were underage. Katrin dashed off to fetch Uncle Sebastian who was chopping firewood. She urged him to accompany her to town hall in his work clothes to provide his signatures.

"I have to send your applications to the district office in Homburg and will notify you when they have returned," the clerk said in conclusion, dismissing the siblings.

* * *

During the following weeks, Katrin and Nikolaus were busy with travel preparations. Katrin had already knitted stockings and mended underwear and clothing over the winter. Friedrich Weber's suit and his wife's Sunday dress were at the seamstress's house for alterations. Brother and sister now visited the cobbler for a fitting of new shoes. Nikolaus packed the most necessary household goods in a wooden crate he had built for the journey.

Katrin received an old suitcase from Uncle Sebastian and a new goose quill from Aunt Minna. With trembling lips the young girl promised to write to the homeland regularly.

The first one to use the new quill was Nikolaus. He wrote a detailed letter to Martin about their plans and promised his friend to visit him.

In early March, a municipal servant appeared at the Weber farm and handed Nikolaus a note from the secretary. Mantes had summoned brother and sister to the town hall because their documents had arrived. Katrin quickly tied on a clean apron, put the purse in her pocket and the siblings ran off in good spirits.

They were out of breath when they reached the office, but their smiles vanished when Mantes looked at them gravely. The secretary searched through the files that were strewn over his desk and put several records on top.

"The petition for release from the subject federation, made by Katharina Weber, age nineteen years, residing in Moorbach, is hereby approved. The fee for this certification is one Gulden twenty Kreuzer and is to be paid at once," he read. "Furthermore, a passport for an indefinite duration has been issued to the applicant. The cost for this amounts to twenty-four Kreuzer."

After Katrin counted out the money to the official and received the important documents he turned to Nikolaus.

"The emigration permit of petitioner Nikolaus Weber, twenty years of age, residing in Moorbach, has been rejected with the explanation that the above mentioned is to be available to perform his military service. A new petition may be filed when the person willing to emigrate can find and pay for a substitute. The applicant will be issued a passport for the duration of one year so that he may accompany his sister on the long journey. The fee therefor amounts to thirty-nine Kreuzer."

Without a word, Nikolaus accepted the document, paid the money, and strode home with his sister. Noticing Katrin's long face, he said cheerfully, "At least we have saved one Gulden and twenty Kreuzer."

"What are you talking about?" asked Katrin.

"If they refuse to give me permission to emigrate, I'll just emigrate without permission. Surely, I will not be the first one to do that. I have paid my taxes and therefore I have nothing to fear."

* * *

The next morning Nikolaus and Katrin called on several shipping line agents in Kaiserslautern. They finally accepted Friedrich Müller's offer of eighty-five Gulden for a passage from Mainz via Rotterdam to New York. He referred them to his main agent Schönborn in Mainz to sign the contract. The boat was to depart from Mainz on March 20.

The siblings had a week's time to acquire provisions and pack their possessions. Food was cheaper in the Palatinate than in harbor cities and they stocked up on potatoes, salted meat, biscuits, bread, vinegar, oil, and wine.

A day before their departure the siblings went to visit their parents' grave one last time before entrusting it to the care of Aunt Minna.

"Oh God, I hope we are doing the right thing," Katrin whispered in a choked voice.

She would have remained longer at the cemetery if Nikolaus had not insisted on taking her home, trembling from exhaustion and cold.

Chapter 25

On the morning of their departure, Nikolaus helped Uncle Sebastian load his wagon after a quick breakfast. Sebastian would drive them to Mainz to deliver his niece and nephew and the remains of their worldly possessions before returning to complete the sale of the farm.

Meanwhile, Katrin walked from room to room and said good-bye to all the things a nineteen-year-old girl could grow fond of. She ran her hand over the scratched slate on which she had arduously scrawled her first letters before she caught sight of the first potholder she had knitted. The memories of the parents who had died in such quick succession descended on her soul like a nightmare. She moaned as she placed the potholder back on its hook.

Finally, Nikolaus stomped into the house. "We're ready. Are you coming?"

Katrin straightened up, locked the front door behind her, and handed the key to Aunt Minna. The dear woman blew her nose noisily. Aunt and niece kissed each other's cheek, blinking away tears.

Now Nikolaus understood why Martin had said to him during their farewell, "Go on because I cannot bear it anymore."

Nikolaus even envied Martin because he had emigrated without a last visit home. Leaving one's home deliberately was much harder if you were there.

Uncle Sebastian urged the travelers on. Aunt Minna waved good-bye to them until the wagon disappeared behind a bend in the road. Katrin and Nikolaus did not speak much on the long journey to Mainz. They huddled together on the board, taking in the villages and rolling hills they would never set eyes on again.

* * *

In Mainz Uncle Sebastian remained with the wagon while the siblings searched for the shipping agency.

Schönborn's tiny office was located in a narrow house in a side-street of *Rhein Allee*. On the walls of the office hung a world map and a map of the United States.

The agent, a short man who constantly whistled, was seated behind a huge oak desk. After Nikolaus stated his request, he proceeded to fill out the ship contracts. Five minutes later Nikolaus and Katrin were one hundred and seventy Gulden poorer and two tickets to New York richer. When looking at the vouchers, they began to grasp that they were embarking on the greatest adventure of their lives. This was much more exciting than Katrin's escape from the parental home and Nikolaus's involvement in the revolution. Uncle Sebastian helped them carry their luggage on board and shook hands with his wards one last time before he disappeared from their lives.

* * *

When they reached Rotterdam after a journey of two and a half days, they had to wait in the harbor city for nine days to catch a passage to London. During the crossing, the square-rigged brig experienced heavy seas and all passengers became seasick within a short time. In London they realized with distress that they had made little progress on their long journey to the New World. One of the passengers had already lost heart and decided to return to his home in northern Germany.

Katrin and Nikolaus enjoyed their idleness on board for a while. After several days, however, they were seized by mind-numbing boredom because the only distracting occupation was watching their fellow travelers. At mealtimes Katrin not only cooked for Nikolaus and herself but also for a man who was traveling alone. She felt sorry for the lonely passenger and wondered more than once whether Martin had found a companion on the ship to pass the time.

On May 15, 1850, the three-master *Andrew Carroll* entered the Narrows between Staten Island and Long Island. Katrin and Nikolaus greeted the forest of masts in the harbor with relief over the end of their idle sea voyage. Their longing for land was almost as great as their appetite for fresh bread and a glass of milk.

Two days later, the thoroughly cleaned *Andrew Carroll* berthed at the pier and a stream of immigrants poured forth into the crowded streets.

"Are you looking for a place to stay tonight?" a young man asked Nikolaus in German.

"Yes."

"I can take you to a German boardinghouse," the runner offered. "It's really clean and the food is German, just like home. Wait for me over there."

He pointed to a family that had gathered on the quay.

"How much does it cost?" Katrin asked, yet the stranger had disappeared to hustle some more travelers.

Katrin, who had always been more suspicious in money matters than her trusting brother, said, "I have a bad feeling about this."

Nikolaus shrugged. "Come on, he's a German. He wouldn't take us for a ride, would he?"

Still wary, Katrin sighed and they joined a group of sixteen passengers to the inn. The landlord locked his guests' trunks in the cellar before they knew what was coming.

"I want to leave tomorrow," Katrin insisted as the siblings devoured a dinner of pot roast and potatoes.

"Very well, we'll look for provisions as soon as we're done eating," Nikolaus gave in.

Together with a man from northern Germany, they marched off to purchase tickets for the steamboat to Albany. On their way back, they bought bread, cheese and smoked meat for the trip.

Katrin breathed a sigh of relief when she climbed aboard the steamer which was to take her and her brother upstream. Nikolaus was still fuming over the exorbitant price their landlord had charged at the rooming house before handing over their luggage.

"Let this be a lesson to you," Katrin said. "You're much too trustful and think that Germans cannot be dishonest. Be on your guard in the future."

"Oh, I will."

"Look," cried Katrin. "How neat these white farmhouses are when they peek through the fruit trees. Do you think we could settle here?"

Nikolaus weighed his head. "I don't know. The land here is probably expensive and most likely spoken for."

"I guess you're right. Everybody says 'go west,' so that's where we're going."

Chapter 26

Ohio

Nikolaus and Katrin disembarked their canal boat in Dayton and strode along Main Street until they came to a tavern with red and white checkered curtains. While the landlord poured their beers, Nikolaus asked if any of the customers were German. Most of the men, apparently Irish, shrugged their shoulders without comprehension. One patron rose from his window seat, though, and approached the newcomers.

"My name is Jakob Biehl and I live in Manheim, a few miles south of here. Are you looking for someone?"

Nikolaus introduced himself. "Do you know a German farm where my sister and I could find work?"

"Sure I do," Biehl replied. "I'm a farmer myself and am looking for someone to help with my wheat harvest. That's why I came to Dayton today. I pay fifty cents a day with free room and board until the harvest is over. When can you start?"

"At once," Nikolaus said. "We have to pick up our luggage first. It's still on the canal boat."

"My wagon is outside. Climb up and we'll pick up your things."

At the mooring, Biehl also hired a young Swiss lad named Hans before driving over bumpy roads back to his farm. The wagon had not covered more than half a mile when Biehl already knew the life story of the siblings because, like all immigrants, he was eager for news from the home country.

"You're from Moorbach?" he asked. "I think my neighbor is from that town."

Nikolaus pinched Katrin's arm, grinning about their good fortune to find a job on their first day of searching. Now he was sure that they had made the right decision to come to America.

* * *

Manheim, a small prairie town settled by Irish and German immigrants, was a welcome sight for the weary travelers. Businesses along Main Street bore German names. Covered sidewalks protected the shoppers from the elements while the columns served as hitching posts for the horses.

Tears began to well in Katrin's eyes at the sight of the red and white brick houses. The strain of the long journey had finally worn her down. She was gripped by an attack of homesickness as the wagon left the town behind.

Biehl's farm was larger than Katrin had expected. A spacious vegetable garden and orchard stretched from the road to the one-story house, protected from the roaming hogs by a split-rail fence. Across the farmyard stood the pig pen and the massive barn that glowed fiery red under the scorching sun. A log cabin of pioneer origin, obviously serving as a chicken coop, and a springhouse completed the homestead.

It was suppertime when Biehl drove up to the house with his newly hired hands and a stern-looking countrywoman invited them to a hearty meal. The three Biehl children joined the three strangers at the long table and everybody took their seats without ceremony.

"Are there many Germans in the area?" Nikolaus asked while helping himself to smoked sausage and bread.

"Yes," Biehl said keenly. "Didn't you notice all the women working in the fields?"

Katrin and Nikolaus stared at him.

"American women don't have to help in the fields," the farmer explained. "But our women aren't so delicate, are they?"

He looked at his wife.

"As long as I have time to cook dinner," Frau Biehl replied with a shrug. "I'll help if it means bringing in the wheat before it rains. It's food for winter, after all."

Not long after the flaming sun disappeared behind an ocean of wheat, the siblings turned in for the night. Nikolaus shared a bed of hay with Hans in the barn while Katrin sank on a straw mattress in the kitchen, exhausted from the arduous journey.

* * *

At the crack of dawn everybody marched out to the field where forty acres of wheat were ready to be harvested. Nikolaus, Biehl, and Hans walked ahead with their scythes and mowed the grain while Katrin, twelve-year-old Franz Biehl, and his mother followed behind, bound the wheat into sheaves, and piled them up in heaps.

Biehl advised Nikolaus and Hans not to bend over as low as they were used to at home since the stubbles were used as fertilizer in America. During supper Nikolaus told Biehl about his plan to buy a farm.

"Don't buy Congress land under any circumstances," Biehl said. "It only costs one-and-a-quarter dollars per acre, but it is usually of a lesser quality than federal land and it has to be cultivated before you can grow anything. Do as I did and buy an established farm. They are more expensive but are situated in a more populated area and will much sooner bring in a return than a farm on Congress land. By the way, the taxes are insignificant."

Nikolaus and Katrin listened attentively to Biehl's words and Katrin's thoughts revolved around the anxious question where they would earn enough money to acquire an established farm.

"Why would a farmer cultivate his land just to sell it later on?" Nikolaus asked.

Biehl slurped his coffee before replying. "Americans are not as attached to their house and farm as we Germans are. They don't make a fuss about selling a piece of land they have worked for twenty years to start anew out West. The farther away, the more Americans like it, be it Indiana, Illinois, Missouri, or even Oregon."

* * *

After the grain was delivered to the gristmill, Biehl drove his three helpers to the nearest landing stage where they boarded a canal boat to Cincinnati to find employment.

In the city, Nikolaus soon found work as a teamster. Each day during the winter, hundreds of pigs and cattle were slaughtered and processed in the city on the Ohio River. It was Nikolaus's duty to drive the carcasses from the slaughterhouses at the outer edges of the city to the processing plants where they were salted and placed in barrels. The stench was nauseating, even in the open air, but the pay of one dollar a day rewarded him handsomely and he was able to put money aside for his farm.

Through an employment agency, Katrin found a position as a domestic servant in the house of a banker. She earned a meager four dollars a month with board and was glad that at least Nikolaus was earning a living salary, even if the work was unappealing. She spent her precious free time writing letters to Aunt Minna or mending her clothes. Sundays were the only days when the siblings could meet and talk about their experiences of the past week.

Katrin listened intently when Nikolaus told stories about the Germans he met in the course of his work or during his evening strolls. For the most part, though, their conversations revolved around the future. Both had resolved not to touch their reserves and to save as much of their wages as they could. They considered the time in Cincinnati as a transition but were unsure about their future.

In April, Nikolaus asked Katrin, "Is there anyone in this city you feel attached to?"

"No." Katrin shook her head. "Why do you ask?"

"I want to travel to St. Louis to see Martin again. Will you come with me? I don't want to leave you alone."

"Why, I. . ." Katrin stuttered, flushing slightly. "I'll be glad to go with you. Nothing keeps me here."

Nikolaus clapped his knee. "Well, that's settled. I wasn't sure how you felt about meeting him again. You didn't seem to like him back home."

Katrin turned her head away from him so he could not see her burning cheeks. "That was just because our circumstances were so different. I have nothing against him personally, I just never had much tolerance for rich people."

"I'm glad to hear that." Nikolaus let out a sigh. "I'll write to him that we're coming. Perhaps you can become friends after all."

Katrin nodded, hoping that her brother could not hear the rapid drumming of her heartbeat.

Chapter 27

Spring 1851

Dozens of bright white paddle-steamers with crowned, smoking chimneys were moored on the levee in St. Louis, forcing the *Thomas Jefferson* to anchor in the middle of the river. The deckhands threw thick ropes to the neighboring ship and put two gangways across.

Nikolaus and Katrin left their luggage aboard and went ashore by carefully crossing the two ships that berthed between the *Thomas Jefferson* and the shoreline. They spoke enough English now to ask about the way to Flaherty's Inn without inhibition.

Flaherty greeted them as friends of Martin and immediately put a mug of lager and a mug of cider on the counter.

"Martin hasn't worked here for a while," he told his baffled visitors. "I think it was last year in February when he quit his job here."

"Do you know where he moved to?" Nikolaus asked.

"He moved to Illinois because he heard that many Germans had settled in the town of Belleville. If I remember correctly, he said that he found work in a general store."

"How do we get to Belleville?" Katrin asked, relieved that the Irishman had remembered that much.

Ray explained the way and Katrin and her brother headed back to their ship to fetch their luggage.

* * *

Katrin anticipated the upcoming meeting with mixed feelings. She remembered their last encounter in Kaiserslautern all too well when she had reproached Martin for the wealth of his family, as if it were his fault.

Now he had to earn his living as an ordinary store clerk. She was curious to see if the change in circumstances had agreed with him.

The heavy rain of the last few days had turned Belleville's Main Street into a large morass. When Nikolaus and Katrin descended the stagecoach in late afternoon, their shoes sunk to their ankles in the mud. There were not too many general stores in the small town and the siblings began their search on Main Street.

The third store they entered was Oscar Ellis's Country Store. Ellis opened the trapdoor and called into the cellar, "Martin, you have company."

* * *

Martin closed the trap, shook the dust from his clothes, and looked around the store. He had expected to see Anna and was now speechless at the sight of his two best friends from the old homeland.

"Guten Tag, Martin," Nikolaus said with a grin on his face and Martin emerged from his paralysis. He almost ran to Nikolaus and slapped him on the shoulder, laughing even louder than his friend did.

Martin hesitated before addressing Katrin, whose honey-colored hair was held up by pins in the back of her head. She was even lovelier than the last time he had seen her. Her eyes sparkled as brightly as his mother's amber necklace. Was she as delighted about the reunion as he was? Martin wanted to kiss her cheek but instead gazed deeply into her hazel eyes while holding out his hand to her. She took it without hesitation and shook it firmly.

Martin turned slightly to Nikolaus. "I'm so happy that you have come to visit me. After I hadn't heard from you for a whole year, I thought I would never see you again."

"Our letters must have crossed each other. But we're here at last," Nikolaus exclaimed.

And I am lucky that I have not proposed to Anna, Martin silently added. *She will be hurt but she will soon forget me. There is only one girl for me.*

* * *

Surprised at the firmness of Martin's formerly soft hands, Katrin wriggled her hand out of his.

"Oh, I'm so sorry," Martin cried, blushing as he unclasped her hand.

Katrin and Nikolaus admired the store's offerings while they waited until Martin closed up the store and counted the day's takings. Ellis took the money and let the three friends out the back door.

"You must be very hungry," said Martin when they stood on the wooden sidewalk.

"You're right. Now that you mentioned it, I can hear my stomach rumbling," Nikolaus replied with a laugh.

"Let's go out for dinner to celebrate. The food at the Maus Tavern is very good."

The restaurant was popular, but they were able to find an empty table in a corner. The landlord himself took their orders of roasted chicken with fried potatoes and peas.

"You haven't changed at all. It doesn't seem like it has been two years since we saw each other last," Martin said.

"Maybe we haven't changed on the outside, but time has left its mark on us," Nikolaus replied and told of the deaths of their parents and their life in Ohio.

Meanwhile, dinner was being served and the young people silently devoted their attention to the chicken. From the corner of her eye, Katrin took a good look at Martin. Apparently, the transition from the spoiled patrician's son to the lowly clerk had agreed with him. His features had become more masculine, the eyes clearer, and his hands appeared as if they could lift a barrel with ease.

There was a sadness around his eyes, however, that she could not explain. Perhaps he had been very lonely in the years since they had last met. After all, Martin had been all by himself while she had had Nikolaus as a companion. Katrin realized that she was staring at Martin and lowered her head before anyone noticed her pink cheeks.

* * *

Martin's eyes lit up when Nikolaus told of his wish to buy a farm.

"I have also thought about purchasing a farm as soon as my inheritance arrives," he said.

"Have you made peace with your parents?" Nikolaus asked.

"My mother died last December, and it was her last wish that I should finally get my inheritance. I won't receive the bill of exchange until summer, though. How long are you planning on staying here?"

"If we like it, we'll stay forever," Nikolaus replied.

Martin leaned back in his chair and looked from Nikolaus to Katrin.

"This is the happiest day since I stepped off the ship in Baltimore to conquer America," he said. "And I have to admit that I started way down at the bottom. But things will all be different now. Let's buy a farm together! A piece of land in a free country. But, what will you live on until then?"

"We'll start looking for a job tomorrow," Nikolaus replied. "When it comes to buying a farm, Katrin and I can contribute the money we received from the sale of our farm."

"First we'll have to find lodging for you tonight," Martin said, "You must be tired from the journey."

"Oh yes," Katrin admitted, "I'm fit to drop."

They paid for their meals and stepped outside, where Martin offered Katrin his arm to help her avoid the largest puddles. While they walked side by side, Martin thought feverishly where they were heading. Nikolaus would probably find a bed at Glanig's boardinghouse, but he had to find accommodations for Katrin somewhere else. She could not stay with one of his acquaintances because most were lodgers themselves.

Suddenly Martin remembered that he had promised to visit Anna that evening. He had never been late before and assumed that the girl would kindly overlook this one incident.

An idea flashed through his brain: he would ask Anna's parents whether Katrin could spend the night in their house. Nikolaus and Katrin agreed with his suggestion.

"Where is your luggage?" Martin asked.

"We left our suitcases at the stagecoach station since we didn't know whether we would find you," Nikolaus replied.

"No matter, I can give you what you need until tomorrow," Martin said.

* * *

Anna opened the door at the Ruppelius home. Two steep furrows creased her forehead when she recognized Martin. He hastened to say, "Good evening, Anna. I'm sorry that I couldn't keep our appointment, but I had some surprise visitors. Imagine, my two best friends from Germany have arrived today."

He introduced Nikolaus and Katrin. Anna gave Nikolaus a friendly greeting while curtly eyeing Katrin.

"Can I talk to you alone?" Martin asked. They walked a few steps along the porch.

He twisted his hands behind his back and faced Anna. "I've no doubt that Nikolaus can sleep at my rooming house, but Katrin can certainly not sleep among all these men. I know this is rather sudden, but could you ask your parents whether she can stay in your house tonight?"

His eyes begged her, yet her face remained sullen at the intrusion.

"Who is it, Anna?" Elisabeth Ruppelius appeared in the open door.

"It's Martin, Mother."

"Where are your manners, child?" she scolded Anna when she saw the assembly on the front steps. "Since when do you make your guests wait on the porch?"

"I'm sorry, Mother," Anna whispered, repeating Martin's plea.

"Of course, the girl can sleep here," the mother replied with enthusiasm. "We will prepare the living room couch for her right away."

Martin and Nikolaus thanked her effusively and left. As Martin had predicted, Widow Glanig did have a bed available for Nikolaus and the friends retired for the night.

* * *

Nikolaus made his way to B-Street right after breakfast the next morning to pick up Katrin. His sister was washing dishes when he arrived. Anna was nowhere to be seen, but Katrin's eyes had lost all of last night's glow.

"Did you have an argument with Anna?" he asked when they were alone.

"Yes," Katrin replied in a low voice. "I guess you couldn't call it an argument since she was the only one talking. Imagine, she said she is engaged to Martin and I shouldn't hold out any hopes for him. I never even said one word about Martin."

"She was probably just cross with him because he forgot to visit her last night," Nikolaus said, trying to calm down his sister.

"But do you think that Martin would want to buy a farm with us if he wanted to marry Anna?"

"No, I don't think so. Perhaps she is imagining things," Nikolaus said. "Don't worry about her anymore. Our most pressing concern is to find jobs."

"You're right. I don't want to take advantage of the hospitality of Anna's parents longer than absolutely necessary."

At this early morning hour, the streets were quiet. The older children were in school while some younger children played marbles or took their dolls for a walk. A woman was hanging laundry out to dry and one lady was shopping with a little girl in tow.

Nikolaus and Katrin walked without a word for fear of destroying the idyll of this sunny April morning. At last Katrin said, "It's even prettier here than in Manheim. Let's stay here."

"That would be nice. I'm looking forward to being my own boss again, aren't you?"

"No," Katrin replied with a flat voice.

"Why not?"

"Every time I am looking forward to something it doesn't come true. If I don't get my hopes up, though, everything will be fine."

Nikolaus and Katrin roamed the streets of Belleville for two hours, passing breweries, oil mills, stove manufacturers, and blacksmith shops. At last, they rested on a bench in public square.

"Well, has the walk made you smarter?" Katrin asked.

"Yes. I think I'll start looking at Washington Brewery."

"What do you know about beer brewing?"

"Nothing, but maybe I could work as a teamster just as I have done in Cincinnati. What will you do now?"

"I'm sorry, but I don't feel very well today and would like to lie down. Anna is at the bookstore, so I should have some peace right now."

"Alright, I'll come by this evening."

Chapter 28

The buildings of the Washington Brewery extended half a block on South Second Street. Wagons drawn by four horses rolled into the large courtyard or left to take countless barrels of beer to the Mississippi River. An American flag fluttered in the spring air above the massive brewery building and a high chimney puffed black smoke out of the boiling house.

Nikolaus took heart and stepped through the office door. He waited patiently while the bookkeeper added a long column of numbers. The clerk looked up and asked indifferently, "What can I do for you?"

Nikolaus told him that he was looking for work and the bookkeeper pointed his quill at a bulletin board next to the door. While Nikolaus studied the few bilingual notices, the door flung open and a well-dressed, stout gentleman stepped inside.

"Well, Fischer, are you finished with the accounts yet?" he bellowed in German.

"Yes, Mr. Eimer. We can check them at once," the clerk hastened to answer.

"What does this young man want?" Simon Eimer asked when he stood next to Fischer. The latter explained Nikolaus's situation to his supervisor and Eimer rubbed his chin pensively.

"Come here, young man," he called to Nikolaus. "Can you handle a horse and cart? What have you done so far?"

Nikolaus told him his work history and the brewery owner said, "I could use a hand in the brewery. Fischer, send Tom to the outbuilding. Tell him to fetch the Irishman whose name I cannot pronounce and send him over to me. As far as I heard, he would like to learn the brewery trade, but he probably won't have much more to learn. All Irishmen know plenty about beer. He'll start working in the brewery tomorrow and this young fellow will take his place as a teamster. You," Eimer said, looking over his shoulder toward Nikolaus, "report to Mr. Stuhlfauth in the outbuilding tomorrow morning at seven o'clock."

* * *

In the evening, Nikolaus met Martin at the store, and they strode to the boardinghouse together. Martin was pleased that Nikolaus had found a position so soon. Yet his smile faded when he learned that Katrin was not feeling well.

"I hope it's not a fever but simple exhaustion," he said, hiding his concern from his friend.

"I will go see her after supper." Nikolaus turned to face his friend. "Are you engaged to Anna?"

Martin jerked back. "No. What gives you that idea? Did she say that?"

Nikolaus told him of Katrin's problem. "It was not a good idea to put Katrin up with Anna," he criticized his friend.

"I don't know anybody else in Belleville," Martin defended himself.

Nikolaus looked sharply at him. "As far as I can tell in such a short time, Anna seems to be a sweet girl. Why are you hurting her?"

"Am I?" Martin asked and then answered his own question, "Anna wants to get married and it doesn't seem to matter much whom she marries. Some girls are like that, they're fun to dance with but marrying her—no! I like her very much, but I often feel cornered in her presence and you know that I cherish my freedom above anything else. She has already declared that she has no intention of living on a farm. Sooner or later we would have parted ways and it is probably the best for both of us."

"Does Katrin have anything to do with your decision?" Nikolaus asked relentlessly.

Martin gave a slight nod. "I still love Katrin."

"Why don't you tell her that?"

Martin shrugged. "She never had a very good opinion of me."

"Maybe she has changed her mind over the years."

"Two years is a long time and I have tried to forget her. But when she stood in front of me, I knew it was all in vain," Martin said more to himself than to his friend.

"She didn't seem to object when you held her hand for ten minutes yesterday," Nikolaus teased him. "And during supper she couldn't keep her eyes off you."

"Really? Do you think I could win her heart after all?" Martin brightened up.

"Come, friend, you're a man now. Act like one. If you want to win her, fight for her. Court her! She hasn't had an easy time these past few years and deserves some happiness."

A faint smile crept over Martin's face when he heard these words.

"There are people who take life more seriously than it already is," Nikolaus philosophized. "I for one think that we shouldn't let our supper wait any longer. And afterward we'll both go and see Katrin, is that understood?"

* * *

They found Katrin alone on the porch while her hosts had gone to a church meeting. Martin asked how Katrin was feeling and she told him she was merely exhausted from the arduous journey.

Nikolaus sat on the bench next to his sister while Martin settled in a wicker chair facing them. At this time of year, night closed in early and the threesome sat quietly in the dark.

Martin finally broke the silence and told them how he had fared after he bid good-bye to Nikolaus in Lorraine. When he told of his jobs as a street sweeper and dock worker, Nikolaus shook his head in astonishment. He admired Martin's resilience and desire to be his own master.

"When can we start looking for a farm?" he asked when Martin had finished.

"Hold on a minute, we'll have to wait until my money arrives from Germany," Martin said.

"No matter," Nikolaus replied unmoved. "First, we'll have to find out which farms are up for sale. By the way, what is the quality of the land in this area?"

"As far as I've heard, the soil in St. Clair County is fertile and productive. The best fields are in the Mississippi valley, of course, and they are all spoken for, but they're also unhealthy. I suggest that we rent a wagon and look around the countryside as soon as the roads dry up."

* * *

Katrin found a position as a maid at the *Belleville House*, a hotel on Public Square. Several small stores were located on the ground floor of the two-story Greek Revival building while the guest rooms were situated on the second floor. A spacious balcony stretched above the entrance of the hotel.

Katrin's predecessor had married a baker, leaving the hotel short-handed, and Katrin was able to begin work the very next day. The tiny attic room she was to share with the kitchen maid was barely large enough for two beds, a washstand, and a wardrobe. Katrin sank on the straw mattress and thought about the first time she had worked at an inn, during the first days of the revolution. How young and inexperienced she had been. She had learned to stand her ground in the two years since the day of the public assembly in Kaiserslautern.

Katrin also reflected how much her feelings toward a certain young man had changed for the better during their separation. Free from the shackles of an unwanted engagement to a man she did not love, she realized that she had never disliked Martin, just the social class he represented. How dashing he and Georg had looked on the day of the assembly, dressed in black coats and silk ties, so hopeful for the future. On that day Katrin had first developed a crush on Martin that she could not even admit to herself. And now Martin wanted to buy a farm with the siblings. Did that mean that he liked her?

* * *

After Katrin moved out, Martin paid a visit to the Ruppelius home. Anna was bent over embroidery in the living room while her mother was writing a letter.

"How nice to see you here again," the clueless book dealer exclaimed. "Come, join me in a chat about politics."

"I'm sorry, but I don't have much time." Martin faced Anna. "Can I speak to you alone for a moment?"

She rose and stepped out on the porch with him.

"My friends and I want to buy a farm and operate it together," Martin said with a flat voice, avoiding Anna's eyes. It would be easier to say what he had to say without looking at her.

"Nikolaus is my best friend and he knows a lot about farming. It has long been my wish to own land, but I didn't know how to do it all by myself. But now it happens that I have inherited money and that Nikolaus and Katrin came to visit. We have decided to make a go of it together. I don't believe that farm life would be very pleasant for you and I therefore think it best if we part our ways."

Anna covered her ears although Martin had spoken with a low voice.

"Look at me, for God's sake, look at me," she cried, clutching Martin's arm. "Don't you care for me anymore?"

Martin's face contorted in pain as he remembered the day when he bid good-bye to his mother. She had had the same tone in her voice as Anna, like an animal in the throws of death. Why did he always end up hurting the women he cared about?

"I've never raised your hopes and you know that," Martin said when he had regained his composure. "Perhaps we would have become a couple if Katrin had not come along. But I've always been in love with her and seeing her again made me realize that you and I were not meant to be together. I don't know if Katrin will return my love, but she would always stand between us. Don't you understand? You deserve better than that. You're young enough to find a man who loves no one besides you."

Anna sniveled as she let go of his arm.

"Goodnight." Martin said and turned to leave. She jerked around and banged the screen door behind her when she entered the house.

Several days later, Martin met Wilhelm Ruppelius on Main Street. He wanted to step into a store to avoid him, but the book merchant blocked his way.

"Anna went to visit her brother in St. Louis," he said with a trembling voice.

"I'm sorry," Martin said, "I never meant to hurt her. But Anna and I are too different to be happy together."

Ruppelius bowed his head and trudged away. Martin looked after the man who seemed to have aged since his beloved daughter's departure. He felt sorry for Ruppelius but consoled himself that St. Louis was only seventeen miles away while an ocean separated Martin from his family.

Chapter 29

In late July, Martin received the long-awaited letter from Carolina.

> Dear Martin,
>
> I have followed all the recommendations of your last letter and send you hereby a bill of credit by Philipp Hauck und Söhne of Mannheim to Mssrs. Wagenknecht & Leppert in New York in the amount of 1,230 Dollars or 3,000 Gulden, payable eight days after sight. I am happy to learn that you intend to use the money to buy land. As you have learned from our father, land is always the safest and most proper investment.
>
> Please write to me soon and let me know whether you have found an adequate property yet. Here in the Palatinate we all enjoy the best of health. Ludwig and I have welcomed a little daughter into our family last fall and baptized her Augusta Margarethe. She gives us nothing but joy.
>
> Your loving sister, Carolina

Martin was so ecstatic that he twisted and turned the bill of credit back and forth until he had memorized the text by heart. The next morning, he walked to Russell Hinckley's bank at Public Square before starting work and waited impatiently until the banker opened the heavy padlock and the three bolts.

"Can you collect this bill of credit for me?" Martin asked in his best English when he entered the building.

"Why, of course," the tall banker replied affably.

Hinckley carefully studied the bill of credit and then said, "If you need the money right away, I'll have to charge you eight percent interest."

"How long would it take for me to receive the money?"

"You can count on it in no later than fourteen days."

"I don't need the money right now. I would like it to be paid into my account as soon as it arrives."

"May I ask what you intend to do with it?" Hinckley asked with businesslike curiosity. "If you would like to open a business and need a loan, we could discuss it at the appropriate time."

"I want to buy a farm but haven't heard of one that is for sale even though my friends and I have asked around everywhere. Do you know anyone who wants to sell his farm?"

"Wait, I have to think about that," the banker replied. While he deliberated, his hands performed their morning tasks. He opened the safe, took out the cashbooks and several bills and coins which he put into the desk drawer. He looked up while sharpening his pencils.

"Last week a farmer of Shiloh Valley was here and mentioned that he would like to move to Iowa. Why don't you ask him how much he wants for his farm? You can buy a large piece of land with buildings for one thousand dollars."

Martin began to feel impatient because he should have reported for work by now. "What's the name of this man and where does he live?"

"His name is Owen Ames and you may find his farm on the road from Belleville to Mascoutah. On the left there is a small copse and about one hundred yards behind it a dirt road leads to Shiloh. The farm lies on this track. It's a white two-story house."

"Thank you very much, Mr. Hinckley, I will come back in about two weeks to check on the money," Martin said and hurried away.

"I'm sorry for being late but I had something very important to do," Martin apologized to Ellis, but the shopkeeper shrugged his shoulders.

"That's alright. After all, it is the first time that you've been late."

Martin counted the hours until evening so he could tell the big news to Nikolaus and Katrin. They were as enthusiastic as he was.

"Let's take a day off from work the day after tomorrow and ride out to the farm," Martin suggested. Nikolaus had seen the farm from the main road he traveled on the brewery wagon and agreed it was worth a closer look.

* * *

On Thursday morning Martin and Nikolaus headed to the stable and rented two horses. Martin enjoyed the ride immensely since he did not leave the boundaries of Belleville very often. Yet Nikolaus, not a seasoned horseman, was bouncing helplessly in the saddle.

"I hope there's a wagon on this farm, so I don't have to ride all the time," he moaned.

Martin roared with laughter. "I can assure you, when we buy a farm, we'll also get a wagon."

"This must be Ames's farm," Martin said when he caught sight of a white farmhouse partially hidden behind a huge oak tree. The fields surrounding it rose gradually toward the hamlet of Shiloh.

A harvested wheat field spread to the right of the road bordering on an extensive orchard. A covered porch stretched along the front of the house, which was set back from the road. Behind the driveway a herd of five or six cattle was grazing in the fenced-in pasture.

The two friends hitched their horses to a fencepost and Nikolaus followed Martin into the barnyard with stiff legs. There was nobody outside except a four-year-old girl who was playing with a tattered corn husk doll on the porch steps. They approached the child and Martin asked, "Where is your father?"

The little girl appeared not in the least frightened. "He's in the cornfield."

"And where may we find the cornfield?"

"Over there."

Her arm pointed to the east, beyond the white barn and outbuildings.

"Thank you."

Nikolaus and Martin tramped to the cornfield on foot. At the sight of the dark green corn, tall as a man, Martin's heart instinctively beat faster. Owen Ames was clearing the weeds from the edge of the field with a scythe. He did not look up from his work until the two friends were less than ten yards away.

"Mr. Ames?" Martin asked.

"Yes."

Martin introduced himself, then declared, "I've heard that you want to sell your farm."

"Who says?"

"I heard it from Mr. Hinckley at the bank."

Ames set his scythe on the ground and stepped closer to the young men.

"It's true, I'm moving to Iowa in the fall," he replied. "Do you want to buy my farm?"

"It depends how much you're asking for it."

Ames scratched his head. "Well, the farm is one hundred acres big, plus ten acres of forest. I thought I'll ask for eight hundred dollars. That includes the land, the house, barn, cowshed, and some of the livestock and implements."

Nikolaus took Martin aside.

"The price seems reasonable from what I have learned in Ohio," he said. "I doubt that we'll find cheaper land around here. But I have to know if the soil is of good quality."

He turned to Ames. "Where do you draw your water from?"

"There's a well in the farmyard and, should it ever run dry, we get our water from the creek over there."

He pointed to the edge of the cornfield.

"May we look around your farm for a while?" Martin asked.

With Ames's approval, the young men moved on. Nikolaus touched the cornstalks, which were as thick as his wrist, and beamed. Ames hurried ahead of them to the house while they remained motionless on the track.

The elevation they were standing on commanded a view of the plain for several miles to the east and south while a copse restricted their view to the west. Most of the land had been cleared but a few woodlands were obviously too thick to be penetrated by an axe. Far apart from one another, several farmhouses were overshadowed by their huge barns and Nikolaus said dryly, "We won't have too many neighbors here."

Countless chickens were roaming around the farmyard and the orchard in search of food while the vegetable garden was protected from them by a fence. Ames showed his two visitors the outer buildings after they joined him by the house.

Martin was inclined to purchase the farm on the spot, but if his friend disapproved of it, he would put the thought out of his mind.

"What do you think?" Martin asked anxiously when they stepped aside.

"So far, I'm impressed," Nikolaus said. "Let's give him our address so he can let us know when he decides to sell."

They bid good-bye to Ames and rode uphill.

"Do you know what we'll do now?" Nikolaus asked.

"We'll look at the surroundings."

"That too, but I had something specific in mind. Let's ride to the nearest farm and find out how fertile the soil in this area is. I would also like to know how far away the nearest town is."

They rode on the bumpy track until they met a narrow road running from west to east. Instinctively they turned west and soon spotted a red farmhouse nestled among extensive cornfields. The farmer was repairing a fencepost when the friends approached him.

"Do you know Owen Ames's farm?" Martin asked him.

"Of course I know his farm. He doesn't live far from here."

"We're thinking of buying it, but we want to be sure the land is healthy."

"You have not made a bad choice, I reckon," the farmer said. "The land is very fertile, and it includes a forest so that you will always have firewood and lumber. If I had enough money, I would buy the farm myself, but I don't."

He shrugged. Nikolaus and Martin thanked him for this information and rode further west toward the village of Shiloh. Before they reached the settlement, they stopped on the side of the road and unpacked the sandwiches they had brought along.

"Well, what do we do next?" Martin asked when they had finished their paltry meal.

"Sleep." Nikolaus stretched out in the grass.

"What about the horses?"

"One of us will have to stay awake," Nikolaus retorted with a yawn and rolled over to his side.

* * *

The road from Belleville to Lebanon was Shiloh's only street. Business life and social life took place on the main street of this hamlet, the core of Shiloh Valley. A church, a gristmill, a tavern, a wheelwright's shop, a smithy, a general store, a hotel, and a one-room schoolhouse were located along the dusty thoroughfare.

While Nikolaus was mainly interested in the wheelwright's shop and the smithy, Martin was drawn toward the general store with professional curiosity. This store surpassed everything the two friends had seen so far. Its shelves were bulging from the weight of dozens of cotton bales, linen cloths, coarse woolen material, hats, thread, lace, and ribbons. Pots, teakettles, and bowls were displayed nearby. In addition to soap, nails, and harnesses, Jakob Wehrle stocked dozens of books, both in German and in English. Every tiny space in the jumble was crammed with books.

With big eyes, Martin and Nikolaus read the titles of these books because all famous authors—from Goethe, Schiller, and Lessing to Shakespeare—were represented in this general store in the Midwest.

Wehrle followed the questioning looks of the young men and explained, "I carry these books for the Latin Farmers. Even though they have established a library on Schott's farm, some people want to own their own books."

"Latin Farmers?" Nikolaus asked.

"They're revolutionaries who attended universities in Germany," the store owner explained. "We call them Latin Farmers because they know more about Latin than about farming, but they're learning."

The sight of books satisfied Martin's concern about the location of the farm. Perhaps life in Shiloh Valley would not be lonely after all.

Chapter 30

The following Sunday, Ames appeared at Widow Glanig's house.

"We've decided to set off by the end of the month," he said to Martin and Nikolaus. "Are you still interested in my farm?"

"Yes, we are," Martin said.

"When can we go to the courthouse to sign the papers?"

"It'll take a few more days to get the money," Martin replied. "Can we look at the farm one more time before we decide to buy it? There is one more person who wants to see it."

"Yes," Nikolaus said, "if my sister doesn't like it, the deal is off."

Ames said, "Of course. My wagon is right outside."

Ames showed the young men the boundaries of the farm while Katrin followed Mrs. Ames through the house. When Nikolaus and Martin returned, they looked anxiously at Katrin.

"When will we move in?" Katrin asked with a smile.

"You like it?" Martin shouted and Nikolaus chimed in. They beamed as they took Katrin's hands and danced with her in the farmyard while chickens and turkeys hastily took flight.

I don't know if we're making the right decision, but I am finally going to have a home again, Martin thought. *The years of living in rooming houses are over.*

Mrs. Ames prepared sandwiches and invited the three friends into the house. It was not long until the merry company had cleared their plates.

"Why are you moving away even though you own such a nice farm here?" Martin asked the American.

Ames filled his pipe with great deliberation. "Moving around is in our blood. My grandfather was born in Virginia, my father in Tennessee, and I in Kentucky. Maybe my grandchildren will reach the Pacific Ocean one day."

The friends gaped at him. Such a way of life was entirely foreign to them. In Germany, many families lived in the same village for generations. Katrin was the first one to regain her voice.

"When will we go to the courthouse?" she asked her brother.

"The last Tuesday in August. I have only local deliveries that day."

"I don't think that's a good idea. Why don't we all give our notices on Wednesday and sign the deed on Thursday," she suggested.

"She's right," Martin agreed. "It is more sensible to quit a day earlier instead of taking a day off two days before we quit our jobs."

"But where will I sleep on Thursday if I'm not working anymore?" Katrin asked.

"You can sleep here with us," Ames suggested, accepting the date they had set.

They agreed that Katrin would go to the farm with the Ames family after signing the deed and stay there overnight. On Friday morning, the Ames family planned to leave at the crack of dawn and Katrin could pick up the young men in Belleville with the buckboard they had also purchased from Owen.

* * *

That Thursday, Katrin accompanied Nikolaus and Martin to the courthouse where the young men and Ames solemnly placed their signatures under the document acknowledging the sale of the land in Shiloh Valley. Then all four of them made their way to Hinckley's bank where Martin withdrew eight hundred dollars from his account and handed it to Ames.

Katrin picked up her belongings at the Belleville House and climbed on Ames's wagon. A huge Conestoga wagon stood in the center of the farmyard after gathering dust in the barn for years. Gradually, the house emptied while the family carried bedding, plates, and pots outside.

Ames would drive a team of four horses and had bought two more horses for this purpose, leaving two horses behind for his successors. Two cows, two oxen, ten pigs, and twenty-five chickens would also stay behind.

It was still dark when the family rose and invited Katrin to share their last meal on the farm. Afterward, she stepped outside to watch their departure as the faint light of dawn made the contours of the farm buildings barely visible.

There they go, she thought. *They are so hopeful for their future, just like we are. What fate will await me here? Will Martin propose to me or reject me?*

Chapter 31

Once alone, Katrin took a deep breath. She roamed through the barn, garden, and orchard, touching walls and fence posts to take possession of the farm. At last, her long journey had come to an end.

Their parents would have never imagined that their children would own a big farm one day. Hot tears welled in her eyes at the thought of her parents, but there was no time to mourn their loss today. She dried her cheeks with a handkerchief, hitched up the horses to the wagon, and drove to Belleville to pick up Nikolaus and Martin. They were waiting in front of Widow Glanig's house with their luggage.

"Do you have any money?" Katrin asked.

"We have our wages for this week," Nikolaus replied.

"That won't be enough. I need to buy pots, pans, plates, and a thousand other things."

Nikolaus took over the reins and drove first to the bank to withdraw money from their savings account and then to Oscar Ellis's store.

"I'll stay with our belongings," Nikolaus turned toward Martin. "You go in with Katrin and help her carry everything."

Katrin took her time choosing household items. When she handed Martin a pot, their hands touched briefly. His hands felt comfortable and reassuring, not like Alfons's clammy fingers. On the drive out to the farm Martin and Nikolaus incessantly sang all the freedom songs they had chanted during their campaign. Friedrich Hecker would have been overjoyed if he had heard them.

"Go on now, get to work," Katrin said when they arrived at the farmyard. Nikolaus set the brake and shot a reproachful look at his sister.

"But first we need to eat something. I'm hungry."

Katrin smiled mischievously. "I'm sorry, but I can't offer you anything but lettuce."

When she saw the young men's horrified faces, she added quickly, "See if you can find some eggs."

Martin and Nikolaus headed to the chicken coop while Katrin carried a basket with groceries into the house. The ashes in the stove were still aglow and she had soon kindled a fire with a few sticks and wood. She fried bacon and the young men burst into the kitchen with a basket full of eggs.

"Oh my goodness! These must be at least a dozen eggs," Katrin exclaimed.

"Fifteen," her brother beamed, "that makes five eggs for each of us and if you can't finish your portion, I'll help you."

Katrin clapped her hands with feigned dismay. "I forgot what a healthy appetite you always had. I can imagine that you two will soon eat the hair off my head."

Martin helped Katrin to crack the eggs into the pan, but it was soon apparent that they could not fry all of them at once.

"Let Nikolaus eat first because he is the hungriest," he suggested. "We'll eat later."

Nikolaus set the rough-hewn sawhorse table, cut off a thick slice of white bread and thumped the end of his fork on the table.

"If I could have a cool glass of beer right now, I would be content," Nikolaus said.

"You're not working for a brewery anymore," Martin gloated. "But you're right, we should have picked up some beer when we passed the tavern to celebrate."

Before they rose from the dinner table, Katrin said firmly, "this afternoon I want you two to stay out of the house. I am going to clean it thoroughly before we move in. Would one of you get me a bucket of water from the well?"

Martin obliged and the young men disappeared for a thorough inspection of the farm while Katrin rubbed her hands together and began to work.

* * *

Arranging their living quarters was not difficult. The room off the kitchen became Katrin's bedroom. That way, she could get dressed and start the fire before the men rose. Nikolaus and Martin slept upstairs in the second bedroom. The third room would serve as a storage room and also provide space for drying herbs, fruits and other provisions for winter.

Katrin hung up the blue-and-white checked curtains she had brought from Germany and felt right at home.

On Saturday evening, the three youths had a surprise visitor. A stocky man of about forty years drove into their farmyard and introduced himself as their neighbor, Daniel Meidinger.

"I've heard that Owen Ames sold his farm," he said. "So I thought, 'Go and ask your new neighbor whether he needs your help.'"

He faltered and looked from one to the other. Martin hastened to introduce everybody and Meidinger invited the newcomers for a visit.

"How will we find your farm?" Nikolaus inquired.

"If you drive from here through the woods, you'll come to the Shiloh road. Make a right turn and you'll see our farm on the left."

"I don't expect that we'll have time during the next few weeks to visit our neighbors. We have a lot of work to do around here, but we'll come as soon as possible," Nikolaus replied.

At the supper table, Katrin addressed an issue they had avoided so far.

"People are going to talk about our living arrangements," she addressed Nikolaus while glancing at Martin.

"Why? You're my sister and keep house for us," Nikolaus quickly retorted. "We can't possibly do all the work ourselves."

"Of course not," Katrin said. "The work is not the problem. It's the fact that we are living in the same house together that people are going to talk about. I saw the curiosity in Meidinger's eyes."

"Alright," Nikolaus said, after considering, "maybe we should build a separate cabin for Martin when we have some free time."

"That might be a good idea."

* * *

During the following weeks, Nikolaus, Martin, and Katrin worked from sunrise to sundown without respite. While the men harvested the cornfields, Katrin's responsibility was the garden's bounty. She canned vegetables and bundled herbs together to hang in the spare room. The day was not long enough for all the fall chores: peeling apples, slicing apples for *schnitz,* and making applesauce. Everywhere in the house the inhabitants seemed to trip over apples.

Nikolaus and Martin helped Katrin harvesting their bounty before the insects devoured their crop. Martin picked an unblemished apple and offered it to Katrin.

"A beautiful apple for a beautiful girl," he said. She took the apple and gaped after him while he turned away to empty his sack into a basket.

When the corn cobs were finally piled up in the barn it was high time to plow the land and to turn over the earth in the garden. After this bountiful crop, Katrin's pots were filled with many delicious meals. Her hard work was rewarded every time the always hungry lads stepped into the kitchen, inhaling the aromas deeply before gobbling down their meals.

"Do you know what we need now?" Katrin asked one night during supper.

Nikolaus and Martin looked up from the apple sauce they were savoring. They shook their heads simultaneously.

"We need a dog!" she exclaimed. "A dog that will announce visitors and protect me when you two work in the field all day."

"That's a very good idea," the young men agreed. "We'll ask around if anyone has puppies."

* * *

One day, Martin drove to Belleville to purchase some items that were not available in Shiloh. When he returned, he had a small package in his pocket.

After supper, Martin led Nikolaus to the barn and pulled out the box. "What is it?"

"It's a brooch," Martin said while he opened the lid.

"Is it for Katrin?"

"Yes. Do you think she'll like it?"

"Of course, Nikolaus reassured him. "It's beautiful. She'll love it."

Martin smiled. "Aren't you interested in girls at all?"

"No," Nikolaus said, shaking his head. "Most girls are silly and give you nothing but heartache."

Martin chuckled, wondering whether his friend ever had any experience with a girl or was just talking from observation.

"What did you think of Meidinger's girls?" he asked, watching Nikolaus's face twist in dismay.

The evening before, they had all paid the overdue visit to their neighbor. The farmer and his wife had spent all evening displaying their two daughters to the young men while the girls stared at Katrin with open jealousy.

"The whole time we were there, Meidinger danced attendance on us to offer his dull, witless daughters," Nikolaus gave vent to his feelings.

"Well, I wouldn't quite call them dull. It's just that one of them seemed ready to drag you to the altar and the other one is dumb as straw," Martin said bluntly, causing them to snicker like schoolgirls.

Chapter 32

On a sunny Sunday in October, Katrin, Nikolaus, and Martin put on their best clothes and drove to the service at the small church in Shiloh. After the last hymn had faded away the congregation streamed outside to picnic on the grass next to the church.

Unaware of this custom, Katrin, Nikolaus, and Martin had not brought any food and lingered around their wagon until a man of about forty years approached them.

"I guess you are newcomers to Shiloh since I have never seen you here before," he said kindly. "Would you do us the honor of sharing our meal?"

The young people nodded and followed the stranger.

"My name is Gottfried Weisgerber and this is my wife Gertrud," the tall, lean man introduced his plump, dark haired wife. A ten-year-old girl sat by her side and chewed absent-mindedly on a sandwich.

Frau Weisgerber generously offered the friends the food and cider she had brought along. Martin had already noticed that settlers in the thinly populated areas of the Midwest were very interested in their neighbors and knew all farmers within a radius of several miles, so he was not surprised to be quizzed by the Weisgerbers. When they told of their work on the farm, the couple marveled at their zeal.

"You would set a fine example for Friedrich and Gustav, our sons," Weisgerber said while glaring at a group of adolescents. "Will your parents follow you soon?"

"Our parents passed away," Nikolaus replied.

"I'm sorry," Weisgerber said, turning to Martin, "You're lucky that your sister has accompanied you to keep house for you."

"Katrin isn't my sister."

Weisgerber fell silent. Martin guessed his thoughts and hastened to steer the conversation to a more harmless subject. "Have you lived in Shiloh Valley very long?"

"Yes, I came here in the summer of 1833. I have spent half of my life in America," the farmer replied.

"Then you should know Gustav Körner."

"Of course, I know him. We sailed on the same ship to New York."

"I met him at the town celebration last year," Martin said. "Were you also involved in the storm on the Frankfurt guardhouse?"

"No, my father had lured me to Darmstadt under a pretext so I could not take part in it. When I saw through him, I rushed back to Frankfurt, but I was too late. I then asked my father for my inheritance and emigrated to America."

"Herr Körner told me that you were about one hundred people on the ship. Did all of you settled here in Shiloh Valley?"

"Most of them live here on their farms but some live in Belleville or St. Louis."

Now Weisgerber asked why the young friends had emigrated, and Nikolaus and Martin reported briefly about their adventurous campaign and Martin's flight to France.

Weisgerber said, "I believe your neighbors would like to hear about your adventures. We are all eager to learn news from the old homeland. We still feel attached to Germany even though many people don't want to admit it. If it's alright with you, I would like to invite you to our house on one of the following Sundays so you may tell our friends about your adventures."

* * *

After supper, Nikolaus collected kindling in the grove, leaving his sister and friend alone. In the meantime, Martin and Katrin fed the animals and gathered eggs. Then Katrin put three chairs on the porch and sat down to watch the last light of day as it painted the sky a vivid orange.

Martin realized that Nikolaus deliberately stayed in the woods and went upstairs to fetch the brooch. He poured some water from the ewer into the washbowl and wetted his face. Then he ran a comb through his tousled hair and slowly descended the stairs. Taking a deep breath, he timidly placed the cameo in Katrin's hand.

"What's this?" Katrin asked.

Martin stepped back and leaned against the porch railing. "It's a brooch."

"Is it for me?"

"Yes," Martin said.

Katrin twisted and turned the ornament in her hands.

"You can use it to pin your scarf together," he muttered.

"No man has ever given me a gift," she whispered, not meeting his gaze.

At last, Katrin rose and stepped over to Martin who was anxiously searching her features for signs of rejection. Her eyes glowed as warmly as the setting sun and a faint smile stole over his face. He gently placed his arms around her waist and kissed her tenderly. Her mouth tasted like a fresh glass of milk and his kiss grew more passionate as she folded her hands around his neck. When their lips parted, Katrin said, "I thought you would never find the courage to tell me that you love me."

"Well, I haven't said that."

"Then say it now," she demanded.

"I love you with all my heart," Martin said. He pulled the combs out of her hair so that her honey-colored curls fell over her shoulders. His fingers moved slowly through her locks while she rewarded him with another long kiss.

"When did you first realize that you didn't hate me anymore?" Martin asked.

"I never hated you," Katrin said with mock indignation.

"Well, you made it seem like you did," Martin said as he wrapped his hands around hers.

"It was back in Kaiserslautern after the public assembly. You gave up your room for me even though I was flattered by Georg's gallantries. I thought highly of you for that, but I didn't fall in love with you until you shook my hand when we arrived in Belleville. You seemed so much more grown up and suddenly there wasn't the barrier of money and class between us anymore. I felt wretched when you put me up with Anna."

"It's all over now," Martin consoled her, "and besides, I was devastated when I learned you were promised to another man."

"Did you love Anna?"

"No, but she was fun to be with, and I thought I would never see you again."

Nikolaus returned from his walk as the sky grew dark.

"Congratulations," he said when he saw the couple standing on the porch with their arms wrapped around each other. He stepped inside and lit the tallow candle in the kitchen.

"Come into the house, I have a surprise for you," he called a little later.

Martin loosened his embrace and took Katrin's hand while they followed him.

"But this is Palatine wine," Katrin exclaimed when she spotted a bottle of wine and three mugs.

"Yes, it's the last bottle of our stock," Nikolaus beamed. "I've saved it for a special event, and I believe an engagement is such an occasion."

Neither Katrin nor Martin had thought about an engagement just yet. Katrin's eyes searched Martin's and he lowered his lids in approval. He took both her hands in his and asked, "Will you marry me, Katharina?"

She nodded, unable to utter a word. The threesome emptied the bottle of wine and indulged in reminiscences of their homeland. Before they all went to bed, Katrin said, "We'll keep this bottle as a reminder of this day."

* * *

As they were getting dressed the next morning, Martin said to Nikolaus, "Don't tell Katrin, but I want to drive to the store today to buy a ring for her."

"Was I out of line to talk of an engagement?" Nikolaus said with a grin.

"No. I guess I'm a little slow where girls and marriage are concerned. I still feel too young to get married just yet and hope for a lengthy engagement."

"Don't wait too long or Katrin may lose patience and marry someone else." Nikolaus winked at his future brother-in-law and climbed down the steps as the smell of flapjacks and eggs wafted from the kitchen.

* * *

Jakob Wehrle never gave Martin a chance to speak.

"I think I have found a dog for you," he said.

Martin gaped at him.

"Your sister was here about a week ago and asked me whether I knew anybody who owns young dogs. I've just learned that a farmer west of here had another litter of puppies. He doesn't think that he'll be able to get them all through the winter and wants to give them away."

Martin asked him about the location of the farm and then addressed his main concern.

"Do you carry any wedding rings?" he muttered even though nobody else was in the store.

"I have a small assortment in stock." Wehrle disappeared in a back room and returned after a few minutes with several jewelry boxes.

"Are you engaged?" he asked with the curiosity of his trade while he spread the rings in front of Martin. "Who is the lucky girl?"

"My sister."

"Your sister?"

"I mean the girl you mistook for my sister."

"Oh, I see," Wehrle said.

The shopkeeper's face reflected his curiosity, but Martin remained silent.

Martin chose a plain gold ring, bought a few staples for Katrin and proceeded to the farm of the puppy owner. It was difficult to choose between the six pups that were part sheepdog, part undefinable mutt. Finally, Martin picked a gray bitch with a white triangular spot on her face.

* * *

Katrin beamed when she took the puppy in her arms, despite Martin's warnings that it was not yet housebroken." When he led the horse to the barn, he coaxed a small bowl of milk from the cow and took the dish to the kitchen. The whelp cautiously approached the bowl but then hunger won over all doubts and she lapped the warm liquid until the plate was empty.

"I think we should leave her in the kitchen for now until she is big enough to sleep in the barn," Katrin said. "Here she can get used to us and doesn't have to be afraid of oxen and pigs."

"We have to think of a name for her," urged Martin.

"What do you think of Cora?" Katrin asked at last. "That was the name of our first dog when we were children."

"Cora it is," Martin replied.

After supper, Martin remembered the ring which was still tucked into his pocket. When he put it on Katrin's ring finger he was surprised to see that her eyes were moist with tears.

"What's the matter?" he asked.

"I wish my parents could have lived to see this day," Katrin whispered and softly put her hand on his. Martin reflected on Frau Weber's frosty demeanor toward him but did not express his thoughts. He kissed Katrin's cheek and said, "I wish you had met my mother. She was a wonderful woman."

Chapter 33

On Sunday, they drove to the church in Shiloh as promised. Weisgerber greeted them warmly while his wife met them with visible reserve.

After the service, Weisgerber's friends gathered in front of the church and the procession of wagons slowly started moving. It was a select group of people that finally assembled in Weisgerber's living room. All male guests, except Martin and Nikolaus, had attended a prestigious university and their wives had obtained their education in a Swiss or English boarding school.

"Gottfried has told us that you two fought in the Palatine uprising two years ago," Johann Scheel said. "Do tell us how you fared. We are very interested in the revolution because we only know what the newspapers reported."

"Yes, I know," Martin replied, "Friedrich Hecker told me that you gentlemen even collected money and sent it to Germany, but it was already too late."

They seemed surprised that Martin knew the famous revolutionary and Martin began his narration. He was sometimes carried away by the fire of youth and the series of events unfurled before his eyes: the public assembly; the proclamation of a provisional government; the unsuccessful weapons purchase in Belgium and his father's role in its failure; the disastrous battle near Rinnthal; the retreat over the Rhine River; Georg's death; and finally the realization that the revolution had been defeated once and for all.

The party listened for the first time to an eyewitness account of the uprising, and the ladies were especially indignant over the Prussian army's cruelty.

"Do you think that there will be another revolution in Germany in the foreseeable future?" asked a man named Theodor Hilgard.

"I think it is highly unlikely," Martin replied. "Now I realize that a small country like the Palatinate is unable to free all German states. We would probably have had a chance, though, if we had had enough weapons early on and had ambushed the Prussians in the Palatine Forest. First and foremost, our leaders made the mistake of not pulling the armies of our neighboring states to our side. Nikolaus and I were ordinary rebels and even we recognized with a heavy heart that our cause was lost."

"I see you are thinking just like us," Hilgard said. "We gave up hope in 1833 and immigrated to America so that we could finally live in freedom. We were, however, just a small group compared to the thousands of democrats who emigrated after the revolution of 1848. These days, a rebellion in Germany is impossible for the very reason that all leaders of the insurgents are either dead or living in exile."

"Would you have returned to Germany if the revolution had succeeded?" Nikolaus asked.

Anton Schott scratched his chin. "The American culture is on a much lower level than the European culture. Unlike us, Americans don't know museums, theaters, galleries, and good universities. We even brought almost all books we collected in our library from Europe. I believe that I would have gone back to Germany, had the revolution succeeded."

The group remained silent for several moments.

"You said that you have a library," Martin said. "I would like to read books but can't afford to buy any right now. Could we use your library even though we haven't contributed to it?"

"Of course," Schott said. "The library is open to everybody and I would be happy to welcome you and your friends on my farm. There is a small fee of five cents per book, however."

Martin was pleased. Books would help to pass the time during the approaching winter. After coffee and cake, Weisgerber led Martin into the garden.

"I have been tasked to talk to you about your conduct," he said.

Martin jerked back, although he had half expected a rebuke. "Would you make yourself clear?"

"It's quite simple. You're living under one roof with an unmarried young girl. We cannot possibly tolerate your behavior."

Martin's face began to burn. Annoyed with the berating, he decided not to reveal the engagement just yet. "And what should I do in your opinion?"

"Either you marry the girl, or you sleep on one of the neighboring farms from now on," Weisgerber demanded.

"I bought the Ames farm with my inheritance and I intend to sleep on my property," Martin said with unintentional harshness. "I don't need to sleep in a barn when I own a whole house. Besides, all the farmhouses I've seen are hardly big enough for one family."

Martin turned away. Before he stepped onto the porch, he said to Weisgerber, "Just so you know: Katrin and I are engaged."

"Then I trust you will do the right thing," Weisgerber said.

Martin stomped into the living room and told Katrin and Nikolaus that it was time to leave.

Katrin gave him a perplexed look, but she remained silent until they were on their way.

"What did he want from you?"

Martin told them about his conversation with Weisgerber.

"He's not entirely wrong," she said quietly.

Martin shook his head. "I didn't say that he was wrong, but I can't agree with his demand. Why do people always tell me what I should or shouldn't do?"

"I'll talk to him because I don't want to quarrel with our neighbors. We now live in a country where we depend on them."

"Alright, you do that," Martin said gratefully and patted her arm. "You're much more patient than I am anyway."

* * *

After finishing their chores Katrin and Martin took a stroll in the woods.

Katrin took a deep breath before she spoke the words that might alter their relationship forever.

"Do you know what I was thinking this afternoon?" she asked with a quivering voice.

"No."

"I was wondering whether we did the right thing by getting engaged. I love you very much and because of that I don't want you to be unhappy because of me. You may not know it yourself, but you belong to the people we saw today in Weisgerber's house. You have good manners and can express yourself while Nikolaus and I sit there quietly. The only thing that separates you from them is your connection with us."

She bit her lower lip before continuing. "I was embarrassed when I saw how their wives were dressed today. Those people can start afresh again and again, they will always fall on their feet. Museums! Theaters! That's what these rich people think about while we are struggling to feed ourselves year in and year out."

Martin stopped and embraced his pink-cheeked betrothed. "Don't worry about them. I don't belong to them anymore than you do. I will always love you and I need you so much. You have no idea how lonely I was before you and Nikolaus came to live here. I have always enjoyed being alone, but I have spent the most wonderful hours of my life with you, Nikolaus, and Georg. You may not have attended a fancy boarding school, but you have common sense and you are more competent than all the Latin farmers' wives together."

Katrin still looked skeptical.

"There will come a day," Martin said, "when we will all be part of the great American nation and will speak nothing but English, regardless of our background. The American Constitution guarantees us life, liberty, and the pursuit of happiness. That means we are masters of our own fate."

They continued their walk silently while Katrin mulled over his words. "Nikolaus and I know almost nothing about America even though we have lived here for a year. Who told you so much about American history?"

"Anna's father gave me several books and he often discussed politics with me. I'll drive to Schott's farm soon to borrow a book so we can all learn together."

Just a few days later, Martin helped Katrin onto the wagon and dropped her off at Weisgerber's farm before continuing to the library.

Weisgerber appeared surprised to see Katrin but graciously offered her a stroll through his orchard.

"Martin told me that you asked him to sleep on another farm until we're married," she said.

"That's right."

"We have been so busy since he bought the farm that it would be very inconvenient for us to follow your advice."

"You could get married, that would solve the problem," Weisgerber suggested.

Katrin ignored his remark. If Martin wanted to wait before getting married, she would not argue. After all, they were both still very young. "We don't have parents who could follow us here. Nikolaus and Martin are my family and a family usually lives together in a home. Martin has bought the farm with his money since our savings weren't nearly enough.

It would therefore be my brother's and my turn to move out. This would not only mean that Martin would live alone on the farm, but Nikolaus and I would be a burden in a stranger's house. You have my word that we are living together as siblings."

Weisgerber's expression softened after hearing her words. "I'm glad we had this talk," he said. "Will you have a cup of coffee with us?"

When Martin drove up to the gate, Katrin parted from Weisgerber with the promise of another visit.

"It seems that you have twisted him round your little finger just as you twisted me," Martin teased.

"That's not how I remember it," Katrin said, causing Martin to grin from ear to ear. "I'm so relieved that I can choose my own husband. Not many girls can do that."

"Time will tell if you're lucky with your choice of a husband. But it was very brave of you to end your engagement."

Katrin shrugged. "I didn't have any other choice since I didn't love Alfons. I didn't even respect him. I already knew that his mother and his spinster aunt pulled the strings on the farm and I would rather have died than move into that house. I wanted to determine the course of my own life and had not given up hope yet to find a man who I loved as much as he loved me. When Nikolaus suggested immigrating to America, I was so relieved because I feared that my uncle would find a husband for me. I think I already loved you back then, but I didn't know it."

"I've known for a long time that I loved you, but I never had the courage to say it," Martin said and turned toward Katrin. Her lips reached up to his face and their mouths met with a tenderness and passion Katrin had never felt before in her life.

* * *

After the fields were plowed, Nikolaus and Martin cut firewood and performed some necessary repairs. The roof of the cow barn had to be mended and several boards were loose on the side of the barn. The tools that had been strewn all over the barn were now stored on shelves or hung on hooks. Nikolaus built a sturdy doghouse for Cora and made two snow shovels for the imminent winter weather.

One Sunday, Nikolaus set out on a lonely walk. About a mile away, he came to a farm he had passed while driving to Shiloh. A slim young fellow with flaxen hair was sitting on the porch steps, reading a newspaper. When he became aware of Nikolaus, he waved him over.

"I've never seen you around here," he said, "and I know just about everybody in the valley."

"I just moved here," explained Nikolaus. "My sister's future husband bought the Ames farm and we help him operate it."

The young man introduced himself as Peter Kolb. He lived on the farm with his parents and his younger sisters Susanne and Marie. Nikolaus soon found out that Peter was just one year younger than him and also lamented the lack of amusements in the valley. Peter's mother invited Nikolaus to share their Sunday cake with the family and he gladly accepted. Before he left the Kolbs, Peter promised to drive to Belleville on one of the following Sundays with his new friend.

* * *

A letter from Germany was a rare occurrence on the Dupree farm and the opening of it resembled a ritual. Most of the letters came from Uncle Sebastian and Aunt Minna, and Nikolaus usually read them out loud after dinner.

Uncle and aunt told their young relatives of the happenings in Moorbach including births, weddings, and deaths, and the siblings also learned who had immigrated to America in the meantime.

"Don't you ever write home?" Nikolaus asked his friend one day.

"I rarely write letters," Martin admitted. "I'm glad you reminded me because I have not announced news of our engagement to Carolina yet."

He fetched paper, ink, and a quill and slowly drafted his letter. While he considered what to write, his gaze fell on Katrin, busily knitting. His heart welled with pride that this lovely and sensible girl would become his wife.

Chapter 34

In late November, Katrin was invited to the Biehl farm for a quilting bee. An American neighbor, Mrs. Scott, had offered to show the new settlers the unfamiliar custom. Nikolaus offered to give her a ride before continuing to Peter's farmstead. They wanted to build a primitive sled for winter outings. Martin stayed behind by himself for the first time since he had purchased the farm.

When Nikolaus and Katrin returned in the evening, Katrin stumbled into the kitchen, visibly shaken. She almost ran to Martin and threw her arms around his neck.

"Oh, Martin," she sobbed, "it was awful."

"What happened?" he asked, startled by the outburst.

"The girls and women all gave me a hard time about living here like this. They said that we are living in sin and that you are just using me as a cheap worker until you get tired of me and dismiss me. What should we do?"

Martin pulled a handkerchief from his pocket and dried her tears away.

"Well, there is only one thing we can do," he said with resolve. "We'll drive to Belleville tomorrow to get married."

"Get married?" Katrin asked, her eyes growing wide. "So suddenly? We have not discussed a date yet, but I expected to get married next spring at the earliest."

Martin helped her out of her coat and said tenderly, "I was alone all day and I had a lot of time to think. It occurred to me that I don't want to live without you for even a day. So, let's put on our best clothes and get married tomorrow. Or did you have other plans?"

* * *

176

The next day, Katrin, Martin, and Nikolaus finished their morning chores before dressing in their finery. Martin placed Katrin's ring into the pocket of his new charcoal suit while Katrin donned a rose-colored dress and proudly clasped her brooch on her chest.

In Belleville, Martin steered the wagon to a livery. He helped Katrin off the wagon and offered her his arm for the short walk to the courthouse. Before entering the building, Martin faced Katrin. "Are you sure about this?"

Katrin nodded. Inside, the clerk of the court escorted them to the office of the justice of the peace. Nikolaus took a seat on the wooden bench that hugged the rear wall of the sparsely furnished office. Too nervous to sit down, Martin stood rooted in the center of the room where Katrin joined him. Martin took Katrin's hand in his left and whispered, "I promise, you will not regret this day."

Katrin's glowing face was answer enough for him. With her at his side he could face whatever the future held in store for them.

The tall, lean justice of the peace looked up from his papers and gave a faint smile. Martin stammered slightly as he explained their intentions. The justice nodded and ordered the clerk to fetch the appropriate document.

Minutes later, the justice rose and said solemnly, "I hereby certify that on this 28th day of A.D. 1851, I have joined in the Holy State of Matrimony Martin Carl Dupree to Katharina Weber, both of St. Clair County, according to the Customs and Laws of Illinois."

He signed the document with a flourish, and the clerk verified it as a witness. Then both officials shook the couple's hands while Nikolaus jumped up from the bench to cover their hands with his. If Katrin was disappointed at the brief ceremony she didn't show it. Indeed, her face glowed with such love that Martin did not hesitate to kiss her soft lips. Nikolaus whooped and ushered them out of the office. "Come on, I'm starving. Let's go eat."

Clasping the envelope with the document, Martin guided his new wife and brother-in-law to the Maus Tavern where they feasted on pork roast and potatoes.

It was growing dark when they arrived at their farm. While Martin lifted his young bride from the wagon, a fiery-red sun was about to disappear behind the rolling plain and he faced the western horizon as if spellbound. Katrin followed his gaze and whispered, "How beautiful! As wonderful as the whole day has been."

Then she kissed Martin and the bridal pair stood in the farmyard with their arms tightly round each other as if they were reluctant for the day to end.

"I'll feed the animals," Nikolaus said while he unhitched the horse, "and I'll sleep in the barn tonight."

Martin shot him a thankful look. He had been wondering how to persuade his brother-in-law to leave the house for the night.

"Come," he said to Katrin, took her hand softly into his and led her into the house.

In her bedroom, he clumsily opened the many hooks on the back of her dress. When it dropped to the floor, she bent over to pick it up, but he grasped both her arms.

"Leave it, it can wait," he said and led her to the bed. He pulled a comb out of her coronet and her braids dropped on her back. Gingerly, he loosened her braids and buried his hands in her hair that enveloped her upper body.

"I love you," he whispered while he covered the nape of her neck with kisses. "Do you love me?"

"I love you with all my heart," Katrin said breathlessly.

"Don't be afraid. I promise I won't hurt you."

"I'm not afraid," Katrin assured him but her voice was trembling slightly.

Martin motioned her to sit on the edge of the bed and continued to caress her neck while his other hand wandered to her body. Katrin soon relaxed and began to unbutton his shirt.

Martin smiled. "There, that's better. Now, could you possibly help me with this corset?"

Chapter 35

In December, a blizzard swept across the Midwest for two days and brought icy cold from the polar regions of Canada. In one night alone, the temperature dropped thirty-six degrees.

The next morning, the snow drifts reached as high as the windows of the farmhouse. Martin reluctantly rose from the bed, still warm from his wife's body. Katrin already had a fire going in the stove and he and Nikolaus sipped a cup of coffee before they bundled up to venture to the barn. The animals were screaming in their anxiety. The young men sank up to their thighs into the snow and had much difficulty clearing a narrow path to the barn. The wind whipped around Martin's hands until they were so stiff that the shovel slipped out of his fingers.

"I've never been so cold in my life," declared Martin when he stomped into the kitchen to warm his frozen hands over the stove before continuing to clear a path.

The storm penetrated every crack of the barn and the animals were huddled together as closely as the chains allowed.

Nikolaus and Martin filled the troughs with a whole day's ration of hay for the cattle and horses and corn for the hogs and chickens. Then they spread straw in the compartments to protect their livestock from the cold.

Winter closed in on the small family, but they were not idle. The men were busy caring for the animals, bringing in firewood, sealing the windows with rags, and grinding corn. Whenever she had a break from housework, Katrin occupied herself with sewing or knitting. The windows were darkened by drifting snow and a candle was burning in the kitchen throughout the day.

During a break in the weather, Martin harnessed Lisa to the primitive sleigh to take Katrin to the store. The sleigh consisted of a triangular board at the bottom and a footboard to cut through the snow. Katrin stood behind Martin and placed her arms around his waist to keep her balance.

"Yoo-hoo, this is fun," she shrieked and huddled closer to him, eliciting hoots of laughter from Martin.

At Wehrle's store, they hurried to the coal stove in the center of the room. As they rubbed their icy hands together, Wehrle moved in closer.

"Congratulations," he said and shook Katrin's hand, "I heard you got married recently."

"Thank you," Katrin said, bending her head slightly at the unusual attention.

"Who got married?" asked Mrs. Kolb who had been looking at calicos. "Why didn't you tell us? We would have come to church with you."

"We got married at the courthouse," Martin ended all speculation.

Soon they were surrounded by people who shook their hands and clapped Martin's back. Katrin basked in the attention of the women while the men made jokes about Martin's secrecy. They stayed for hours, talking to old friends and new ones, and catching up on news from the outside world.

* * *

Several days later, the tingling of sleigh bells sounded through the still valley.

The sleigh turned into their barnyard and the chatter of several voices sent Martin outside.

"Good day," yelled Peter over the din. "Mother told me you got married, and so I brought my sister Susanne and some friends along to celebrate."

Katrin was quite startled when she became aware of the invasion. While she accepted the congratulations and small gifts of their friends, she thought feverishly what to offer the surprise visitors. She sent Nikolaus to the smokehouse to pick up some sausages and began to cut slices of bread.

Peter's sister Susanne motioned her to a corner of the kitchen. "I brought a couple of cakes. And you don't have to worry about drinks. We brought enough wine and beer for everybody. We even brought chairs."

"Thank goodness," Katrin exclaimed. "I'm a bad hostess since I have almost no refreshments in the house. How could I possibly have known that we would have so many guests in the middle of winter?"

"Did you really think you could keep your marriage a secret? What in the world for? Go on to see your friends. I'll set the table."

"Thank you so much," Katrin said with a grateful sigh. "Ever since we moved out here, we have had so much to do before winter that we have barely had time to meet our new neighbors. And when Martin and I became engaged, well, we were content with each other's company."

Susanne winked and motioned her to take a seat next to Martin.

Meanwhile, the first bottle of wine had made the rounds and a cheerful chorus song filled the kitchen. When Susanne put a platter with sausages and a breadbasket on the table, Peter was singing a tune from home and the rest of the party joined in.

The day passed by with eating, storytelling, and drinking. The sun was touching the horizon when the unexpected guests climbed on their wagon with some difficulties and drove off. Katrin had dipped into the wine more than usual, almost tripping over Cora, causing the dog to give a startled whelp while the men roared with laughter.

* * *

When Katrin awoke the next morning, Martin was already preparing breakfast.

"How are you feeling, *Schatz?*" he asked tenderly.

"Oh, I have a headache," she replied, eliciting a grin from Martin.

Katrin quickly dressed herself and entered the kitchen, ignoring her throbbing head and nauseated stomach. Nikolaus was already seated at the table while Martin poured coffee and placed a plate of flapjacks and bacon in front of her. Katrin was overwhelmed by the lavish care and forced herself to eat with slow bites.

"Have you seen our gifts yet?" Martin asked.

"No."

He wiped his hands on his pants and showed her two white handkerchiefs that were embroidered with their monograms.

"Oh, how beautiful," Katrin exclaimed, "Who made them?"

"Susanne gave them to me."

"What a dear girl," Katrin fell into raptures. "I'm glad you found a friend in Peter, Nikolaus. It must be awfully lonely for you here with us."

"It isn't easy living with two lovebirds," Nikolaus admitted while he wiped his plate.

"Would you rather live with an employer who yelled at you from morning 'til night?" Katrin teased him.

"I suppose not. Peter and I want to go to Belleville next Sunday if the weather holds. It would be nice to get out for a while."

Katrin felt a pang of guilt. "Yes, do that. And tell Peter he is welcome here anytime, especially if he brings his sister along. I could use a bit of female companionship."

* * *

On winter evenings, Martin often read aloud from *The Last of the Mohicans*," a book he had borrowed from the Schott library.

"Are there still any Indians in Illinois?" asked Katrin once.

"There used to be several Indian tribes. One of them called themselves 'Illini' which means 'the people,'" Martin replied. "Nowadays there are no more Indians east of the Mississippi."

"What happened to them?"

"They were pushed off to the West."

Katrin paused. "What will happen when the white Americans settle the West?"

Martin shrugged helplessly.

"But it is their land and we have driven them off."

"As far as I know there are boundless, sparsely populated areas in the West. Surely, there is enough room for everybody."

Katrin had to be satisfied with his answer, even though she could not share Martin's opinion when she thought of the many ships that spewed out immigrants onto the streets of New York.

* * *

In early spring, a thaw transformed roads into mud baths, making even the shortest distances difficult because wagons became stuck in the morass quite often.

Still, the young family had to drive to the store quite often to replenish necessities. Katrin needed everything from kitchen staples to fabric and other sewing supplies.

One day, Martin rode to Belleville to be measured for a pair of shoes. Afterward he strolled along Main Street and paused in front of Wilhelm

Ruppelius's bookstore. Before he could change his mind, he stepped through the bright red door. It was time to make amends with an old friend.

"Good morning, Martin," Anna's father greeted him without any sign of ill feelings. "How nice to see you again. Are you making good progress on your farm?"

Martin talked about life on the farm and his recent marriage before he finally asked, "How is Anna?"

"Anna is fine, but I miss her very much," the book dealer confessed. "She now lives in St. Louis and is married to a young lieutenant. In three weeks, my son-in-law and his soldiers have to accompany a wagon train to California. My wife and I have asked Anna to move back with us until her husband returns."

He sighed softly and Martin quickly changed the subject. He bought an English grammar book and, bidding good-bye to Ruppelius, went to an agricultural machinery store where he looked around with great interest. The implements Owen Ames had left behind were without exception in good condition, but an American farmer had to be open to all innovations.

At home, he told Katrin of his encounter with Ruppelius. "One can really feel sorry for Anna. Now she's married to a man who is away for most of the year and she never knows whether he will come back alive because the wagon trains run through dangerous Indian Territory. But she was dead set on getting married and now she'll have to be content with the life she has chosen."

"Would you have married her if I hadn't come around?" Katrin asked.

"No," Martin hastened to answer, "I can't imagine Anna milking cows."

"That's not what I meant."

Martin chided himself for telling Katrin about his encounter with Ruppelius. Katrin still seemed to be jealous of her even though he had assured her that he had never been serious about Anna.

"You know there is only one woman for me, and that is my lovely wife," Martin said and planted a kiss on her cheek. "After all, you were my first love and will be my last."

Chapter 36

Martin and Nikolaus were in the wheat field cutting the golden treasure that would feed them through winter. Suddenly, Nikolaus turned around in alarm as Martin's scythe slid out of his hands.

"What's the matter?" Nikolaus asked.

A shiver traveled through Martin's body and he was barely able to whisper, "I don't feel good."

Nikolaus dropped his scythe and caught his brother-in-law before he sank to the ground. "Do you think you can walk home if I support you?"

Martin muttered, "I'll try."

Katrin looked distressed when she caught sight of her ill husband. Together with Nikolaus, she led him to the trundle bed and covered him with a down comforter. Martin shivered so violently that the entire bed rocked back and forth.

Time stood still for Martin as he was gripped in the clutches of ague, the Midwest farmer's nemesis they had heard so much about. Katrin fed Martin quinine and soups despite his weak protests. After a few days, he was able to get up long enough to finish his morning chores before dropping on the bed like a sack of flour, but he would not be able to complete the harvest. Nikolaus drove to the stagecoach station in Belleville to hire a farmhand until the harvest was completed or Martin was well enough to help.

From his sick bed, Martin watched Katrin going about her chores. She looked haggard as she bent over the iron stove canning vegetables for winter. Yet, she always found time to wipe Martin's sweat-soaked face or cover him up when a convulsion of chills shook his body. The love he felt for Katrin grew even stronger during those weeks of illness. When

184

Martin began to feel better, he wondered how he could repay her for her selfless nursing.

"What do you think about going to St. Louis for a few days this fall?" he suggested during dinner. "I would like to see my old friend Ray again."

"That's a great idea," Katrin exclaimed, "but—"

She gave Nikolaus a questioning look.

"Don't worry about the farm," Nikolaus said. "I'll get along just fine by myself."

"And who will cook for you?"

"I'm not as helpless as you think I am. After all, I learned during the campaign that a man can feed himself quite well without female help."

Martin smiled at Nikolaus's obsessive dislike of girls.

"Won't such a trip be too expensive for us?" Katrin asked.

"Not if we fetch a good price for our wheat."

* * *

One evening, Daniel Meidinger stopped by with a letter from Carolina. Katrin and Nikolaus hurried to the porch while Martin carefully opened the letter.

> My dear Martin,
>
> Ludwig and I send you and your wife our sincerest congratulations on your marriage. We are so happy that you have found a nice girl to share your life with.
>
> Since I wrote my last letter, two things happened that concern our father. The second news especially will probably not meet with your approval, but I beg you not to judge him too harshly. Well, first things first: Although father had been sentenced to death in absence in April 1851, he returned from Paris in December and was immediately arrested upon crossing the border. To our great joy, however, he was released after just a few days and came home at last.
>
> I've been told that a great many curious people awaited him outside of town. After father had inspected the house and outbuildings, he rushed to Mother's grave. But the mourning did not last long because last week he married Johanna Arendt of Kaiserslautern.

Martin dropped the page. How callous his father was to get married so soon again. Didn't he grieve his wife and mother of his children at all?

"What else does the letter say?" Katrin urged him.

"'Of us siblings, only Joseph remains in Landstuhl. He still plans to take over Father's businesses while Karl is studying law in Heidelberg. I often think of you and hope that you are as happy as I am. Your loving sister, Carolina.'"

Martin frowned, his lips tightly pressed together.

When they went to bed that night, Katrin said, "I understand that you're annoyed that your father has remarried so soon after your mother's death. But after all you told me about him, he's a man in love with life. Did you really think he would remain a grieving widower forever?"

"I loved my mother very much," Martin said, still upset. "He and I, however, have been estranged long before I left."

He swallowed hard. "I feel responsible for her death."

"You mustn't talk like that," Katrin implored. "You know it isn't true."

"My emigration broke Mother's heart."

"Other mothers have to cope, too, when their children leave their homeland," Katrin said while she tenderly stroked her fingers through Martin's black locks.

"Why don't you try to forget about your father since the thought of him bothers you so much?" she suggested.

"I would love to, if Carolina would stop writing about him," Martin grumbled.

"I think that, if I were to lose you, I would never get married again but live out here with Nikolaus as a hermit," he declared and took Katrin's hand. She shook her head skeptically.

"If I know the Meidinger girls at all, they will pounce on you like hawks while you're still at the cemetery."

Chapter 37

Fall 1852, St. Louis

Raymond was so pleased to see Martin again that his embrace almost crushed him. He even recognized Katrin even though he had only met her once.

"You're married?" he cried. "Splendid! I'll give you my best room."

The young couple spent the evenings in the lounge where quite a few patrons talked to them after Ray's introductions. The Irishmen were surprised to hear that such a young couple owned their own farm debt free. When Ray had a few minutes to spare he reached for his old, well-worn fiddle and coaxed enchanting ballads and reels out of it.

During the day, Martin and Katrin strolled along the streets and entered almost all the stores in the business district. Katrin tried on hats and examined fabrics she would never buy. Once she tried on a nut brown and yellow checkered tweed shawl.

"Do you like it?" Martin asked, giving her an adoring look.

"Yes."

"I'll buy it for you."

Before Katrin could object to the cost, Martin asked the salesclerk to wrap the shawl and they gleefully left the store.

They also visited businesses that carried agricultural machinery and hardware, gathering ideas to improve life on the prairie. The young couple had intended to spend only a little money, but the stocks in their bedroom grew larger every day. Katrin bought wool, calico, sewing needles, thread, and several essential medicines, while Martin purchased books, nails, a saw, and a few other tools.

With a heavy heart, Katrin and Martin left St. Louis after three days. Bidding good-bye to Ray was not easy for Martin but there was so much work waiting for him at home that their departure was inevitable.

"It was lovely," Katrin sighed when they stood aboard the ferry and looked back at the lively city on the banks of the Mississippi. As they drove to Belleville, a flock of Canada geese soared high above their heads in vee formation. Their mournful honks were a reminder how aware the wildlife was of the seasons.

"Look. They're flying south for the winter," Katrin pointed at them.

Her face darkened at the thought of the approaching lonely winter months, but she reminded herself that their community would host harvest celebrations and corn husking bees before being snowed in.

* * *

Before winter began in earnest, Martin drove to the gristmill with a wagonload of corn. Instead of waiting at the mill he decided to pass the time by visiting Wehrle's store. The store owner joined him as he lingered by the bookshelf.

"We just received a shipment of new books. Here is a German translation of *Uncle Tom's Cabin.*"

Martin weighed the book in his hand. "What is it about?"

"It's about the life of Negro slaves in the South. A lady from the East has written it, Mrs. Harriet Beecher Stowe. I read it in one night."

"Alright, I'll take it."

* * *

During the long winter evenings, Martin read Uncle Tom's Cabin to his wife and brother-in-law, the book that was absorbed by opponents of slavery in the North as well as in the South. Martin shivered when he remembered his brief stay in Baltimore, where he had observed Negro slaves being hit with leather whips on the way to the slave market.

The book made a lasting impression on the German settlers in the area, who were fierce opponents of slavery. After all, they had fled the yoke of sectionalism and despotism to build a new life for themselves in a free country.

From newspaper reports they had learned that the planters of the South declared that they were treating their slaves humanely and provided them with food and clothing.

"Negroes are second-class humans and must be led and cared for by the white race," they claimed.

Resistance against this inhumane system increased in the North. Yet, it was still not strong enough to secure the majority support in the Senate and the House of Representatives.

Chapter 38

Late Winter 1854

Katrin sunk onto the bed and nestled into Martin's arm. "I have to tell you something," she whispered.

"Hm?" he uttered drowsily.

"Next year at this time we'll have another mouth to feed."

Martin turned to face her, suddenly wide awake. "You mean to tell me. . ."

Katrin nodded. "We're going to have a child."

"That's wonderful news." Martin kissed her. "How long have you known?"

"A few weeks. I wanted to be certain before saying anything."

"I wish you had told me this earlier," Martin chided her. "I would have helped you more with your heavy chores."

Katrin chuckled. "I'm not as delicate as you think I am. If I need help, I promise I will ask."

Secretly, she was relieved that Martin was excited about her pregnancy. Considering the strained relationship between him and his father, she had not been sure whether he felt ready for parenthood. Now she could enjoy Martin's caresses without reserve before drifting off to sleep.

* * *

At breakfast they made the announcement to Nikolaus, who beamed from ear to ear.

"I'm going to be an uncle," he exclaimed, clearly proud of his new role.

"That's right," Martin said.

"There will be some changes around here. When Katrin's confinement nears we are going to need help in the household."

"Won't that be too expensive?" Katrin protested.

"Nothing is too expensive for my love." Martin covered her hand with his. "It doesn't have to be all the time, but I think you will need help with heavy chores like washing and harvesting."

Katrin considered his words. He was right, of course. When she and Nikolaus were children their grandmother and mother had shared the household chores while women here on the prairie had to make do without such help. How did they cope until their children were grown enough to assist them?

* * *

Martin had just washed himself at the trough when he jerked at the high-pitched cackle of a chicken. Alarmed, he ran to the coop and was almost knocked over by a young boy with tawny matted hair. The chicken still flapped its wings violently while running away from its would-be captor.

Martin grabbed the boy by his wrist. "What are you doing?"

The boy remained silent and Martin repeated his question in English.

The youth stared at his shoes. "I'm hungry."

Martin looked the young thief up and down. His shirt sleeves and pant legs were much too short for his size while his shoes appeared too big. A picture appeared in front of Martin's eyes: Two young, unkempt men fleeing through France, begging for bread at every door.

"What's your name?" he asked in a softened tone.

"Jim Harper."

"I've never seen you around here. Where are you from and who are your parents?"

"My mother is dead, and I never met my father. I'm from Salem, but I ain't never going back there, ever."

Martin let go of the arm when Jim's stomach began to growl.

At this moment, Katrin called from the house, "Martin, breakfast."

"Come with me," Martin said, and Jim followed without a word. He told Nikolaus and Katrin how he had found Jim. Nikolaus gave the orphan a wary stare, but Katrin smiled encouragingly and cracked three eggs into the frying pan. After Jim wolfed down his breakfast, he wiped his mouth on his sleeve. He pushed his empty plate away from him, beaming at Martin.

191

"Thank you."

Martin chuckled. At least Jim had been taught some manners. He began to ask the boy questions and learned that Jim's unwed mother had worked as a serving girl until she had died of scarlet fever when Jim was just three years old. On a judge's order he had been brought up by a woman who disliked small children. She had been all too glad to pass him on as an apprentice to a carpenter who paid Jim very little and whipped him with his belt for the slightest mistake.

Martin swallowed hard when he contemplated an upbringing so different from his own privileged home.

"Where are your parents?" Jim asked when he had finished.

"Our parents are also dead," Martin replied. "We work our farm alone."

Cora, who usually barked at strangers, sat still as Jim stroked her behind her ears. He seemed to contemplate Martin's answer. "Could I stay with you for a few weeks? I'm very young, but I can work, and I can sleep in the hay loft. Please don't send me back to Salem."

Nikolaus, Katrin, and Martin looked at each other and nodded slightly.

"Alright," Martin said, "if you promise not to steal any more chickens you may stay here."

"That I'll promise you. As you just saw, I'm a bad chicken thief."

* * *

Life on the farm changed after Jim's arrival. The three young people, who had lived among their fellow countrymen, were now forced to speak English every day. They did not want to ignore their mother tongue, however, and began to teach Jim German. In a short time, the boy was able to speak some broken German and even a few words in the Palatine dialect. No one talked about him sleeping in the hay loft anymore and he moved into the kitchen. Jim was not just a cheap farm laborer to Katrin, Martin, and Nikolaus but an orphaned boy looking for love and security.

One May morning they rose to discover that Jim had disappeared without a trace. While the men searched barn and cowshed, Katrin counted her provisions.

"I'm missing a loaf of bread and a ring of sausage," she reported.

"Well, he won't get too far with that," Nikolaus said.

"I never thought that I could misjudge a person so completely," Martin said, his face clouding in despair. He would have to be more careful when approached by strangers in the future.

A week later, Martin was mowing the grass on the wayside when he heard a sound.

"Psst! Psst!"

There it was again. He followed the voice and found Jim cowered in the grass.

Relieved that the boy was safe, he asked, "Where did you go?"

"I wanted to see the Mississippi and St. Louis so badly," Jim murmured, his eyes pleading with Martin. "Are you mad at me?"

"We aren't mad, but we're disappointed in you. Don't you have any confidence in us?"

"I'm sorry," Jim said, "You're the kindest people I know, and it was very foolish of me to run away like that. I wanted to see the Mississippi."

Martin shouldered his scythe and put his free arm over Jim's shoulder. "Come along. Katrin is probably waiting with dinner."

When he caught Jim's questioning look, he added, "Oh yes, she always cooked for four as if she had known you would come back. Please, stay with us. We need you."

Katrin and Nikolaus's faces lit up at the sight of Jim, but Cora bested them all. Without tiring, she jumped at him and did not want to let go. Jim had to give her a big piece of sausage before she retired to her usual place next to Katrin's chair.

During dinner Katrin said, "If Jim stays with us to help with the chores, then maybe we could attend the firemen's ball in Belleville on Saturday evening. What do you think?"

Martin and Nikolaus clapped their hands, loving parties above all else.

"Won't you mind being alone all evening?" Nikolaus asked the boy.

"It'll be a pleasure," Jim replied. "Besides, I couldn't find it in my heart to deny you the fun."

In the evening, Martin and Katrin strolled through their orchard, sharing a few moments alone together.

"Are you sure you are up to visiting a ball in your condition?" he asked.

Katrin patted her belly and looked up to him, her face radiating a glow that rivaled the setting sun. "I don't feel any discomfort lately and would like a diversion very much."

"Very well, if you're certain. It will probably do your brother good to get out." He took her hand in his as they strolled back to the house.

Chapter 39

When the threesome entered the ballroom, they found almost all tables occupied, but Peter and his girlfriend had saved three chairs for them. Martin made the rounds to greet old friends and shake hands before the music began playing a polka. Peter and Sabine danced almost every dance while Katrin and Martin danced only to slow tunes. Only Nikolaus remained behind by himself.

"Why aren't you dancing?" Peter asked him during a break.

"I can't dance," Nikolaus lied.

He made his way to the bar to join some acquaintances. A deep groove formed on Katrin's forehead as she observed her brother ordering a mug of beer. Suddenly she felt flushed in the closed atmosphere of the packed room and asked Martin for a stroll through the garden.

"I'm worried about Nikolaus. He isn't interested in girls at all and is well on his way to become an old bachelor."

"Some men become interested in girls at a later age than others," Martin replied with a smile. "Not everybody marries as young as I did."

"But that doesn't mean he has to get addled every time we go out."

"Perhaps he's unhappy with his life?"

Katrin wiped a strand of hair out of her face. "Exactly. That's why we have to help him."

"What do you have in mind?" Martin asked, sounding lightly irritated. "Do you want to find him a wife?"

"No. I'm his sister, not his mother. Perhaps you could talk to him. If he doesn't want to look for a girlfriend, he should at least have a pastime that goes beyond cows and chickens. When we still lived in Moorbach he went to the linden tree almost every night and had numerous friends. I don't understand why it can't be the same here."

Martin sighed. "Very well, I'll talk to him." He lifted her chin up and looked deep into her eyes. "Are you happy with your life here?"

"Yes," Katrin answered. "I never imagined that I could be so happy."

Martin replied with a tender kiss.

* * *

The following evening Martin beckoned Nikolaus into the garden.

"Katrin and I are worried about you," he began. "Is something amiss?"

After a brief silence, Nikolaus said, "I have no friends. You have Katrin, and Jim is much too young to be company for me. Even Peter is deserting me now. He spends every free minute with Sabine. Nobody cares how I'm doing."

"Why don't you find yourself a girlfriend, too?"

"Nobody would want me."

"How do you know that? You never tried to find one."

Nikolaus turned away and stalked off, his chin jutted in defiance.

Martin decided to take things into his own hands. Nikolaus's birthday was just a few days away and Martin planned to invite all of their friends in Shiloh Valley. Katrin agreed and he used a shopping trip to Shiloh to invite the far-flung guests. When he steered the wagon toward home in the late afternoon, he was content: about a dozen young people had promised to come.

To keep the extensive preparations a secret from Nikolaus, Martin stayed out in the fields with his brother-in-law until nightfall. A day before his birthday, Nikolaus asked his sister, "Why are you baking cakes? I didn't invite anybody."

"No birthday is complete without a cake," Katrin said.

On his birthday, Nikolaus started to saddle a horse after dinner and Martin asked, "Where are you going?"

"I'm riding to Shiloh to get drunk."

Martin seldom raised his voice against his brother-in-law, but on this occasion, he could not contain himself. "No, you're not. Now listen to me: you will lead Lotte back to the paddock and then you will lie down and take a nap. Katrin is cooking a special meal for your birthday and you'll do her the courtesy of appreciating it."

Nikolaus took in a deep breath before he slogged into the house without uttering a word.

Martin breathed a sigh of relief and beckoned Jim for help because there was still much to do before the guests arrived.

An immense pork roast sizzled on the stove while the aroma of sauerkraut wafted through the small house. When the preparations were almost completed, Martin woke Nikolaus and asked him to put on his Sunday clothes. Before Nikolaus could object, the first wagon rolled into the farmyard, guided by Peter. He lifted a laundry basket full of plates from the wagon down to a waiting Martin while the other youths crowded around Nikolaus.

"What's going on here? Who invited all these people?" Nikolaus asked. He shot Martin a suspicious look.

"I'm guilty as charged," Martin said, casting a mischievous look at his brother-in-law. "Since you didn't make any effort to celebrate your birthday, Katrin and I felt we had to do something."

Nikolaus bowed his head before he approached Martin and pressed his hand.

"You're the best friend I've ever had," he said in a low voice.

Meanwhile, the rest of the visitors had arrived. Jim looked after the horses while the girls helped setting the table. Martin introduced Jim to their friends, and they made room for the boy in their midst. The party devoted themselves to the pleasures of coffee and yeast cake.

"Your cakes are always the best," Peter praised Katrin after he had consumed five pieces.

Later, a young man named Andreas fetched an accordion from a wagon and soon cheerful songs filled the porch.

"It's a shame that we don't get together more often," Peter said.

"Next week is my birthday. You're all invited," said Henriette Müller, the girl who had helped setting tables. "I live on the Belleville-Mascoutah road. The Americans call my father 'Cider-Müller' because we sell our apple cider throughout the area each fall."

"We'll gladly come," Peter assured her, "But I had a different goal in mind. I was thinking of something fun to do that would benefit the whole community."

For several minutes, the party brooded.

"I have an idea," Martin said. "What if we published a newspaper for Shiloh Valley?"

"Have you taken leave of your senses?" Katrin asked. "With all your obligations, how would you find time to write and publish a newspaper?"

That was a reasonable argument and Martin yielded without a word. Katrin probably suspected that he would have to bear most of the workload.

Finally, Karl said, "I suggest that we will meet regularly from now on, each time on a different farm. The host will have to supply food and drink. The next meeting will be held on Henriette's birthday."

Everybody laughed about this announcement since Karl was notorious for being a good eater. The proposal itself was accepted unanimously.

Katrin, Susanne, and Henriette served supper. The party drank to the health of the birthday boy and the competent housewife before they filled their plates.

Later the friends went for a stroll until nightfall forced them to return. Andreas hammered at his accordion until late in the evening when the last wagon left the farmyard.

"Do you think Nikolaus had a good time?" Martin asked when he was alone with Katrin.

"Of course, he always sang the loudest," she said. "But you, were you serious about the newspaper?"

Martin shook his head. "It was just an idea. I wanted us young folk to do something meaningful."

"Isn't it enough to run a farm and provide for your family?"

"Not entirely," Martin said.

Katrin took his hand. "If life on the farm is too boring for you, we could move back to Belleville."

"That's not what I meant," Martin interrupted her. "I came here looking for freedom. It concerns me that this freedom is denied to so many others because of the color of their skin. I am not certain yet what I want to do but it might mean getting involved in politics."

Katrin gave him a worried look. "I can't stop you but think about it carefully. I wouldn't want you to get disappointed again."

"Back then, a lot of important people believed in a victory," Martin protested. "And besides, when we once talked about slavery you were just as opposed to it as I am. We don't want our children to grow up in a country where humans are held in bondage, do we?"

"Of course not."

"That's not all," Martin continued. "I want to get my citizenship papers as soon as I am eligible, and I hope that Nikolaus will do likewise. We can never go back to Germany anyway and it is my deepest wish to be able to vote."

"I will support your wishes, as long as you don't neglect us," Katrin said.

Martin was relieved that Katrin had not opposed his wish to get involved in public life. She was right, of course, that publishing a newspaper would be impossible considering their workload. He was unsure how to proceed and resolved to discuss his thoughts with his acquaintances. Perhaps they could give him insight into current events like the Kansas-Nebraska-law. The newspapers had even mentioned a movement to form a new political party, the Republican Party.

Would they be able to quench the turmoil that embroiled the nation over the question of slavery in newly formed states?

Chapter 40

Fall 1854

Autumn brought much work and anticipation to the Dupree Farm. Peter's sister Marie had offered to help Katrin with the heavy work during the harvest season. While Katrin stayed busy peeling apples and preparing meals, Marie picked more of the bounty or worked in the garden. Jim helped her out whenever he was not needed in the fields.

On a crisp October day, Marie and Jim were carrying a basket of apples into the kitchen and found Katrin doubled over the table.

"I think it's time," she gasped. "Can you fetch Martin and the doctor?"

Jim sprinted through the courtyard to the far end of the corn field where Nikolaus and Martin were working. "The baby is coming," he yelled at Martin before taking off toward the barn to saddle a horse.

* * *

Martin paced between the house, the barn, and the road, unable to sit still or perform any meaningful work. Marie had banished him from the house, claiming that he made her and Katrin nervous. Finally, the doctor drove into the courtyard in his buggy. With his red hair and red beard, the burly Scotsman resembled a sailor more than a doctor. He grabbed his bag and strode toward the house without needing much explanation from Martin.

While Nikolaus finished their chores, Martin retreated to the orchard. Being among the trees calmed his anxiety for Katrin. After a while he was ready to return to his vigil in the house. Jim had returned from town, but not before riding by the Kolb farm to tell Marie's mother about the impending birth. She stepped into the kitchen to take command, advising her daughter to prepare supper for the men while she assisted the doctor.

Night had fallen and a screech-owl whinnied in the grove when the doctor finally treaded down the stairs from the bedroom.

"Congratulations! You have a son," he said, wiping his forehead with a handkerchief.

Martin's face broke into a grin. "Thank you. How is my wife?"

"She is very tired, but you may see her for a few minutes. In the meantime, I wouldn't mind a bite to eat."

Martin stormed up the stairs. Beads of sweat glistened on Katrin's face as she smiled wanly at the sight of Martin. "We have a son."

* * *

Martin and Katrin named the baby Philip. During the long winter they remained in the cocoon of their home, reveling in their new role and responsibility of raising a child. The outside world would intrude on their bliss soon enough, but for now their lives seemed complete.

Chapter 41

Spring 1856

Martin entered Jakob Wehrle's store to buy some much needed supplies.

"What's new?" he asked the merchant who was stocking shelves in the back of the store.

"Haven't you heard the news yet?" Wehrle replied while approaching him. "Last night, Friedrich Hecker's house burnt to the ground. Thank God that the barn and cowshed could be saved."

"That's horrible. I'll have to ride over to see if they need anything."

Martin hurried to make his purchases and drove home. There, he saddled a horse and rode to Hecker's farm.

The entire Hecker family was sifting through the smoking rubble when Martin rode onto the farmyard.

"You've heard what happened," Hecker said, wiping a handkerchief over his bloodshot eyes.

"Yes, and I have come to offer you my help. If you need a place to stay overnight or anything else, just let me know."

"Thank you." Josephine Hecker wiped away a tear and put her hand on Martin's arm. "We'll be fine. We can sleep in our neighbor's house until ours gets rebuilt. Besides, we were able to save some clothes and household goods."

Martin addressed her husband, "Do you know what caused the fire?"

Hecker sighed. "It was quite possibly arson."

"Arson? But who could do something like that?"

"There are people who hate Republicans like me. I don't think it's a coincidence that I just gave a speech for Frémont."

* * *

201

In early October, Friedrich Hecker drove up to the Dupree farm looking for Martin.

"How is your farm doing?" Martin asked after they had exchanged greetings.

"Very well. The house is now rebuilt, thanks to the help of my friends. I came here to tell you some news. On October 18, an associate of mine, Abraham Lincoln, will give a speech in Belleville in front of Johann Scheel's house. Would you like to accompany me to listen to him?"

Martin did not have to think twice. "It would be my pleasure to come with you."

On Saturday afternoon, Hecker and Martin arrived at South Illinois Street where banners reading "Lincoln and Hecker" hung on several houses.

On the small balcony above Scheel's front door, Abraham Lincoln finally appeared to face his audience. Martin's jaw dropped at the sight of the Springfield lawyer. He had never seen such an odd figure, not even during his revolutionary days. Lincoln's tall, scrawny body was dressed in an ill-fitting suit and atop his small head sat a high, slightly wrinkled top hat.

It was Lincoln's third visit to Belleville, but his first appearance as a Republican. He praised the Germans and the noble position they held and asked the Almighty to bless these hardworking settlers. A shiver of delight traveled along Martin's spine. Here was a politician who did not rail against immigrants but appreciated the Germans' contributions to their new country. Yet, as the applause of the crowd abated, Martin overheard several critical remarks.

"Too bad that Frémont hates us Germans. I don't know if I should give my vote to such a man," said a sonorous voice behind Martin.

"I've never heard that Democrats like us any better," another man replied.

"None of them are as loathsome as the Know-Nothings," a third one chimed in. "They don't even want us to vote until we have lived here for twenty-one years."

Martin cringed. He had been furious when he first learned of the Know-Nothings' plan to exclude foreigners from voting. If the Republicans wanted to gain a foothold in the North, they should welcome the votes of German immigrants.

In his opinion, Lincoln was well advised to flatter the German voters. As farmers, it was in their basic interest to prevent the spreading of slavery to the new territories. That would inevitably ruin small farmers.

After Lincoln concluded his speech, he stepped in front of the two-story brick house to greet his associates.

"Hello, Fred. How're you doing?" he exclaimed in a falsetto voice.

A lively conversation about the campaign arose between the two politicians. Deep grooves ran through Mr. Lincoln's hollow cheeks, emphasizing his image as a rail-splitter.

Martin began to ease away, but Hecker held on to his arm. He introduced Martin as a former freedom fighter. Martin grasped Lincoln's huge outstretched hand, worried that the lawyer would crush his palm.

They exchanged a few words and Martin scrutinized Lincoln's deep-set, melancholy eyes; eyes that radiated so much simplicity and kindness.

On the drive home, Martin said to Hecker, "I didn't know you were good friends with Mr. Lincoln."

"Yes, we are," Hecker said, tilting his head at a passer-by. "Abe even raised a fund to rebuild my house. I'm grateful that I could finally thank him in person."

Martin felt honored that Hecker had taken him along. The former revolutionary leader could have easily found older, more respectable gentlemen to accompany him. But perhaps he had intentionally asked a young, impressionable man like Martin to witness this historic event in hopes of stoking his interest in politics?

* * *

Martin was bursting with desire to discuss current events further. The occasion arose weeks later when he visited the Belleville library.

"One thing I don't understand at all," Martin said to Mr. Schmitt, the librarian. "Why does the Republican Party only want to prevent the spreading of slavery? Why doesn't anybody talk about abolishing slavery? It's an appalling injustice."

"I am convinced that slavery in the United States will end eventually," replied Schmitt. "The question is: how can this goal be achieved without endangering the unity of the nation? We must not forget that slavery is the basis of life in the southern states and if we want to take away the foundation of their livelihood we will meet with bitter resistance."

"Do you think," Martin scarcely dared to say it loud, "Do you think that there will be a war?"

"I did not speak of war but of resistance, in whatever form. By the way, are you an American citizen yet?"

"Not yet," Martin admitted, "But I want to apply as soon as I am eligible."

"You should do it. A lot of Americans look down on us Germans because many of us are still German citizens even though we will never go back home again."

Martin cocked his head. Schmitt was right, it was time to quit dragging his feet on the matter of citizenship. And he wished very much to vote. Martin drove straight to the courthouse to file a declaration of intent, the first step toward naturalization. He was disappointed to learn that he had to wait at least two years before petitioning for second papers.

Afterward, he entered the office of county treasurer Johann Scheel who also managed the local office of the Republican Party. Scheel smiled when Martin stated his request.

"You are the tenth person this week who wants to join the Republican Party," he said.

After paying his dues, Martin headed to Oscar Ellis's store. It was his habit to buy something for Katrin and Philip when he was in town. Ellis was delighted to see Martin again and proudly showed him an assortment of candies. Martin chose some gumdrops and pralines before driving home.

* * *

The settlers in Shiloh Valley eagerly followed the outcome of the presidential election which ended with a surprise. Democrat James Buchanan won the election while John Charles Frémont was short a half million votes. Martin was crestfallen about the results because Buchanan shared Southern views about slavery. Would the Republican Party dissolve faster than it had been formed?

Katrin was more pragmatic. "Every fruit will ripen when the time is right. It's not good to rush into things when the people aren't ready for them yet. People don't like change."

"So, we should just accept that slavery will expand into new territories instead of being abolished?" Martin objected.

"Let's be honest: your so-called revolution was doomed to fail from the beginning because it was never properly planned. Your father went to purchase weapons when you should have marched on Frankfurt already."

Martin nodded reluctantly but then he could not stop himself from saying, "Mistakes were made on the other side too, otherwise it would not have taken three months to crush the rebellion. At least we were capable of fighting for ourselves while the slaves can't do that."

"Do you think that the South will secede from the North like the newspaper suggests?" Katrin asked with a sigh.

Martin raised his hands helplessly. "Who knows what's going on in their heads."

Katrin picked up Philip and put him on her lap. "Sometimes I wonder if we have done the right thing coming here. What kind of a world are our children going to grow up in?"

Martin looked deep into her eyes. "In Germany we would have never been allowed to marry, so please put such thoughts out of your mind."

Chapter 42

Nikolaus rode to Jakob Haag's residence and shoemaker's shop in Shiloh for a fitting of new work boots. He entered the one-story annex where Haag was busy pegging a sole onto a boot.

"Good morning, young man," said the shoemaker without interrupting his work. "Would you like some coffee while I finish this boot?"

"Yes, thank you very much."

"Barbara," the shoemaker called toward the house. A vivacious young woman of about twenty years appeared in the door. Blonde braids formed a crown at the back of her head, accentuating her slender neck.

"Yes, Uncle?"

"Can you bring us two mugs of coffee?"

"Of course," she replied and disappeared into the kitchen with light steps.

"Who is that girl?" Nikolaus asked, glancing at the door. "I've never seen her around here."

"She's my niece," the beaming shoemaker replied. "She came here from Germany two weeks ago to visit us and other relatives. If she doesn't like it here, she'll go back in a year."

At that moment Barbara returned with the coffee. Nikolaus felt as if the shop brightened like a spring morning when she entered the room. She blew a strand of hair out of her face and smiled at Nikolaus. His cheeks grew hot, but he continued to follow her with his eyes.

"Drink up," Haag encouraged him. "It's only barley malt coffee, but at least it's hot."

While Haag measured his feet, Nikolaus cast glances at the door, hoping in vain for Barbara's reappearance.

On the ride back, Nikolaus was so lost in thought that he could not recall how he had gotten home.

* * *

For the next few days, he could not give one comprehensible answer when his family addressed him. Martin believed Nikolaus was in one of his moods again.

After taking a bath on Saturday evening, Nikolaus asked Martin, "Can I have the buckboard tomorrow after dinner?"

"Of course," Martin said, not daring to ask more.

Nikolaus put on a clean white shirt, a freshly starched collar and combed his hair with water. Then he polished his shoes, climbed on the wagon seat and drove off.

"Do you understand that?" Katrin said, shaking her head.

"There are two possibilities. Either he has really snapped now or— he's in love."

"Do you think so?" Katrin's voice revealed her doubts.

"Of course. I know the symptoms," Martin said with a laugh.

"Well, then everything is alright. I was afraid my brother would become an old bachelor."

Martin's laugh faded. "I was afraid, too. Even after his party, he seemed to have no other interests than the farm and Peter."

* * *

Nikolaus drove up to the Haag residence, descended from the wagon and smoothed the creases of his suit. Timidly, he knocked at the front door, hoping for a moment that nobody was home. Barbara opened the door before he could slip away.

"Good afternoon," she said with a questioning look. "Is there a problem?"

"No," he stammered. "I was in the neighborhood and wanted to stop by to see how you're doing. My name is Nikolaus Weber, by the way."

She asked him into the kitchen where her uncle read the paper and her aunt knitted socks. Unlike his niece, Haag did not appear in the least surprised about Nikolaus's visit.

"You're lucky that Barbara is still here," the shoemaker said. "Tomorrow she'll go visiting her cousin in Randolph County."

They talked for an hour about the old homeland and Nikolaus learned that Barbara lived in Haßloch in the eastern Palatinate. Nikolaus admitted that he had only seen that part of the region during the revolution but had liked what he saw.

At last Nikolaus rose and Barbara accompanied him to the door.

"May I see you again when you come back?" he blurted out.

"Alright," Barbara replied, making his heart jump. "I should be back in two or three weeks."

While Nikolaus waited for Barbara's return, he could barely contain his impatience. Yet, he did not want to reveal his feelings by constantly asking about her. Now he could understand Martin's anguish when he learned that Katrin was promised to another man.

* * *

Three weeks later, chance was on Nikolaus's side. Their Sunday morning chores had taken longer than usual, delaying their arrival at church. From his aisle seat in the last row, Nikolaus spotted Barbara on the other side. Relieved that she was alone, he bowed his head in greeting. She gave him a smile that made him blush. From then on, he was unable to concentrate on the sermon.

After the service concluded, Katrin and Martin talked with friends. Nikolaus ambled over to Barbara who stood forlorn in a corner. Now that he was near the object of his dreams, he twisted his hat in his hands, desperately searching for words.

"When did you come back?" he said at last.

"The day before yesterday," Barbara replied, "And I have come at the right time. My uncle is ill, and my aunt stayed home today to nurse him."

"I hope he feels better soon. Do you need any help?"

"No, that's not necessary. I believe he's getting better. I'm glad to help my family because it gives me something to do. I am not used to being idle and feel like I have too much free time on my hands. At least uncle lets me do simple chores in his shop."

"I'm glad that you're here," Nikolaus said. "Is there someone in Germany who's waiting for you?"

"No. The boys I liked were not interested in me and I didn't want the others."

"Didn't your parents choose a husband for you?"

"They have tried more than once, but I was always able to get my own way. The men they had picked for me were impossible. One of them was forty years old and bald. Brrr!"

She shook herself. "I think they were glad when I went to America because my mother's health is not the best. While I'm gone, she has time to recover from those excitements."

She laughed in relief and Nikolaus joined her. He glimpsed at Katrin and Martin who hovered near the door. He felt embarrassed that they may watch him courting a girl. "I think I have to go now. Can I see you again when your uncle has recovered?"

Barbara's eyes sparkled. "Yes, come pay us a visit in a little while."

"Goodbye," Nikolaus said, shaking her hand.

* * *

Nikolaus had learned about an upcoming dance in Mascoutah and rode over to the Haag house to invite Barbara. While he was not as fond of dancing as his brother-in-law, he would make his best effort to impress her.

Barbara was busy washing clothes when he arrived, but she promised to accompany him to the dance.

Precisely at six o'clock he knocked at Jakob Haag's front door where Barbara awaited him in a dove blue dress. He held his breath when he saw her and stood up straighter. Suddenly he had second thoughts about taking her to an event where she might meet other young men. He had never felt about a girl like he felt about her. The thought elated and terrified him at the same time.

On the drive Barbara said, "Now that we're finally alone, tell me something about you."

"What?" Nikolaus said, dumbfounded.

"I want to know everything about you. I've told you so much about me, but I don't know much more than your name."

He obliged and told her of his childhood, his friendship with Martin, the deaths of his parents, and finally the immigration and the new beginning in America.

"Could you imagine going back to Germany?" asked Barbara after he had ended.

Nikolaus paused. "I don't believe so. Katrin and I did not make the decision to emigrate easily. If we had stayed in the Pfalz, we would not only have to go into service for a rich farmer, we wouldn't have a home anymore. And besides, I emigrated illegally. My family is here in Shiloh now, and I plan on staying here until they get tired of me. Of course, I sometimes get homesick, but there are many Palatines here and when we get together, we like to talk about old times."

They remained silent for a while. The clatter of hoofs and the creaking of the wagon were the only sounds that broke the silence of the night. Then Nikolaus asked, "What's your father's profession?"

"He's a baker and has three marriageable daughters."

"Are they all as pretty as you?"

"Both are prettier. I'm the oldest and most difficult of them. Helene, my middle sister, is engaged to a baker journeyman, but my parents didn't want her to marry until I had left the house. That's why I came to America. I wanted to take time to think about my future."

"Do you think you'll stay here?"

"I haven't made up my mind yet. I don't want to live off my uncle too long."

Nikolaus took a deep breath. "Could you imagine marrying me?" he blurted out. Had he really said that to a girl he barely knew?

Barbara gaped at him without uttering a word.

"My sister and my brother-in-law are the nicest people you could find anywhere," Nikolaus continued, desperate to make a good impression.

"I would like to meet them before I answer your question," Barbara said finally. "Maybe they won't like me at all and then there is nothing more to be said."

"Alright, I'll pick you up for dinner next Sunday."

"Why do you want to rush into things?" Barbara asked, sounding slightly irritated.

I would like to tie you to me before you meet another man whom you like more than me.

Barbara faced him. "I didn't come to America to allow other people to run my life. I thought I had made that very clear."

"Then I won't pick you up," Nikolaus pouted. This was not as easy as he had expected.

"I didn't mean it to sound like that. I just like to be asked."

* * *

At the meeting hall, Nikolaus introduced Barbara to all his friends and the evening passed with cheerful chats and dancing.

That night, Nikolaus lifted her off the wagon in front of her uncle's house and kissed her softly on the mouth. She did not shrink back, as he feared, but returned his kiss.

"I'll see you Sunday," she whispered and disappeared into the house.

At breakfast the next morning, Nikolaus wanted to announce the news, yet he could not utter a word. At last, while Katrin cleared the table, he muttered, "I think I may get married soon."

The cup Katrin held in her hand shattered on the pegboard floor while the whole family gawked at him. Katrin was the first one to speak again while picking up the pieces.

"My beautiful cup," she complained in feigned seriousness, "it's much too early in the morning for jokes."

"It's not a joke, I'm quite serious," her brother assured her.

"Is it the girl we saw at church?" Martin asked.

"Yes."

Nikolaus told them everything he knew about Barbara and closed with the remark, "Next Sunday, she will have dinner with us so she can meet you."

* * *

On Sunday morning, Nikolaus spent at least an hour washing, shaving, and putting on his Sunday best. Then he went into the kitchen to tyrannize Katrin. He moved furniture, straightened out potholders, and sorted kitchen tools and mugs by size. Finally, Katrin lost her patience.

"Out, or we won't have any dinner at all."

Nikolaus complied because it was time to drive to Shiloh by now. As they pulled up to the farm, he noticed a look of consternation on Barbara's face as she took in her surroundings.

He hastened to say, "Don't worry, it's not as lonely as it looks. We have plenty of friends now and drive to Shiloh almost every weekend."

During dinner, Barbara asked, "Isn't it difficult to manage a farm without the advice of an older adult?"

"No," Martin assured her, "Young people have to learn to live their life according to their own ideas. Besides, it helps a lot that Katrin and Nikolaus grew up on a farm. I could not manage without them."

While Barbara helped Katrin wash dishes, Katrin asked her, "Would you like to see our garden when we're done here?"

"Yes."

The young women strolled down the garden path, carefully holding up the bottoms of their dresses.

"Your garden looks as neat as any I've seen in Germany," Barbara said.

"Thank you," Katrin said. "Jim or Martin help me turn over the soil, but I do the rest of the work myself. I like watching things grow and I can keep an eye on Philip while I work. We all carry our load."

She studied Barbara's face and was pleased that the girl did not shrink back at the mention of work. She decided to probe carefully what her intentions were. "Will you and Nikolaus get married?"

"Did he tell you that?" Barbara said, her eyes betraying her astonishment.

Karin chuckled. "Yes, that's what he said the other day, but I'm afraid he hasn't asked you yet."

"He did ask me, but I wanted to meet his family first before I made a decision."

They had reached the honeysuckle fence and inhaled the beguiling scent.

"Is your father well off?" Katrin asked.

"No. He's a baker and is struggling to provide for my mother and my two sisters and me."

"That's good," Katrin said. "It is often better when a couple comes from the same social class. That was not the case with Martin and me. In Germany, his family would have never consented to our marriage but we both ended up in America where all class differences between us disappeared. I hope that you will be just as happy with Nikolaus as I am with Martin."

"Are you so sure that I will marry him?"

"Yes."

"I think you're right," Barbara said in a measured tone, "But you cannot guess the reason for my decision. When we were eating, I looked around the kitchen and the most astonishing thing I saw were books. They looked well-worn, as though someone were actually reading them. So, I said to myself: You won't fare badly in a house with books."

"It's true that the books are read," Katrin admitted. "On winter evenings Martin reads to us while we work. I have much mending and sewing to do while the men repair tools or do other chores. We don't have much time for reading, on the contrary. Whoever doesn't work doesn't get to eat."

Barbara laughed. "You can't scare me with that. I often got up at three o'clock in the morning to help my father in the bakery. Later, I stood in the store and sold the bread. No, I'm not afraid of work."

Katrin smiled, pleased with the answer. She liked Barbara already and looked forward to the prospect of having female company. Barbara had a pleasant personality, but there was a spirit about her that betrayed a trace of willfulness and determination. Nikolaus could fare much worse when it came to a partner. "Come, let's go back to the others."

* * *

An hour later, Barbara asked Nikolaus to drive her home. When they were about to leave, Cora begged until they allowed her to come along. She pushed herself between Nikolaus and Barbara and put her paws in Barbara's lap.

"See, she likes you too," Nikolaus said tenderly.

Barbara petted the dog and remained silent. Nikolaus wanted to ask the girl whether she had made a decision yet, but he shied away from it. If Barbara did not want to marry him, he would learn it soon enough. It was too much to ask for her to say yes after such a short time and he therefore decided to wait.

* * *

From then on, Nikolaus often visited Barbara at her uncle's house, but they were seldom alone with each other. It was autumn now and too dark and chilly to go for a walk in the evenings.

As they bid each other a good night at the front door several weeks after her visit to the farm, Barbara asked, "Aren't you curious to hear my answer to your proposal?"

"It depends," Nikolaus said, averting his eyes. "I wouldn't hold it against you if you turned me down. A pretty girl like you has enough opportunities to find a husband who doesn't live on a remote farm."

"But I'm not refusing you," Barbara said, laughing at his discomfort.

"Really?" Nikolaus could barely believe that his greatest wish was coming true. He secretly vowed that he would do anything to make this spirited girl happy. He wrapped his arms around her and kissed her tenderly on forehead, cheeks, and mouth.

"What do I do now?" he asked, still holding her tight. "Do I write to your father asking for your hand?"

Barbara quivered slightly.

"What's the matter? Are you cold? Did I say something wrong?"

"It isn't that. You just reminded me that I will never see my parents and sisters again."

"But you said yourself that you had difficulties at home."

"I still love my parents," Barbara insisted.

Nikolaus thought feverishly. "Would you like to visit them before we get married? I think I might just have enough money for the trip."

Barbara bit her lip but then shook her head vigorously.

"That's very generous of you, but I couldn't do that. Parting from them again would be too difficult. It's best if I stay here and get ready for the wedding."

"You can take your time," Nikolaus said dryly. "We won't be able to get married before next spring anyway."

"Why not?"

"Our little house is too small for all of us. We'll have to put an addition on it or build a cabin. Things are already getting tight. I'm sharing a room with Jim right now while Philip still sleeps with his parents."

* * *

The next morning, Nikolaus told his family of his plans. He was surprised to learn that Martin and Katrin had already discussed the space problem and had even drawn up a crude plan.

"Would you rather live in an annex or have your own house?" Katrin asked her brother.

"An annex may do. We could share the kitchen for eating and sitting room. I haven't asked Barbara yet, but I think she would like the company in winter when we're snowed in."

"Right after breakfast we'll go into the woods and pick the best trees," Martin said. "Let's hope we'll have a mild winter because we have a lot of work ahead of us."

"Before you begin building you have to harvest the corn," Katrin added.

"That goes without saying. The harvest comes first."

"Have any of you ever built a house?" she asked.

The three males looked at each other and shook their heads.

"I'm sure that our friends and their fathers will help us when the field work is done," Nikolaus said at last.

Then he studied the plan and said, "Do you think that two rooms are enough for us?"

"We'll share the kitchen and larder. Besides, the roof truss should be high enough that someone could sleep in the attic," Martin replied.

Chapter 43

When the annex was finished, Barbara and Nikolaus got married in the Shiloh church. Barbara's relatives had come from a nearby county and joined Nikolaus's friends at the place of worship.

After the ceremony, Nikolaus kissed Barbara in front of the applauding crowd. The party took place in Jakob Haag's lounge because it was bigger than any room at the farm.

The coffee table was already set when the hungry guests arrived at the shoemaker's house.

They ate and drank well into the night. Several of the women helped with the cooking and dishes, but Katrin was excused since she was the groom's sister.

"What a beautiful day," Katrin said to Martin after supper. "I hope we will live to see many more days like this. Wasn't it nice of Peter and Sabine to invite us to their wedding?"

She faltered when she noticed Martin's sad expression.

"What's the matter? Aren't you feeling well?" she inquired with a worried look in her eyes.

Martin shook his head. "I just thought of the past. Today, everything reminds me of Carolina's wedding. I had hired three Mackenbach musicians and she was immensely happy about it. It was the last time I saw her, and I wonder how she is doing now."

"Write to her, then you will know," Katrin suggested.

"Yes, I will. After all, I have much news and many blessings to share," he said while glancing with pride at his son who was seated at the children's table. The little boy already bore a more than fleeting resemblance to Martin's beloved grandfather.

216

It was long past midnight when the last guests drove home or settled on straw mattresses all over Haag's house. Martin sank on the wagon board and steered the wagon with its six passengers homeward. Jim had fed the animals in the evening before returning to Shiloh. The farmstead sat peacefully in the darkness of the March night when Martin turned into the farmyard.

"Welcome home," Nikolaus said to his young wife.

Jim wanted to help unharnessing the horse, but Martin turned him down.

"I'll take care of it. You must be dead tired."

Jim beamed and wished everybody a good night. Martin stared after him and shook his head.

"The boy is thankful for every good word," he said to Katrin. "I wonder what would have become of him if he hadn't found us. When I look at him, I always have the feeling that for once I have done something good in my life."

"You've done many things right, you pessimist. After all, you married me," Katrin replied, smiling mischievously. "Now, take care of the horse while I put Philip to bed. Tomorrow is another day."

* * *

During the same month, a court decision shook the Republican Party in its very foundations. It concerned the slave Dred Scott who had come into a slavery-free territory and, once there, sued for his release. The case proceeded all the way to the Supreme Court. Two days after the inauguration of President Buchanan, Supreme Court Judge Roger B. Taney of Maryland pronounced his verdict.

He decided that slaves had no civil rights and therefore could not sue before a federal court. Besides, according to the Constitution, Congress was not authorized to deny U.S. citizens their property without "due process." Dred Scott had been born a slave and therefore should remain one for the rest of his life.

Taney further remarked that the Missouri Compromise was unconstitutional, that slavery in the territories was indeed in accord with the U.S. Constitution and that no federal state had the right to free Negro slaves.

When Martin read these cruel words to his family, he closed his eyes in agony.

"How is it possible that a country with a liberal constitution approves such inhumanity?" he said with a trembling voice. "I immigrated to America because it seemed to be the paragon of freedom. But I fell out of the frying-pan into the fire."

Katrin and Nikolaus agreed with him, but the others gave him blank looks. Barbara had been in America for too short a time to understand the correlations and spoke only rudimentary English. Jim, an American by birth, had never uttered an opinion about the growing unrest over slavery. He was too busy with his own survival.

"What can you do about it?" Nikolaus asked with a shrug. "The rich always get their way. It's been like that forever."

Martin sighed. "You may be right. But there are thousands of people in the North who think like us. I joined the Republican Party because I believe that one day slavery will be completely abolished. What we need is a strong leader who will lead our movement to victory. I think that's why our revolution eight years ago foundered: we had rushed into it and did not have enough support from the conservative population. And we sorely lacked weapons. Some of us didn't even have pitchforks. The biggest mistake was made by our leaders, though: instead of marching to Frankfurt straight away we had to wait in Kaiserslautern until the Prussians arrived and then it was too late."

"Do you think there will be a war because of a few slaves?" Nikolaus asked, sounding incredulous.

"I hope not. I just wanted to say what could happen when the wrong men are at the top. And besides, they are not "a few slaves," there must be several millions."

For a moment, the room turned so silent that only the clicking of knitting needles could be heard.

"Cotton," Nikolaus said at last, "It's all cotton's fault. The planters fear for their wealth and are fighting with all their might against the abolition of slavery."

"And they do it even though cotton exhausts the soil," Martin added. "It would be far better if the fields lay fallow for several years. The planters overexploit nature and the consequences cannot be foreseen. The South has been sleeping for a long time, but one day there will be a rude awakening."

* * *

218

Soon after their conversation Martin had to pick up supplies at Wehre's store and returned with the mail and the newspaper. After dinner it grew quiet in the kitchen as everybody was reading letters, except for Jim, who busied himself feeding and petting Cora.

"My sister Helene has married her baker," Barbara said. "My mother is doing better and can now do all her housework. Father writes, 'We all miss you very much!'"

She dropped the letter and wiped away a tear.

"Aunt Minna and Uncle Sebastian are very pleased about your marriage," Katrin quoted from the letter she was studying with Nikolaus. "They only regret that they can't meet Barbara in person."

Katrin put the letter on the table and turned to Martin. "How is your sister doing?"

"She and the children are doing well. But her father-in-law passed away in October and now Ludwig has to manage the business by himself. My brother Karl is now an assessor at the county court in Rosenheim. He is engaged to the daughter of a prosecuting attorney from München. Not bad! He probably has a splendid career ahead of him while Joseph waits at home until my father gives up his reins."

Martin folded the letter and placed it back into the envelope. He was about to rise from his chair when Barbara asked everyone, "Do you ever get homesick?"

Katrin was the first to reply. "I often think of the friends I had back home and of the games we played as children. But I don't long for the life I would have to lead if I had stayed there."

"I miss the food most of all," Nikolaus said, earning laughter from everyone. "There is nothing like the bread we ate at home."

"True," Katrin admitted, "but our bellies are fuller here than they ever were at home."

Martin covered her hand with his. Ever more practical than Martin, she had pointed out what was most important for families like the Webers: to have enough to eat and a roof over their heads while leaving romantic notions of freedom and abolition to Martin and others like him. Martin still pondered such thoughts when he noticed Barbara's eyes on him.

"And you?" she probed. "Do you ever get homesick?"

"I sometimes get homesick for my childhood," he said. "the games I played with my friends and the walks I took with my grandpa. I hope we can give Philip such happy memories too."

Chapter 44

Autumn's fruit harvest was more plentiful than usual, and the dozen apple trees bent under their golden load.

"We can't possibly eat all our apples ourselves," Martin remarked one evening, "I think we should sell some apples at the market in St. Louis. Nikolaus, would you like to take Barbara and Jim to St. Louis next week?"

Jim's eyes grew wide. "Can I really come along?"

"Yes, it's time for you to see a city."

* * *

Over the next few days, the young farmers sorted apples and carefully packed dozens of eggs in straw-filled baskets.

At last, the wagon rolled off the farmyard in the early morning. Hours later Nikolaus parked the wagon at a creek and helped Barbara down. Her cheeks seemed less rosy to him than usual, but he attributed it to the bone-chattering drive over rutted roads. When they reached the Mississippi River, Nikolaus paid the ferryman sixty-two cents for the passage. During the crossing, the group marveled at the hustle and bustle of St. Louis since they had not seen a larger city than Belleville in years. At the wharf, Nikolaus met a driver of Eimer's Brewery who still recognized him. He had just unloaded a load of beer kegs destined for New Orleans. They chatted briefly and Nikolaus proudly introduced his wife before the driver drove off.

Nikolaus suggested finding a place to spend the night. Following Martin's description, he steered the wagon into Pine Street and the courtyard of Flaherty's Inn. Leaving Barbara and Jim to watch the load, Nikolaus went inside to look for Ray.

The Irishman and a young fellow were busy serving their thirsty customers. Nikolaus stepped to the counter and waited until Ray asked for his order.

"I'm Martin Dupree's brother-in-law," he introduced himself. "Do you have a room for my wife and I and a young man?"

"Of course," Flaherty assured him and shook his hand, beckoning top a young man. "Andreas, take your fellow German upstairs."

Raymond started toward the bar, but Nikolaus held him back. "We have a load of apples in the backyard. Where can we leave the wagon overnight, and what do I do with our horse?"

"The wagon can stay where it is because I'm locking the gate to the courtyard right now. The stable is right across the yard. There's plenty of water and hay for your horses."

Nikolaus thanked him and followed Andreas to the upper floor. He strode through the simply furnished room with two separate beds and looked down onto the gas-lit street.

"I'll take it," he said. "But first I want to take care of the horse."

* * *

Barbara, Nikolaus, and Jim entered the lounge, looked for a vacant table and ordered a supper of fried potatoes and pork chops. Nikolaus suppressed a chuckle as Jim shot shy glances at a young girl with auburn hair who sat at the neighboring table with her parents. It would not be much longer now until he might want to leave the farm and enter a profession that could support a family of his own.

Jim got up early the next morning to tend to the horse while Nikolaus and Barbara got washed and dressed.

At the breakfast table Jim bubbled over with excitement. "Can we take Kate to the market with us? Her parents have already agreed."

"Who's Kate?" Nikolaus asked, even though he already guessed the answer.

"I met her in the hallway and she's real nice. Please say yes."

"Alright, if her parents agree, she can come with us."

Despite the early hour, the streets of St. Louis bustled with activity. This late in the year, no more wagon trains gathered here for the long journey west. Instead, the streets teemed with farmers and their grain loads; horse carts on their way to the harbor; business travelers; and immigrants who had just arrived from Europe.

At the market, the young people set up their wares and waited for customers. By the time the midday sun warmed their backs they had sold a good part of their apples.

"Lunch break," Nikolaus exclaimed and lifted a wicker basket with their provisions from the wagon. Kate and Jim ate their lunch perched on overturned boxes and watched their display. Nikolaus and Barbara wanted to sit on the wagon seat, but when he helped her up she sank into his arms. Nikolaus's heart began to drum as he looked into her ashen face. Together with Jim he carried her into the shade on the other side of the wagon and opened the top buttons of her blouse. After several moments, Barbara opened her eyes.

"Are you feeling better now?" Nikolaus asked.

She nodded but still looked exhausted. Jim returned to their goods and his sandwiches while Nikolaus brought the basket to Barbara.

"Would you like to eat something?"

"Not now."

Growing increasingly worried, Nikolaus did not take his eyes away from her. Could she have the fever that was so common here? "What's wrong? Should I send Jim for a doctor?"

Color rose in Barbara's pale cheeks. "Nikolaus, I have to tell you something: I'm expecting a baby."

A weight of worry dropped from Nikolaus's chest. A baby? Was it just a year ago that he had been a lonely bachelor? And now he had a pretty wife and a child on the way. Life was indeed grand. He hugged Barbara and placed a tender kiss on her cheek.

"Why didn't you tell me that earlier?" he said. "Had I known this I would have never taken you on this trip."

"I didn't want to disappoint you and Jim. I felt fine until today, but the heat must have knocked me out."

"Stay here in the shade until we leave. We're almost sold out anyway."

Barbara nodded and closed her eyes.

Nikolaus returned to their display of apples and thoughtfully finished his sandwich. He would be a father soon and Philip would get a playmate. Katrin and Martin would be thrilled.

* * *

The next day Barbara was well enough to stroll the streets of St. Louis with Nikolaus. They paused in front of every store window, whether a barber shop, an apothecary, a bookstore or a watchmaker. Nikolaus was particularly interested in agricultural machinery. Barbara had to pull him away from the farming equipment to buy fabric and yarn for the baby; a bonnet; a few yards of lace and braid trimming; and other necessities.

When they spotted Jim and Kate across the street, Nikolaus said, "Poor boy. He's in love for the first time and has to leave her so soon."

"He'll get over it, he's young. I think we should go home tomorrow. The earlier we leave, the sooner he'll forget about her."

"Yes, I believe you're right."

Jim's face drooped when he learned of this plan during supper. All his pleas fell on deaf ears. Each day in St. Louis cost money that could not be retrieved by selling goods, Nikolaus explained to him.

* * *

As expected, Katrin and Martin were elated about Barbara's pregnancy. The women spent the winter and spring preparing for the baby's arrival by sewing and mending clothing that Philip had outgrown. Meanwhile, the men built a bed for Philip, whose crib was needed for the baby. Caught in the frenzy, the little boy darted from one adult to the other and enchanting them with his boisterous laughter.

Barbara gave birth to a healthy girl in the spring of 1858, and the proud parents named her Charlotte after Barbara's grandmother. Life on the Dupree farm became more frantic than ever that year.

Martin never lost sight of the outer world, though, and longed for taking part in it. Much as he loved his family, sometimes he yearned to escape the monotony of farm life. That year he would have an opportunity to do just that.

Chapter 45

1858

When the term of Illinois' Democratic senator Stephen Arnold Douglas expired, the Republican Party nominated Abraham Lincoln as their candidate, sparking a heated election campaign. For weeks, the two opponents fought verbal battles in six towns across Illinois.

Martin read and reread the newspaper that related Lincoln's speech during their first debate, in which he quoted a parable of Matthew 12:25, "A house divided against itself cannot stand. I believe this government cannot endure permanently half slave and half free. I do not expect the Union to be dissolved—I do not expect the house to fall—but I do expect it will cease to be divided. It will become all one thing, or all the other. Either the opponents of slavery will arrest the further spread of it, and place it where the public mind shall rest in the belief that it is in the course of ultimate extinction; or its advocates will push it forward, till it shall become alike lawful in all the states, old as well as new—north as well as south."

Douglas had countered that Lincoln wanted to unify the house against the will of many of its inhabitants. Lincoln retorted that the Republican Party did not intend to abolish slavery but hoped that it would confine itself to the original slave states again.

* * *

One day in October, Martin drove to Shiloh past a color palette of yellow and crimson trees. After looking in on Barbara's aunt and uncle, he stepped into Wehrle's store.

"Good day, Martin," said Friedrich Hecker from a corner. "I'm glad I met you here. My son Arthur and I are taking the train to Alton next week to hear one of the debates the whole country is talking about. You remember Mr. Lincoln from his visit in Belleville, don't you?"

"Of course I do," Martin said, stepping closer to his famous acquaintance.

"Would you like to come along with us?"

Martin rubbed his chin. "How long would I be gone?"

"The debate is on October 15, but we want to leave the day before to be sure we won't miss anything. So, we shouldn't be gone for more than three days."

"Can I think about it for a moment?"

"Yes, of course," Hecker said. "But please let me know before I leave here today."

Martin stepped toward the canning jars he was supposed to buy. There was plenty of work on a farm in autumn, to be sure, but he longed to see one of the great debates he had heard and read so much about. The newspapers related the speeches that the opposing candidates made about the subject of slavery. Slavery! It always came back to that. The wretched institution was beginning to tear the country apart at its seams. Katrin would understand that he did not want to miss this event. He stood up straight and strode over to Hecker.

"I'll come with you," Martin said.

"Good. We'll pick you up at daybreak next Thursday."

* * *

The overcrowded train sighed as it shuddered into the station at Alton, spewing out spectators into the cool autumn day. A friend of Hecker had arranged that he and his party could stay at the home of a business acquaintance, Mr. Beard, and that's where the weary travelers aimed their steps next. The following morning, the streets were choked with farm wagons and buggies. As Martin walked closer to the town center, the animated strains of a brass band kept rhythm with his steps. Dark clouds threatened rain as a procession of flag-bearers and drummers marched through town.

The festive atmosphere reminded Martin of the public assembly in Kaiserslautern that had aroused his youthful passion. Nine years older now, his ardor had not diminished over the years. On the contrary, his eagerness in a new cause had only increased since he had first shaken Mr. Lincoln's hand. *This time, we shall win.*

Martin wondered whether any of the onlookers who gathered in the streets today were Forty-Eighters. The number of beards and slouch hats told him it must be so. The Heckers wandered off to have a word with Mr. Lincoln while Martin and Mr. Beard ventured out into the throng.

Farmers and townspeople, newspaper reporters and slaveholders, Republicans and Democrats had traveled to Alton to hear the last of the now famous debates. The sidewalks resonated with Irish brogue and German tongues as well as Swedish singsong and the American English Martin had grown used to by now. Hecker and his son joined Martin and Mr. Beard at a predetermined spot before the speeches began.

At last, Senator Stephen A. Douglas addressed the crowd of thousands from the balcony of Town Hall. From the beginning, Martin took a dislike to the stocky, white-haired senator. He had never seen a duke or king in person, but the mannerisms of this haughty politician reminded him of tales he had heard about European princes. The senator's voice sounded hoarse as he once again stressed that each state should have the right to decide whether to allow slavery or not.

"Our Government can endure forever, divided into free and slave states as our fathers made it, each state having the right to prohibit, abolish or sustain slavery, just as it pleases," Douglas stressed repeatedly. "But the moment the North obtained the majority in the House and Senate by the admission of California, and could elect a president without the aid of Southern votes, that moment ambitious Northern men formed a scheme to excite the North against the South, and make the people be governed in their votes by geographical lines, thinking that the North, being the stronger section, would outvote the South, and consequently they, the leaders, would ride into office on a sectional hobby. I am told that my hour is out. It was very short."

The audience erupted in cheers when Abraham Lincoln rose. Like the keep of a medieval castle, the former rail-splitter towered above the crowd. This was a man of the people who had worked the land just as his listeners did day after day. Where his opponent had relied on theatrical gestures and vanity to convince the spectators of his greatness, Lincoln exuded self-assurance by his very presence.

Even from a distance, Martin could feel the earnestness in the deep-set eyes he had once seen up close. They had made a lasting impression on him. Today, he was not the only man who hung on every word the lanky politician spoke.

"That is the real issue," Lincoln emphasized. "That is the issue that will continue in this country when these poor tongues of Judge Douglas and myself shall be silent. It is the eternal struggle between these two principles—right and wrong—throughout the world. They are the two principles that have stood face to face from the beginning of time; and will ever continue to struggle. The one is the common right of humanity and the other the divine right of kings. It is the same principle in whatever shape it develops itself. It is the same spirit that says, 'You work and toil around and earn bread, and I'll eat it.'"

When the last applause subsided and the spectators dispersed to the taverns, hotels, and stores, Hecker asked, "Well, Martin, what do you think?"

"I think that, if ever a man will put an end to slavery, Mr. Lincoln is that man," Martin replied with sincerity.

Hecker nodded. "It appears so, even if he insists that he doesn't want to abolish slavery, only to contain it. Moreover, he does not seem to care how many enemies he makes in the process."

* * *

In November, Martin waited anxiously for the newspaper that announced the results of the election. Although he had seemed to win the debates against his opponent, Abraham Lincoln lost the senate race against Stephen A. Douglas. Yet, no one could deny that Lincoln had won the popular vote and that his political star was rising. Despite his disappointment, Martin was convinced that he had not seen the last of Mr. Lincoln yet.

Chapter 46

1859

Martin, Katrin, and Jim dressed in their Sunday best to attend the Schiller Festival in Belleville. Too young to come along, Philip looked forward to spending the night at the Kolb farm.

"Are you sure you would rather stay home?" Martin asked his sister-in-law for the last time.

"Yes, Charlotte has a slight fever," Barbara replied.

"Couldn't your aunt watch her for a day?"

Barbara's eyebrows rose with her voice. "I'm not a bad mother."

Martin plowed his fingers through his hair, wishing he could take back his words. He had not meant to upset her. "I just wanted you to have some amusement."

"I know," she said, her voice softened now, "have a good time."

"What's keeping you?" Jim called from the wagon seat where he sat next to Katrin. Martin lifted Philip up and climbed on the wagon, adjusted his slouch hat and let Jim have the reins. As they approached Belleville, more and more wagons closed in on them.

Much had changed in the appearance of the town since Martin had first arrived in Belleville. Office buildings occupied once empty lots along Main Street. The corner of North High Street and East Main Street had once housed a small blacksmith shop. Now, the massive Thomas House stood in its place, rising four stories high and stretching a whole block.

Driving further, they reached Public Square with its two-story courthouse. A smile crept over Martin's face when he remembered the two significant events in his life that had taken place in the courthouse: his wedding and his citizenship oath ceremony.

Jim parked the wagon on a side street, set the brake and hung a fodder bag around the horse's neck. Foliage and German flags adorned all houses along the parade route. Despite the early hour, the citizens of Belleville promenaded through the streets in their finery, often stopping to greet acquaintances.

Martin, Katrin and Jim entered the National Hotel and sat down at an empty table.

"Good morning, Katrin," called Sabine from the back, where she sat with Peter and her sister. The Dupree family joined them in a lively conversation about the upcoming festive ball.

At dinnertime, Martin, Katrin, and Jim savored juicy pork chops before heading for Public Square to watch the parade. The square swelled over with people and Martin often came to a halt to greet friends. It seemed as if everybody in the county had come to Belleville on this Sunday. The German population in particular never missed an opportunity to celebrate.

A trumpeter and a vanguard of four men led a parade of riflemen, singers, and musicians. At the conclusion of the parade, Lieutenant Governor Gustav Körner gave a speech in which he urged the German settlers to preserve their cultural heritage and to keep the memories of their homeland alive.

"I thought we came here today to observe Friedrich Schiller's birthday," Martin complained, shaking his head. "But I can't recall hearing his name more than two or three times."

"They could have made a bigger effort," Katrin admitted. "But you know that Germans like to celebrate, no matter what the occasion."

"Did you have a good time?" Friedrich Hecker asked as he and his wife approached.

"We'll go to Körner's house now and wait until the ball begins. Will you join us?"

"I don't think so," Martin said. "We're not invited."

"That doesn't matter. There will be so many people that nobody should notice a few more."

Martin searched in Katrin's face for her approval.

"Very well, we'll come with you," he said.

"Wait, I'll fetch the wagon," Jim said and hurried away.

Körner's white-washed, two-story brick house stood at the corner of Abend Street and Mascoutah Avenue. A long balcony created a covered porch in the back of the house. Martin cringed when he parked his wagon behind the fine carriages that lined the roadside. Despite his upbringing in a prosperous family he felt out of place among strangers, especially when they were leaders in the community and beyond.

He took a deep breath as he entered the house together with Katrin and the Heckers. Martin recognized the host, who was moving around greeting his guests. He had only spoken with Körner once when he had attended the celebration of Belleville's town charter with Anna. As expected, the politician did not remember Martin when Hecker introduced him.

"Let's go into the garden," Katrin suggested after the host moved on. "It's crowded in here and the weather outside is so beautiful."

Several people were already strolling through the garden, where a maid served raspberry juice and cookies.

The young servant handed them refreshments and asked, "You're from the western Palatinate, aren't you?"

"Yes," Martin replied, "I'm from Landstuhl and my wife comes from Moorbach."

A smile crept over the maid's face. "Then we are from the same county. My name is Hildegard."

Pleased to meet someone from home, Katrin chatted with Hildegard when she was not busy.

"Do you get homesick often?"

The maid sighed. "Yes, sometimes. Once a week, I get together with several other Palatine girls who are in service. It is nice to speak in my dialect."

"It gets easier after a while. At least you have found friends," Katrin assured her, thinking back to the lonely time she had spent in Cincinnati. *I am so lucky to have a loving family and plenty of food to eat every day. What more could I ask for in life?*

* * *

The evening ball took place at the brightly lit City Park Hall. Gentlemen dressed in tailcoats and suits were accompanied by ladies in beautiful robes of tulle and silk.

"Oh, Martin," Katrin whispered, "I feel shabby in my dress."

Martin suppressed a smile. "But this is just the second time you're wearing it."

A seamstress in Belleville had sewn the forest-green dress with its tight bodice, long sleeves, and flowing, ankle-length skirt for Nikolaus and Barbara's wedding. Katrin had opted not to bow to the fashion of hoopskirts since they were impractical when one traveled on a wagon. Instead, she had draped her dress over a couple of petticoats. Martin had ordered himself a new midnight blue suit and Jim a gray outfit on the same occasion.

Martin could therefore not understand Katrin's reservations. He thought his wife looked enchanting in her new ensemble.

He beamed and linked arms with her as they entered the ballroom. They stood near the entrance when Jim cried, "Look, I see Peter, Sabine, and Marie."

They rejoined their friends while Martin looked around the ballroom. Flower bouquets adorned each table and the band on the platform seemed to drown in a sea of flowers.

When the first tunes of a waltz resonated through the hall, Martin led his wife to the dance floor.

"I hope Jim doesn't get too bored tonight," Katrin said.

Martin laughed. "I doubt it. He's already dancing with Marie over there."

A smile played around Katrin's mouth. "Do you think he'll find a nice girl and get married someday?"

"Well, the only reason he may not get married is that he likes too many girls."

"I believe Jim will have an easier time in life than we did. You and I made our lives unnecessarily difficult before we finally got married."

"We sure did," Martin agreed. "If you and Nikolaus had not been forced to leave home, then I would be living on my farm like a hermit. And all because we come from different backgrounds. Jim should be spared such a fate. He's an American through and through and class differences don't exist for him. He will probably leave us soon and I'm happy for every day he is still with us. I love Jim like a younger brother, and he has considered us his family for quite some time."

After the music ended, they took their seats again and drank to each other's health. During the evening, Katrin danced with Jim and Peter, but most of all she danced with Martin.

* * *

While Martin joined an acquaintance at the bar, Katrin watched the dancers. She flinched when she detected Anna, Martin's old girlfriend, dancing with a man in his late twenties. Not far from his daughter, Wilhelm Ruppelius whirled his wife over the parquet. After the music ended, he led his wife to her seat and approached Katrin to greet her. Katrin's back stiffened as she placed her palm into the book dealer's outstretched hand.

"Well, well, I do believe you're Martin's little girlfriend."

Katrin averted her eyes. "We have been married for quite a while and have a son."

"I'm happy for you. Our Anna, on the other hand, has not had much luck with her first husband. As a lieutenant in the US Army, he spent most of his time in the West while Anna lived all alone in St. Louis. When he drowned in the raging waters of the Missouri River two years ago, she came back to live with us. Four months ago, she remarried and this time she seems to fare better. Her husband is an insurance agent, and they live here in Belleville, so she is always close to us."

Katrin suppressed the jealousy that arose within her. *It must be nice to still have parents to go back to. But I should not complain. I have so much to be thankful for.*

* * *

Katrin stared at the center piece when Martin returned.

"What's the matter?" he asked.

"Oh, it's nothing. I just realized that people who seem to have everything going for them often have the biggest worries."

She told him of her conversation with Ruppelius.

"It wasn't my fault," Martin said. "Even if I had wanted to marry Anna, she is not cut out to be a farmer's wife. And you and I, we are very happy together. Aren't we?"

"Of course we are."

Katrin's gaze floated through the room. "I believe this is the first time we've gone to a ball without Nikolaus." She sighed. "I'm getting worried about Charlotte. I think we better drive home now."

"Very well, it is rather late."

They found Jim in a cozy lounge. A group of young men sat at a round table, each with a full glass of lager in front of him. The merry group sang one drinking song after the other and Jim sang the loudest.

"Do we have to go home already?" Jim asked.

"Yes," Katrin replied, "I have a hunch that Barbara and Nikolaus need us."

Chapter 47

Their wagon turned into the barnyard when they recognized a lone figure at the fence gate.

"There you are, finally," Nikolaus said with a croaking voice. "The baby has a high fever. We have to go fetch a doctor right away."

"I'll do it," Jim offered.

While Katrin and Nikolaus hurried into the house, Martin unharnessed Lisa and led her into the stable where Jim saddled Grete.

"Do you know where Doctor McGregor lives?" Martin asked.

"I believe so," Jim replied and swung himself over the saddle.

"Tell him to hurry."

Martin stood in the farmyard and stared at the starry sky, afraid to enter the house. Just a few hours ago, he had twirled his wife around a dance floor. Was this a punishment for a rare night of amusement? A great horned owl hooted in the distance, making Martin shiver. It was the loneliest cry he had ever heard. At last he bowed his head in resignation and stepped over the threshold.

The little girl's condition was indeed serious. Barbara's ashen face spoke volumes about the agony the young parents had experienced. Nikolaus placed a hand on her shoulder and urged her to lie down. Katrin joined her brother at his child's bed and put cool compresses on the forehead of the screaming baby. Feeling useless in the house, Martin trudged to the barn to take care of the horse and livestock. He was still there when Doctor McGregor appeared.

He examined Charlotte thoroughly and motioned Katrin aside.

"I don't want to upset the mother. The child has severe pneumonia which can be very dangerous at his age. Does she eat?"

"My sister-in-law has tried several times to feed her mash, but she doesn't keep any food in. She also hasn't been drinking for hours," Katrin said.

"See to it that she will take in some liquid," McGregor said.

He gave Katrin some instructions and filled out a prescription.

"I'll stop by tomorrow morning again," he promised before he drove away in his buggy.

Martin sent Jim to bed, gave Grete some water and rode to Belleville. At the apothecary's store, Martin jumped off the horse and thudded at the door several times. No one answered.

It occurred to him that the apothecary might be at the ball and he remounted to hurry to the theater. He asked everywhere for Mr. Kempf, hoping to find the apothecary reasonably sober. He finally located Kempf in the same lounge where they had found Jim a few hours before. The bearded apothecary, while not entirely clear-headed, seemed capable of understanding his plea. Martin explained the urgency of his errand to Kempf and the two rushed away.

Meanwhile, Barbara and Nikolaus had fallen asleep from exhaustion while Katrin sat up with Charlotte. At the sight of Martin, her face brightened for a moment.

"I'm glad that you're back," she whispered. "Did you get the medicine?"

"Yes."

While taking off his jacket, Martin's eyes met Katrin's. He saw naked fear in them.

"Do you think. . ." he stammered, "Do you think she will not come through?"

She slumped her shoulders in resignation.

"I'm going to make some mush," she said. "The doctor said the medicine is very bitter and I should mix it with mush."

It took two attempts for the girl to take the mixture. A few minutes later she vomited everything. Katrin picked up the dirty pillow, changed the cover and put the pillow back under Charlotte's burning head. Then she sank on a chair and wept.

"What should we do? What are we to do if she doesn't even take the medicine?"

Martin, who was himself fatigued and at a loss, approached her and put his hands on her shoulders to calm her.

"Maybe we should give her the medicine without mush?" he murmured.

"I'll do that. What can it matter now?"

She dripped the remedy onto a spoon and gave it to Charlotte, expecting her to get sick again. This time she kept it in, and her uncle and aunt exchanged glances of relief. Martin pulled up a chair for himself because he was exhausted from the events of the night. They sat together until early morning when Katrin climbed on unsteady feet to their bedroom. She returned with a bundle of sheets draped over her arm.

"Let's wet a sheet and hang it over her crib. Perhaps she might be able to breathe easier that way."

When Nikolaus and Barbara rose, they were despondent over the unchanged condition of their child. They took turns caring for Charlotte while Martin and Katrin ate a hasty breakfast. Unable to remain on their feet any longer, they climbed to their bedroom, but sleep eluded them for a while.

"I feel it is our fault that Charlotte is so ill," Katrin said with a trembling voice. "If we hadn't gone to the festival, then Barbara and Nikolaus wouldn't have been alone, and we could have fetched the doctor sooner."

Martin cradled her in his arm, comforted by her warmth. He was also tortured by such thoughts.

"Oh, Martin, I'm so scared. These last few years we have been as content as anyone can be and I have always wondered what I have done to deserve this. What are we going to do if Charlotte does not survive? I don't know if Nikolaus and Barbara can endure the pain. I fear for our future."

"Haven't we suffered enough?" Martin said after pondering her words. "We have lost our parents and our homeland. We should not give up hope yet. As long as you and I are together, nothing will happen to us. Our love will give us the strength to endure anything. Do you believe that?"

Katrin looked up at him with tear-filled eyes and said, "Yes, I believe you."

Her lips briefly touched his before she turned over to sleep. Unable to ignore the sunshine that intruded through the drawn curtains, Martin lay quietly on his back and brooded. He was now preoccupied with the somber thoughts he had tried to dispel in Katrin. The illness that had descended on the small family without warning oppressed him like a nightmare.

Would they be punished now for being so happy the last few years? Was this the beginning of a streak of misfortunes? And Philip? Would he become ill, too? He played with Charlotte every day, after all.

I have a right to some amusement just like everybody else. Things were different when I lived in Belleville, but here on the farm there is always so much to do that one doesn't have much time to visit friends, another voice within him said.

The next few days taxed the strengths of the entire family. Jim completed most of the chores while Martin asked the Kolbs to take care of Philip until Charlotte was out of danger. Because Katrin was needed at home, Martin visited his young son every day, well aware that Philip had narrowly avoided a severe illness.

Finally, after a week of exhaustive care Charlotte's fever dropped and she began to breathe easier. Barbara cried tears of relief when her baby smiled at her at last.

Chapter 48

1860

In early May, Martin drove to the mill in Mascoutah. While he waited for his order to be ground, he stopped by the store and happened upon Friedrich Hecker.

"Good thing I've run into you," he said to Martin. "Tomorrow I'll take a train to Chicago to attend the Republican Party convention. We will nominate a candidate for the presidential elections in November. Do you want to come along?"

"How long would the trip take?"

"Well, I reckon I'll be back in eight to ten days."

Martin scratched his head, sorely tempted. "I don't think I can get away for such a long time. We have so much work at the moment that we all have to lend a hand."

"That's a pity, I would have loved to take you along," Hecker said. "I have always hoped to stir your interest in politics."

"You have, but unfortunately I don't have the time to be absent for more than a week," Martin hastened to say. "Please let me know if I can help in any other way."

Hecker pursed his lips. "There is one thing you could do. You could impress upon all your friends to vote for the Republican Party."

"But most of my acquaintances aren't even American citizens yet and aren't allowed to vote," Martin objected.

"Then convince them to become naturalized."

"I'll do that."

"I have to go now. When I come back, I'll tell you all about the convention. Auf Wiedersehen, my friend!"

* * *

Martin did not have to wait for Hecker's return to learn the results of the party convention. The newspaper indicated that Abraham Lincoln had been nominated as their presidential candidate after days of debating. The lawyer from Springfield who had spent his whole life at the frontier and had not even enjoyed an education won with the image of 'Old Abe—the rail-splitter.' With these qualifications he projected the vision of a man of the people.

He owed his nomination above all to the German-Americans who supported him in order to protect their own interests. Martin had even heard rumors that Lincoln had bought the *Illinois Staatszeitung* to promote his agenda. The Germans were firm in their demands: 1.) the party program was to oppose slavery; 2.) the party should pass more liberal naturalization laws; 3.) the generous Homestead Act should be passed through Congress—and would therefore be beneficial to German settlements in the West; and 4.) that Kansas was accepted into the Union as a free state. The Republican Party submitted to these requests to secure the German votes needed for a victory.

* * *

During the fall, Martin rode over the rutted country roads around Shiloh whenever his time allowed.

"There he goes again," Nikolaus said, shaking his head. "Good thing I'm here to do his chores for him."

"Leave him be," his sister scolded him. "Without him, we wouldn't have a farm at all. Have you ever considered what would have become of us then? Politics are in his blood and there's nothing we can do about it. He has promised Friedrich Hecker to round up support for the Republican Party in the coming election, and Martin keeps his word."

And it keeps him from getting too restless.

"Well, I hope he doesn't cause any bad blood among our friends," Nikolaus said, rising from the table.

"No. Three people have already joined the Republican Party since he started his rounds."

"There's one person he will never convince to join."

Katrin turned away from the sink where she was washing dishes. "Even if you aren't interested in politics, someday they will catch up with you and you'll have to take a stand, whether you want to or not."

With a dismissive wave of his hand, Nikolaus stepped over the threshold. "Until then, I will tend to the farm and livestock, as usual."

Katrin gawked after him. Sometimes she wondered how Martin and Nikolaus had ever become friends. Her brother was a good farmer, though, and a great help to Martin. If only Nikolaus could be an equal conversation partner to his brother-in-law. . .

* * *

Nikolaus even stayed home when Carl Schurz, the German revolutionary and lawyer, visited Belleville to campaign for Lincoln. Katrin and Philip accompanied Martin to town to listen to their compatriots Schurz and Hecker. Wagons, carriages, and buggies clogged the streets as Martin steered the wagon toward the center of Belleville. Banners and wreaths hung from all buildings, houses, and stores while a brass ensemble blared out German marches. Cannons boomed as town officials and maidens in white dresses crowded around the platform from where the two German politicians would speak.

"Oh, wasn't it exciting?" said Katrin on their way home. "I haven't seen so many people since the Schiller festival last year."

"The speeches were very moving and I'm glad that we went," replied Martin.

"Did you notice how gray Hecker's hair has become since we last saw him?" Katrin rambled on. "Why, his beard is almost white now."

Secretly, she was glad that Martin had refrained from growing a full beard like most Germans had. He only wore a mustache that was as black as his hair.

* * *

Martin anxiously awaited the weekly trip to the general store to pick up mail and the newspaper. Finally, the papers announced that Abraham Lincoln had won the election.

News of the electoral results had scarcely reached Shiloh Valley when the farmers began to host victory parties. Martin and Katrin were among the many settlers who invited guests to a celebration on the Sunday after the newspaper announcement. Jakob and Amalie Haag came as well as Peter and Sabine with their little boy.

Martin had purchased a demijohn of wine and Katrin and Barbara cooked a typical Palatine meal: pork roast with sauerkraut.

"You're a good cook, Katrin," Peter said, licking his lips. "Your food tastes just like home."

Everybody understood that by "home" he did not mean his parents' home in Shiloh Valley but the Palatinate. Martin raised his glass and declared, "A toast to Abraham Lincoln."

"Long live Lincoln!" the company replied.

They sat together all afternoon, chatting about their families and the old homeland. At last, Martin and Nikolaus were urged to sing Hecker songs. When the last drop of wine was gone, their guests finally headed home.

* * *

Christmas was barely over when Barbara and Nikolaus drove to Shiloh to visit her uncle and aunt. Before heading home, they stopped at Jakob Wehrle's store to buy staples and thread.

Wehrle stood behind the counter, engaged in an agitated conversation with three men. With strained ears, the couple approached the group.

"Did anything happen?" Nikolaus asked the man closest to him.

"Yes. South Carolina has seceded from the Union."

"It's true. I heard it from a peddler who delivered merchandise this morning," Wehrle added.

"What does that mean for us?" Nikolaus asked.

One of the three men fixed his eyes on him. "It means that there may be a war soon."

Barbara's hand touched her lips as she suppressed a cry. She and Nikolaus finished their shopping, picked up a newspaper and hurried home to tell Martin the news.

* * *

Martin's face drained of all color as he listened to their report. He knew from Wilhelm Ruppelius's history lessons that more than one state had threatened to secede before. Besides, there had been several attempts for the foundation of independent states; the Giessen Society strove for it in Arkansas and Brigham Young and his Mormons in Utah. But so far, no state had taken the final step of secession.

This situation was unprecedented for the United States and Martin felt a growing sense of dread with each passing day. Wasn't this situation similar to the uprising in the Palatinate and Baden? And yet, the southern states were not occupied by the army of another state as was the case in his Fatherland.

By February, the cotton states had declared their secession from the Union. President James Buchanan could not prevent the schism since the constitution granted this right to the states. On February 4, 1861, the renegades founded the alliance of the "Confederate States of America." As president they elected Jefferson Davis, a planter from Mississippi.

* * *

It was a winter like no other before on the Dupree farm. A breathless suspense seized the young immigrants, Martin in particular. Sensing his uneasiness, Philip followed his father everywhere. His presence calmed Martin and he patiently answered Philip's questions while allowing him to perform simple chores.

When the weather allowed it, they drove or sledded to Shiloh to pick up their mail and to catch the latest news at Wehrle's store. They eagerly questioned the storekeeper about information from the outside world. One day, Martin received a letter from his sister Carolina.

"What is she writing?" Katrin asked after Martin had finished reading.

"My brother Karl is dead," Martin said with a flat voice. "He fell off his horse while on a ride. Three days later he died without ever regaining consciousness."

"I'm sorry," Barbara said. "I would feel awful if one of my sisters died."

Martin placed the letter on the table and began pacing the kitchen. "Strange, the longer I live here, the less I am interested in my family's lives—with the exception of Carolina. Mother is dead and my father never writes to me. You are my family now and I feel happier in this little house than in a large estate with many servants."

Martin avoided Katrin's gaze as he paced the room. She was the only person who knew how hurt he had been when his older brothers had belittled him and excluded him from their adventures. Carolina was closest to him in age and it had seemed natural to play with her instead. After she was sent away to school, he had become close to his grandfather, who had given him the attention he had craved. Together they had roamed the hills and woods near home, creating memories he would cherish forever.

* * *

Martin was well aware how fortunate he was. Neither he and Katrin, nor Nikolaus and Barbara had parents or parents-in-law who told them how to operate their farm and run their lives. Without the reluctance of the older generation, it was easy to adopt new methods on the Dupree farm.

Martin's biggest concern was Jim. When the two were mucking out the barn, Martin used the opportunity to talk with the boy.

"Listen, Jim," he began. "I know that life can be monotonous out here, especially in winter. I've been watching you for a while and feel that you are not entirely happy. You probably feel like the fifth wheel among us two couples. If you want to look for a job in town where you can meet more young people, I won't stop you."

Jim let go of his pitchfork and fixed his sad eyes on Martin. "Aren't you satisfied with my work anymore? Do you want me to leave?"

"I don't want you to go away," Martin hastened to say. "You're like family to us. That's why it saddens me when you're unhappy. When I came to America, I was miserable because I didn't know anyone. Finally, I came to Belleville because there are many Germans here and I was hoping to make friends. As you can see, my wish has been granted. Many Americans have the false opinion that happiness equals wealth and power. They're mistaken, because I come from a rich family, but I was not happy because I had not found my place in life yet. Besides, I was in love with a girl who was promised to another man. Are you lovesick?"

Jim bowed his head. "Quite frankly, I've never been able to forget Kate."

"Kate? Who is Kate?"

"She's an Irish girl I met in St. Louis when I was there with Barbara and Nikolaus."

"But she may be married by now," Martin said.

Jim's eyes grew wide. "She wasn't more than fourteen or fifteen years old."

"Well, then you may stand a chance," Martin said with the trace of a smile. "But before you make any plans to go to St. Louis, I advise you to wait until the political situation has calmed down."

"Alright, I'll wait." Jim picked up his fork. "I'm glad we had this talk."

* * *

Deep in his heart, Martin was glad that he had persuaded Jim not to travel to St. Louis because times were indeed troublesome. The question had arisen in the border states whether they should side with the Confederates or the Union.

Such was the case in Missouri, which was officially a slave state. The German population of St. Louis firmly rejected slavery while a large part of Missouri's inhabitants wanted the state to remain neutral. It was therefore no surprise that the Unionists were recruiting militia companies among the Germans in St. Louis during the winter. These companies were drilled in the halls of the turners. Both parties—the Unionists and the Secessionists—kept a watchful eye on the US arsenal, where 60,000 muskets, 1.5 million cartridges, and a number of old-fashioned cannons and lathes were stored.

* * *

On March 4, 1861, Abraham Lincoln assumed office as President of the United States. Martin joined a throng of excited farmers at the general store to buy the newspaper with details of the event. The sun had dipped low on the horizon when Martin finally reached the farm. After supper, he read the inaugural address out loud. The new president stressed once again that he did not want to abolish slavery but wanted to restrict it to the original states. Furthermore, he expressed the opinion that the union of the United States was permanent and that it required the consent of all members to dissolve this union. *If anyone can solve this thorny problem, it will be Mr. Lincoln.*

But the Confederates turned a deaf ear to all his assurances. Just a few days after the inauguration, Jefferson Davis had assembled one hundred thousand volunteers under his flags. More and more southern states joined the Confederacy until the federal flag fluttered only above Fort Sumter, a fortress in the Charleston harbor.

On April 12, the Confederates began to bomb Fort Sumter. After a thirty-hour long, bloodless battle the garrison's soldiers had to lower the federal flag and leave the fortress by sea. *Even a lumberjack in the woods must know that the country is headed toward a civil war*, Martin thought glumly.

The very same day, Lincoln asked the federal states to supply a militia contingent of 75,000 men for the duration of ninety days. Lincoln had to rely on the volunteers since the federal army only consisted of 16,000 men, who were needed elsewhere. In response to the mobilization, Virginia, North Carolina, Tennessee, and Arkansas declared their withdrawal from the Union.

Chapter 49

Martin, Nikolaus, and Jim were working in the field when a small group of horsemen approached them. As they came across the field, Martin recognized Friedrich Hecker as the first rider.

"*Guten Morgen*, Martin," Hecker greeted him. "We came to invite you for a ride. The turners of St. Louis want to occupy the federal arsenal and have asked us for support. Are you with us?"

Martin did not have to think about it long.

"Very well," he said, shouldering his hoe. "I'll be ready in a short while."

He found Katrin alone in the kitchen and told her the news. Dropping her cooking spoon on the floor, she whirled around to face him, her face ashen.

"Make a few sandwiches for me; I'll pack my bag in the meantime," Martin said without concealing his excitement as he climbed the stairs to the bedroom. When he stood before her with the leather bag slung over his shoulder, she could not hold back her tears.

"Oh, Martin," she cried, "do you really have to go?"

He embraced her with his muscular arms. "Don't worry about me. You'll see, I'll be back soon."

He kissed Katrin one more time and stepped out onto the farmyard. Philip came running from the chicken coop and Martin tousled his son's hair before he saddled his horse. As the group rode off, Martin forced himself not to look back even though he knew that Katrin and Philip stood on the porch gazing after him. It was the first time in their marriage that Martin had left his wife for more than three days. The further he went away from home the more his heart pounded in anticipation of the adventures that lay ahead.

Martin recognized Hecker's son Arthur from the trip to Alton. The other two men were Jakob Stuhlfauth and Daniel Wagner, two farmers of New Baden. In Belleville, another half dozen turners joined the group at the station where they left their horses behind and boarded the train. Hecker's farmhand would take the horses back to their homes.

St. Louis revealed an unfamiliar image to its defenders: instead of the usual crowds of immigrants, travelers and merchants, the streets were teeming with militia soldiers, turners in their club uniforms, and federal soldiers. Some storekeepers had even boarded up their shop windows to protect them from destruction.

Hecker led his companions to the hall of a turner club whose president he knew personally. When they entered the hall, a unit of turners performed a drill under a lieutenant's command. A small man with black hair, a goatee, and mustache sat next to the door.

"Franz," Hecker cried and shook his fellow countryman's hand. Then he put a hand on Martin's shoulder and led him to the stranger.

"May I introduce Franz Sigel to you?" Hecker said.

Martin extended his hand to Sigel while scrutinizing the famous revolutionary. Sigel's eyes faced different directions, which lent a strange expression to his countenance.

"Martin was a rebel in the Palatine revolution of 1849," Hecker told his friend, then addressed Martin. "You probably know that Sigel was the general of the Baden rebels before he was relieved by General Mieroslawski."

So that's what a man looks like who took part in two revolutions and failed both times. Here we stand, three failures, remnants of a long-forgotten rebellion, and are preparing for a new war. Will the upcoming clash finally end in a victory for us? Martin tried to wipe those gloomy ideas away. *This time, everything will be different. This time, millions are standing behind us and we have money, provisions, and weapons.*

Weapons? Martin recalled that he carried nothing on him but a pocketknife. He had left the hunting rifle at home so that his family could fend for themselves. At last, he faced Hecker who was engaged in a lively conversation with Sigel.

"Where did the turners get their weapons?" he asked.

"Most of them have brought them from home. When they're finished with their drills you may ask one of them whether he can get a musket for you. You know how to shoot, don't you?"

"Of course," Martin replied and treaded off to find a turner.

Soon he was in possession of a musket, some ammunition, and a sack of straw which he dropped in the quietest corner of the gymnasium. Exhausted from the journey, he ate only one slice of bread before dropping on the straw. He soon fell asleep and did not wake up until a turner dressed in white exclaimed, "Come on, get up."

It was long before daylight and Martin wondered what was so important in the middle of the night. He did not need to wait long for an answer because the news spread like a wildfire.

"The time has finally come. We are to occupy the arsenal!"

Martin learned from Stuhlfauth that Sigel and Hecker would each assume command of a Home Guard regiment and that he and Stuhlfauth belonged to Hecker's regiment. After a hasty breakfast, the Germans marched across town to the federal arsenal. Other regiments joined them on the way, and they all passed the gates of the arsenal unchecked by the militia. Inside the fence, the Home Guard fell into line in regiments and sentries were detailed. Captain Nathaniel Lyon, the commander of the few federal troops who had so far guarded the ammunition depot, greeted the Home Guard warmly.

During the following days, Martin's routine consisted of two hours' guard duty and four hours' rest. The German brewers in town sent a fresh supply of beer every day and the turners' songs filled the night air.

Three days after they marched into the arsenal, Lyon ordered his soldiers to load all available wagons with weapons and ammunition and drive them to the ferry mooring. All in all, he was able to slip 30,000 muskets and 10,000 pounds of powder over to Illinois to arm their volunteer regiments.

Martin was among the escorts who guarded the wagons on their way through town under cover of darkness. Even though he kept a watchful eye on his surroundings he enjoyed the march like an unexpected outing. Contrary to expectations, the secessionists kept quiet.

The longer the defenders of the armory had to wait, the more restless Martin and the others grew. He wondered whether he had made the right decision in following Hecker while his chores awaited him at home. Just when he didn't expect it anymore, something did happen.

Governor Jackson had gathered the state militia and fellow secessionists at the edge of St. Louis per order of Governor Jackson under the guise of military maneuvers. After long negotiations, Lyon was allowed to lead his soldiers and the Home Guard against Camp Jackson on the tenth of May. After he had forced the commander to surrender, the federal soldiers marched into the camp and disarmed the militia while the Germans surrounded the grounds.

Martin was part of the German militia escorting the prisoners to the arsenal. Jackson's supporters formed a mob along the way and swore at the Germans. "Damned Black Guard," "long-eared Germans," and "Hessian Mercenaries" were the kindest expressions they used. Martin's heart pounded when faced with such hatred, but he did not let it show. Nobody should think that he was scared. Out of the corner of his eye, he peeked at his comrades. He could not read their thoughts because their facial expressions were as stoic as his own.

Everything went well until Lyon's horse kicked him after he dismounted, throwing him to the ground. The column came to a standstill and the mob used this moment of uncertainty. They surged toward the German militia who pushed them back. Somebody in the agitated crowd fired a revolver, hit a captain, and the rabble began to throw sticks and cobblestones at the troops.

Nobody gave orders to shoot since Captain Lyon was still dazed from his fall, but as if by command the German militia soldiers opened fire. Martin did not lift his musket, not wanting to shoot at civilians. Suddenly, he touched his head in surprise where a small rock had hit him. A cacophony of angry voices surged through his head while he fought to stay on his feet. After regaining his posture, he dabbed at the affected patch, but it was just a harmless laceration. Still a little dazed, he watched the wild gun battle as if he were an indifferent onlooker.

After the last shot had died away and some order had been restored, twenty-eight bodies lay on the cobblestones. Captain Lyon, once again firmly in the saddle, instantly ordered his troops to keep marching to the arsenal. Sentries were posted immediately after the gates closed behind the Unionists and the prisoners.

Martin and a group of fellow soldiers occupied the flat roof of the arsenal to report any approach of the enemy early on. The mayor ordered all saloons to stay closed that day, but the city experienced no further disturbances.

During the night, the Home Guard men on the roof talked very little and Martin lost himself in his thoughts. This was the just the second time during their marriage that Martin and Katrin were separated and he longed for her more and more every day. Above all, he valued her sound advice and felt certain that she would understand his decision. She knew that Martin would have lost all self-respect if he had remained on his farm during the fight for Missouri.

In the days following the street battle, the Home Guard once again sank into idleness. Martin grew more and more restless when he considered all the work on the farm. At last, he approached Hecker and asked if he could be excused. Hecker regretted Martin's request, yet he admitted that the struggle in the city was probably quenched for the near future.

Martin packed his bag and boarded an omnibus. A few blocks from Pine Street he got off and strode toward Flaherty's Inn. At this time of day, the lounge was still empty. It had not changed at all since he had given his notice.

"Hello, is anybody there?" he exclaimed.

At last, Ray entered the room through a back door. He appeared absentminded, but he perked up when he recognized Martin and rushed to greet him.

"Martin! How nice that you came to visit me. You're lucky to catch me."

"Why? Are you going on a trip?" Martin asked.

"Well, you may call it that: I'm going to join the army and am sorting through my papers."

"You're joining the army?"

"Yes, I've leased the tavern to enter an Irish brigade. Fighting is nothing new to us Irishmen. Every Irishman fights at least once in his lifetime against the British or against starvation, like I did. I want to fight for freedom because that's the greatest good of mankind."

Martin told him that he taken part in the campaign of St. Louis before he took his leave.

During the journey home Martin was in a pensive mood. The idea that Raymond would be fighting as a soldier while he sat on his farm disturbed him. Did he love his new country less than the Irishman? On the other hand, he had just resigned from the Home Guard because his sense of duty had called him home to work. Unable to reconcile his conflicting feelings, Martin focused on his reunion with Katrin and Philip.

Katrin was turning over soil in the garden with Philip by her side. She gave a startled cry when Martin peeked over the fence.

Philip dropped his trowel and scrambled to his feet. "*Papa*, you're finally home!"

Katrin's smile faded when she stepped closer to the fence. "Are you injured?"

"No, it's just a tiny cut," Martin assured her and hurried into her arms.

"Are you hungry?"

"Yes."

"Well, it's a good thing that I cooked extra food today. We had dried meat, beans, and fried potatoes."

"Wonderful," Martin said and followed Katrin into the kitchen.

While she warmed up the food, he fetched his work clothes and washed up in the trough. He told Katrin and Philip all his adventures after eating and did not withhold his encounter with Flaherty.

"Where are the others?" he finally said.

"Nikolaus and Jim are weeding in the big cornfield and Barbara took Charlotte to visit her aunt and uncle."

After finishing his meal, Martin set out to help Nikolaus and Jim in the cornfield. They broke into grins when they recognized his figure and asked many questions about his adventure. By evening Martin's back hurt just as much as if he had moved across the field on his knees all day long.

The weekly newspaper kept penetrating the domestic peace in Martin's house with disturbing news. Its pages were filled with reports about the volunteer regiments that had already been raised in St. Clair County. Abraham Lincoln had not only requested 75,000 militia soldiers for a service of ninety days, but also called for over 42,000 volunteer soldiers.

* * *

Martin often wondered whether he should enlist. The decision was much harder than it had been twelve years ago. Back then he had been young and independent. Now he had a wife, a child, and a farm which he could not abandon overnight. On the other hand, Nikolaus and Jim were still here and the women would not be left without help.

While Martin found a thousand reasons for his actions to justify them to himself, his decision had long been made. Four weeks after his return from St. Louis he said to Katrin, "I need to talk to you. Sit down."

Katrin dried her hands on her apron and approached him.

"I've decided to enlist," Martin said, avoiding her eyes.

Katrin's face was crestfallen, her shoulders slumping as she collapsed onto a chair. She had coped with many great misfortunes in her life and had told him that she was sure that someday she would get used to being a soldier's wife. For now, though, she looked like she was suppressing the urge to cry out. She glared at Martin without saying a word.

"I knew it," she finally whispered. "When you went to St. Louis, I knew it."

"But I didn't know it myself at that time," Martin said.

"We women have a feeling for that sort of thing—especially when it involves the man we love. But if you think you have to go, then go! I won't hold you back, as much as I want to."

"There are moments in my life when I just don't know how to go on," Martin said in a toneless voice. "Sometimes I have to make a decision and no matter what I do, I always seem to hurt someone. I obviously have a special talent for making the people I love unhappy."

"Oh, Martin, don't say that," Katrin cried. "You have made me very happy."

After dinner, Martin rode to Belleville to sign up at the recruiting office. A young man in the uniform of a sergeant sat behind a desk leafing through papers. Martin stated his request and the sergeant shook his head.

"I'm sorry, I have orders not to sign up any more volunteers," he said with a shrug. "Illinois has fulfilled its quota. We cannot accept any more volunteers since we don't have enough weapons and equipment. But if you want to enter the regular army, that's something else."

"No, no, I'm a farmer and want to remain one."

He turned away and walked out. On the ride home, he felt like someone whose toothache had driven him into a dentist's chair and who was almost sad when his pains had disappeared.

* * *

During the summer, Nikolaus and Martin often had heated discussions about the war when they sat out on the porch in the evening. Exhausted from work in the muggy summer heat, they rested on the wooden bench Nikolaus had built years before.

"It's our duty to volunteer for our new country," Martin insisted.

"I'm a farmer, not a soldier," Nikolaus said, swatting at a fly.

"Don't you care about the Union?"

"Why should I care about it? What is it to me?"

"They gave you shelter when you needed it," Martin said. "Now it's time to return the favor."

"Is that so? Well, the first battle at this place called Bull Run didn't go so well for the Union, did it?" Nikolaus retorted. "And besides, who would help the womenfolk on the farm if we all went to war?"

Their voices became so passionate that Katrin rose from her rocking chair, put down her mending, and escaped to the orchard. Martin followed her soon afterward.

"I cannot stand this war talk anymore," she said, rubbing a leaf between her fingers. "All you two do any more is arguing. Oh, I wish this terrible war were over. Why do brothers want to fight each other? Can't they solve their differences any other way?"

Martin took her hands in his. "Did you never fight with Nikolaus?"

Katrin bowed her head. "You're right, families do squabble more than any other union. But why does it have to disrupt our lives like this?"

"I don't know, but I do know that we can't choose the time we live in any more than we choose the family we are born into. Here we are and we'll have to make the best of it without losing our soul."

"You're thinking about the revolution again, aren't you?"

"Yes, I think about it every day. Had we won we might not be here at all. But sometimes I believe that we were destined to lose the fight in Germany and come here instead. Maybe we weren't meant to bring freedom to Germany, but here we can and will make a difference."

Chapter 50

Martin learned from the newspaper that former Lieutenant Governor Kőrner had begun raising a volunteer regiment. The next morning, Martin rode to Belleville and soon found the attorney's office on Main Street. Kőrner himself was seated at the simple walnut desk. Behind him on the wall hung a Merian engraving of Frankfurt, the politician's hometown. An American flag and a picture of Abraham Lincoln completed the office decor.

"I read that you are raising a volunteer regiment," Martin said.

"That's right," Kőrner replied.

"Why did the recruiting office reject me three weeks ago if now you're looking for soldiers?"

"Abraham Lincoln is a good friend of mine and I wanted to personally put this regiment at his disposal. With his promised support, we will get enough weapons and outfits."

After writing down Martin's personal data, he said, "That'll be all for today."

Now that he had made the decision, the tightness in Martin's chest had lifted and his steps quickened as he fetched his horse. On the ride home, his thoughts wandered back to the public assembly in Kaiserslautern and the euphoria he had experienced on that fateful day. Only two events in his life had evoked the same excitement in him: his wedding and the Lincoln-Douglas debate in Alton.

Martin received orders to report to the railroad station in three days. He took Philip aside and explained as best he could that he would be going to war. Philip's eyes filled with tears before he wiped them away with fierce determination.

"Look after your Mama for me," Martin said with more composure than he felt.

Philip nodded. "I will."

Word got around and several of his friends called to bid him farewell. Jakob and Amalie Haag, who had become as fond of the Duprees as they were of Barbara and Nikolaus, came to visit from Shiloh.

Martin and Katrin had little opportunity to be alone with each other, but that was perhaps for the better. Everything had been said between them.

On the day of departure Katrin paced the porch, wringing her hands into her apron. She had refused to accompany Martin to the station because she did not want to part from him among strangers. Philip remained rooted by her side.

The wagon stood in the barnyard when Martin stepped out of the house. Saying good-bye to Katrin was much harder than a few weeks ago. This time he might not return for years, if ever. He kissed Katrin one last time, patted Philip's head and climbed on the wagon board next to Jim. Martin's gaze lingered on the fields that had become his purpose in life for the past ten years. He could not help but look back at his house and the two figures on the porch. How would they fare without him? Doubts clawed away at his determination to help his new country in times of need.

* * *

Martin had hoped to enter the train unnoticed by strangers, but he had not reckoned with the enthusiasm of Belleville's citizens. A band stirred up the crowd with patriotic marches, forcing the gentlemen to raise their voices to be heard while the ladies handed out pieces of fruit pie, sandwiches, and cider. Jim parked the wagon a block away from the train station and Martin shook hands with the young man. A lump formed in Martin's throat when he observed Jim's sparkling eyes. It would not be long now until Jim might want to enlist.

The volunteers did not wear uniforms yet, but the tearful embraces of their female companions set them apart from other civilians. Martin accepted some pie and looked for an empty compartment on the train. He wanted to sit quietly and relive the past few months.

Soon, however, the compartment filled with noisy young men who behaved as if they were going on a Sunday picnic. One of them brought out a bottle of wine and Martin got his share during its round while they introduced themselves. Before long, the boisterous mood of his fellow travelers lifted Martin from his somber thoughts.

* * *

The troop train arrived at Camp Butler, six miles east of Springfield, and the volunteers marched into the camp that was to be their home for several weeks. In this training camp, officers would turn farmers and artisans into soldiers—not an easy task by any means. To make matters worse, many of the officers had no prior military training and consulted training manuals to instruct their soldiers.

The vast area was surrounded by a tall wooden fence guarded by sentries around the clock. The smell of freshly cut wood drifted through the air while carpenters were busy erecting row after row of barracks. Martin had never been in a camp before. He jerked back when the gate closed behind the companies that had arrived with him, shutting out the outside world. The great square inside the fencing served as a parade ground surrounded by the barracks, the kitchen, mess hall, chapel, hospital, and lavatories. A private showed Martin and his comrades their quarters. In the mess hall, the men received their mess tins and ate dry bread, cold ham, and coffee.

During the following days, more and more troops arrived at the camp. An army surgeon examined the men before they were sworn in by an army officer. When they came back from drilling, they found light blue trousers, a dark blue sack coat and equipment spread out on their cots.

"There you have it," said John, a mason from East St. Louis, to Martin. "A thin coat, a couple of wool shirts, a gray blanket, a black leather belt, a forage cap, and heavy shoes. That's all the army thinks you need. Let's hope we get a greatcoat before winter sets in."

"Winter? Don't you think the war will be over by then?" asked a sixteen-year-old boy.

John chuckled. "No. We signed up for three years, remember? Well, I plan to make the best of it and will start at the mess hall."

"But we already had our dinner."

"Do you think anybody will remember this mug?"

"You better hurry, we're supposed to be drilling in fifteen minutes," Martin yelled after him while he looked over the gear. He ran his fingers over the cartridge box, knapsack, haversack, and canteen. These, more than the clothes, brought the realities of war to the forefront of his mind.

I'll have to carry all this? Guess one gets used to it as time goes on. I better hurry or I'll be late for drill.

Chapter 51

October 5, 1861

Dearest Katrin,

I hope this letter finds you well. My days are so busy that I can hardly find time to write. I am glad that you urged me to take paper and pencils with me (and stamps!). And write I must, because there is so much to tell. Many men have begun a diary and I will probably do so myself. We spend our days with drills, drills, and more drills. We are drilling six to eight hours each day. In our free time, the men play cards, fight over the few newspapers we receive here, or write home.

Yesterday, we elected our officers. In my company there are many men from St. Clair County. I didn't recognize any of them except Peter Weis, who I have seen at Wehrle's store before. I soon got acquainted with many fellows in my company and don't feel so lonely anymore. I miss you very much, though, and I hope to be back again soon. Rumor has it that we will be moving to St. Louis soon and maybe I can come home for a furlough or you and Nikolaus could come to St. Louis. Has Nikolaus sowed any wheat yet? How was the apple harvest this year? How is Philip doing?

Write soon if you can find the time.

Your loving husband, Martin

* * *

October 21, 1861

Dearest Katrin,

It was good to hear from you and I am glad you are well. I know you are very busy with canning and preserving fruits and vegetables and don't have much time to write.

On October 12, my regiment was mustered into service. The next day, we traveled by railroad to Benton Barracks in St. Louis. The journey was a pleasant one and the trees we saw were dressed in their glowing autumn colors.

We have finally been given weapons. My Harpers Ferry musket looks like a dangerous weapon indeed. That is, dangerous to me.

Benton Barracks is a huge camp and they say it can house 30,000 soldiers. The food is alright as far as army food is concerned and we are all in good spirits.

I hope we will remain in St. Louis long enough that I can see you. I will apply for a weekend pass and will write to you as soon as I know. Please come for a visit since I don't know when we will see each other again. There are some little photo galleries outside the camp. Bring enough money because I would love to have our likeness taken by a photographer. Many men have done so already and sent theirs home. The photographers are enjoying a brisk business indeed and so are the saloons and restaurants that sprung up nearby.

By the way, if you come, can you bring me a needle and some thread to mend my clothes? I would also appreciate some apples and pears from our orchard.

Send my love to all.

Your loving husband, Martin

* * *

Katrin and Nikolaus watched the docking of the Mississippi ferry to St. Louis from the deck. The wharf was livelier than ever as the blue Union uniforms mingled with the mellow clothing of farmers and merchants. Katrin pulled her brown scarf tighter around her shoulders. The late October air felt chilly, especially on the river. It had not been easy for her and Nikolaus to get away for several days during the busy autumn season.

Barbara's Uncle Jakob and Aunt Amalie had arrived from Shiloh to help with the chores while they were gone, and Jakob drove the siblings to the train station in Belleville. Nikolaus had to accompany Katrin because times were too unsafe to let a woman undertake a trip by herself. Moreover, Nikolaus had wanted to see his brother-in-law again.

Katrin strained her eyes to make out faces in the bustle, hoping against hope that Martin awaited them at the landing. The five weeks since she had last seen him seemed like an eternity. How was she ever to survive a whole war without him?

* * *

Martin paced in front of Krumbacher's restaurant where he had arranged to meet his wife. He wanted to enjoy every minute of his twelve-hour furlough with Katrin. The smoke that wafted from the chimney smelled of beef and pork, causing his stomach to grumble. Martin had never eaten here because he had not been paid yet, but he intended to take out his wife and brother-in-law. Katrin would have enough sense to bring along some money. Besides, he hadn't had a decent meal since leaving home and who knew what the winter would bring. This war would not be over as soon as everybody hoped.

Finally, the omnibus from the levee arrived and Katrin waved excitedly at Martin. He beamed as he lifted her from the vehicle.

"My, my, you look handsome in a uniform," she admitted while looking him over.

"You look pretty good yourself, Frau Dupree. Wearing my favorite dress, I see."

"Well, if I'm supposed to have my picture taken, I have to look as good as I can."

"We'll do that, but first I want to take you two out to dinner."

They waited for a group of men to leave and hurried to take their places on the wooden benches. Martin and Nikolaus ordered beef stew and fresh corn bread while Katrin chose pork roast with dumplings and white bread.

"Ah, that tastes good," said Martin and wiped his mouth after drinking from his beer. "I have become quite a coffee drinker lately."

"Tell me about army life," Nikolaus asked his brother-in-law.

Martin did not need much coaxing and began to chat about his comrades, the routines of camp life, guard duty, and the possibility that they would move out soon.

"But I'm forgetting the time. We should be going to the photographer now."

Nikolaus kept them company while Martin and Katrin took their place in a slow-moving line. Martin wanted to know all the news from home. He was especially eager to learn about Philip's well-being and Katrin happily obliged.

Finally, they entered the tent where a skinny man of average height greeted them. He wore a mustache and spoke in a hasty tone. His English was heavily accented, and the couple looked at each other, not comprehending.

"Swedish?" he asked.

"No, we're German," Martin answered while Katrin looked around.

Mr. Baker placed a coated plate into his camera. "What size photo would you like? The *carte de visite* is very popular as it fits into an envelope. But the young lady may want to have a larger picture of her husband?"

He showed three different sizes of photos. One was so tiny that it fit into a locket, while another was big enough to be a centerpiece on a chest of drawers. They decided on two cartes de visite for the prize of one dollar each, one for Martin to take with him to the field.

"I would like a frame, please," Katrin insisted.

"That'll be another dollar."

He showed them where to stand and pose. The background behind them depicted a tent, a musket, and knapsack.

"Now, please stand perfectly still. Do not move until I say so," Mr. Baker said and disappeared under a black cloth.

Martin and Katrin hooked their arms and froze in their position until they began to itch. It seemed like an eternity but had only lasted about thirty seconds when the photographer emerged and pulled the plate out of its slot. He disappeared behind a curtain.

For the first time that day, the couple was alone, and Martin quickly planted a kiss on Katrin's lips. Katrin blushed and looked around before she returned his kiss fervently.

"Oh Martin, I don't know how I'll live through the winter without you. Jim is talking about enlisting and I think even Nikolaus is having doubts now. If he goes, there will be nobody but me and Barbara and the children. Who is going to help with the farm work?"

"Why don't you ask Uncle Jakob and Aunt Amalie to live with you?"

"That's a very good idea," she said, brightening.

"Write to me often, even if I can't answer right away," Martin said and took her hands in his. "And if you have time, could you knit a couple pairs of socks for me? I'm sure I will need them before long."

Tears began to well in Katrin's eyes as she nodded.

"Come, come, don't cry," Martin said, wiping a tear from Katrin's cheek. "We only have a few hours together and I want to make the best of it."

Mr. Baker appeared at last with a framed photograph in his hands.

"It's very small," Katrin exclaimed while inspecting the tintype.

"It'll be easier to carry it home with you," Martin said. They paid the money, thanked Baker and left the gallery. A young private was next in line.

"He couldn't have been older than sixteen," Katrin whispered as they went to meet Nikolaus. "He hasn't even started to grow a beard yet."

"Some of them lie about their age when they enlist."

"Their poor mothers. What must they be going through."

Martin laughed dryly. "Always thinking more of others than yourself, aren't you?" He hooked his arm in hers so he wouldn't lose her in the crowd.

"It isn't easy to stay behind while you men rush off to war. There are no bands playing for us, no rallies, no parades. Just work, work, and worry."

"I know, *Schatz*," Martin said softly and touched her chin with his thumb and forefinger. "I know how hard this is for you, but I feel it is something I have to do. I found a new home here in America. And now that my country needs me, I cannot refuse the call. I couldn't live with myself if I did."

Katrin said feebly, "I know. I have known all along that you would join up sooner or later. Don't worry about me. You'll have enough to think about."

"They keep us very busy here, but I'll think about you every night."

* * *

The next day, on the ferry to East St. Louis, Katrin thought about the dashing figure of her husband who stood there waving good-bye as they boarded the omnibus. Pride and heartache fought within her. At least she had a photograph of him. She did not dare to unwrap it now, fearing that the moisture of the river would damage it. But at home, in the privacy of her bedroom, she would look at it without being ashamed of her tears.

Her gaze followed a great blue heron as it glided over the mud-colored waters on its majestic wings. At last, it swooped down to the surface, seizing a slimy fish with its long bill. Nature was the only aspect of life that remained unaffected by the war.

"Well," Nikolaus said, rousing her from her daydreams, "If the war is still going on after the next harvest, I may join up too."

Katrin fixed her eyes on him. "I thought you were opposed to the war?"

"I am, but I don't like people to think of me as a coward. Did you see the way those soldiers looked at me? No, you wouldn't have. You only had eyes for one of them. But I felt their stares on my back and they said 'Coward.' Why isn't he in uniform, they must be wondering. An able-bodied man like him should have signed up by now." He sighed and clenched his fists. "I don't want to be the laughingstock of women and children."

"You want to enlist because you're afraid people will talk about you?"

"Yes. You know how much people talk."

Katrin sighed when she remembered the time of her engagement with Martin.

"I don't even want to go to the store or the gristmill anymore because of the dirty looks I get," Nikolaus said through clenched teeth.

"Well, let's hope the war will be over by next summer."

"Don't count on it."

Tears began to well in Katrin's eyes.

"I'm sorry," Nikolaus said, taking her hands in his. "About my enlisting, please don't tell Barbara anything yet. There's no need to worry her before it's necessary."

"I promise," Katrin said, her eyes resting steadfast on the city that was once more her husband's home for a short while.

* * *

January 31, 1862

Dearest Katrin,

We are back at Benton Barracks but not for long, I think. On December 30, we had our first march from Otterville back to Tipton and from there by rail back to St. Louis. This march through mud and snow gave me a taste of what is yet to come. Marching is harder when you're no longer nineteen years old.

Two new companies have been added to our regiment. The other day we received new Belgian rifles. It is a very heavy rifle but supposed to be an excellent weapon. When I first held it in my hands, I could not help but think of the time when my father was sent to Belgium to purchase rifles and bungled the whole affair. I was so embarrassed I wanted to change my name. I kept thinking what would have happened if we had gotten those rifles. Would the revolution have been successful? We might still be living in the Pfalz and would not be affected at all by this war of brothers. But what is the use of thinking what if when the deed is done. We are here and I am a soldier now.

We have not been paid yet and many of the men are beginning to grumble. Their wives keep writing them to send them money and they don't have any. I am very glad that we have a farm and you have enough food to eat.

There is talk that we may be moving to Tennessee soon. Whether our destination will be Fort Henry or Fort Donelson, no one knows. The soldier is the last to know anything.

I miss you very much and wish I could see you now that I am so close to you, but I know it is not possible. My thoughts were with all of you at Christmastime and I remembered the Christmas tree we used to decorate together. We are in high spirits, though, and hope this affair will be over soon.

Love, Martin

Chapter 52

With flying colors, fixed bayonets, and bugles playing, the Forty-Third Illinois Infantry regiment marched to the landing where the steamer *Memphis* awaited them. By the lack of enthusiasm from the people in the street it was clear that they sympathized with the South.

Martin stepped on deck to contemplate the countryside passing by. Back in 1849, when he had first traveled the Ohio and Mississippi River, autumn trees had been afire with golden, orange, and crimson colors. Now, a gray blanket seemed to be draped over the whole world, matching his somber mood.

He wondered what would lie at the end of their journey as the steamer turned into the narrower mouth of the Tennessee River. God only knew. The heavily wooded land was as flat as the Illinois shore before giving way to steep banks. The river flowed slowly, almost sluggishly, belying the great depths beneath its surface. Occasionally, a landing for the cotton boats jutted out into the river, but there were no towns to speak of near the riverbanks.

* * *

Martin pulled up the collar of his great coat against the cold.

"Better go downstairs, private. You don't want to be shot dead before getting to battle, do you?" A soldier on guard approached him, hinting at the sharpshooters that were likely hiding in the thicket of trees.

Martin gave a curt nod and went under deck where numerous card games were in progress. He moved toward one of the stoves that provided heat and a place to cook the salted pork and coffee they had received as rations.

"Come join us," Private Karl Arendt cried over the din of the crowded boat.

"Not now," Martin replied, "I want to write a letter to my wife."

The invitation had sparked a memory of another card game back at his father's inn when he had met Nikolaus for the first time. Nikolaus had come into town for the annual fair and had invited Martin to visit him at home. So much had happened since then. The young and naïve boys, now grown and married men, were once again caught in a tumult they could not control or contain.

With his sense of civic duty and disgust of slavery, he was the first one to go to war. Jim would probably follow soon, leaving only Nikolaus as a neutral. Katrin had hinted in her last letter, however, that her brother was thinking about enlisting after the next harvest. He would not do it out of a conviction of the righteousness of their cause, she added, but because he did not want to be ridiculed as a coward.

Poor Nikolaus! He has always shied away from fighting for any cause but gets pulled into them in the end.

* * *

The regiment arrived at Fort Henry two days after the Confederate rebels had surrendered and retreated to Fort Donelson. The reports of Donelson's fall on the sixteenth of February brought cheers from the Union soldiers who were starved for good news. Martin's regiment left Fort Donelson in early March when another steamer brought them to Savannah and then to Pittsburg Landing. They finally arrived near a chapel named Shiloh where they pitched their tents.

Spring arrived with warm days. Violets burst into bloom, carpeting the woods around the Union camps. Martin wore short sleeves while he and the others searched for wild onions. Every morning, Martin woke to the *what-cheer cheer cheer* of a cardinal perched in a black oak tree near his tent. He thought back to the ride on the Pennsylvania Canal when he had first spotted the beautiful red bird and attempted to sketch it. How young and full of expectations he had been.

In the days that followed, the men went leisurely about their routines of cooking, cleaning their rifles or inspecting their clothes for graybacks. Martin had ample time to ponder over the familiar name of the church. The densely wooded area bore little resemblance to the rolling prairie of Shiloh Valley, however, and he fought hard to shake off the sense of foreboding that crept up in him whenever he was alone. After all, nobody from the generals down to the ranks expected the Confederates to attack here. Convinced that there were no rebels in the area, the officers had not even posted one picket.

* * *

On Sunday morning, April 6, the sun rose bright and warm, lighting up a camp of resting soldiers. The dull boom of distant guns shook the earth and aroused Martin's company from their slumber. Without breakfast, they hastily took down their tents and gathered their accoutrements on wagons. Before their lieutenant could bellow a command, Martin and his fellow soldiers loaded their rifles and formed the color line.

Hearing the wild yells of the rebels for the first time, Martin's heart pounded in his chest like a hammer striking a fencepost. Now he understood just how close the enemy was. Why hadn't anybody noticed their presence?

Martin took a deep breath to overcome his impulse to run for cover as fast as he could. Calmer now, he raised his rifle to his shoulder, took aim and pulled the trigger. He unfastened his cartridge box and fumbled for another cartridge.

Steady. It would do no good if he bungled the loading of his weapon out of haste and fear. While bullets flew all around him, the trembling of his hands subsided as he recalled the steps he had learned in months of drilling. He tore the cartridge open with his teeth and poured the contents into the barrel. Then he pulled the ramrod and pushed it down the barrel. A rifle shot exploded next to his left ear, deafening him for a few moments. He pivoted to face the rude rifleman but could not make him out in the smoke.

Soon, the regiment's lines wavered like a wheat field in a summer breeze. The rebels' attack was so massive and unexpected that many Union recruits began running as soon as the first shots were fired.

Dense, acrid smoke filled the air like a giant cauldron and Martin was unable to detect the enemy lines through the billowing fog. He knelt down to penetrate the smog near the ground, but it was hopeless.

"Why are you kneeling on the ground?" Lieutenant Riehm yelled behind his back. "Stand up and fight like a man!"

"But I can't see anything," Martin stammered.

"Shoot, private, shoot anyway."

Martin's face grew hot as he clambered up. He could not bear the thought that his lieutenant believed him to be a coward. He lifted his rifle to his shoulder and fired into the miasma. Before he could reload his weapon, a shriek tore through the haze to Martin's left. He turned to find a young private on the ground, clutching his thigh. Martin hastened to his side and saw that the wounded man's hipbone was exposed. Another private had rushed to the injured soldier's side and, together with Martin, they carried him behind an oak tree.

"I'll go see if we can carry him to an ambulance," the soldier said. He soon returned. "No, we're supposed to leave him here and get back in line on the double."

Martin obeyed, wondering what would happen to the unfortunate soldier. He did not have much time to ponder the man's fate as he realized that the majority of the Confederate's rifle shots came from the direction of his regiment's right and left flanks. Within seconds, Lieutenant Riehm gave the order to fall back to the Corinth road.

Confusion ensued. Martin stumbled into a fellow soldier who seemed puzzled about the direction of the road. Officers shouted orders, soldiers repeated them to each other with hoarse voices, and above all, minié balls and grape shots whirred through the air, searching their unlucky target. A bullet passed Martin's arm so closely that he smelled the burning threads of his sleeve. Beads of sweat formed on Martin's forehead when he inspected his arm. He had narrowly escaped becoming one of the first casualties in his company.

As the panting soldiers gathered in a line, Martin asked the stocky fellow next to him, "What's happening?"

The man shook his head. "I don't know. I heard that the rebels have overrun General Sherman's position."

The officers seemed to be just as surprised by the Confederate attack as the soldiers were. Martin couldn't do much more than follow orders and shoot at the enemy before they shot him.

By mid-afternoon, Martin and his comrades ran out of cartridges. Lieutenant Riehm sent the two worst shots in the company to the nearest deserted Union camp to look for ammunition. When they returned, they brought the wrong caliber of bullets. With the rebels at their heels, Martin's company had no choice but to retreat. Martin's fear of being taken prisoner subsided when the men spotted a wagon full to the hilt with cartridges.

Please, let it be the right caliber. It was a disadvantage that the Union had purchased all kinds of different rifles, each requiring different calibers. Whooping cries told Martin that they had been spared from being overrun by the rebels this time. Grateful for the incredible luck, he stuffed the ammunition in his cartridge box and in his pockets before falling back in line.

* * *

Nightfall brought a welcome break in the fighting. The day had clearly ended in favor of the Confederacy.

Martin's regiment dropped to the ground as they were. Martin chewed on his last piece of hard bread and washed it down with the remaining water from his canteen. He had not eaten all day, the excitement of battle alone sustaining him. Even though he was completely exhausted, sleep did not come easy this night.

Throughout the night, Federal gunboats shelled the Confederacy's positions from the landing. The roar of explosions broke the nervous silence of the night that blanketed the soldiers.

"Are you awake?" whispered the soldier who lay next to Martin, Private Peter Müller.

"Yes."

"What are you thinking about?"

"I was thinking about my wife and son and how much I miss them," Martin replied.

"I never was married. Had a sweetheart once, back in Germany. We wanted to get married, but she died of consumption. I never looked at another girl since. Guess I never will now."

Müller's voice quivered and he fell silent.

Martin sighed. He could not imagine a life without Katrin. She was the anchor in his life, his whole reason for being. He was glad that this terrifying battle had not made her a widow yet. He was determined for it to stay that way.

Around midnight, a thunderstorm rolled in, replacing the roar of battle with nature's own earthshaking explosions. The rain fell in torrents, soaking Martin to the bone. A flash of lightning revealed a group of three men holding a blanket over their heads. At their encouragement, Martin joined them. The soaked blanket did not provide much protection as it dripped on the fatigued soldiers.

"To think that I joined the army to have an adventure," lamented one man. "Lord, how I wish to be back on my father's farm now."

The soldiers grunted in agreement. Martin did not need to see their faces to know that they shared his thoughts. The skirmishes of Rinnthal and Ubstadt had not prepared him for a battle of this magnitude, even as

266

he had lost a dear friend. He was as green as his comrades when faced with an overwhelming enemy. He felt that he had not been as brave as he had expected himself to be. Yet, only a fool would not be scared in battle. It would have been suicide to remain in the vulnerable position his company had been in. Had not Lieutenant Riehm himself ordered his men to retreat?

After a while, Martin's legs seemed to pull him earthward and he eased away from the blanket. He shoved his bayonet into the soil and curled up in the mud. Soon, the rainwater gushed over his face, forcing him to rise on unsteady feet. He rested his lower arms on his rifle butt, pulled up the collar of his fatigue coat and lowered his chin on his arms. Müller soon joined him when any rest on the sodden ground became impossible. Occasionally, Martin lifted his open mouth skyward to let the rain wash away the burning taste of the cartridges he had opened all day. He thought of the warm bed he had left behind on his farm. How he wished he could lie next to Katrin one more time!

Flashes of lightning revealed dark contours near the ground. Martin shuddered when he realized they were turkey vultures feasting on the bodies of fallen soldiers. He felt ashamed that he had thought of his own comfort when those young men would never feel a drop of rain or the kiss of a woman again.

He could hear the cries of the wounded men between crashes of thunder. How close had he come to joining those miserable soldiers when the projectile singed his shirt sleeve?

Oh Katrin, I wish had listened to you. If I survive this war, I shall never leave you again. Whenever Martin drifted off, the booming shells from the gunboats pulled him out of his trance. To pass time, Martin tried to remember when he had last eaten a full meal. Despite the lack of food, his stomach had stopped rumbling as if it had reconciled itself with its empty state.

Martin wished that the downpour would end soon. Yet, he thought with trepidation of dawn lighting this miserable group of soldiers. Was the battle lost yet? Would he soon be marched off to a prison camp? Or would tomorrow be his last day on earth?

* * *

Morning broke with heavy clouds weighing down on the weary soldiers. The long, luring call of a bugle roused Martin and his comrades from their short rest. A company that had arrived on the battlefield during the night shared their ration of hardtacks with the hungry and sodden soldiers.

The thick underbrush slowed their progress westward. Martin often had to use his knife or his bayonet to cut through the tangle of untamed forest. Coming around a tree that was covered with Spanish moss, he tripped over the stretched-out legs of a dead rebel. A fat crow feasted on the soldier's intestines which were spilling from his abdomen. Martin began to retch and stumbled backwards to gag behind a tree pierced with grape shots.

The day wore on as incessant musket firing mingled with the roar of cannons. The earth's resulting tremors traveled through Martin's body, making him feel confident, almost giddy. Had it not been for the pulsing charges, he would certainly have fallen over from hunger and fatigue.

Around four o'clock, the decimated regiment staggered across a battlefield littered with knapsacks, blankets, shredded tents, canteens, and splintered rifles. Dead horses were scattered everywhere, and the stench of their decay mingled with the reek of rotting human flesh. Although the company's tents and accoutrements were still on a wagon somewhere in the rear, Martin stacked his rifle together with his tentmates' and sank to the ground. Unless the wagon returned before nightfall, they would not have any protection during a rainfall such as the one last night.

At least Martin still had his most precious possession. He pulled a tin container from his inner coat pocket and opened it to look at the *carte de visite* he and Katrin had posed for in St. Louis.

"Well, your husband has survived his first real battle, and it looks as if the war will take longer than anyone imagined," he whispered. "Pray that I will live to see the end of it."

Martin replaced the photograph into the container and rolled up his coat to rest his head on the muddy soil. He hastened to cover his head with his coat when a quick-moving storm drenched him again. Unable to wait any longer, several of the younger soldiers set out to find the wagon containing their tents. The sun had already reached the western horizon when they reappeared at last.

"Hurrah," Martin joined the whoops of the German soldiers, but it sounded more like the caw of a crow from his parched mouth. The men hoisted their shelters and were soon overwhelmed by a surge of soldiers from other regiments looking for protection from the elements.

Within the tent, Martin had barely enough room to sit upright. Once the men stopped talking over each other, the course of the attack became clearer. Last evening, Major General Buell's Army of the Ohio had begun to arrive at the battlefield to enforce the battered Union troops. Thus, the Union was able to drive the rebels not only back where they had begun their assault yesterday morning but force them to retreat to Corinth. Martin quietly thanked the general for appearing in time to save his hide.

Chapter 53

With Philip by her side, Katrin turned over her vegetable garden, generously working manure into the fertile earth where she intended to plant lettuce, carrots, cabbage, potatoes, cucumbers, and herbs. When she heard hoofbeats on the road nearby, she dropped the spade handle against the fence that surrounded the garden. Always hoping for news of Martin, she ripped off her leather gloves and ran out to the road to see who was passing. It was Wilhelm Beinhart, a farmer who lived about a mile away.

"Good day, Katrin," he said in a grave tone as he reined in the horses. His wagon clattered to a halt. "Have you heard the news?"

"What news?" Katrin asked. Her hand trembled as she reached for her throat. She tried to contain the fear that made her heart beat faster.

"There's been a major battle at a place called Shiloh in Tennessee. I'm on my way to the store to buy a newspaper. Say, isn't Martin out that way?"

"Yes," Katrin said softly, "His last letter came from a town called Savannah or something like that."

"Shall I bring you a newspaper then?"

"Yes, please. Wait, I'll go and get the money."

"I'll also ask if there is a letter for you at the post office."

Katrin fetched the money, thanked him and trudged back to the garden. She continued her work as Philip prattled about their animals while her thoughts were at a place in Tennessee she had never heard of before. She remained silent during dinner until Nikolaus asked her, "You're awfully quiet today. What's the matter?"

Katrin stepped to the window and motion for him to join her, away from the unsuspecting children. "There's been a big battle in Tennessee and I'm afraid that Martin may have been in it. Wilhelm Beinhart drove by this morning and promised to bring me a paper when he comes back from the village."

After dinner Katrin returned to her garden. Every time she heard a hoofbeat she hastened to the road, but none of the passersby knew anything concrete about the battle. They had only heard of huge casualties. Around supper time Beinhart finally approached.

"Have you got my newspaper?" Katrin pleaded.

"Here you go, girl."

Katrin barely thanked him as she scanned the columns of the paper for the casualty list. When she did not find the name she was looking for, she lowered the paper and let out a cry.

"His name is not on the list, so he must be safe, right?"

"Yes, one would think so," Beinhart said. "But others weren't so lucky. Well, here's a letter from your husband. I'll be on my way now."

He handed Katrin the envelope and, thanking him, she hastened to the kitchen.

"It was written three weeks ago," she uttered as she dropped on a chair to read it. Martin wrote that she could expect to receive money soon since he had finally been paid. As a private, he received thirteen dollars per month and had allotted most of it for her.

When she had finished the letter, Katrin took up the newspaper again and read the report about the battle. It had indeed been a great battle and the losses on both sides were staggering.

Even though the Union had eventually won, their casualties amounted to 13,000 soldiers while 10,700 Confederates were killed, wounded, captured, or missing. The toll on Martin's company was proportionately high: six officers had been killed on the battlefield and its Colonel Raith was mortally wounded and not expected to survive. Forty-nine wounded soldiers had been left on the field to be dragged off by the rebels.

Katrin grasped the paper and ran to the field where Nikolaus and Jim were sowing wheat.

When she was within earshot, she cried, "Martin is safe."

The men wiped their hands on their trousers and looked over the casualty list.

"Oh my God, Peter's brother's name is on it," Nikolaus exclaimed. "Martin never mentioned meeting him. He was probably in another company."

"Maybe he is just wounded or was taken prisoner," Katrin suggested.

Two weeks later, they finally received word from Martin about his first battle. His regiment was now en route to Corinth, an important railroad junction in northern Mississippi. Here, the Mobile and Ohio line intersected the Charleston and Memphis railroad.

* * *

Martin was digging trenches near Corinth when he doubled over with cramps. As he collapsed to the ground, he pulled his knees toward his body in an attempt to confine his pain. Draping his weak arms around their shoulders, his messmates Fritz and Gustav helped him to a hospital tent. Too nauseated to move by his own will, Martin spent a miserable day on the filthy cot. He could barely lift a finger when the two privates returned in the evening to check on him.

"I have dysentery," Martin muttered, trying in vain to swat a fly from his moist forehead. The next time they visited, the young men brought a fan they had made from playing cards. Martin laughed feebly about his comrades' ingenuity, appreciating their thoughtfulness.

Several days later, Gustav came alone.

"Where is Fritz?" Martin asked.

"Fritz is sick with a fever."

"Oh no! I hope he didn't catch it from me." While he had much enjoyed the visits of his messmates, he would not forgive himself if he had caused Fritz's illness.

"No, it's not your fault," Gustav assured him. "The men are falling like flies and everybody wonders whether the rebs or the Union will pull out first. They may send Fritz to a hospital up north because they are overwhelmed here. How are you doing?"

"The doctor thinks I'll be on the mend in a few days if I don't get dehydrated. I guess I'm one of the lucky ones."

"Yes, you sure found a way to avoid digging. I'm sick and tired of it."

"What else is new in the regiment?" Martin asked.

"Anton Weis deserted last night. Good for him. Sometimes I think about deserting myself. At home, they're paying a mason three dollars a day. Here we only get thirteen dollars a month and have to wait forever to get paid at all."

"You mustn't talk like that. We have volunteered and it is our duty to stay. Do you want to be an outlaw for the rest of the war?"

Gustav shrugged. "I guess you're right. I wouldn't be able to go home if I deserted and I don't know where else to go, but I sure wish we would leave this place."

Gustav's wish was soon granted since the Union army was not the only one whose ranks were thinned by disease. After the Confederate troops quietly slipped away, Martin's regiment returned to Tennessee. Too weak yet to work on the fortifications near Bolivar, Martin was assigned to picket duty. When his health improved, he also participated in reconnaissance expeditions.

One day, Martin and a corporal rounded a corner of a plank road when they came upon two barefoot rebels hiding behind a rhododendron bush. Their hands shot up in the air when the Union soldiers surrounded them. One of them remained silent, while the other one, a young fellow with carrot-red hair, began to plead in German.

"Please, don't hurt me," he whined, "I had no other choice."

Martin almost dropped his rifle. This rebel was a Palatine if he ever saw one.

"What's your name and what are you doing here?" he asked in his German dialect.

The rebel's jaw almost touched the lapel of his threadbare butternut coat. "My name is Ernst Bollinger. I'm from a village in the northern Palatinate. I arrived in New Orleans just as the war began," he said. "I searched and searched, but I couldn't find a job. Then someone told to me to join the army. They would surely feed me. So that's what I did, but they didn't feed me so well, did they?"

Still amazed over the unexpected encounter with a fellow countryman, Martin said, "Come with us."

"What's going to happen to us? I'd like to join the Union army. At least I'd be able to talk to my comrades and officers. I almost got killed because I couldn't understand my captain's orders."

Martin addressed his corporal. "I don't think we need to bind them. He's my fellow countryman and wants to join our side."

"I gathered as much, but I did not understand everything you two were talking about. Can you come to Captain Holtz with me and these two fellows?" the corporal asked and gave orders to return to camp.

Captain Holtz did not hesitate to allow the unusual request. If the Union had to feed these soldiers, they might as well earn their keep. Bollinger requested to be put in Martin's tent and the two newest Union soldiers were dismissed.

"Can I speak to you for a moment," Captain Holtz addressed Martin who was about to leave.

"It has come to my attention that you speak English very well," the captain said.

"Yes, I practice it as often as possible," Martin said.

"Since you are the only soldier besides our colonel who speaks English fluently, I would like to promote you to corporal when the next promotions are announced."

A smile crept over Martin's face. "Why, thank you very much."

"Don't thank me, you've earned it. And now, I would like you to talk to the Confederate prisoner who doesn't speak German."

* * *

"The Southern boys speak a language that resembles English in name only," Martin wrote to Katrin.

> Since our regiment consists almost entirely of German-born men or sons of German immigrants it is just about impossible for us to understand the rebels. One cannot help but feel sorry for them. We just captured a rebel from Kentucky, and he is the most backwoods creature I have ever met. He asked me to write a letter home for him and I obliged even though it was highly improper. He has the utmost respect for me because I can read and write. When I told him that everybody can read and write where I come from, he said he had to start working in the mines when he was nine years old.
>
> Tennessee is a pretty country, but I don't think I would want to make a home here. There are three classes of society: the rich planters who own slaves, the slaves, and the poor whites who are worth much less than slaves. I was most appalled, though, to see that many ladies here chew tobacco and drink whiskey. All in all, I am very glad that we live in a more civilized society.

Katrin looked up from the letter she had read aloud.

"Imagine that, ladies chewing tobacco."

"What do you expect from people who keep others in bondage," exclaimed Amalie, who was helping with chores whenever she could. She never looked up from the bread dough she was kneading but instead pounded it harder.

"I've heard enough of that. What else does he write?"

"He has now fully recovered from dysentery. Other men were not so lucky. His friend Gustav has been so sick with typhoid fever that he has been discharged."

"Well, you wouldn't cry if Martin were discharged, would you?" Amalie said with a twinkle in her eye.

"No, I wouldn't. But Martin has too much of a sense of duty to be pleased about a discharge. Only an injury could keep him out of the war."

"Well, one has to take men as they are. Your brother, on the other hand, seems to be more reluctant to serve. Has he enlisted yet?"

"No, but he heard a rumor that Friedrich Hecker is raising another regiment. I don't know why Nikolaus would be interested in him. It was always Martin who adored Hecker. Probably because he was a hero of the Revolution of 1848 and Martin still dwells on that conflict a lot."

"Why didn't Martin join Hecker's regiment last year?"

"He didn't want to travel to Chicago to join a regiment. His company is from St. Clair County and he feels less homesick that way."

* * *

As they were mucking out the cow barn, Nikolaus said to Katrin, "I'm going to enlist after the harvest if they're calling for volunteers again."

"Does Barbara know about this?"

"Yes, and she's very upset about it. But I'll be damned if I'm going to wait until I get drafted. Only cowards do that."

Katrin rested her arms on her fork handle. "But how are we going to get along on the farm without you? Jim is anxious to join and it's only a matter of time until he does."

"We'll have to leave some of the land fallow. I spoke to Uncle Jakob and he agreed that he and Amalie will move out here for the time being. And I'm afraid you and Barbara will have to do the farm work together with Jakob. Maybe we should think about buying some farm machinery. I heard that the John Deere reaper is doing a fabulous job."

Katrin pursed her lips, deep in thought. She could not comprehend why Nikolaus would want to leave the baby they had almost lost. "Why are men always so eager to go to war? It seems like only women keep a level head these days."

"Sometimes things happen, and we are powerless about the outcome."

Chapter 54

Nikolaus bid farewell to his family at the station in Belleville. The atmosphere was less cheery than a year earlier when Martin had enlisted. With tearful eyes, women waved goodbye to their husbands or sons while a young girl handed a note to a clean-shaven boy of no more than eighteen. Even the band's spirited marches seemed subdued. Everybody realized that the country was engaged in a lengthy war with no end in sight.

* * *

Training at Camp Butler consisted of endless drills. After electing the noncommissioned officers, the soldiers were mustered for a three-year service. In early November, the streets of Springfield were lined with people as the regiment marched to the train station. Box cars awaited the recruits to take them to Virginia where the Second Hecker Regiment was to join the Army of the Potomac.

"Box cars?" cried the man next to Nikolaus, "Are we cattle?"

"Did you expect to travel first class?" Nikolaus retorted, hiding his own surprise.

* * *

In December, the regiment assumed its winter camp near Aquia Creek, Virginia. Here, the soldiers built log huts with fireplaces made of brick or stone. Most companies gave their streets and tents elaborate names. Nikolaus and his five messmates named their tent "Hotel Pfalz." The

Germans stuck together to cope with the prejudice of the American-born soldiers.

Rain and storms soon turned the ground into ankle-deep mud. This took a toll on their shoes, which fell apart quickly. The men did not leave their huts except for drills, roll calls, fatigue labor, and guard duties. Before long, boredom and homesickness tugged at the hearts of the soldiers. What bothered Nikolaus and his comrades more than the monotony was the lack of pay. Christmas brought a welcome surprise in the form of sauerkraut, sausages, and beer.

Then, on January 20, the regiment was ordered on the move. The soldiers had doubts about the successful outcome of a mid-winter campaign. They had not advanced far when heavy clouds descended upon the men. A slow drizzle started dripping on the Union soldiers, wagon trains, and supplies. It soon changed into a steady, pouring rain that did not let up for days. The downpour transformed roads into a quagmire that seemed to swallow the wagon wheels, caissons, and guns. The soaked soldiers worked themselves to sheer exhaustion. Their only reward was a cup of coffee at night to warm their stomachs and hands. After spending two nights in the woods, the regiment was ordered to return to their winter encampment. Nikolaus and his comrades had to build a corduroy road all the way back to camp. The rain finally subsided when the exhausted troops entered their huts.

Morale was at a low point when one of Nikolaus's messmates rushed into the cabin with the news, "The paymaster has arrived."

The paymaster set up his table in the open and the companies assembled for roll call. Nikolaus was one of the last to get called. He signed on the allotment roll that he wished to send his wife ten dollars of his pay each month.

Many men headed straight for the sutler's tent to buy whiskey, pies, sweet potatoes and other delicacies they had missed for a long time. Nikolaus decided to get a haircut and go back to his hut to write a letter to Barbara.

The next mail call brought a welcome surprise for him: a box from home. His curious messmates surrounded him while he unpacked the products of his farm: canned meat, liverwurst and blood wurst, brawn, smoked ham, and a huge marble cake. Barbara had also packed thread, needles, bandages, paper, and stamps. At the bottom of the box lay a couple pairs of wool socks.

The soldiers' diet typically offered little variety, so Nikolaus followed custom and shared the contents of the box with his mess.

"Too bad my wife could not send any wine," Nikolaus said with regret and bit into a piece of ham.

"I would drink nothing but water for a whole year if I could eat another brawn like this one," one private said. "It tastes a lot better than hardtack."

* * *

By April, the regiment was still encamped near Aquia Creek. Waiting was the order of the day. The men waited for the paymaster, the mail, boxes from home, and most of all, the beginning of another campaign. But the weather remained unpredictable. One day a snowstorm blew through the camp and the next day heavy rains washed away the white blanket.

In an effort to boost morale, President Lincoln himself visited the Army of the Potomac and the troops spent days preparing the parade ground for inspection. Glad to have something to do, Nikolaus filled ditches and puddles until he feared his arms would fall off. The parade in the president's honor was such an exhilarating sight that Nikolaus was sure he would never forget it. The wind lashed around his frozen ears and Nikolaus had lost all feeling in his toes as he impatiently waited for his regiment's turn. Over 100,000 soldiers passed by the president, accompanied by the rousing music of drums and marching bands. "Now I have seen the president, too," Nikolaus wrote home the next day.

Conditions in the army had improved much since General Hooker took charge. Instead of salt pork and hardtack, the men were now able to feast on fresh beef, onions, peas, potatoes, and turnips. The only blow to the spirit of the XI Corps was the appointment of Major General Howard to replace General Franz Sigel. The temperamental German revolutionary had been forced to accept lesser duties during the past winter.

Anxiety and anticipation fought within Nikolaus when he thought of the approaching spring campaign. He and his regiment had not seen any battle yet, not even a skirmish. His only experience was that long-forgotten battle in Baden. Yet, he dreaded boredom even more than a fight. Ever since he was a boy, he had worked on the farm. It was not his nature to be idle.

The men were ordered to keep eight days' rations in their knapsack and haversack together with sixty rounds of ammunition. All other clothing and blankets were packed and sent into storage for the summer. And then it rained nearly every day.

* * *

Finally, on April 27, a beautiful spring morning, the X, XI and XII Corps were on the march. The delicate white dogwood blossoms that dotted the Virginia countryside seemed to beckon the men to stop and admire them. *It's much too pretty here to go into battle,* Nikolaus thought glumly while he trudged through the deep mud.

The soldiers pressed on, crossing a ford over a pontoon bridge. On the third day of marching, the XII Corps took over the lead from the XI Corps.

"Why are we changing places now?" Karl Haimbach asked no one in particular.

"Because they don't trust us. We're just ignorant Dutch peasants to them," Johann Müller replied and spat on the ground.

"Quiet," hissed Lieutenant Schmitt, "I'll shoot the next man who shouts."

The men progressed in silence as they knew the lieutenant made no empty threats. Just the other day he had shot a man, believing he was a deserter, when in fact he was trying to forage food from a nearby house. Luckily, the man had survived.

* * *

On the morning of May 2, Nikolaus rose stiffly from his hard dirt bed. They had not been allowed to put up tents and he had wrapped himself in his only blanket. Now he flapped his arms against his body to get warm. After breakfast, his regiment was ordered to picket duty and he stayed close to Karl Haimbach.

"Do you see what I see?" whispered Karl while he pointed to a distant hill in the southwest.

"Those look like muskets glinting in the sun," Nikolaus said. "Do you think those are the rebels?"

They reported their sighting to Lieutenant Schmitt.

"That's probably another corps of our army," he said. Then he wheeled around in the direction of the staff officers.

In the afternoon, Nikolaus's regiment was relieved from picket duty. The men stacked their rifles while they cooked meat for their dinner. Before they could eat a bite, however, a volley whirred past them on their right.

Nikolaus jumped up to grab his musket from the stack while Karl calmly said, "Don't worry, that's nothing. You'll get used to it after a while. I'm going to eat my meat first."

Nikolaus scratched his beard. "Don't you think we're too exposed? Between the embankment in front of us and the thick woods in our rear, where are we supposed to go if we're attacked?"

"If our officers aren't worried, why should I be?" Karl said.

Nikolaus sat down again and began eating while casting occasional glances at the horizon.

In late afternoon, the forest came to life. Rabbits and deer scurried out of the woods, followed by the terrifying yell of the rebel soldiers. Nikolaus felt a chill traveling down his spine at the unfamiliar sound. He dropped his coffee cup on the ground and rushed to grasp his musket from the pile. The pickets who had relieved his regiment came running toward them with the enemy in quick pursuit. Firing a shot was impossible unless they wanted to shoot their own troops. Row after row of Confederate soldiers progressed over an open field. Their color bearer was one of the first to fall.

As soon as the pickets were out of the line of fire, Lieutenant Schmitt gave the order to shoot. Nikolaus took aim and pulled the trigger. There was no time for fear. No time to think of his wife and child. He found himself calmer than ever and loaded his musket as he had learned during drills. Two cannons fired their charges into the thick mass of attackers before they fell silent, their operators abandoning them.

"Fall back! Double quick!" shouted Lieutenant Schmitt.

Nikolaus tried to change direction, but he was wedged in by soldiers.

"*Dummköpfe*," he yelled, "You want to get us all killed?"

At last, the men untangled their muskets and knapsacks and began to withdraw to their new position near the crossroads. Before they arrived there, Nikolaus saw Colonel Hecker fall from his horse.

"Fire away, Eighty-Second," the colonel screamed before two men carried him to the rear.

Nikolaus gave a faint smile. Martin would be proud of his hero when Nikolaus told him about the incident.

The volleys kept falling from the sky like hail and the incessant rifle fire soon intermingled with the screams of wounded soldiers, whinnying horses, and creaking wheels of ambulances. The corps withdrew to a shallow rifle pit near Dowdall's Tavern. Nikolaus had lost contact with his regiment when the order was given to fall back into the woods. He was fighting his way through the thicket when a shell exploded no more than six feet from him, leveling the underbrush. As debris went flying, a branch struck Nikolaus on the cheek. He struggled to stay upright as a trickle of blood began to flow down his face. He touched the wound briefly, but determined it was nothing more than a scrape and kept moving.

At last, nightfall descended on the unfortunate corps and the shooting became scarce. Relieved that his first day of battle was almost over, Nikolaus began to breathe easier. He never saw the stray musket ball that hit him in the lower right leg. He slumped to the ground, clutching his injured leg in desperation. Fearing that the rebels would hear him and drag him off, he suppressed a loud cry when the ball began to burn his flesh. Aware that he was defenseless, he sat up and moved his upper body until he retrieved his dropped musket. If the rebels approached him now, he would at least be able to fire a shot before getting captured.

"Help," he called into the semi-darkness, "I'm hurt and can't walk."

After several minutes, a retreating soldier came to his aid.

"Lean on my left shoulder for support," the stranger said. Together they began to make their way to the nearest ambulance.

"You're lucky you didn't get wounded earlier. The rebs would surely have captured you."

Nikolaus winced in agony at every step he took while they passed a field of horrors. Men who were torn apart by shells or had been shot in the abdomen and lay dying cried out for water or assistance. The XI Corps was in complete disarray.

"What's your name?" Nikolaus asked at last when he was lifted on an ambulance cart.

"I'm Anton Hussack. Good luck to you. It looks like the war is over for you."

Nikolaus waved a weak good-bye to Anton as the cart began rolling. The ambulance crossed the fort under cover of night, taking Nikolaus back to the winter camp which had been set up as a hospital. The bullet remained lodged in his flesh. Nikolaus tried to get some rest, but the screams of the other patients kept him from drifting off. He thought with dread of the upcoming examination. *Will I be able to walk again? Why didn't I listen to Barbara and stay at home? I would be a coward, but at least I would be in one piece.*

After hours of waiting in agony he was finally lifted on a table.

"I'll have to remove your leg," the surgeon said matter-of-factly.

"Over my dead body," Nikolaus replied. "I'm a farmer and can't do my work with one leg."

"Pick him up," the surgeon said to the stretcher-bearers.

"I said NO!" Nikolaus yelled, lashing out as the orderlies tried to grab him by his arms and upper legs.

At that moment, a cavalryman in the cot next to Nikolaus pulled a revolver from its hiding place under his pillow, cocked it and pointed it at the surgeon.

"You heard him. If you try to cut off his leg, you will have to deal with me."

The men obeyed although the threat was voiced by a man who was unable to walk. The surgeon gave Nikolaus a generous shot of whiskey and removed the slug.

Within a short time, Nikolaus was back in his hospital tent. As the effect of the whiskey subsided, searing pain engulfed his leg. Before he parted his cracked lips to call a nurse for a drink of water, he had to know for sure that he was indeed feeling the extremity. He cautiously lifted the soiled sheet that covered his lower body and nodded. The wound itself was covered in a blood-soaked bandage, but for now he was satisfied that he still had all his limbs. *I hope Barbara is not too fond of dancing because I may never be able to twirl her around a dance floor again. At least I should be able to put food on our table and that is no small thing, if the wound does not get infected.*

As the hours dragged on, more and more wounded soldiers arrived at the hospital tent. Too overwrought to sleep and desperate for a diversion, Nikolaus asked several conscious men about the outcome of the battle. Their downcast glances spoke volumes.

Colonel Hecker was also conveyed to the hospital with a serious leg wound. Overwhelmed with injured soldiers, the field hospital placed Nikolaus on a Washington-bound train where he shared a car with Hecker.

"We have given away victory," Hecker declared. He told his listeners about headquarters' chilly attitude toward the German officers who had warned them about the dangers of an attack from their unprotected left. Several fists went up in the air.

"Hooker has ordered the retreat this morning," an aide said to Hecker.

Fourteen thousand Union soldiers had sacrificed their lives or were wounded during the battle of Chancellorsville while the Confederates counted 10,000 casualties. Nikolaus learned from an orderly that General "Stonewall" Jackson had been shot by his own men during a night reconnaissance. On May 10, the most celebrated soldier of the

Confederacy died of the resulting pneumonia. The South had paid dearly for their victory.

Chapter 55

Katrin broke into a wide smile when Daniel Meidinger brought two letters to the Dupree farm. One was from Martin and the other one from Washington. She concluded that it must be from Nikolaus and hurried to show it to her sister-in-law. Barbara was putting Charlotte down for a nap when Katrin entered. Her face drained of color while she fetched a knife from the kitchen to open the envelope.

"Oh my God," she whispered, touching her lips with her hand, "Nikolaus was wounded at Chancellorsville. He's in a hospital in Washington now. He almost lost his leg and will be discharged when he's well enough to travel."

She shot Katrin an anxious look. "I don't know what he would do if he couldn't walk anymore. This farm is his life. Without it, he would be lost."

Katrin patted her arm. "There's plenty a man can do with one leg. After all, he's lucky that he survived at all. Let's be content with that until we know more."

"Yes, of course. I was just thinking how much he loves to move around. He can never sit still for more than a moment."

Barbara picked up the letter to read it again.

"I almost forgot, I got a letter from Martin. I wonder what news he has?" Katrin said and slipped out the door. She needed some time herself to absorb the news about her brother. Minutes later, she rushed back in, waving Martin's letter in mid-air.

"Martin is coming home on furlough for thirty days," Katrin cried. "This is such exciting news. I wonder if Nikolaus will be home yet during his visit. My, they would have such tales to tell each other. I must find Philip right away to tell him his Papa is coming home."

* * *

Martin picked up his furlough papers and his pay, packing just enough clothing for the journey. The remainder of his outfits and accoutrements stayed with his regiment. In Memphis, he boarded a steamer to St. Louis. At the train station in Belleville he met a farmer from Shiloh who gave him a ride on his wagon. The closer he came to his farm, the broader his smile became. It still looked exactly as he had last seen it.

Martin absorbed the image of his farmstead as if to capture it for eternity. He was surprised to realize that the grandiose sandstone mansion in Landstuhl had never conveyed such a strong feeling of home as this simple frame house on the Illinois prairie did. Here he had worked every inch of his land with his sweat and muscle power while everything at his parents' house had fallen into his lap.

Since the family did not know exactly when he would arrive, no one greeted him at the gate. Katrin had written him that Cora had died soon after Martin had left for war. Their new dog alerted the family with its barking. Katrin, who had been weeding a cornfield, flew along the furrows as fast as her long skirt allowed, her straw hat pushed all the way back to her neck.

"Welcome home," she said, out of breath. Her cheeks were flushed from running.

Martin hugged her wordlessly and smacked a kiss on her cracked lips.

"Well, that's a fine way of greeting a soldier," he said dryly. "Nobody was at the train station to welcome me."

"We had no idea what day you would arrive."

Katrin wriggled herself out of his embrace, stepped back and looked over her husband with a disapproving eye.

"Do you like my dress uniform?" Martin said with a smirk.

"You do look a little ragged," she said without the hint of a smile.

"Let's go inside. I'm hungry," Martin urged.

"I'm sorry we don't have anything special for you. I can get you a nice green salad and some carrots from our garden, though. And Tante Amalie baked bread this morning."

Martin perked up at the mention of fresh vegetables.

"What do they feed you men in the Army these days?" Amalie asked when they were all seated around the table.

"Well, if you're lucky, you'll get salt pork or beef, coffee, sugar, salt, vinegar, and flour and—of course—hard bread. Sometimes we get dried fruit or dried vegetables such as beans."

"Hard bread? What's hard bread?"

"It is sort of like a ship's biscuit and it tastes quite good when it's fresh. But it seldom is fresh. Some men call them worm castles."

The women wrinkled their noses at the mention of worms.

After dinner, Martin undressed and took a bath. He put on his old trousers and was startled to notice that they were much too wide for him now. The concerned look on Katrin's face showed him that he had changed more during the war than he had realized. That night, Martin's and Katrin's lovemaking was more desperate and passionate than ever.

"I've missed you so much," Martin confessed and buried his face in her hair.

"Not as much as I've missed you."

"How are you getting along with Uncle Jakob and Aunt Amalie?"

"Uncle Jakob is a darling. He and I had to work in the fields since Nikolaus and Jim left. Aunt Amalie, however, can be trying at times. She took over my kitchen and I have nothing to say anymore. I'm quite fed up and am glad when I can go outside. I can't wait until this terrible war is over and I'll be mistress in my own house again."

* * *

During the following days, conversation at the dinner table revolved around the laws that had been passed on January 1.

One was the Emancipation Proclamation, which guaranteed freedom to all Negro slaves even though President Lincoln held no legislative powers in the Confederate states. The second law, the Homestead Act, allowed each person over twenty-one years of age to acquire a quarter section of public land. All they had to do was become citizens of the United States and live on the land continuously for five years. After that, the land was their property without any restrictions.

"Did you hear about the draft?" Amalie asked.

"It was the talk of the day on the steamer. They say that, instead of serving, one may hire a substitute for three hundred dollars."

Jakob snorted. "So, this is a war of the little man."

"Aren't all wars?" his wife countered.

"Let's hope it'll be over soon," Martin said. "Our Union has just had two important victories with the fall of Vicksburg and victory at Gettysburg. How much longer can the Confederacy hang on with such losses?"

"That's true, but the South has better generals," Jakob said.

* * *

Martin and Katrin walked over their property and through the woods. There was much to tell and too little time to tell it.

"During our campaigns, we march over the fields left and right of the road to keep the roads free for the artillery. My heart bleeds every time we trample down a wheat field," Martin said.

Katrin whirled around to face him. "Has this war fulfilled your expectations? Does the army give you something that I can't give you?"

Martin stood agape as he gathered his thoughts. "I would rather come home to you sooner than later. When I volunteered, I believed I could help to end the war quickly. Since then I have fought more against boredom than against the rebels. I have made many friends, but they are disappointed too. On the other hand, I could not live with myself if I had paid other men to fight for me while I sat quietly on my farm. It's my country now, just as it is theirs. As soon as this war is over. I shall never leave you again, I promise you."

"Dear God, please let this bloodbath be over soon," Katrin said in a choked voice and rested her head on his chest. "We need you here, whether you're a hero or not."

* * *

Nikolaus wrote from St. Louis that he had been transferred from Washington to the hospital at Benton Barracks.

"I'll bring him home," Martin declared.

Barbara wanted to go with him, but Charlotte felt under the weather and she decided to stay home with her precious little girl. Katrin, eager to spend every minute with Martin during his furlough, offered to go along instead. They spread straw on the bottom of the wagon so Nikolaus would not get jolted around during the ride home.

Martin donned his uniform and put Nikolaus's letter in his pocket. They rose before sunrise and were on their way right after breakfast. Martin's gaze took in all the subtle changes that had occurred in his absence. Most men were away at war and building construction had almost come to a standstill.

* * *

"Where are you going?" a burly sergeant asked as Katrin tried to enter a hospital building.

Martin stepped forward and pulled out the letter.

"I think he arrived a couple days ago," the sergeant said.

He motioned Katrin and Martin to follow him as he pointed out the soldiers in his charge. Some of them were amputees, others had dysentery, ague, or typhoid fever. Although Martin had warned her that army hospitals were dreadful places, Katrin had to suppress the urge to flee the overpowering stenches of sweat, dried blood, and vomit.

She barely recognized her brother when they came to a halt at his cot. Her lips quivered as she observed Nikolaus's hollow cheeks. Gone was the naïve private who had climbed the troop train last year. In his stead was a mature man whose thick beard was speckled with fine strands of gray.

Nikolaus perked up at the sight of his sister. "Katrin, what are you doing here? And Martin. Are you home on furlough? How long can you stay here?"

"We've come to take you home," Martin said. "Have you received your discharge papers yet?"

"No, not yet. The doctor who examined me here said that there's no chance of me returning to my unit. He says my lower leg will probably remain stiff."

"Then it shouldn't be any problem to get your discharge papers. I'll see to it."

Martin hastened away in search of a doctor.

"The doctor will have his paperwork ready by tomorrow morning," he said when he returned. "There is a tent for visitors where Katrin and I can sleep tonight."

Katrin carefully sat on the edge of her brother's bed and dried the sweat pearls on his forehead with a towel she had brought. Tears moistened her eyes as she contemplated that she had almost lost her only brother.

"Don't cry," Nikolaus begged her.

"They're happy tears," Katrin assured him. "I'm so glad you made it back."

"The war is over for me now and I'm not sure if it's made any difference whether I was part of it or not," Nikolaus said with a smirk. "I was in battle for less than two hours. Some hero, eh?"

"Shhh," Katrin admonished him, "You mustn't talk like that. You're alive! That's all that matters. We have read some dreadful reports about that battle."

"I'm sure you have. When we get home, I'll tell you all what really happened."

* * *

"You mustn't believe what everybody says about the XI Corps," Nikolaus said when Martin visited him on his sickbed back on the farm. Charlotte played nearby and her proud father watched her every move.

"They say that the Union would have won the battle if the XI's had not run away like chickens," Martin said.

"Is that so? Well, here's what I saw. . ."

Nikolaus told his brother-in-law how the XI Corps had been left far out, its only reserve withdrawn and the headquarter officers ignoring all warnings from the lower-ranking German officers.

"I was on the same hospital train with your friend, Colonel Hecker. He told me how the higher officers brushed off all cautions about our exposed flank."

"He's been good to me, but I wouldn't consider him a close friend."

Nikolaus cast a doubtful look at Martin. "Come on, you worship him, don't you?"

"I guess we all need heroes, especially in these trying times. But I'm through idolizing him after what I've heard about his behavior during the war."

"He does seem to be rather hot-headed at times, doesn't he?"

Martin sighed. "Well, if the officers stopped playing politics, maybe this war would be over by now."

* * *

All too soon, Martin's furlough was over, and the family assembled on the porch to bid him farewell.

"Good-bye, old friend," he said to Nikolaus. "Take care of my wife until I come back."

Flanked by Philip and Katrin, Martin sat on the wagon bench and took the reins. It was a quiet ride since even Philip seemed overtaken by the solemn occasion. As the wagon rumbled along the rutted road, Martin drank in the sight of the green cornfields left and right of the highway. The golden faces of black-eyed Susans adorned many a fence while majestic purple coneflowers pointed their spiky crowns toward the sun and the bees that savored their nectar. *How could I ever think that my life was dull? How much would I give if I didn't have to leave it behind.*

"I forgot how peaceful it is here until I saw the destruction in the South," Martin said aloud. "Even though they brought it on themselves, it hurts to see a family's home destroyed or their animals taken away for forage. Would you believe that many of the small farmers have never been more than ten miles away from their home and cannot read or write?"

"Let's not talk about the war anymore," Katrin said, nestling against him.

Martin swallowed hard when the train pulled up. Once again, he wrangled with his fate that always separated him from a dear loved one when he needed her the most.

He kissed Katrin one last time and hugged Philip tightly before climbing up the carriage steps. A deep sigh escaped his lips while he watched his wife and son disappear from his life as the train pulled away from the station.

Chapter 56

December 1863

The Forty-Third was the first regiment to enter Little Rock on September 11, 1863, after the Confederates withdrew. Martin's regiment had been encamped here ever since. The officers had done everything they could to keep the men busy. They were only allowed to walk the streets of Little Rock when they were on patrol duty. Roll call, guard duties and, most of all, fatigue duty kept the soldiers occupied while they waited for winter to pass. Fatigue duty comprised everything from policing camp to gathering firewood and water or digging sinks.

Martin stepped out of his log hut and closed the door behind him. As he walked to his guard duty post, he breathed in the fresh, crisp air until his lungs hurt. He found that he enjoyed the solitary watches after spending much of his time in cramped winter quarters.

Martin had time to think about his life while on sentry duty. He missed Katrin and Philip every day. Yet, he had never been closer to a group of men than he had to his messmates. With the exception of his wife and sister-in-law, he had always felt shy and self-conscious in the company of women. He preferred social contact with men of similar interests.

Sharing a tent for months did not leave any opportunity for secrets. The men revealed their plans and dreams about the future after the war ended. They also shared many tales about their past lives.

One of Martin's messmates was Ernst Bollinger. The twenty-one-year-old Palatine had barely left Martin's side since his capture near Bolivar. Apparently, he thought that he owed Martin his life or, at least, his presence in the Union Army. They often swapped stories of their childhoods back in Rhenish-Bavaria.

After sentry duty, Martin went to the sutler's tent. With longing eyes, he contemplated the assortment of pies, butter, condensed milk, tobacco, and canned preserves.

"What will it be for you today, Corporal? Some condensed milk maybe?" the stout man asked Martin.

Martin licked his dry lips and counted his coins. "No, that's too expensive for me. I'll just take six of your cookies."

"That'll be a quarter."

Martin paid and tramped back to his log hut. The molasses cookies would taste good with coffee—a welcome change from the perennial hard bread. He did not allow himself the luxury of visiting the sutler's tent very often, but he just couldn't take the monotony of Army rations anymore.

Darkness descended on the camp. A silvery soprano sang *"Hinaus in die Ferne"* to the skillful play of a harmonica as he slogged through the encampment.

"There's a letter from your little wife on your bunk," Ernst said when Martin stepped into his hut.

Martin filled his tin cup with coffee and settled down to read the letter while munching on his cookies.

"Any news from home?" Mueller asked.

"Well, only that Arthur Lang of Shiloh has been excused from the draft because of his bad teeth," Martin replied absentmindedly.

"Come join us for a card game, we need another man."

Martin obliged, his mind elsewhere. Katrin had written him the most wonderful news. . .

* * *

April 30, 1864
Jenkins' Ferry, Arkansas

In an effort to fight the French threat in Mexico and to gain Texas with its cotton for the North's famished cotton mills, the second Federal Army under Major General Steele had moved south toward Shreveport, Louisiana, on March 23. They wanted to rendezvous with General Banks's army on the Red River.

Martin, whose regiment was part of this army, quickened his steps when news of the upcoming campaign reached them. The men broke camp in high spirits, elated that the monotony of the past few months finally ended. Their excitement did not last long.

Troops were on half-rations when they occupied the city of Camden in mid-April, but the expected food supplies never materialized. Hunger began to gnaw at the men and their nine thousand horses and mules. After foraging troops were defeated by Confederate soldiers at Poison Spring and Marks' Mills, Steele had no choice but to order a retreat to Little Rock.

Martin and his fellow soldiers spent the day destroying everything they couldn't take back to the garrison: tents, wagons, mess chests, and even hardtack and bacon. Martin was issued two pieces of hardtack and half a pint of corn meal. He was still staring at his meager portion in disbelief when Ernst passed him.

"Back home I used to eat this much between meals," Ernst said with a sneer. "Maybe I should have stayed with the Confederates. They didn't feed us much, but it was more than this."

While their bugles sounded taps in the deserted camp to deceive the rebels, the Federal troops slipped out of Camden and crossed the Ouachita River over a pontoon bridge. After midnight, Martin's company was one of the last to leave town. Toward evening, the expedition finally halted several miles north of Camden and Martin tumbled to the ground like a felled tree. The next day, they hurried along the Princeton Road toward Jenkins' Ferry. As the day wore on, Martin began to stagger more than he marched. With visions of hardtack in his head, he threw out pieces of clothing from his knapsack to lighten his load. Excess garments and equipment littered the roadsides. That evening, they camped near several springs where the men could at least secure fresh water.

Rain began to fall in sheets before they reached Jenkins' Ferry. Soon, the old trunk road turned into a mire, sucking in wagon wheels as well as the soldiers' legs. The Saline River was swollen and too deep for guns and wagons to cross. A detachment stretched an India rubber pontoon bridge across the river while another one corduroyed the road. Artillery and supply wagons soon clogged up the road as well as the pontoon bridge, and the infantry had to trudge forth through a swampy forest.

Martin was up to his knees in water and the sodden ground threatened to suck in his battered shoes. With nothing but coffee in his stomach to sustain him, his feet grew heavier with every step. His thoughts turned to the end of his enlistment in August. During the winter he had considered reenlisting, but this disastrous expedition changed his mind.

I'm thirty-four years old. Why am I laboring through this miserable swamp in disintegrating shoes when I could be sitting high and dry on my farm?

* * *

Lieutenant Hartmann rounded up his scattered soldiers. "You're probably aware that the Confederates are hard on our heels. To allow our wagons and troops to cross the river, we have been ordered to stay in back to fight the rebels and buy us time. We will position ourselves behind the crest of the ridge south of the Jiles house. We expect them to attack at dawn, so try to get some rest tonight."

Martin snorted when he was out of earshot of the lieutenant. Rest. How could he rest when he had to fight yet another battle? And why did it always have to rain during an attack? It was as if nature's forces were taking revenge for disrupting the courses of rivers and stands of timber.

Glad to get to a field where his unraveling shoes would not sink into the morass anymore, Martin stiffened as he followed his comrades to their battle positions. He dropped to the ground where Ernst soon joined him. Martin pulled his last half piece of hardtack out of his haversack and chewed it slowly. Ernst let his finger run through his empty pouch.

"I'm so hungry, I could eat a horse," he said.

"Please, don't talk about food anymore," Martin said. "I don't know why we had to throw out our hardtack in Camden. What do they carry in all those wagons?"

"Quiet," hissed their sergeant.

Ernst moved closer to Martin. "You look spent, my friend."

"Sure am."

"Try to get some sleep tonight. And tomorrow, we'll stay together if we can."

Martin nodded feebly. He wished he had his younger friend's unrelenting energy.

* * *

The Confederate Army's attack came in the early morning as expected, but the Union forces fought with desperate bravery. The rebels had to cross an open field which was not wide enough to line up all the Confederates at the same time. Meanwhile, Martin's company lay hidden behind the crest of a timber-covered hill.

Early morning mist rose from the swamp and mingled with the dense smoke from hundreds of rifles and guns. Salvo after salvo of shots flew into the throng of rebels but they kept coming.

Is this what hell is like? Martin fired another bullet into the fog. He could not even see Ernst who had trudged alongside him just a few minutes before. He almost stumbled over a fallen soldier. Noticing his fatal wound, Martin quickly emptied the dying man's cartridge box. He loaded his rifle and looked around to take aim.

How could he tell if he was shooting at a Confederate or a Union soldier? The flash of a musket that appeared for a moment out of the smoke gave him the aim he needed as he fired. At the same moment, a great force smacked into his right shoulder, sending him tumbling to the ground and into darkness.

* * *

Martin awoke when someone shook his upper body. As his vision cleared, he saw that Ernst was kneeling next to him.

"Come on, Martin. We've got to get out of here."

"What happened?" Martin asked, feeling his shoulder. "I thought I was shot."

"I think it was the recoil of your rifle that felled you. As far as I can tell in this rain, your shoulder appears to be fine."

Martin sighed. "How long have I been out?"

"Long enough to miss that we whipped the rebels this time. They've retreated for now, but I'm sure they'll be back. We've been ordered to cross the river. Here, I'll help you get up."

With Ernst's aid, Martin rose on shaky legs and looked around. He pulled up the lapels of his coat since the downpour had not let up. Dense gun smoke still enveloped the battleground and he barely spotted mangled bodies strewn across the former cornfield. That would almost have been his fate in his weakened condition.

"Let's go," Ernst said. "I'll take your knapsack for you. Can you carry your rifle?"

"I'll manage."

Ernst stayed close to Martin as they hobbled across the pontoon bridge. By mid-afternoon, they arrived safely on the other side of the river.

On the road back to the capital, Martin's shoes finally gave out, forcing him to continue the march barefoot. None of the wagons the

Federals had abandoned along the way contained any shoes. Martin felt more dead than alive when he stumbled back into the garrison. Blisters covered his cracked, bleeding feet. Without much urging from Ernst he headed to the hospital.

The next day, Ernst visited him on his sickbed.

"Our messmates are very concerned about you," he said. "Look what I brought for you."

He pulled a piece of paper and a pencil out of his pocket. "I'll help you write a letter to Katrin, who I'll hopefully meet someday."

Martin dictated a short letter to Katrin before his head sank back on his pillow.

"Why are you doing all this for me?" he asked.

"Because I'm grateful that you rescued me from the rebel army. I was so lonely there, you wouldn't believe. And besides, you would do the same for me if the tables were turned."

Martin gave a wry smile. "That's true, I would. And if you ever decide to settle in Illinois, I'll be glad to give you all the help you need. My brother-in-law has been injured and walks with a limp. Would you like to work on a farm?"

Ernst scratched his beard. "I'll have to think about that. I would rather prefer to work in my old job as a tailor again."

"Very well, this country needs craftsmen. But my invitation stands: when this terrible war is over, I want you to visit us on our farm, no matter where you choose to live."

Chapter 57

December 1864

Katrin and Nikolaus stood on the platform of the train station in Belleville, waiting for the train that would finally bring Martin home. An icy wind howled around the station building and Katrin's teeth began to clatter.

"I wish the train would come soon," she said. "I'm almost frozen."

Nikolaus laughed. "I told you we were too early. You should have waited in the hotel where it's warm. I would have come to get you as soon as the train arrived."

"I just couldn't wait. I'm too nervous to sit still. But I can't stand out here much longer."

At that moment, a train whistle pierced the clear winter air. Katrin and her brother were not the only ones waiting for the soldiers. Children shrieked while their mothers and grandparents tried without success to appease them. At last, the train came to a halt and the doors swung open. Martin was the second soldier to emerge from his car. How much he had changed since his furlough! His once black hair now showed fine streaks of silver and his cheeks still had not filled out after the deprivations of the spring campaign. His gray eyes searched the crowd until Katrin waved at him.

* * *

Martin descended the train with heavy steps. He hoped that Katrin would not shriek when she saw him. His recovery from the expedition had been a long one. After his release from the hospital, he had returned to his duties as a corporal in the Little Rock garrison. The regiment was still stationed there when his three-year enlistment expired. It had been hard to say good-bye to Ernst who had promised to visit Martin when the regiment was mustered out of service. Martin was sure that he would regain his former strength under Katrin's loving care. He had to look after his family now, and it was time that younger men than him took over his duties in this war between brothers. It could not last much longer at any rate.

Martin spotted Katrin and Nikolaus in the crowd and hurried over to take his wife's gloved hands in his.

"Home at last," he said. "My, have I looked forward to this day."

"Let's go to the hotel for a cup of coffee before we drive home," Nikolaus suggested. Martin and Katrin agreed, their eyes locked on each other.

A few minutes later, they were seated at the hotel and Katrin warmed her red fingers on a steaming mug.

"How is everybody at home?" Martin asked.

"They're all fine," Katrin said. "Barbara is expecting again. She stayed home with the children and Uncle Jacob and Aunt Amalie moved back into their house yesterday."

"They didn't have to leave because of me," Martin said.

"Well, it was getting crowded in our house. And besides, Jakob is anxious to start working in his shop again. I think he missed it during the past few years although he worked in it when work was slow on the farm. We're all very grateful for his help."

"I hope they visit us over the holidays so I can thank them personally," Martin said. "And now, I'd like to go home."

The sun had disappeared over the western prairie when their wagon finally turned into the yard of the Dupree farm. The once white paint of the house had faded into a light gray. Martin would have to paint it after he regained his strength. Nikolaus led the horses into the barn while Martin and Katrin headed for the house. The kitchen smelled of stew and apple *schnitz* when they entered. Martin scarcely greeted Barbara who was mending a sock at the table.

"Where is he?" he whispered to Katrin. She pointed to a cot near the stove.

Martin dropped his knapsack on the floor, tiptoed to the crib and peered down. Two large hazel eyes, the eyes of his mother, looked up at him. Martin held out his finger and the little boy took it and broke into a smile.

Katrin stepped next to him and lifted the baby out of the crib.

"Can I hold him?" Martin asked.

"Of course," Katrin said. "Sit down first, you must be dead tired."

Martin did what he was told, and she cradled little Carl in his arms. Carl began to cry and Katrin picked him up to sooth him.

Martin suppressed a sigh. "I'm a stranger to him."

"Of course you are," Katrin said. "Don't take it to heart. He'll get to know you soon enough."

Martin ate two heaping plates of stew for supper, licking his lips afterward. "I haven't had such good food since I was home on furlough."

Nikolaus laughed. "I won't cry if I never see another piece of hardtack in my life."

Martin's face hardened. "Still, during the Red River campaign we would have been happy to eat hardtack if we had had any, worms and all."

After supper, Martin took a bath before he and Katrin went to bed. He cradled his head on Katrin's chest and she drove her fingers through his still moist hair.

"Was it really as awful as you wrote me?" she said after a while.

"It was even worse. I didn't want to scare you too much, but I don't know if I would have made it without Ernst." Martin said in a throaty voice. "Let's not talk about the war anymore. I don't want to think about it right now."

They lay in an embrace until Katrin had to get up to feed the baby.

At breakfast the next morning, Martin said, "Tomorrow is Christmas Eve, and I don't even have any gifts for you and the children."

"Shhh," Katrin said, "you're the best gift I could have wished for. So many women have lost their husbands. It makes me feel almost guilty that I have you and two healthy children."

"Yes, you're right, as usual. My biggest wish still remains unfulfilled: peace. I truly hope that this will be the last Christmas of the war. The South cannot hold out much longer. While I disagree with General Sherman's tactics of burning crop and supplies and killing livestock, I understand his motive. It should break the South's back once and for all. No one can understand how they can hold on this long without the North's industry and farm production."

"Everyone says they have the better generals," Katrin replied.

"That is unfortunately true," Martin said, looking around. "Say, where is everybody today?"

"Nikolaus and Barbara thought we might enjoy some time alone together, so they took Charlotte and Philip to Aunt Amalie while they'll go to the store in Shiloh to buy some foodstuffs for the holidays. Everything is so expensive, you wouldn't believe. I told Nikolaus to bring some coffee for you even though it costs three times as much as when the war started."

"That wasn't necessary," Martin said.

"It's just because it's Christmas. And now, eat your breakfast. I don't want to see those ribs much longer. You need to fatten up so you can help Nikolaus with the farm work," Katrin said with a twinkle in her eye.

"I would start working today if I could buy you a new dress for my labor," Martin said, looking at the frayed cuffs of Katrin's house dress.

"Never mind that," Katrin said, "Other women are much worse off than I am. At least we have enough to eat on the farm. City people are not so lucky."

"True. By the way, what's for Christmas dinner?"

* * *

The new year brought the welcome news that Sherman had captured Savannah before Christmas. Martin and Nikolaus eagerly followed the course of the war. Since Martin's regiment was still in Little Rock and therefore out of harm's way, they followed the progress of the Army of the Tennessee through the Carolinas in the newspapers. Whenever the weather allowed, Martin and Nikolaus hitched a horse to the sleigh they had bought before the war began and drove to the store in Shiloh to hear the latest news. Other times, Martin and Katrin visited a neighbor whose son served in Sherman's army. Martin was deeply disturbed when they read one of their boy's letters aloud.

"This isn't the army I know," he said when they were back home. "We never had a quarrel with the civilian population in the South. We only took what we needed in order to survive. Sure, we stole chickens or a pig from time to time, but smashing pianos and china, that's just not right."

"Surely the South can't hang on much longer," Nikolaus said.

"It's hard to understand how they could hold out as much as they have," Martin agreed. "But I'm afraid that the hatred that divided this country four years ago will only get stronger as more destruction happens in the South. Each railroad tie that's twisted and destroyed will make the people of the South more bent on hating us."

"So, you think the North should have mercy on the South?" Nikolaus asked.

"Yes, I believe it would be best for the future of the country," Martin said. "I sincerely hope that Mr. Lincoln can reunite the nation. If anyone can, he will."

* * *

April 1865

Martin and Nikolaus were ploughing when Katrin came running across the field.

"Daniel Meidinger just came by," she said, out of breath. "He said the war is over! General Lee surrendered at a place in Virginia I cannot pronounce."

The men reined the horse and whooped. Martin threw his cap in the air and clapped Nikolaus's shoulder.

"That's reason to celebrate," Martin said. "Let's end work early today and visit the Kolbs. They must have heard the news, too."

The following Saturday, the entire family drove to Belleville to watch the victory festivities. Just like before the war, bunting hung from the houses that surrounded the square and flags fluttered from almost every building. However, this time many men were missing arms or legs. Veterans of the Mexican War marched along Main Street to the spirited melodies of the ever-present brass band. A child shrieked in the crowd, competing for attention with the French horn in pitch and volume.

Peter and Susanne were there with their children. Peter had lost an arm after the battle of Chattanooga, but he had learned to compensate for his missing limb.

Nikolaus grinned from ear to ear when he met one of his former messmates, Johann Müller.

"What are you doing here?" he asked. "I thought you were still soldiering."

"I got discharged after I contracted typhoid fever. Took a long time to recover but I'm alright now. I'm back working as a tanner."

While the men exchanged news of their former comrades, Martin led Katrin and Philip to a booth that sold cider. Despite the noise, Carl slept soundly cradled in his left arm.

"Guten Tag, Martin," said a well-known voice behind him. It belonged to Colonel Hecker, who had resigned during the spring of 1864. "I see you've had an addition to your family. Congratulations, he's a strapping child already."

"Thank you," Martin said while they shook hands.

"You weren't in Virginia, were you?" Hecker asked.

Martin went on to tell his old friend about the battle of Shiloh and the Red River campaign. There was no getting away from the war. Katrin wandered off to talk with Susanne and they agreed to meet at the Maus Tavern for dinner. That evening, they returned to the farm in a festive mood.

* * *

Martin's high spirits lasted all week. While working in the fields, he hummed the songs he had listened to so often in camp and during marches. His good mood infected Katrin and Nikolaus.

One day while eating dinner, they heard a wagon screeching to a halt, followed by heavy steps on their porch. Soon Peter filled the frame of the open door. He kneaded his hat in his hand and seemed reluctant to come into the kitchen.

"Peter, what brings you here at this unlikely hour?" Katrin asked. "Come in and have a seat."

"I can't stay long because I have to go to several more houses today," Peter said and sank on the chair. "I'm afraid I have some bad news."

"The war is over. What bad news could there be now?" Nikolaus said.

"I had to go see your uncle about a wheel that needed fixing."

"Oh, how are he and Aunt Amalie doing?" Katrin asked.

"They're fine but let me finish."

He hesitated.

"Well, what is it?" Martin asked.

"The store just got the latest paper from Chicago and it said," he paused before he continued, "it said that President Lincoln has been shot."

Martin blanched. "Shot? Is he. . .dead?"

Peter nodded without looking at him. "Yes, he died the next morning."

Martin, Katrin and Nikolaus remained silent until Martin asked, "Did they catch the shooter?"

"Not yet, but they're chasing him. I have a paper for you on the wagon because I thought you would want to read it for yourself. I'll go and get it."

Katrin rose to fetch money for the newspaper. Martin was unable to move until he had read the entire article. Then he rose heavily and walked out the door without uttering a word. He trudged to the orchard where the apple trees were about to open their white blossoms to the world. He stepped to a tree and buried his face in its bark. Martin had no idea how long he had been standing there when he heard Nikolaus's limping steps behind him. His brother-in-law laid a hand on his shoulder, forcing him to turn around.

"Martin, I'm so sorry," Nikolaus said. "I know you held Mr. Lincoln in high esteem. There are many people in the South who just can't forgive him for freeing the slaves. You and I cannot understand that, but that's the way it is. We live here now and there are certain things we just have to accept as a way of life."

Martin's hands tightened in fists in an effort to control his grief. "Don't you see what consequences his death has? I think Abraham Lincoln would have been able to bring the North and the South back together, but what's going to happen now?"

He gripped Nikolaus's shoulders tightly. "Now all the sacrifices and killings have been in vain. Did you get a lame leg for nothing?"

Nikolaus shook his head. "No, I don't suppose that my injury was for nothing. I believe now that we fought for the right cause and that the nation will be united again, even if it takes years."

Martin gaped at him. "Do you really think so?"

"Yes. I refuse to accept that our sacrifices were for naught. And now, come back to the house. Katrin is worried about you."

* * *

Every evening after supper, Martin disappeared among the fruit trees until he was out of sight.

"Where is he going?" Nikolaus wondered.

"I don't know," Katrin said.

"Should I go after him? He hasn't been himself since Mr. Lincoln got shot."

"No. I think he needs to be alone right now. Even I cannot get through to him."

"I've never seen him like this," Nikolaus said. "Not even when Georg died."

"You and Martin didn't have time to grieve when his friend died," Katrin said. "Now, despite all the spring planting, there seems to be too much time all of a sudden. I feel as if all the joy of spring has left me. Don't you feel it too?"

"Yes," Nikolaus said with a sigh.

"I asked him if he wants to go to Springfield when the train with the President's body arrives, but he said no. He would rather remember Mr. Lincoln the way he last saw him in Alton."

Nikolaus's fingers forked through his hair. "Sit down, sister. I have to show you something and I can't tell it to Martin right now."

Katrin sat down, her face distraught by Nikolaus's tone.

"I've never kept anything from Martin, but he got this letter the other day and I knew right away that it carried bad news. The letter was from a private in Jim's company. He writes that Jim got killed during the battle of Nashville. Jim was like a son to Martin and I just can't bring myself to give him more grief right now. Maybe in a few months he'll be able to deal with it, but not now."

Katrin wiped away two tears with the corner of her apron. "Poor boy. He had an awful life, and then he died so young. God, how I wish this terrible war had never happened."

Nikolaus patted her hand. "There's no sense wishing that; what's done is done. We have to get a grip of ourselves for the sake of our children."

"Yes, of course. But if Martin doesn't come around soon, could you please talk to him?"

"Very well," Nikolaus said. "Give him a few weeks, though. Remember, this is the second time that he fought for a cause and been disillusioned."

"But, so have you."

Nikolaus said, "Not quite. I was only a soldier for a few months and just one battle. Martin was in the war for three years and almost starved to death. That takes its toll on a man."

* * *

The following Sunday after they came home from church, Martin addressed his family. "I know I haven't been quite myself lately and I apologize for that. Come along, I want to show you something."

"Shall we leave the children here?" Barbara asked.

"No, they can come," Martin answered before taking the baby into his arms. Katrin and Philip stepped beside him, followed by Nikolaus who was walking on a cane today. Barbara was last with Charlotte. They made their way through the orchard where the cherry trees turned their beguiling blossoms upward and buttercups and phlox bloomed in the grass beneath the trees. After they left the copse behind, they came to the highest elevation of their property. Martin came to a halt underneath a gnarled oak tree. He pointed to a rock that was smaller than a wagon wheel. The words "A. Lincoln +1865" had been scratched on it with a knife. A look of understanding came over Katrin's face.

"So that's what you've been doing all these days," she said and moved to face him. "You could have told me. I wouldn't have stopped you."

"I know, but I wasn't ready to talk about it yet."

Martin's gaze wandered from her face to the trees they had just passed. A robin gathered nesting material under a pear tree while a goldfinch sang on the tallest branch of an apple tree. Suddenly he envied the birds. They knew nothing of the grief men caused each other but followed their instincts as thousands of generations had done before them.

"I've brought you all here today to pay tribute to our late president," Martin began. "The murderer has already been brought to justice, but that can never erase what happened to Mr. Lincoln and our country. I say "our country" because, by swearing an oath, I have joined my fate to that of the United States of America. May they be united again, under one flag, before long. Because the longer this nation remains divided in the hearts and minds of the people, the longer it will take Southerners to treat us like brothers again. Even though Mr. Lincoln has emancipated the slaves, it will take great effort by all of us to open our hearts and doors to men and women who have been kept in bondage for so long. Right now, I feel as if all our hardships have been futile."

Martin looked deep into his brother-in-law's eyes. "Nikolaus says that isn't so. I'd like to believe him, but at this moment I'm too grieved to understand it. Someday, we may look back to this war and say that it has made the nation better for it. There was plenty of discord before the war, to be sure, but the states should have settled their differences without cannons. Today, I ache not just for our President, but also for the thousands of soldiers who have died in this war. May their sacrifices never be forgotten!"

Martin cleared his throat. "And now I'd like to be alone for a while."

Katrin's eyes glistened when she took Carl from him. Martin looked after her as she followed Nikolaus, Barbara, and the children through the orchard. He had fought through blinding fog, relentless rain, knee-high mud, heat that wrapped him like a blanket, and snowstorms so fierce that a man could not even see the hand before his eyes. He had seen mansions and barren fields where even a raccoon would have been hard-pressed to find a meal. After all this, he found that his destiny lay here, in the neatly plowed fields that would soon be waving with rows of corn and wheat. No one could take his land from him.

He placed his hat on his head and started walking back to the house to join Katrin and their children. It was time that he gave his sons his full attention. He could already sense how Carl looked up to him, eager for his love and guidance. Someday Martin would perhaps regain his interest in politics, but for now he was content with the love of his family and friends.

Halfway through the orchard, he turned to look at the stone one last time and saw that a cardinal had landed on it. He smiled and hurried through the copse toward the house where Katrin waited for him.

Timeline of Events in the Pfalz (Palatinate)

1794 – 1814:	The *Pfalz* belongs to France. French laws leave their mark in parts of the legislation (especially the judicial system and press law) and give the opposition an opportunity to organize themselves in press clubs.
1815:	After the Congress of Vienna, the kingdom of Bavaria gains control of the *Pfalz*. But the Rhenish Palatinate is geographically isolated: there is no immediate connection to the rest of the kingdom. This isolation and the unfavorable customs and politics create problems for the economy. It is extremely difficult to export tobacco and wine, while crop failures and poor wine harvests cause food prices to climb. The poorer regions experience famines and discontent.
May 27, 1832:	A festival at the Hambach castle near Neustadt draws almost 30,000 people. Attendees are mostly from the lower and middle classes, including many women. They demand a unified, free Germany as a federal republic. The *Deutscher Bund* (alliance of German states) reacts with arrests and a total suppression of press and assembly freedom. The black-red-and-gold flags that flutter here would later become the flag of the Federal Republic of Germany.
1848:	Revolutions break out all over Europe, beginning with France in February.
April:	In Baden, Friedrich Hecker demands the establishment of a German Republic, resulting in the "Heckerzug" (Hecker Campaign). The rebels lose a battle and Hecker seeks refuge in Switzerland, then in the USA.
May:	The National Assembly gathers in Frankfurt.

March 28, 1849:	The National Assembly approves the imperial constitution. Friedrich Wilhelm IV is elected as Emperor of all Germans.
April 3:	Friedrich Wilhelm IV declares that he will accept the crown only with the consent of the other rulers.
April 14:	Twenty-eight German states consent to the constitution and imperial election. Prussia, Austria, Bavaria, and Hannover do not.
April 28:	Friedrich Wilhelm IV declines the imperial election.
May 2:	Ten thousand people attend a public assembly in Kaiserslautern and approve the formation of a state defense council.
June 17:	After a defeat near Rinnthal, the rebels retreat to Baden.
July 23:	Fortress Rastatt falls to the Prussian army. The rebellion is defeated.

Glossary

Kaiserstraße:	Emperor Road, named after Napoleon, who moved his troops on this road toward Russia.
Stiftsplatz:	Public square in Kaiserslautern, next to the Stiftskirche
Fruchthalle:	Grain exchange in Kaiserslautern
München:	Munich
Tagwerk:	Approximately 3,407 square meters (0.84 acre). An area that could be plowed in one day.
German mile:	4.7 American miles
Gymnasium:	High School
Turner:	Nationalistic gymnast. Since political clubs were prohibited, men met in gymnastics clubs to discuss the events of the day.
Friedrich Hecker:	Most famous revolutionary of 1848. Emigrated to America after the revolution failed.
Bundschuh:	Name and insignia of the peasant uprising during the 15th and 16th centuries.

About the Author

Doris Dumrauf is an award-winning author and bird photographer. She grew up in the Cold War era West German state of Rheinland-Pfalz, a region with a long history of emigration resulting from poverty and political turmoil. She was inspired to write *Shiloh Valley* following a trip to American sites of German settlements and an article about the revolution of 1849. Since moving to the United States in 1995, Doris has published nonfiction articles, her novel *Oktober Heat*, and three nature books. She divides her time between writing, nature photography, and public speaking. Please visit her website at dorisdumraufauthor.com.

Other Books:

Oktober Heat

Create Your Own Backyard Wildlife Habitat
Common Backyard Birds
Life In A Wetland

Made in the USA
Middletown, DE
29 April 2025